THE DRAGON GEISHA

INDIA MILLAR

The Dragon Geisha

THE DRAGON GEISHA

India Millar

ALSO BY INDIA MILLAR

The Geisha With The Green Eyes

The Geisha Who Could Feel No Pain

This book is humbly dedicated to Benzaiten, the Japanese goddess of good luck for both writers and geisha. May both she and you enjoy the words herein!

"Living only for the moment, giving all our time to the pleasures of the moon,
the snow, cherry blossoms, and maple leaves. Singing songs, drinking
sake, caressing each other, just drifting, drifting. Never giving a care
if we had no money, never sad in our hearts. Only like a plant moving
on the river's current; this is what is called The Floating World."

Tales of the Floating World
Asai Ryoi, 1661

PROLOGUE

The smaller vessels scudded before our larger ship like flustered children, disturbed in their games by the arrival of an unexpected but much-loved elderly relative. I sucked in a breath, sure for a moment that a particularly tiny ship had been taken down by our bows; but no, there it was, popping out on the far side, unharmed. Even though I could see the harbor in front of us, growing larger by the minute, I knew from a past journey that it would be hours before we actually docked in San Francisco, so I took the chance to go back to my cabin and changed from my kimono and obi into Western dress: a long skirt and a blouse topped by a jacket. I pulled the combs out of my hair and rearranged my curls so that they could be topped by a hat and a veil. I scrubbed my traditional makeup off and replaced it with no more than a dab of face powder. I checked myself in the mirror and frowned at my reflection, wondering—not for the first time, and no doubt not for the last—which woman was the real me?

Back on deck, I smiled at my dinner companion from

the journey. He was leaning on the rail, watching San Francisco speed toward us. He raised his hat to me uncertainly, and it was clear he had no idea who I was. I watched the expression in his eyes change from puzzlement to greed in a second, and my smile froze on my lips. He had been an avuncular companion on the long sea journey across the Pacific, regaling me with stories of his travels the length and breadth of America, telling me constantly how glad he was to be back, and how I would soon come to love his country as much as he did. Politeness forbade me to explain that I had lived in America for the last two years, and no longer regarded it with any terror at all. Instead, I nodded and smiled and allowed him to pick out the choicest dishes at dinner for me.

Experience should have told me that I ought not to have been either surprized or hurt by the change in my new friend, but I was.

"Henry-san?" I murmured hopefully, watching as his mouth opened and closed but no words came out. He wore dentures—I had often hidden a smile as I had watched him fight with the tougher cuts of meat—and now his upper set slipped and collided with the bottom teeth with a distinct click.

"My God. Midori No Me? I barely recognized you in those clothes, and without your makeup."

I smiled sweetly and thought, *Liar. You didn't recognize me at all. You thought I was some woman who had popped up out of nowhere. Some woman who was...available.*

I didn't say anything. I simply lowered my head and watched him from beneath my eyelashes. Obviously flustered by his mistake, Henry-san took my hand and guided it through his arm, giving it a little pat of reassurance as our ship bumped and nuzzled into the harbor. It was unforgivably rude of him to touch me uninvited, and I stiffened, fighting the urge to pull away and reclaim a respectable distance from him. Apart from anything else, from this close, his body odor was overwhelming and I closed my nostrils, trying to appear I had not noticed.

And then I realized the mistake was mine, not his. We were no longer in Japan, where such a public gesture of affection between mere acquaintances would have been unthinkable. No longer in Japan, where it was a constant joke that one could smell the gaijin before they could be seen. We were back in America. Back in my new home.

I had only spent a couple of months back in Japan, and already I had to remind myself I was no longer a geisha. I frowned at my own mistake.

Henry-san was chattering away, but I barely heard him. I nodded and smiled automatically, my thoughts dancing like fireflies as my mind was caught and pulled here and there by my two worlds.

I searched the quayside for Danjuro, my husband. Useless, there were too many people ranked there to make out a single figure. I thought I saw him, and half raised my hand to wave, and then decided I was wrong. It wasn't him. Never mind, in a few minutes I would see my husband, and then I would truly be sure that this *was* my home.

My breath hitched as panic consumed me with a physical pain, gripping my stomach and squeezing so that bile rose in my throat. Home? Was this really home, this country that was suddenly foreign to me again? I wanted to turn, to run back to my cabin, to stay there until the ship turned around and went back across the great ocean.

Back to Japan.

Back to where I belonged.

I stared at San Francisco, growing larger by the moment. It shone in the sun and the sunbeams winked off the windows of the high buildings all along the waterfront. In spite of my worries, at least it was comfortingly familiar.

It had all been so very different, the first time.

1

Fish swim in the depths
For them, there is no difference
Between day and night

That first journey had been a terrifying leap of hope. We were rats, caught in a trap of our own making. Time and time again, Danjuro told me that we were doing the right thing, the only thing. Did I want to stay in Edo, remain a prisoner in the Floating World? Did I really want to stay as Akira's slave? I sensed jealousy in his words, and in spite of the terror and confusion that gripped me constantly, I was comforted by his possessiveness.

No, of course I didn't want that. None of it, and especially not Akira. Every moment that passed carried me further away from that terrible man. Even if Danjuro had not been by my side, I would have been happy at the thought that I would never see Akira again. With Danjuro miraculously restored to me, and Akira becoming more and more just a terrible nightmare with the motion of every wave, I should have begun to look to the future, and forget the past.

But I couldn't settle. Everything was so terribly strange. Apart from a short trip on a pleasure boat on the river in Edo, I had never been on a boat before. Never even seen open water. And now, we were imprisoned in a tiny cabin and I began to wake in the night, sure that the walls were moving in to crush us. Danjuro explained to me that until we were well out of Japan, it was unwise to go on deck. He didn't have to go into details; I knew perfectly well that for a Japanese person to attempt to leave Japan was a capital offense. If the authorities could be bothered to chase us, if we were caught and taken back, we were both likely to be beheaded for our crime. I choked back a moan of fear at the thought. But my cat—who had escaped with us—soon made it clear that he would be pleased to take the opportunity to go outside. I let him go; what danger was there for a cat? Surely nothing worse than a scrap with the ship's resident feline, and Neko was well able to take care of himself when it came to rival toms or even the ship's rats. But we two dared not move outside our cabin.

The knowledge that my husband was frightened gave me pause, and no mistake. Danjuro, afraid? Danjuro, who had been the leading actor in the Edo kabuki theater? The man who had enchanted the notoriously hard to please Edo audience night after night? Danjuro, who had nearly been killed by the yakuza Akira, yet had lived to tell the tale and had been brave enough to come back for me; he was afraid to go out into the light? If my husband was afraid, then I decided that we were indeed in great danger, and I prayed that we would reach our new world quickly and safely.

No matter what awaited us.

I soon had other things to occupy my mind. As we

cleared the waters around Japan's main island, the sea became rough and we were both terribly seasick. For days we could not eat, and only drank when we were desperately thirsty. I envied Neko, who wandered in and out and stared at us smugly, as if wondering what all the fuss was about.

I barely remembered changing ships. At least this second one was a little larger than the first, but the force of the sea was hardly less. I held on to Danjuro as if my life depended on it, but even the joy of finally being together constantly couldn't stop the seasickness, or the nightmares.

It began to seem to me that Akira visited me every time I slept. Time and again I felt the pain he had inflicted on me when his tattooist had engraved the symbol of his yakuza on my back. A huge rearing dragon, claws out and screaming defiance to the world in a riot of reds and yellows. Akira had gloated over it, telling me that I was the only woman he had ever honored with the symbol of his clan. But I knew he had done it for possession. For pleasure. Not for honor. Certainly not for love.

There were nights when I heard myself moan in my sleep, desperate to push Akira away before he forced himself into my body. In reality, I had not dared to defy him. Akira owned the Hidden House where I had been a geisha —a very special geisha—in Edo's center of pleasure, the Floating World. And even in the Floating World, where money could purchase almost anything, we geisha in the Hidden House were very expensive and very special.

In fact, we were unique.

Each of geisha was flawed in some way. Kiku was monstrously fat. Poor Carpi—who left this world with my help—was born without arms, her hands sprouting straight from her shoulders. One of the geisha was as tiny as a doll. Mineko—who I looked upon as my sister—was unable to feel pain. And me? I carried the sins of my mother in my face and my body, plain to be seen.

My mother, who was said to be the most beautiful and talented geisha of her generation, had eloped with my father, who was a foreign barbarian, on the day I was born. They had left me behind, and I was reared in the Hidden House. I knew no other home. I grew up to become Midori No Me—The Geisha With the Green Eyes. I had reddish hair as well, and was taller than many Japanese men. Truly, as blemished a jewel in my own way as all the other girls who were the treasures of the Hidden House.

And Akira owned all of us. We were all his property, to do with as he fancied. But for me, it was even worse.

The other geisha were convinced Akira loved me. That I was special to him. I laughed at the idea. A famous yakuza like Akira—head of the greatest gangster clan in Edo— actually loving a woman? This wicked man, who would punish and even kill at a whim, in love with a lowly geisha? If my situation had not been so tragic, it would have been funny.

Akira always had an eye for the main chance. When trade with the foreign barbarians—as we called them in those days—began in earnest, Akira realized there was money, easy money, to be made out of them. He made me learn to speak English so he would have a translator he could trust. So when I escaped from him, he not only lost his woman, it hit him where it really hurt, in his money chest.

And now it seemed Akira had his revenge on me. I could not forget him. No matter how far we fled from him, he haunted me. When the nightmares were at their worse, I clung to Danjuro, forcing him to wrap his arms around me as I hung on to his neck. Sometimes he reassured me, stroking my hair until I fell asleep again, holding me tightly. Other times he was angry at being awoken, and hugged me only briefly before turning over. I was lucky, I knew. Any other Japanese man would have shouted at me to be quiet, even thrown me out of the berth to sleep on the floor.

But Danjuro was a very special man. Akira had tried to murder him, both because he was jealous that I loved him and because he knew that Danjuro had stood in his way when he had tried to buy the kabuki theater. Just like me, Danjuro would bear Akira's mark forever. In his case, a thick scar that ran from his ribs down into his groin, caused when Akira had ordered his men to hold him down and inflict the ritual seppuku suicide cut on his poor body, leaving him for dead. But Danjuro had survived. He had not only survived, he had come back to the Floating World and snatched me away from Akira.

And now both of us were starting a new life in a new country.

And I knew that neither of us had anything to fear from Akira again.

But still I dreamed of him. And I thought that Danjuro did, too.

2

The best porcelain
Shatters easiest. Take great
Care with my heart

On that first, terrifying journey, it was only when we docked and changed ships yet again that my nightmares began to fade. This vessel was bigger; on the other ships, we had huddled in a make-shift cabin, the only passengers aboard. Now, our cabin was larger, and either I was becoming used to the motion of the sea or the waves really were smoother. Strangely, I became sure that I heard Japanese voices again. Instantly I was seized with an intense longing to demand of Danjuro that we abandon our plans, turn around and go back to the Floating World again, even if it meant facing Akira's vengeance. I was lost and bewildered and terrified of our unknown future, and I hated myself for it. But I couldn't help it.

It was my mother who saved me.

I had no memory of her at all. She had been a geisha, but unlike me, she had been flawless.

Like any traditional geisha, she had been free to take a lover of her own choosing. But unlike any other geisha, she fell deeply in love with a foreign barbarian. In those times, the whole of Japan had been almost closed to the outside world. Foreigners of any kind were few and far between, and those who were allowed into the country for trade were largely restricted by the authorities to the man-made island of Dejima. How my mother met her lover I never knew, but meet him she did. He was obviously an exceptional man, as I had learned that he both spoke and wrote Japanese like a native of Edo. In fact, Big—the feared enforcer in the Hidden House who had known and loved my mother—told me that if you closed your eyes against the glare of his fox-red hair and pale skin, and just listened to him speak, you would have thought he was Japanese.

My mother must have had immense courage as well as great beauty. When I was born, it would have been natural for her to expose me, her half foreign-devil daughter. But she did no such thing. It was not long before I left the Floating World myself that I came into possession of a letter she had left for me. I should have been given the letter as soon as I was old enough to understand what had happened, but Big—for reasons of his own—had kept it from me. He had left me thinking that my mother had hated me and had abandoned me before running away with her lover, with not a care about what would happen to me.

When I read her letter, it was as if everything that had happened in my life until that moment no longer mattered. I knew then that my dear mother had left the Floating World because she had to; because she knew that if it were discovered that she had given birth to me, then she would have been forced to expose me. And also because she knew it was certain that her lover would have been driven out of

Japan, or possibly even executed by the authorities for the dishonor he had brought on her. She didn't want to leave me behind and had always intended to come back for me as soon as she could.

But alas, that day had never come.

That barely mattered to me. The essential thing was that she loved me. And because of that, her letter gave me hope for my own future—a future that was as uncertain as her own had been on that fateful day when she had left Edo behind her.

When I had been forced to flee from Japan, my mother's letter had been one of the few things I had been able to bring with me. I read it from time to time, when I was sure that Danjuro was asleep. He knew of it, and I had always meant to share it fully with him, but somehow it never seemed to be quite the right time. Besides, reading it made me long for the familiar world of Edo, and I knew he would reprove me; tell me that we should look forward, not back.

Now, hearing the familiar Japanese voices unsettled me all over again. I longed to be back in the Floating World, with my friends in the Hidden House. Even the thought of Akira seemed less terrible than it had. Danjuro was dozing, muttering and frowning in his uneasy sleep. I put my hand on his forehead, but he shrugged me away. Lost and alone, I unfolded my precious letter and re-read it yet again. I hardly needed to see it; I had read it so many times I knew it by heart. But I needed to touch something that had been my mother's, to know that her hand had once touched the same paper I held.

And as I read it, I wondered.

I had always assumed my father was Dutch. The letter didn't say, but at the time of my birth almost all the gaijin in Japan were Dutch. There were a few Portuguese, but from my limited knowledge of them I doubted that they would have red hair. But was my father Dutch? Could he have been English, perhaps? Or even—and the thought took my breath away—American? Was it possible that I might be traveling to the same country where my mother had taken refuge so many years ago?

I asked Danjuro what he thought as soon as he woke up. I was greatly surprised when he was immediately interested.

"American? It's possible. There were a few of them in Edo years ago, I remember. Long before the black ships arrived in Edo harbor and the gaijin pushed their way into our lives. They were important men who were associated with the shogun. It would be very good for us if your father were American. If he was, he must have been wealthy. A man of position."

He stared into space, and I could see his mind working. I wanted to shake him, to tell him it wasn't important *what* my father was, just *who* he was. But I did nothing of the sort, of course. I bowed my head humbly and let him take my mother's letter from my hand. I watched him read it with pursed lips.

"No real clue there." He crumpled the letter in his fingers and it took all my willpower not to snatch it away from him. "Your father's name was Simon. A strange name, but it may be common amongst the gaijin. Still, it will do us no harm to hint that your father was a great man in America, that only courtesy prevents us naming him. In fact, the more I think about it, the more sense it makes. Your mother was the most famous geisha of her generation. She would never have been able to make his acquaintance if he was a nobody. She certainly would never have taken him for her lover."

He was pleased, I could see. He was nodding and humming to himself. Neko chose that moment to yowl to be allowed out, and Danjuro glared at him.

"I'll let him out," I said hurriedly. "In fact, if you would allow it, I would like to go with him. Some fresh air would be pleasant."

He shrugged, tossing my precious letter aside. Although he seemed to be looking at me, I guessed his thoughts were far away, back at the kabuki. Perhaps he was working on a twist to one of his famous roles, or reviewing a favorite play. I had no way of knowing which, but it didn't matter. I felt a flash of irrational jealousy; Danjuro would never be home-sick. Never really miss Japan. He had no need; he carried it in the depths of his soul, recalled it fondly every time he thought of his beloved kabuki. Ah, lucky man!

He nodded. He wanted to concentrate, and for the moment I was a distraction.

"Yes, do. We must be well out of Japanese waters by now. We should be safe. Don't be too long."

I grabbed my precious letter as I got to my feet, tucking it away in the chest that contained all our possessions. I turned at the door, hoping for a word of encouragement—after all, it had been a long time since I had ventured beyond the cabin door—but Danjuro was already lost in the play unwinding in his mind, and I decided it was better not to disturb him.

The deck was paradise compared to the dark, close-smelling cabin. I paused in the companionway, my feet suddenly reluctant to take me any further forward. And then I saw the sea, and I was lost. It was so big. So blue. So...free.

At first, I saw nothing but sea and sky. I took deep breaths, savoring the sweet, salty air. Neko ran in front of

me, pawing playfully at bits of rope, turning around occasionally and mewing as if to say, "Come on! Nothing to be
afraid of!" I followed him as if I was hypnotized by his
antics, and then came to an abrupt halt.

"Sumimasen deshita. Sumimasen deshita."

I am so very sorry. I am so very sorry. I put my head
down and mumbled the words to my feet. The group of
men I had almost walked into stared at me in surprise, their
gaze licking me from head to foot. I knew their brief
appraisal told them all they wanted—and needed—to
know. They had a geisha on board. A woman who belonged
in the flower and willow world. Odd that I should be here,
but I need not concern them.

"Pass by, geisha."

The man who spoke was turning back to his companions before he had finished the sentence. I bowed deeply
and scampered past as quickly as my hobbling kimono
would allow. Once again, I was terrified. I was shaking with
fear. When Danjuro had spoken of the possibility of us
being taken back to Japan, I had consoled myself with the
thought that we were not important enough to be pursued.
Oh, Danjuro was a famous man; as the chief actor in the
kabuki theater, he was recognized throughout Edo. But
outside his own world, he was not a significant figure. He
was rich, but he had no power. The ordinary people of the
Floating World adored him, but to the upper caste nobles
we were nothing at all. They would look upon as hoi polloi;
in fact, to them we would be nothing but riverbed beggars,
as our class was contemptuously called.

These men were obviously rich. But I knew from the
brief glance I had taken of them that they also had power.
They were nobles. Men of the highest class. Their robes
were subdued in color, but made from the costliest fabrics.

They wore swords, even here onboard a ship. But apart from anything else, it was simply the way they held themselves. These were men who were used to respect. To being obeyed, instantly.

And they were here. Fleeing from Japan alongside Danjuro and me.

I trembled as much with indignation as shock. They had no right to be here! They should be back in Japan, where they belonged. It was well-known gossip in the Floating World that none of the nobles were happy about the invading gaijin. In fact, it was thought that many of them were working to overthrow the mighty invaders. Even those who had accepted the foreign invasion with a resigned shrug would never have contemplated leaving Japan for the West. How could they? It was forbidden. Literally, on pain of death. As the thought came to me, confusion mixed with my fear. Danjuro and I were not important enough for the authorities to go to any great lengths to chase us and take us back. But these men were different. They were great men. For all I knew, even members of the shogun's court. For them, the risk must be ten-fold. Why were they fleeing alongside us poor riverbed beggars?

"Is the wind going to change do you think? Time to trim the sails, maybe? Oh, dammit. You don't understand a word, do you?"

The gaijin words intruded on my thoughts, making me blink with surprise. I was even more shocked when I heard a response in Japanese. The accent was very rough and strange to my ears, but it was, most definitely, Japanese.

"Stupid foreign devil, bleating like a goat. How am I supposed to know what you're talking about? Baah! Baah! Make sure you don't fall overboard and get your beard wet!"

I translated the gaijin sailor's words into Japanese automatically, and spoke without thinking.

"He wants to know if you think the wind is going to change, and if it is, should he trim the sails?"

"Ah." The Japanese sailor spat to one side and shrugged. "Why didn't he ask me properly, then, in Japanese? No, the wind is set fair. Nothing for us to do. Will you tell the bleating goat that?"

I hid a smile at his indignation and spoke quietly to the gaijin sailor. "He says you need to do nothing. The wind is not going to change."

To my amazement, the sailor touched his forehead to me in what I knew was a mark of respect amongst the gaijin.

"Thank you, ma'am. I sure wish I could speak Japanese, or any other language for that matter, a mite as well as you speak American."

I was moved, both by the compliment and his courtesy. But I was also deeply puzzled. Before I had time to really wonder at the strangeness of Japanese and gaijin working side by side, I was shocked yet again, but this time by the nobles. One second, they were drawn apart from me as if the touch of their robes against my kimono might have contaminated them. The next, they were clustered around me and I had nowhere to go. Neko yowled defiance at them, and I scooped him into my arms quickly, afraid one of them might take offense and kick him over the side.

"Geisha." The oldest of the men spoke to me, and I bowed deeply.

"Lord." I made sure that my voice was high-pitched and breathy. I hoped it also sounded sufficiently humble.

"You speak the gaijin language?"

"Yes, lord."

"Where did you learn?"

"In Edo, lord. My master traded with the gaijin, and he needed somebody who could speak the truth of what they were saying."

The silence in the ring of men was unnerving.

"You may raise your head, geisha."

I did so, but took care to ensure that my eyes were carefully downcast.

"You are Japanese? From Edo?"

He sounded deeply suspicious. I wondered about lying, but the sun chose that moment to come out and I heard all of the men draw in their breath in a hiss. My hair. Of course. The sun would bring out the red in it. I gave in and raised my face.

"I was born in Edo, lord. My mother was a geisha, like me, but my father was a gaijin."

The men stared at my eyes in fascination. The older noble who had spoken to me reached out his hand to my face and scrubbed at my eye with his thumb, thrusting his head close to me to see if he had made any change. Instantly, I was back in the Hidden House, with my danna. Kneeling on the tatami in front of the old man who had paid a fortune for my ritual deflowerment, my mizuage.

I was thirteen years old again, and terrified.

Teruki-san had spat on his fingers and taken a tendril of hair in his fist, first tugging it and then rubbing it between his wet fingers. He glanced at his fingers, and then repeated the process with another lock of hair. Appearing satisfied, he had let the hair fall loose and then leaned forward, pushing my chin up with his thumb.

"Open your eyes, wide."

I did so, and Teruki-san leaned forward and pulled my left eye wide open, holding the eyelid tightly between his thumb and first finger. With his free hand, he rubbed the ball of his thumb across my eye, quite hard. It hurt and I tried to blink, but could not as his grip was too tight.

He inspected his thumb carefully, and then repeated the process with my other eye.

I shivered as the long-buried memory came back to haunt me. But things were different now. I was no longer a frightened child. I wasn't even in Japan. I had survived my mizuage, and so very much more. I would not show fear to this man. Neko growled, deep in his throat, and I took courage from his defiance.

I raised my chin and stared back at the noble, refusing to allow my watering eye to as much as blink. He frowned and then one of the younger men laughed, breaking the tension.

"She has spirit, Takishima-san. Are you bound for America, geisha? What is your name?"

He pronounced "America" awkwardly, and it took me a moment to realize what he was asking me. *Oh, well.* I thought. *When one has eaten poisoned food, it was as well to swallow the plate,* as the proverb has it.

"I and my husband are going to America. My name is Midori No Me. And my husband is Danjuro, from the Edo kabuki theater."

I waited for the hiss of a sword leaving its scabbard to punish my rudeness, but there was nothing but an astonished silence for a moment. And then the eldest noble began to laugh. At first, I thought it was the creaking of the ship's timbers, the sound was so dry, so unused. The rest of the nobles immediately followed his lead, tittering politely.

"Well, Midori No Me." He grinned, showing uneven yellow teeth. "You are indeed an unusual geisha. And very well named."

I wasn't afraid of him—after all, what could he do to me that hadn't already been done? Apart from kill me, of course, and I had come so close to that so many times that death had little fear for me now.

I bowed my head and hid a smile.

"Danjuro, you say? And how does a geisha who is half-gaijin and a famous kabuki actor come to be fleeing from Japan?"

"The kabuki theater burned down, lord. Danjuro felt it was worth the risk for us to try our luck in America with a new kabuki. My husband has an important patron waiting for us in San Francisco."

Not the whole truth, but still true. The kabuki had burned to ashes. Danjuro did have a patron waiting for us. I watched as the oldest noble slid the syllables of "San Francisco" around his tongue, trying—and failing—to grasp the strange sounds. The other men exchanged glances, and it was the younger one who spoke.

"Takishima-san. I am sure that this will have no effect on our plans. Although no doubt it will be good to have a reminder of Edo waiting for us, in the form of the kabuki."

His voice was bland, but I understood his meaning immediately, as would any geisha who had spent years listening not just to the words uttered by her patrons, but to the real meaning behind the words. I had been politely dismissed.

"You are right, Shimazu. Of course. It doesn't matter. You may go geisha," the elderly man said. "No doubt your husband is waiting for you."

I muttered gratitude for my escape and turned and dashed for the stairs, clutching a mewing Neko firmly in my arms. I could feel that I was being watched with every step I took.

"Where have you been? What has taken you so long? Did I hear you speaking in English?"

Danjuro had opened the porthole in our cabin—he must have heard me through it. For a second, I was tempted to tell him all about my strange encounter with the Japanese nobles, and then my mouth was speaking without my instruction and the moment was gone. I told myself I didn't want to worry him, yet at the same time I knew it was more a case of not being able to bear being penned in the same cabin with a worried and fretting husband.

"I am sorry I have been so long. One of the gaijin sailors was trying to ask a Japanese sailor for instructions, so I translated for him. That must have been what you heard."

Danjuro frowned, his expression sulky. He spoke a little English, but not nearly as much as I did, and I knew he was jealous of my ability.

"You should not have done that! If anybody had over-heard you, they would have remembered the geisha who spoke English. If anybody came looking for us, it could be very bad."

He spoke so angrily that I breathed a sigh of relief that I had not told him about the group of nobles I had met on deck. If he was furious with me for speaking to a mere sailor in English, what would his reaction have been had he known about them? Apart from that, they worried me. I hoped that the Japanese authorities would not bother to go to the expense of chasing Danjuro and me, but they would certainly be very interested in retrieving the fleeing nobles. We would have been nothing more than small fish caught in the net, but caught nonetheless.

"I am sorry," I apologized quickly. "Danjuro, isn't it strange that this ship should have a Japanese sailor on board, working with the gaijin sailors?"

"Not really." He shrugged. "We are no longer in Japanese waters, but to the gaijin our entire world is strange. They would need a Japanese sailor who knows the seas around here, and I understand that there are now many gaijin sailors in the area. I imagine the Japanese you spoke to was from the Far Islands. They are strange men, a law unto themselves. Nobody cares greatly what they do or where they go."

He was still angry with me, I could tell. I glanced around the cabin, looking for something to distract him with.

Paper was littered all over the floor where he had discarded it. Danjuro's calligraphy was messy. Not because he lacked the talent to make beautiful characters, but more because he lacked the patience. He flicked his characters on the paper carelessly, desperate to get his thoughts down before they were lost. I shuffled the papers together carefully, realizing at a glance that he had been working on a version of *Sonezaki Shinju—The Love Suicides at Sonezaki*. This was the first play I had seen Danjuro perform in the kabuki at Edo and I loved it. I gave a cry of pleasure.

"Ah. Are you going to perform this in America?"

Immediately mollified, he shrugged. "I thought it might be suitable. You've always longed to play in the kabuki, haven't you? Well, do you want the chance to appear in this? Only a very small part, of course. But enough to satisfy your dreams."

I was so excited, I could do no more than gasp. Danjuro grinned.

"We will see," he said superbly. "I understand that the gaijin do not find it strange to see women performing on the stage. If that is so, we should perhaps try it."

He took the papers from my hand and rifled through them, stacking them to his satisfaction.

"You were gone a long time." He returned to his grievance, the play forgotten for the moment. "Were you so happy out there that you forgot about me?"

He was still annoyed with me, then. I bit my lip and looked at his face, searching for a signal. He looked furious. His eyebrows were drawn together, and his lips set in a thin, straight line. His eyes sparked fire. But after a quick glance, I relaxed. I had seen Danjuro perform in the kabuki too many times to be fooled easily. This was the expression he wore when he was playing the villain, sneering at the fools who were trying to get the better of him.

Ah! Two could play this game. I took a deep breath, and when I spoke my voice was soft and trembling.

"Husband, I am so sorry. The air was fresh on deck, and I was interested to watch the sea. I thought I was not gone for long."

"You were forever!" His tone was sulky, and I hid a smile.

"I am sorry," I repeated. "Perhaps I could try and make it up to you?"

Danjuro said nothing, but I risked a quick look at his face from beneath my eyelashes and I saw his expression had changed. Now, he was no longer the angry villain, but rather the wronged lover. His face was noble, wrestling with emotions he was trying not to show. Dear man! I might be his sole audience, but still he was the star of the kabuki, and I loved him the more for it. Neko glanced from me to Danjuro and closed his eyes in contempt for the strange games we humans played. With typical cat disdain, he turned his back, curled nose to tail and promptly went to sleep.

I envied him. I longed for the chance to sit and think about my strange encounter with the Japanese nobles, but I was not given the chance.

"Well?" Danjuro's voice broke my train of thought abruptly. He was tapping his foot impatiently, waiting for me to respond to my cue. "I do not have all day to wait for you, Midori No Me."

I almost laughed out loud. If not time, what else did we have?

"I am sorry," I said yet again. But this time, I accompanied it with action. I kneeled in front of Danjuro and rested my head lightly against his knees, waiting for him to indicate what would please him. When he remained silent and did not move, I raised my head and looked at him hopefully.

The breath caught in my throat. His face was...naked. No actor's expression looked back at me. No heartbroken lover, no menacing villain. I thought I saw tears in his eyes and my own eyes widened in response.

"Danjuro?"

"We are doing the right thing, aren't we?" He spoke hesitatingly, and it was so unlike him that I was frightened. "If we had stayed in Edo, you would have remained Akira's slave, and eventually he would have killed me for sure."

He was talking to himself, not me, and I realized he was trying to convince himself that he was right. Of course he was. Hadn't we talked about this a hundred times, and each time decided that we had had no option? But his worry was contagious and I frowned.

"We could not have stayed," I said firmly. "There was no future for us in Edo, especially not in the Floating World. Even if Akira hadn't killed you, he would have made sure you never got the kabuki back, and we could never have been together. Life will be better in America."

"Yes." The single word was a hiss. We stared into each other's eyes for a long moment, and we both knew the truth.

We were afraid.

Afraid not of Akira, who was far behind us and out of our lives. But afraid of the unknown. In Edo, Danjuro had been a well-known man. Star and part owner of the kabuki theater, he was wealthy and famous. Women—and men—had thrown themselves at his feet. He could not walk the streets without being recognized. I had been nothing but a geisha, kept secret in the Hidden House, but when Akira had taken me to be his mistress there was nobody in the whole of Edo who would have dared to lift a finger against me. In our own ways, both Danjuro and I had been invincible.

Now, we were nothing. We were rats jumping ship. Less even than riverbed beggars.

The knowledge chilled me to the bone. I grabbed Danjuro's robe and hauled myself up with it, flinging myself against him and burying my face in his chest. Far from giving comfort, now I needed it myself.

"We had to leave," I bawled. "Akira would have killed us both."

"Would he?" Danjuro spoke softly. "Would he have killed both of us? Do you really think so?"

I raised my head to stare at him in bewilderment. His face was a blank canvas; only his eyes were alive, burning with an expression I found hard to interpret. Anger, yes. But something more. He gripped my hands, forcing me away from him.

"Take your kimono off. Your underclothes as well."

I smiled hesitatingly, groping for understanding. I knew instinctively that this was not some new love game he was playing, and I was bewildered. But I reacted immediately, as any good geisha—any good Japanese wife or mistress, for that matter—would. I stood and took off my obi, and followed it with my kimono, glancing at Danjuro's face from time to time to see if he was pleased. His expression remained still. My chemise and under things followed until I stood in front of him naked.

Each time we made love it was a joyful reawakening of all our senses. There was little we had not tried. We had no need of pillow books to guide our instinct; we had both known from the first that the gods had meant us for each other. There had been no shyness, no shame. Now, I sensed there was something wrong. I felt awkward and I had to fight the urge to lace my hands in front of my black moss to hide my discomfort.

"Turn around."

I turned, slowly. The skin on my back crawled underneath his stare.

"It's very well done, isn't it? One might almost think it was alive. Will it ever fade, do you think?"

His finger traced the outline of my dragon. I shivered with something akin to pain beneath his touch. I hated that tattoo. The only comfort I could ever take was the fact that it was on my back, where I could never see it. Akira had put it there. The rearing, vengeful dragon that ran from the nape of my neck to the small of my back was the symbol of his clan. He had one exactly the same tattooed on his own back, although on Akira it was less startling since his whole body, with the exception of his hands and his neck and face, were covered in yakuza tattoos. My dragon disfigured me. It marked me as Akira's creature for the whole of my days on earth. It had taken the tattoo artist a whole day to prick it beneath my flesh. It would never fade. I would bear it in all its glory until my dying day.

Akira had been very clever. For Japanese men, the nape of the neck was the most erotic part of a woman's body. Far more so than her breasts, and even more so than her black moss. Only he could see the dragon, but its position meant that I would always make sure that the back of my neck was covered.

"It will not fade." My voice was hoarse. "Akira paid too much to inflict it on me. I will never lose it."

"I hate it." For a moment, I thought I had spoken out loud, then I realized that the voice was Danjuro's, echoing my own thoughts. "It marks you as his. He loved you, you know. Did you love him in return? Is that why you let him put this on your back?"

I was so shocked, I couldn't speak. Danjuro obviously misinterpreted my silence as he snatched his fingers away from my back as if my dragon had truly spat fire at him. I turned to look at my husband and was appalled to see tears running down his face.

"I hated him," I whispered. "Every day I spent with him was torture. I didn't *let* him put his mark on me; I had no choice."

"You could have killed yourself," Danjuro said bluntly. "You always had that choice."

Suicide. The honorable way out of an intolerable situation for any Japanese. I swallowed and shook my head. So many of the kabuki plays ended that way, often with both hero and heroine committing suicide together. The audience loved it. And the theater mirrored real life. Suicide, whether by seppuku—the ritual self-cutting with a sharp knife from chest to black moss—or drowning or taking poison was respected. There were any number of high points around Edo called "lovers' leaps" for good reason.

Yes, I could have killed myself. And no doubt it would have been an honorable death. But I didn't commit suicide. In fact, even in the darkest of days, it had never entered my head. I had always known in my heart that Danjuro was not dead, as everybody thought. Had always known that the gods would not keep us apart forever. Through everything that Akira chose to do to me, I had always clung on to that knowledge. It had kept me sane, had given me hope for the future.

And now that future was here, and Danjuro was asking me why I had waited for him instead of killing myself. I was devastated.

"You loved Akira, didn't you?" he repeated.

Loved him? Loved the monster who had abused me, turned my every waking moment into terror, deprived every night of sleep for fear of the nightmares that would haunt me? I laughed aloud, and then saw the expression on Danjuro's face.

He was suffering. It took me a moment of total confusion before I understood. He thought I had truly loved Akira. And he was jealous. Jealous to the point where he was prepared to show his feelings to me, a mere woman! For a Japanese man, this was unthinkable. I had no words to comfort him with. I had a huge pain between my breasts; I felt as if all the air had been squeezed out of my lungs. I yawned widely, not because I was tired, but because I felt I needed to take a deep breath and could not. Danjuro obviously thought the yawn was boredom because he closed his eyes and his head flinched back as if I had struck him.

My mouth opened and closed, but no words would come out. This was all wrong. It was Danjuro who had snatched me away from the Floating World. Danjuro who had told me that we were both going to start a new life, far, far away from the terrors we had both lived through. I had loved him from the first moment I had seen him, and from that very moment I had hoped and prayed that our fates were entwined. It was Danjuro who should have been telling me what was going to happen. Danjuro who should have been the pillar of strength that would support me through all the strangeness. He was the man, after all. I was nothing, a mere geisha.

Here I was in the middle of a strange ocean, bound for a country I had only ever heard of. I had left behind everything I had ever known to follow my dream with this man. And he was weeping because he thought I loved a man I hated.

I raised my shoulders and let them fall helplessly. In my mind, I was a child again. A very small child who was lost and alone in a huge forest. All around me, strange noises murmured, and wherever I looked, it was all the same. There was no way forward, no way back. I scrunched my eyes up tightly to stop myself bawling alongside Danjuro.

The touch on my cheek was as light as the breeze. I stiffened with superstitious fear, knowing that apart from Danjuro there was nobody else in the cabin. And then, right in my ear, so close I could almost feel the words, came the sweetest of voices.

I came this way before you. Like you, I followed my heart. You are not alone, dearest. You will never be alone. I am waiting for you, just as I have always been. We will find each other. But you must be strong. Depend on no one but yourself. Remember what I wrote to you, so many years ago? Don't let anyone tell you that I and your father did not love you. For that is not true, and never will be. You were the most beautiful baby I had ever seen, and your eyes are the exact color of your father's eyes. We both loved you, and we will think about you every day until we are together again. You have suffered much, my daughter. Don't let it be for nothing. Be strong. Wait.

So real was the voice that I spoke out loud.

"I love you."

Although I spoke to the spirit of my dear mother, Danjuro obviously thought I was speaking to him. He cleared his throat and opened his eyes and sniffed back tears.

"You are sure? You have no wish to return to the Floating World? To Akira?"

I smiled at him, my joy at my mother's voice spilling into my face. "I hated Akira. Hated every second I was with him. Hated everything that he made me do. If I could lose his mark by having the skin flayed off my back, I would do it happily. But the needles went too deep; nothing I can do will erase it. Ever." I reached out and slid my fingers inside his robe, trailing my nail down the wicked scar Akira had inflicted on him. The scar that should never have healed, but should have killed him. He sucked in his breath, and I knew that it was still tender. "Neither of us can lose Akira. His mark is on both of us. But he cannot hurt us again."

My voice was strong, and I think that Danjuro drew strength from it. He placed his hand over my fingers and pressed them hard against the scar. I felt the strange, slippery texture of it beneath my fingertips and I shuddered, feeling the pain he must have endured. Then his hand was forcing my fingers further down his body and my smile widened. We had made love little on the journey so far, and when we had, it had been a swift, unfulfilling sort of affair. Now, I hoped, we might be back to normal.

Danjuro took his hand away from me, but I continued to let my fingers trail down his belly. When I reached his black moss, he grunted with pleasure, but the noise quickly became disappointed when I took my hand away. I leaned forward and unloosed his robe. Danjuro immediately groped for my breast, but I shook my head and stepped back.

"Lie down," I said softly. Strange how even the most dominant of men could become pliable when he foresaw pleasure! Danjuro lay back immediately, his robe falling back to show his thrusting tree of flesh. I ran my fingernail down its length. I knew he was watching me intently, but I refused to be hurried. After all, this was my domain. After my mizuage, I had been taught to give pleasure to men in every way possible; although, until Danjuro had come into my life, I had never known the joy of accepting pleasure as well as giving it. Had Akira also given me pleasure? I pushed the thought away before it could spoil this moment.

Satisfied with my inspection, I leaned forward until my lips could tease the head of his tree. Danjuro could stand it no longer. With a roar of frustration, he pushed himself into my mouth. I allowed my lips to part just far enough so that his flesh scraped against my teeth, and then I bit. Quite hard.

Pleasure and pain are often the twin sides of the same coin. Used properly, together they can give far more than simple pleasure on its own. Danjuro moaned; I released my grip slightly. He tried to pull away, although the attempt was half-hearted. I bit again, just where the flesh is at its most tender, where the hood joins the trunk of the tree. I allowed my teeth to grind together.

His tree of flesh tasted and smelled of the sea. Slightly salty. Fresh. Totally delicious. I wanted to eat him up, but I was not given the chance.

Danjuro grabbed me by my shoulders and lifted me bodily until I was dangling over him. Very slowly, watching my face every second, he lowered me down on to his tree. Suddenly deeply excited, I bit my tongue so hard it drew blood. I licked my lips, tasting him and me together. I wanted more, far more. I wanted to take every fraction of him inside me.

"Who do you love, Midori No Me?"

"You," I said simply. I had learned during the months and years I had served in the Hidden House never to believe a word a man said to me when he was in search of bursting the fruit. But now I wanted to hear my man tell me that I was his love. That I was the one and only. And I wanted to believe him, more than anything.

"Do you love me?" I demanded. I tightened my inner muscles as I spoke, so that no matter how hard he might try, Danjuro could not slide me down any further on his tree. Torture for the both of us, but I needed to hear him say the words. Needed to believe in them even more.

"You are my love. For you I have left behind everything. Our life now is together."

Odd, isn't it? You are given what you long for, and then you doubt it. I devoured Danjuro's face with my gaze, seeking the truth in his expression. His eyes met mine, his whole face open and joyful. Yet still, I wondered. This man had been the star actor in the Edo kabuki theater, the best in the whole of Japan. I had been moved to tears many times watching him perform.

Did I believe him now? I wanted to, so I let hope overcome doubt and relaxed my sex, allowing him to slide me down so that our black moss mingled. But still I watched his actor's face, knowing that my heart would break if I saw any hint of deceit there.

"My love. My life."

His eyes were closed, and even as he spoke, his mouth reached for my neck, nuzzling at the hollow above my shoulder bones. His tongue trailed there and I sighed, knowing that I would never be entirely sure. But after a moment or two, nothing really mattered except the hardness of his tree ramming inside me, and the feel of his hands running over my body, cupping my breasts and scratching at my belly. I thought I might scream when his fingers moved around to my back and slid over my tattoo. Normally, my back was not especially tender, but today I swear I felt my dragon move, its claws scrabbling at Danjuro's hands. Perhaps he felt it too, as he became still.

"One day, I will kill Akira." Danjuro's voice was so deep, it reverberated against my neck. "For the harm he has done to both of us, he deserves it."

"One day," I agreed, wriggling against him. "But not today."

I laughed, and after a heartbeat Danjuro laughed with me and took his fingers away from my dragon and concentrated instead on making both of us happy.

We lay close in the narrow berth, content. Danjuro was dozing, his head on my breasts. I could feel the heat glowing on my back and I wondered with a shiver of fear if somehow Akira was watching us. Was his power truly so great that his dragon could somehow see and hear and report back to its master? The thought made me feel sick, as if my own body was betraying me.

I moved carefully so I did not disturb Danjuro and lay on my back. I was sure I heard my dragon grunt with annoyance and I was pleased. I wriggled down into the mattress, carefully, and willed it to suffocate. When I realized what I was doing, I almost laughed aloud. It was all my imagination, nothing more.

We were free. And I decided at that moment that I would not give Akira a second thought. Ever again.

3

The butterfly sips
His nectar. A short life but
Oh! Such a free one

I kneeled, my head tapping the floor in an excess of politeness. I had realized after a very brief moment that I would have to be careful in paying my respects. The beautifully polished wood block floor was bare, and it would be all too easy to bash my forehead painfully. At my side, Danjuro bowed deeply.

My breath banged against my ribs. I was very grateful for the need to kowtow deeply to our new patron. My legs would have given way if I hadn't been kneeling.

I knew him. Not well, but it would be fair to say that I had been in his company often in the Floating World. Would the past never leave us alone?

I could hear Danjuro speaking from high above me, his voice reverential. I stayed where I was. Sourly, I realized that I knew my place already in this new society—it was exactly the same lowly position that I had occupied in the Hidden

House where our new patron in America had been a regular and enthusiastic customer. Why hadn't Danjuro warned me? Even as the thought came to me, I understood that he could not have known. If he had, he would never have risked bringing me here; rather, he would have hidden me away. The shame would have choked him.

"You may rise, geisha. Welcome to my humble house, Danjuro-san."

His voice was smug. Self-importance rang in every word. I rose to my knees but stayed with my eyes cast down to the floor, my hands flat on my thighs. From a long way away, I could hear our patron speaking to Danjuro, asking him to sit down, to make himself comfortable in a chair. As if that was possible for those of us who were used to sitting cross-legged on tatami matting!

"You are kind, lord," Danjuro murmured.

Not that our patron was a lord, or anything like it, but Danjuro knew the benefits of a little flattery as well as I did. I searched my memory furiously for his name, smiling all the time. Would he recognize me? I had never been his favorite; he had had eyes only for Carpi. If she had not been available, he had refused anybody else. Had she liked him? I pummeled my memory in a desperate effort to recall his name, but came up with nothing except Carpi's sarcastic voice.

They're all the same, she said. *Each and every one of our dear patrons. All they want me to do for them is to twirl the stem with my feet and that's it.*

Out of all us geisha in the Hidden House, Carpi had been the most exotic.

She had been born without arms, her hands sprouting straight from her shoulders. But necessity had made her as able with her feet and toes as the rest of us were with our hands; she could even feed herself with chopsticks, using her toes as fingers. The patrons loved her. Or at least they had, until she had developed a terrible wasting disease. She had begged for release, and finally my friend Mineko and I had helped to free her spirit from this world.

I took a deep breath, trying to jog my memory. *Come on, Carpi. What was he called?* Carpi did not let me down.

That one—Sato-san. That was it! *He thinks because he leaves me a nice present now and then I should fall down and worship at his feet every time he shows his face.*

But even Carpi, courageous as she was, had known better than to answer back to the patrons. She might hate herself for it, but she had still cooed over Sato-san as though she was delighted that he had chosen her. I hoped against hope that he had been so infatuated with Carpi that he had simply not noticed the rest of us. And of course, he would hardly expect to see me here, a world away from the Hidden House. I prayed silently that I was right, and it appeared that the gods heard my desperate pleas.

Sato-san called for sake. Perhaps he finally noticed I was in the way, crouching in the middle of the floor. He called out to me in a voice that dripped with condescension.

"Geisha. You may sit at the feet of your danna."

I waited for Danjuro to tell him that he was my husband, not my danna—my protector—but he did no such thing, so I stood anyway and shuffled over to Danjuro and sat at his feet as Sato-san had instructed.

"Now, Danjuro. To business. I have arranged lodgings for you. Some of your old troupe of actors is already here, and I have no doubt that they will be delighted to see you again. Not a full complement, of course, but they will do. I have already spoken to one of my gaijin acquaintances who owns a theater here. There is a fashion for everything

Japanese amongst the gaijin, and I am sure that you will find a ready audience for the kabuki."

I heard Danjuro murmur his thanks. I bit my lip as I felt the blood rush to my face. We had been so naïve! We had thought ourselves so brave, so special, daring to flee from Japan. Every day on the ocean trip, we had worried that the authorities might, after all, decide to pursue us. Pursue us and make an example of us by dragging us back to Edo, probably to be publicly executed as soon as we arrived. We had not been in San Francisco long before we realized we were not special at all.

There was already a surprising amount of Japanese people in the city. Prosperous merchants like our patron. Men who had been shrewd enough to realize the profits that could be made trading with the gaijin in their own country. And of course, they had brought their families and servants with them. But it was not just rich men who had fled from Japan. It seemed to our astonished gaze that every class of Japanese society was there before us, everybody from common laborers to craftsmen.

At first, we had been bewildered. How, we wondered, was it possible for so many people to leave Japan? How had they dared? How had the authorities come to allow it? Understanding came slowly, although when it did, the answer was obvious.

Many Japanese people had seen the wealth of the gaijin, and had envied it. Sailors and craftsmen were welcomed for their skills; they could work their passage to the new world on the gaijin's ships, and once settled they could send for their families. The merchants, of course, had enough money to pay their way. And the authorities had known all about it but had also known they could do nothing to stop the hemorrhage, so they had simply ignored it. What else could they do without losing face in front of the whole of Japan?

Now, Sato-san was nodding regally. Danjuro had his head bowed, and was looking suitably grateful. I followed his lead.

I managed to keep still until we were dismissed. As we rose to leave, Sato-san glanced at me.

"Geisha, do I know you? You look a little familiar."

"I do not think so, Sato-san." I was so terrified, my voice was barely a whisper. Surely, he had not recognized me at the last moment? "I would have remembered such a distinguished man as you."

He smirked and seemed satisfied. I saw the interest die out of his eyes and I managed to breathe. But I had relaxed too soon. A moment later I could barely believe I was hearing right as he added casually,

"It's as well you have her with you, Danjuro. She's been well-trained in the arts, I take it? Knows how to sing and dance?"

I saw the slight frown between Danjuro's brows. "Of course. She can also play the samisen very well."

"Excellent. The gaijin will expect to see a woman taking the lead female roles. It's the correct thing here. She will do nicely featured in the kabuki, I would think."

He dismissed us with a nod. Sato-san's carriage—the same carriage that had brought us here from the docks—was outside, and we climbed in. I was so relieved that our patron had put aside any thoughts that he had seen me before that I could think of nothing else and barely noticed Danjuro's silence. Had Sato-san recognized me, it would have been the end of all our hopes and dreams. Danjuro would have been so filled with shame that it would have destroyed him. He would have had no option but to walk away from Sato-san, and probably me as well. My release was so great that it shouldered everything else aside and I jumped when Danjuro spoke abruptly.

"What on earth was Sato-san thinking of, when he said you would be expected to take the lead female roles?"

For once, I had no answer for him.

4

Honey cloys; too sweet.
Ginger alone is too hot.
Together? Perfect!

The nature of time was a popular thread of discussion among learned men in Japan. Some said that as time could be measured accurately, then time was always constant. Others disagreed, and insisted that the passage of time varied according to the time of day or night and between seasons. How else, they said, could the day be shorter in winter than it was in summer? At the time, none of the discussions had made any sense to me. Now, I understood that those who had said that time could ebb and flow and that it differed according to many factors were correct.

Although we had landed in San Francisco only hours before we were taken to see Sato-san, it felt to me as though we sat and waited for days. Danjuro had commanded that we would stay in our cabin. I had no idea how long we sat there; I watched the shadows lengthen in the light that came through our porthole, unable to believe that night was not about to shoo away the daylight. When it got to the stage where my stomach rumbled out loud with hunger, I could stand it no longer. I stood and peered out. Even on tip-toe I could see nothing but the sea, but I knew from the steadiness of the deck beneath my feet that we were not moving. Danjuro sat and stared into space, his actor's face impassive.

"Danjuro, we must go on deck." I pleaded. I sat beside him and wound my hand in his robe, tugging gently. "Your patron may be looking for us. If he doesn't find us, what will he think?"

He shook his head imperceptibly.

"We will stay here. He will find us."

I looked at him appealingly, but he was stone. I supposed he was right; what else could we do? We had no idea where to go. Danjuro glanced at my worried face and relented; our patron would be along at any moment, he insisted. But I knew him too well to be deceived. He was as frightened as I was. Perhaps more so. At least I was acquainted with the people from this strange world, could speak their language. Danjuro knew nothing at all about them. In a flash of insight, I realized that that was half the problem. For the first time in many years, Danjuro was nobody. An unknown in an unknown land.

And it frightened him.

His fear was contagious. Neither Neko nor I could keep still. We prowled around the cabin, nearly tripping over each other. Neko planted his claws in the trunk containing all our goods, and for once Danjuro didn't shout at him. I felt sick with fear and hunger, and almost jumped out of my skin when the knock on our door finally came.

Danjuro rose and stretched, sauntering across the small space superbly with only a single, smug glance at me to say "told you so!" I was still on edge, sure that this was one of the crew come to tell us we had to get out. But I was wrong.

"Danjuro-san?" And who else did he expect? I wondered with a flash of irritation. "Welcome to America!"

The man had switched abruptly from Japanese to English. Only his pronunciation was so dreadful, it took me a moment to understand what he was trying to say. I felt Danjuro tense beside me, and I was suddenly annoyed. How dare this man—who from his dress was obviously some sort of servant—try to be superior to us! He would not expect us to speak English; he was doing it on purpose to put us in our place.

I spoke quickly, my head up, my expression condescending. "Thank you for your greeting. You have been a long time getting here. Danjuro was becoming annoyed. You have come to take us to our patron?"

The servant goggled at me. I tapped my foot impatiently as I watched him trying to translate my excellent and rapid English.

"Ah." Getting the gist of my words, the servant bowed deeply. When he spoke again it was in Japanese. And his voice was humble. "I am so sorry I am late. It took me a long time to get here. Please, if you will come this way?"

Danjuro nodded regally and waved at our heavy trunk. The servant was so cowed he didn't hesitate, but hoisted it on his back and—bent double with the effort—grunted his way off the ship in front of us, finally bowing us into a private carriage.

The same carriage where we were sitting once again. Only now, the mood of optimism that had buoyed us up on the journey to see Sato-san had been shattered. Danjuro was frowning, his expression deeply troubled.

"I don't understand. Sato-san is very familiar with the

kabuki. What on earth makes him think that a female could take a major part in it?"

"But you said, when we on the ship, that I might take part in the kabuki," I pointed out gently.

"Yes. You will be an excellent actress, Midori No Me-chan. I am sure of that. But I was thinking that you would be good in the minor roles, where you could show your talents singing and dancing. I understand that our onnagata from the Edo kabuki is already here. He, of course, will take the main women's roles. It is only proper. I will speak to Sato-san again. He will understand."

He sat back, staring out of the carriage window, his face closed. I didn't argue. There was no point. And did it matter? Since I had seen my first kabuki performance, I had been enraptured. Mineko came to the play with me, when she was still a maiko in the Hidden House, and we had laughed and cried and applauded together, both of us so caught up in the action playing out before us that we had left the reality of our world behind us. Ah, we had sighed. If only we could perform on that stage! The smallest, the most insignificant part would do. And now? I had my wish. I was going to perform in the kabuki in this strange new world.

Could I really ask for any more?

I risked a glance out of the carriage, and my eyes widened with amazement.

The Floating World had always overflowed with life and noise, day and night. The streets were crowded, and the noise of carts and animals, of street vendors crying their wares, had been so loud that the people were forced to shout to be heard. But this place was even busier. So many streets. So many people, and each one of them strange and exotic to my eyes. If I listened carefully, I could make sense of snatches of overheard conversations as our carriage pushed its way through the crowded streets. And I peered hungrily at every man I saw who had red hair, wondering each time if this might be my father. I didn't share my thoughts with Danjuro. He had already returned to his professional role; the man beside me was no longer my lover and my husband, but Danjuro, star of the Edo kabuki. Not a stranger to me, nor a man to be feared, but a man who would not be pleased by a woman's idle chatter.

We passed a noisy market, seething with shoppers, and Danjuro frowned as the row interrupted his thoughts. I pulled the blind down on the carriage window quickly, and for the rest of the journey we both sat silently.

5

The bigger the pool
The more frogs gather there. We,
Also, flock as one

*D*anjuro almost vanished from my sight the moment we entered our lodging house. Instantly, he was surrounded by bowing figures, all trying to speak to him at once. I smiled and stood back, watching as Danjuro preened at the actors' ecstatic greetings.

In spite of the fact that they were wearing ordinary robes and no makeup, I recognized all of them. I had seen them perform in the kabuki time after time. That one— taller than the rest—had generally taken the role of the wagoto, the rich young hero who often played the innocent to Danjuro's leering villain. The shorter man, daring to pat Danjuro's shoulder, clearly so pleased to see him, was always cast as the sabakiyaku, the intelligent character who dares to prove the innocence of the falsely accused. Another two men had taken any role that was offered, generally

supporting Danjuro in whatever role he had chosen to play.
And the young, almost pretty, slender man, waiting his turn
on the outskirts of the rest, was the onnagata.

I felt a flare of jealousy as I watched the youngest
member of the troupe. He was bowing and smiling, his long
hair loose and brushing across his face. He, out of all the
kabuki actors, was the most difficult to recognize out of
costume and with no makeup. The onnagata was the man
who took the main female roles, the roles I longed to play. I
caught his glance and managed a smile, and was surprised
when he gave me a huge grin in return. He abandoned
Danjuro and came to stand by me, and I was even more
amazed when he bowed deeply to me.

"Geisha. You have restored Danjuro to us! For that
alone, I am grateful to you."

Out of character, his voice was lower-pitched than I
remembered. He was peering at me through the curtain of
his hair, and his eyes were glinting with laughter. I found
myself smiling at him.

"And what else do you have to be grateful to me for,
onnagata?"

He put his tongue between his teeth so it protruded like
a scrap of pink silk. He reminded me of Neko—who had
already gone for an exploration of his new home—and I
grinned. I liked him. Instinctively, I knew we were going to
be friends. It was one of those rare occasions when you
meet somebody for the first time and instantly there is
harmony between you. A little like love at first sight. Something I had always sneered at, until I found myself in the
same room as Danjuro.

"I am grateful for everything about you, geisha. I have
modeled myself on you, on all of you geisha. You taught me
how to walk and talk like a woman."

I inclined my head, at the same time thinking that this handsome creature was certainly no woman! At the kabuki, he had been second only to Danjuro in the adoration he received from the audiences. And no Japanese woman had been convinced for a second by his kimono and his makeup and his acting skills. I knew he had had his pick of the courtesans and geisha who attended the kabuki, and who had hung around afterward to throw themselves at him. I had a fierce spasm of jealousy, knowing that Danjuro had been even more worshipped than this pretty young man. How many of the women who haunted the theater had tried to force themselves on my husband? I glanced at Danjuro and sighed; he was chattering happily to his long-lost companions, and I wondered if he even remembered I was there.

"Danjuro is pleased to see us." The onnagata grinned at me cheekily. "You must not begrudge the great man to us for a moment or two. You have had him to yourself for many months while we have waited for him." He frowned and shrugged his shoulders. "I would ask you to sit and make yourself comfortable, geisha, but as you can see, we are not blessed with many possessions in our new country."

I stared around the room and my eyes widened with horror.

When we had entered, I had seen nothing but Danjuro's actors, stuttering their pleasure as seeing the great man again. Now, the onnagata stood back, and I had a clear view of the room. It was not large, perhaps eight tatami mats in size, and it took all my training as a geisha not to gasp with outrage. All five of the kabuki actors clearly lived in this one room. There were make-do futons laid on the bare floor, and bowls and chopsticks scattered about. And it stank of unwashed bodies forced to live close together and discarded food. The onnagata saw my expression and his mobile lips turned down at the corners.

"We have lived here for months," he said quietly. "When the kabuki burnt down in Edo and Danjuro disappeared, we thought he was dead. That was hard enough to take, but then we were visited by Akira's men." I shuddered at his name; would the monster never leave us alone? My companion pulled a face, clearly seeing my disgust and sharing it. "They told us that Akira was going to rebuild the kabuki, but that he was going to bring his own actors in. That there was no longer any place for us in Edo. They didn't threaten us exactly, but we understood. We turned our backs on our birthplace. We wandered for a long time, well away from Edo, giving performances for whatever coins the crowds would throw for us. We were truly riverbed beggars during that time."

He smiled wryly, blinking away tears, and I was so moved I leaned over and patted his arm in sympathy.

"I know what Akira is capable of," I said briefly. "You were very wise to get away from him. Tell me, how did you find your way here?"

He grinned again, and I wondered if that face would ever wear a frown for long.

"It was all Daigo-chan's doing." He nodded at the man who took the part of the wagoto. "While we were still performing in the kabuki, he was having an affair with Sato-san's son. When we had to leave Edo, he was miserable. He thought he would never see his lover again, but the young man was more determined than he expected. He sent a messenger to find us—which took him months, of course, as we were on the move so much—with some money and the news that he and Sato-san were about to leave Edo to come to America." His face was serious briefly as he pronounced the syllables carefully. *A-mer-ic-u.* "We thought that it was just a farewell gift from his lover, but Daigo-chan was convinced that there was a hidden message as well, and that he wanted us to follow him here, so we used a lot of the money to smuggle ourselves out of Japan."

"Weren't you frightened that you would be found and taken back to Japan and executed?" I interrupted. He shook his head cheerfully.

"Not really. Why would the authorities be bothered about getting a bunch of nobodies like us back? They were probably pleased to see us go. Daigo-chan made much of how brave his lover was, leaving Japan, but the rest of us weren't convinced about that either. After all, his father might be rich, but he was just a merchant. He had little more standing in society than we did."

I pursed my lips in silent admiration at the actors' bravery, and my new friend preened, tossing his hair out of his face and beaming at me.

"And you ended up...here?"

His lips turned down as he glanced around the squalid room. "We wouldn't have this much if it wasn't for Sato-san," he said reluctantly. "As soon as we got here, we started looking for Japanese faces. We were lucky. We found a man late on the first day who knew where Sato-san lived, so we all just turned up at his door."

Danjuro burst into laughter and we both immediately raised our heads, waiting dutifully to see if he wanted either of us. But he didn't, he was too busy talking to the sabakiyaku actor.

"Go on," I urged him. "What happened?"

"Sato-san's servant opened the door to us. He was a

gaijin." He broke off and rolled his eyes in amazement at the thought of a Japanese merchant employing a gaijin as a servant. "He must have thought all Japanese were the same class, as he let us in and took us straight through to see Sato-san. Everything changed as soon as Sato-san laid eyes on us, though. I thought he was going to burst, he was that angry. He yelled at us to get out of his house and never set foot in it again. It would have been very bad for us if his son hadn't come in to see what all the noise was about. As soon as he saw Daigo-chan, he burst into tears and started wailing that his one true love had come back to him. You should have seen his father's face!"

He giggled and I laughed with him. This was shaping up to be almost as good as a comedy at the kabuki, and I was intrigued.

"No! What happened after that?"

"Well, Sato-san had us all taken out of the way to another room, and we were fed and given tea. I can't remember when I enjoyed a meal more." I remembered the dreadful food we had tried to eat on the ship and I understood perfectly. At least they had been given food; Sato-san had offered Danjuro and me only tea and some peculiar sweetmeats he called "cookies." Hungry as we were, we declined the food. "And then we just sat there waiting. Eventually, Sato-san came in to us and said he would come to a compromise with us. We were to go away. Daigo-chan was never to try and get into contact with his son again. If we agreed he would give us enough money to keep us going until we could find some work, and he would find us lodgings."

I glanced around the truly awful room and raised my eyebrows.

"It's a lot better than some of the places we slept in

when we were forced to leave Edo," he said simply. "We were very careful with the money he gave us, but it was nearly gone when Sato-san sent us a message. We could hardly believe our good fortune. He said that he had decided that America was ready for the kabuki, and that he had asked Danjuro to leave Edo and come to this new world to perform. That we would have the kabuki again."

He was watching my face carefully, and I knew he had seen the amazement I could not hide.

"We didn't understand it either," he said softly. "Apart from anything else, we all thought Danjuro-san was dead. Daigo said he would take the risk of going to see Sato-san to find out what the truth of it was. We all thought it was a trap, you see. That he would have us arrested as soon as we showed our faces and sent back to Japan. But we were wrong." He paused to gather his thoughts and I leaned forward, urging him on silently. "As soon as Daigo arrived, he was hustled into a private room to see Sato-san. Daigo said he could see he was nervous, and so at first he pretended we weren't interested in the offer. As if! But Sato-san believed him, and eventually told him the truth. It seemed that just before we all turned up he had arranged a marriage for his son. A very good marriage, with the daughter of a local gaijin merchant. Both fathers were very happy about it, as they had business interests in common. And it seemed the girl was very much in love with Sato-san's son. Daigo's lover had been happy to go along with things until we arrived, but now he was insisting that he only wanted Daigo."

"Oh, dear." I nodded, understanding at once.

In Japan, it wouldn't have mattered greatly. Whatever the relationship was—men with men, men with women, women with women—what did it matter as long as both sides were content? In theory, men loving men was frowned upon, but in actual fact nobody bothered about it all. At home, Sato-san's son would have married his girl and taken Daigo for his lover and everybody would have been happy. But I knew from my own experience with the gaijin that it was very different outside Japan, and that the gaijin father-in-law would have been appalled at the thought that his new son was in love with another man.

"He believed Sato-san?" I asked.

"Not at first, but he did eventually. Sato-san said that he had kept in touch with some of his old contacts in Edo and he had found out that Danjuro-san was not dead, but was alive and desperate to get away from Edo. And more especially as far away as possible from Akira. I do not like Sato-san, but I will admit he is a clever man. He told Daigo that before he left Edo, Akira had done great damage to him by stealing much of his business in the opium trade. When he heard that Danjuro was not dead, he saw it as a golden opportunity to right many wrongs. If he could spirit Danjuro away from Akira, then he would cause the yakuza a huge loss of face. And if Danjuro could be persuaded to come to America, he would offer him a new theater for the kabuki, here. But of course, all that would only be on the understanding that Daigo would see his son and tell him that everything was over between them, and that he was no longer interested in him. Daigo is not a stupid man. He had enjoyed his affair, but there was no comparison between that and the promise of a new kabuki. He agreed at once, and Sato-san was true to his promise. He got word to Danjuro that he was welcome here, and that another kabuki theater would be waiting for him. Sato-san is a wealthy man, the cost means little to him. And of course, if the kabuki is successful, he will get his investment back many times over. As far as Sato-san is concerned, he can't lose."

Danjuro chose that moment to glance across at us, and I saw his expression tighten into irritation. Superb actor as he was, I knew him well enough to know that the sudden beam of delight he threw at my companion had started out as a look of jealousy. Although which of us he was actually protective of, I had no idea. Danjuro flung his arms wide to greet my new friend, and the handsome onnagata left my side at once and kneeled in front of Danjuro, bowing repeatedly.

"Ryu. My dear Ryu! How good it is to see you again!"

Danjuro put his hands on the onnagata's shoulders, raising him up to embrace him. In Japanese, Ryu means dragon, and I smiled as I thought what an unsuitable name it was for a man who earned his living pretending to be a woman! And then I thought of all the women in Edo who would have been delighted to taste this particular dragon's enchantment, and I changed my mind.

My amusement was upset abruptly as the door banged open. The room was so small that I had to step back quickly or the door would have knocked into me.

"Holy cow, there's more of them!" A tall gaijin was standing in the doorway. He did not have hair on his face exactly, but rather his skin was covered in a nasty, ungroomed sort of stubble that gave him the appearance of a badly plucked hen. "And a woman this time! My God, what have I done to deserve this?"

He glanced at the group of men around Danjuro and then turned back to me. His gaze licked me from head to foot, and his indignant expression turned into a smirk.

"Hey, now. Maybe this isn't all bad. Maybe this one

could be pretty if we scraped off all that paint. Hi there, little lady."

He leered at me, leaning so close that I felt his breath and smelled his stink. Butter and milk and meat, the odor oozing out of his pores. No matter how well washed the gaijin were, most of them seemed to smell the same.

"These are our friends." Ryu stepped forward and spoke carefully, his face serious as he tried to get his lips to form the English words. "Sato-san told you they were to come."

It was a brave attempt, but even I had to listen carefully to make sense of what he was saying. Instinctively, I felt it was better if this man thought we—especially I—couldn't understand him, and I held my tongue. Glancing at Danjuro, I saw him nod fractionally, and stayed quiet.

"Ah, hell. So he did. Give you any money for lodgings, did he?"

The man rubbed his fingers together in the universal gesture for money. Ryu shook his head.

"Sato-san give you money already."

The man's expression turned ugly, but we all simply stood there and looked at him, and he gave way with an exasperated grunt.

"Alright. But I need more, especially if these two are going to have a room of their own. They're next door. Tell them that, will you?"

Ryu translated rapidly and Danjuro bowed stiffly.

"Tell the ugly foreign devil he is very kind." He smiled widely and Ryu cleared his throat of laughter before he spoke.

"Danjuro say we grateful," he murmured.

The man stared suspiciously, and then poked a rice bowl with his boot.

"Get this place cleaned up will you? You two, next door."

We followed the gaijin out dutifully. Daigo hefted our trunk and carried it effortlessly.

Our room was smaller than the main room, but had a large window. It was completely bare and not at all clean and I felt tears prick my eyes as I remembered the elegant rooms I had taken for granted in the Hidden House. The thought stiffened me; I had been a slave there, at the beck and call of any man who had my price in his pocket. Even when Akira had taken me to live in his beautiful house, I had been no more than a bird imprisoned in a golden cage. I was sure I felt my tattoo shiver at the memory and I straightened up, smiling as if the man was showing us a palace.

"You know, you could be real pretty if you made an effort."

Our landlord spoke close to my ear; I had been so concerned with hiding my horror at our new home that I had not noticed he had moved right next to me. He was so close that his arm was pressed against my breasts. Even for a gaijin, I was sure that this was incredibly rude and it took an effort not give him a well-deserved slap.

"Maybe this isn't so bad, after all." He grinned, showing brown teeth in gums that were almost the same color. "I daresay if Mr. Sato doesn't come up with the goods, I could get my money's worth out of your hide any day."

I hadn't been a geisha since I was thirteen for nothing. I kept my head down submissively and smiled at this repulsive creature as if he had flattered me by even noticing me. I could barely believe he hadn't noticed the color of my eyes or my hair, but the lodging house was badly lit and the dirty windows allowed in little light. Or perhaps his eyes had not risen as high as my face. He chuckled, and a breath of tobacco mingled with his bodily odors.

"Hell, you don't understand a single word I say, do you, pretty lady? Just as well."

"What is the ugly foreign barbarian saying now?" Danjuro demanded.

"He's welcoming us to his country," I said sweetly.

6

A rainbow gathers
The sky in its colors. It
Wraps me in its curve

*R*yu woke us early with dishes of rice in his hands. He apologized deeply for the lack of tea, but in this strange place he said green tea was not available, and the tea that was in the shops we would not like. The gaijin, he said, drank it very strong, and often with honey or sugar added. Some of them even put milk in it. We looked at each other and shook our heads in amazement.

Danjuro tucked into his rice with gusto, and I had begun to eat mine before I realized Ryu was not eating. He had rocked back on his heels and was watching us carefully with an odd expression on his face. I put my chopsticks and bowl down carefully.

"Have you already eaten, Ryu?" I asked courteously. He lowered his eyes and I knew he was going to lie to me.

"Yes, Midori No Me. We all ate earlier."

I didn't believe him, but I picked up my bowl anyway before Danjuro could eat his meal and then steal mine.

Ryu looked thinner than I remembered him from the kabuki. Of course, he was not wearing a bulky kimono and obi, but even so, I was certain he had lost weight. In fact, I thought our entire troupe of actors looked thin and slightly bedraggled. I mentioned it to Danjuro as we dressed for the walk to the theater.

"They look all right to me." He frowned. "Perhaps they can't eat the strange food in this country. You know, we barely touched anything they gave us on the ship. Half of it we couldn't work out what was in it and the dishes we could understand tasted dreadful."

I allowed myself to be persuaded. He was right. We had eaten little on the journey ourselves except rice and fish, when we were sure it was fish under the strange sauces. But even so, I felt Ryu had lost not just weight, but something else had changed that I could not quite put my finger on. And he had a cough; every few minutes, he would turn his head aside and bark like a fox. Once we had gotten ourselves settled, I decided I would find a pharmacist and ask for something to make him better. I was greatly taken with our young onnagata and wished him well.

Ryu knew where the theater was and said he would take us there. Had he been inside, we asked? He shook his head.

"We have not been invited in," he said. I was immediately sure there was something he was not telling us.

"Does Sato-san give you all enough to live on?" I demanded. Danjuro glared at me for my rudeness, but I persisted. There was something wrong here, and I was determined to get to the bottom of it. Ryu bit his lip and glanced at Danjuro appealingly, but by then even my husband was interested.

"Does he?"

Ryu gave in. He shrugged. "Sato-san was extremely generous," he said carefully. "He gave Daigo some money when he promised to keep away from his son, and it paid for our lodgings for us, for a while. But everything is very expensive here compared to Japan, and our money soon ran out."

Danjuro and I looked at each other. It was he who began to question Ryu.

"So do you have enough money for food? Please do not lie to me."

Ryu looked up, his lovely eyes glistening with tears. "Sometimes, we are hungry," he said simply. "I am given a little food in exchange for translating for other Japanese in the area, but they are nearly as poor as we are and cannot spare much." He shrugged. "I do not speak a great deal of English but it is more than they do. Sometimes Daigo gets work at the docks. They often need men who will fetch and carry, and he is very strong. There is a Chinese laundry close to our lodgings, and when they are very busy Goro and Choki," the two minor actors I had been introduced to yesterday, "work there." I felt my belly tighten in horror. One glance at Danjuro's face was enough; it had set like stone. Riverbed beggars we might be, but for Japanese to labor for Chinese! We had long felt ourselves superior to our huge neighbor, and this was unthinkable.

"And Tadayo?" Danjuro asked, referring to the actor who took the part of the sabakiyaku, the man about town, swaggering character. "What does he do to help?"

"He helps our landlord," Ryu said simply. "He keeps the house clean for him and looks after his horses."

"I could help, Danjuro," I said eagerly. "Just until we all have some more money. I speak much better English than

Ryu. I could perhaps translate for Sato-san and the other Japanese merchants who are over here, when they trade with the gaijin."

"No."

Just the single word, but it was enough. We had spoken about it yesterday, before we slept. Danjuro was adamant. We would not let the gaijin know how well I spoke their language, and even more importantly, how well I understood them. Part of it was pride, I knew. Danjuro himself spoke no more than a few words of English, and understood little more. I agreed reluctantly. He was probably right. It was better that we should know what was going on without showing our hand.

"It is not necessary," Danjuro said arrogantly. "We will speak to the theater owner today. By tomorrow, we will have a production in place. In the meantime, I have enough money to keep us all. Is there anywhere close where we could get a good meal, Ryu?"

My mouth opened and closed silently. I knew exactly how much money we had, and it was very little. Danjuro had some gold with him when we ran from Edo; the captain of the first ship we had sailed on had exchanged it for what he told us was American money. I had no way of knowing, but I was sure he had cheated us and given us much less than its real value. I bitterly rued leaving my small fortune in gold with Mineko, but I had had no choice. The money had been left to me by my mother, who had intended that I would get it many years before. But fate had not smiled on me, and it had only come into my possession after Akira had taken me to live as his mistress. I had nowhere where he would not have found it, so I had left it at the Hidden House with Mineko, for safe keeping. And it would be safe with her, I knew. But so far away, it might as well be dust.

My stomach chose that moment to rumble; although the rice for breakfast had been welcome, it had been a small portion and I was hungry. Ryu grinned at me and my conscience pinched like a tight sandal. If I was hungry, he must be hungrier still. I had no right to complain.

Let Danjuro spend what we had on a good meal for all the actors. They deserved it.

"There is a restaurant quite close to our lodgings where they have good seafood and fish." He licked his lips at the thought. "Tadayo has worked in the kitchens sometimes, and the food he brought home for us was very good. But I think it is expensive."

Danjuro nodded.

"Then we shall all eat there tonight. Now, Ryu. Please take us to this theater."

Ryu led the way, abreast of Danjuro. I walked behind the two men. At first, I kept my head down, partly from shyness and partly because the road was uneven and I thought I might trip. The theater was much further away than I expected, and I began to look around as I gained in confidence.

I gawped with amazement.

It wasn't just the buildings, although I had never seen anything like them. They were so high, I thought they might be reaching for the clouds. Nor had I ever seen roads as wide as this, and paved with stone. And the shops! They were made so that one could look through glass into them and inspect the goods on sale. I shook my head in disbelief. But more than anything else, I was shocked by the way the gaijin simply accepted us.

In spite of the fact that we were the only Japanese to be seen, and we were all dressed in our finest, we didn't seem to attract a second glance. Danjuro wore a silk robe and sash, and Ryu's robe was less fine but was still handsome. I had put my best kimono and obi on, and that—together with my high geta—meant I could only walk with teetering steps. The streets were crowded with gaijin—men and women and children. But not one of them stared at us or was in any way rude. I found this truly astonishing. One or two glanced at us and smiled kindly, but that was all.

When the first gaijin had appeared in Edo, we had all drawn our robes back so we did not touch them. Politeness stopped us gawping too obviously, but when one passed nearby all conversation would cease. We would look away from them, making it clear that we found them strange. If one came too close to us for our comfort, we took a step away.

And now we were the gaijin in this strange land, but nobody seemed to notice us at all. I hoped this was a good omen. I felt quite cheerful, until we reached the theater.

We stood outside the huge, stone building, looking at it doubtfully.

"This is it? You are certain?"

Ryu bobbed his head. "I am sure," he said. "Perhaps if we knocked on the door, somebody would come and let us in?"

Danjuro frowned. "No. We will start as we mean to go on." He held his head high, and I hid a smile as I realized the actor was back in his rightful place. Preparing to make his entrance, as the great star. "Please, open the door for us, Ryu. We will enter."

After such bravery, it was a shame that the next few minutes were such an anti-climax. The door was not locked, and we simply walked in. The entry hall was very dark, and we stood, blinking for a moment or two, trying to adjust to the dim light. We looked around furtively, waiting for somebody to challenge us, but there was nobody. Eventually, Danjuro told Ryu to call out. And again, when there was no response.

"Yes? Who is it?"

We all jumped as the irritated voice came out of the gloom. Ryu was too surprised to answer, but fortunately it seemed that we were expected after all.

"Ah. I see. My Japanese visitors. William Clay, at your service."

He thrust his hand out and I took it quickly, knowing that this was a polite greeting amongst the gaijin. Danjuro and Ryu exchanged glances and then followed my lead, taking his hand cautiously and dropping it quickly. Courtesy done, we stared at him expectantly. Small and fat with a completely bald head, he looked so much like one of the more amusing characters from the kabuki that I relaxed and smiled at him. He stared at me, his head thrust forward like a turtle peering from its shell, and his eyebrows rose.

"I guess you had better come this way, people."

He gave us tea, and obviously expected us to be pleased about it. It was dreadful stuff, served in enormous cups and so strong it was almost black. It had been sweetened with something that barely masked the taste. We drank it out of politeness, and I was very glad when my cup was finally empty.

"You know, Mr. Sato asked if I would give you a chance. We do some business together away from the theater, so I guess I got to be polite. But I don't mind telling you, if it weren't for my daughter I wouldn't have let you into the place. She's just mad about anything Japanese, and when she heard you were here she just wouldn't take no for an answer. Insisted I had to see you, at least. And here she is, by golly."

The door opened as if thrust aside by a sudden wind and a young woman swept into the room. She stopped dead when she saw us and bowed deeply, staring hopefully at each of us as if asking, *Have I gotten that right?* Her gaze lingered for a long time on Ryu, and he, I saw at once, was equally enraptured with her. It was as if they were bound by invisible threads. They could barely tear their eyes from each other. I was deeply jealous. Not just of the effect that this gaijin was having on my new friend, even more did I envy her freedom. She was probably pretty by gaijin standards, I thought, with a cloud of fair curls and blue eyes. Her skin was as white as the belly of a dead fish, and I thought complacently that Japanese skin would age much better.

"Evelyn, dear. Your friends from the kabuki theater are here, at last. Don't know that I can do much for them, though. We're booked solid all through the spring season."

Neither I nor Ryu had any need to translate that for Danjuro. The regret in his voice was enough. But Evelyn was having none of it. She sprang to her feet and to our astonishment perched herself on her father's lap, nuzzling at his face like Neko when he was feeling affectionate.

"Ah, Papa dear. You got to give them a chance! I know the theater is dark day after tomorrow. Couldn't they have a go for just one evening performance? They'll go down a storm, I know they will. Everybody I know is just crazy for all things Japanese."

And that was it. Truly, it appeared that Papa could not resist his little girl. We were hired, for a single performance. Far from our hopes, but better than nothing.

Evelyn accompanied us as her father showed us the theater. We gawped at it in disbelief. This was the gaijin's idea of a theater? Where was the open stage that stuck right out into the audience like a tongue? At the kabuki, our patrons sprawled in compartments all over the floor. Here, it seemed, they were expected to sit confined in chairs. The only thing that was a little familiar was the row of boxes that rose on each side of the strange stage, and even they were open, not latticed like the kabuki. And worse was to come. I saw Evelyn nudge Clay-san and nod meaningfully at me. He raised a finger as if to say, "Nearly forgot!" and then grinned.

"The little lady will take the female lead, of course. Evelyn tells me that all your female parts are taken by men in Japan, but that's not going to work here. Fine if one of your guys camps it up for the supporting parts, but the female lead has to be a woman. And it would be great if the lady could do an oriental dance or two."

Danjuro raised his eyebrows questioningly, obviously seeking a translation of his words. Poor Ryu looked as if he would swallow his tongue rather than speak. He started to stammer apologies, so I took over and translated as colorlessly as I could. Danjuro waited until I finished, and to my astonishment he simply shrugged.

"Sato-san said the same thing. Well, it's only for once, so I suppose we have to do as the gaijin asks."

He bowed, and Clay-san obviously took it as agreement.

"That's fine," Clay-san said. "What we need is something with plenty of action. A bit of swordplay, maybe. Say, around two hours for the whole thing?"

I put my hand on Danjuro's arm and watched his expression as Ryu translated. Even his actor's face failed him. Two hours! Normally the kabuki began a performance in the morning, and it usually ran through until the evening light failed. Several plays would be performed to the same audience, but each play could last four or five hours easily.

But Clay-san seemed to think everything was settled; he rattled on happily, explaining that he would take his expenses out of the takings from the audience first, and then anything left over would be split equally between him and us.

"I'll see you all for rehearsal tomorrow afternoon, then? See what you got for me? Say about midday? Fine."

Ryu bowed us out with many a backward look at Evelyn.

7

A wave's beauty is
Transient. But still does the
Sand tremble beneath

We ate at Ryu's restaurant, although I suddenly had no appetite, and nor—I suspected—did Danjuro. Ryu darted anxious looks between us, and our companions sat with their heads down, hardly speaking as they obviously guessed that all had not gone well. The food was good, but I barely tasted it. My stomach was rolling in such a ferment of worry.

Rehearsals tomorrow! Rehearse what, exactly? We had nothing to offer. And it was all down to me. Much as I loved the kabuki, I had never set foot on the stage. I would be dreadful. I had expected a tiny part, performed after much rehearsing. Not a starring role, thrust upon me without warning.

As if my thoughts had been spoken out loud, we all stopped eating and laid our utensils down. We stared at the table laden with food and said nothing. Obviously determined to make the best of things, Danjuro picked up the strange implement I had heard the gaijin call a "fork"—and I suppose it did look rather like a miniature pitchfork—and stabbed viciously at a piece of fish. He misjudged the movement, and the fish flew off his plate to land on the floor. A stray cat, obviously a favorite of the customers as he had been rubbing around legs and getting petted since we entered, took advantage at once and ran off with the fish in his mouth.

We all stared at it dumbly, and suddenly I saw the funny side of things. I started to giggle, putting my hand respectfully in front of my mouth. Ryu looked at my face and smiled, and then he was laughing as well. The others tried to keep a stone face, but eventually even Danjuro was wiping away tears of laughter. The other diners glanced at us and smiled and then carried on with their dinner calmly.

"Eat!" Danjuro commanded. "We may well be hungry after tomorrow, so enjoy the food now."

We went to with a will, wielding our strange metal tools with as much care as we could. Nobody wanted the cat to steal any more of our precious food.

Finally, Ryu cleared his throat and spoke softly, his eyes anxious.

"Danjuro-san, I think there may be a way." We all stared at him hopefully. Danjuro waved his hand for him to continue. "If we took a play we all know well, one with plenty of action and a fair amount of singing and dancing, it wouldn't matter if we cut it down a lot. I was thinking perhaps of *The Temple at Dojoji*?"

I knew the play he was thinking of instantly. It was one of my favorites, and Mineko and I had seen it many times at the kabuki. It had perhaps the most imposing female role in any kabuki play, and I guessed that Ryu himself would have loved to play the part. I felt tears of gratitude prickle my eyes, that he should be so willing to sacrifice himself for the rest of us.

But Danjuro was frowning, and shaking his head.

"It wouldn't work. Midori No Me has never performed the part. If you were taking the lead, Ryu, then we could manage. But as it is, no."

My heart sank under the weight of a stone. Or perhaps the weight of the temple bell! But Ryu was not finished.

"We could make it work, master," he persisted. "If we cut out a lot of the dialogue, and concentrated on the action, it would work. It is very dramatic, and there are a couple of good dance scenes for Midori No Me. It is what Clay-san asked for," he added slyly.

I looked from one man to the other, willing Danjuro to agree. But his face was set.

"If we cut the dialogue, the play will not make sense. And no matter how much we cut out, how is Midori No Me supposed to recognize her cues? It would make us all look foolish."

My spirits had soared, listening to Ryu's confident words. I wanted to shout, *I could do it! I know the play well! I could do the main dances, easily! And the songs! Give me the chance!*

But I said nothing. If I tried, it would only make Danjuro more adamant. But Tadayo and Daigo were looking at each other. Tadayo spoke carefully.

"Master, I think perhaps we could do it." Danjuro raised his eyebrows incredulously, but Tadayo continued. "It really doesn't matter what we say, the gaijin will not understand a single word of it. All that matters is the action, and that Midori No Me performs the dances with great spirit. And because the audience will be looking, not hearing, we can give Midori No Me her cues very easily. Even if we shouted, 'turn left!' 'fall down!' and 'start to dance!' they would all think it was just part of the play."

Danjuro stared at his plate and ate a piece of some strange vegetable with great concentration. When he spoke, I knew I had won and my heart lifted.

"You have seen the play, I know. Do you remember the action, Midori No Me-chan? Is your memory good enough to be able to play the part in front of an audience who know nothing about how it should be?"

All I could do was nod. I knew the play inside out. I could even remember the way Ryu had presented the main character, how he had held his head, how he had moved. And certainly how he had danced. I felt a rush of gratitude for Aunty, left behind in the Floating World. She had been a tyrant, who had ruled all us geisha with fierce smacks of her cane and the even fiercer lash of her tongue. But she had trained us well. We had all developed wonderful memories. Memories for the dances we performed, the songs we sang. But even better memories for the patrons, no matter how often they changed. If we didn't see a particular man for a year or more, we would all remember his name. Know instantly whether he preferred tea or sake. Whether he wanted to listen to us play or sing or dance or take us straight to his futon. And—above all else—we knew what he liked, what he expected of us.

Yes, my memory was excellent.

Danjuro stared at me, as if he was trying to read my thoughts. Perhaps he had, as he nodded suddenly.

"Finish the food," he said abruptly. "We will spend the rest of tonight deciding what we can cut from *Dojoji*. I don't care if Clay-san has no idea what we are saying. I want it to be as good as it can be for him."

I concentrated on my plate, hardly able to swallow the food for my excitement. I was so lost in my thoughts that I barely noticed he had moved until Tadayo was actually on his feet. He bowed deeply, and I smiled at him as I saw his beaming face.

"Lilly-chan! How good to meet you again. Please, will you join us?"

Tadayo's English was almost indecipherable, but there was no mistaking the pleasure in his voice. I glanced at the person he was talking to, and my mouth sagged open in amazement.

Just like me, Lilly-chan was obviously half Japanese and half white. Did I look like her, I wondered? I stood courteously and smiled at her, immediately hoping that we might perhaps become friends, as we obviously had much in common.

"Hi there, Tadayo." She spoke in English and ignored me completely. Feeling very foolish I sat down again. "Real nice to see you again. I'm sorry, I don't have time to stop and chat. I got a gentleman friend waiting for me outside."

To my astonishment, she leaned over and kissed Tadayo on his cheek. The foolish man blushed ripely and watched Lilly adoringly as she swept out of the restaurant, waggling her hand in farewell. I noticed she paused in the doorway and glanced back at us, and for some reason I thought her gaze didn't rest on Tadayo.

We all stared at him in amazement.

"And who was that, Tadayo?" Danjuro sounded amused. I smiled with him, even though I thought Lilly had been incredibly rude, particularly to me.

"Lilly-chan is the daughter of a friend of mine. A Japanese gentleman who married an American woman. Lilly was born here and is herself an actress."

"Is that so?" Danjuro said courteously. "Well, that is a coincidence." Tadayo nodded happily. He would, I knew, be teased unmercifully by the other actors about his new acquaintance. Back in our apartment, I immediately forgot about Tadayo's friend. Although I knew I could contribute little, I was too jittery to sit still and I hovered around the men, trying not to get in the way. Ryu had found ink and brushes and paper from somewhere, and Danjuro began to write feverishly, slapping down ideas and comments as they were made. I could take no part in this, but felt that I should stay. My neck ached as my head swiveled back and forth between the men, and my eyes stung from the tobacco breath of their pipes.

"Would you like some tea?" I asked hopefully, and Danjuro grunted what I took to be agreement. I had discovered that if I poured the strange gaijin tea almost as soon as the water had hit the leaves, it didn't taste too bad. Not like real tea, of course, but it was all we had. I rose and slipped out quietly, and I knew not one of the men had even noticed I had gone.

In the kitchen, I heaved the heavy cast iron kettle on the stove and stood with my hands clenched, staring out into the darkness. Was I excited or terrified? Both, I knew. The fate of all of us depended on how I performed; it was in my hands whether we ate or starved. I made a small noise that sounded to my own ears like the whimper of a baby. My reflection wavered back at me from the window, shivering in the glow of the single oil lamp that lit the kitchen.

"I can do this," I whispered aloud. "Of course I can. I may never have acted on the stage, but hasn't every day of my life been an act, since my mizuage?"

Of course it had—except when I had been with Danjuro, of course. All we geisha in the Hidden House were wonderful actresses. We could make the ugliest, oldest patron feel that we were delighted to see him. That he had made us happy by honoring us as his choice of partner. No matter what they wanted to do to us, we beamed with pleasure. Not one of them ever knew that although our bodies were with them, our thoughts were far away.

I took a deep, shuddering breath and straightened my shoulders. And then yelped out loud.

"Hi there, pretty little lady." Our landlord—Mac—was standing close behind me. I had been so tangled in my own thoughts I had not even heard him open and close the door. "All on your own, are you?"

I smiled vaguely at him, and gestured at the kettle. I tried to slide to one side to reach it, but he was firmly in my way. So I did what my training told me to do. I lowered my eyes and looked as submissive as I could, even as my thoughts tumbled over one another like mice scrabbling for the safety of their nest. I could scream, I knew. The men would hear me and come running. But just as I took comfort from the knowledge, Mac's words robbed me of even that small refuge.

"I know you don't understand a word I'm saying, but it don't matter. I'll make it clear enough what I want." He put his finger on my lips in an elaborate mime of silence. "I hope so, anyway, because I'm telling you now, if you make any noise above a whisper, then all of you are out on the streets. Now. And I'll keep your belongings to pay for your rent. And just look, it's started to rain. Won't that be nice for you all? Soaking wet and cold and nowhere to go." He gestured with his head toward the window and then pointed at me, and at the glass.

I kept my face down. I did my best to look as if I had no idea what he was saying.

"But it don't have to be like that, honey. I heard lots of tales about you oriental gals, especially you dancing girls. I heard tell that you know ways to satisfy a man that our women don't know nothing about. Now what say you do something nice for Mac, huh? And if you do, maybe I'll forget this week's rent, if you're good enough. Hell, it'll may be a treat for you! I just bet you're dying to try one of us foreigners anyway."

He stood back, and I eyed the door, wondering if I could get there before he could grab me. Then a sudden gust of wind lashed cold rain against the window and I knew it was pointless. Mac would keep his word, without a second thought.

I lifted my head and smiled at him. After all, what difference was there between this gaijin and any other patron? Danjuro need never—would never—know. If it kept us with a roof over our heads, it would be worth it.

Mac grinned at me and took a step back. He loosened his belt and undid his trousers, letting them fall around his ankles. He was wearing nothing beneath the trousers. His hands were on my shoulders, the pressure forcing me to my knees. He pointed down and clicked his fingers. I ran my tongue over my lips, trying to persuade some moisture into my mouth, but my tongue felt like coarse wool. Mac obviously had no time for hesitation. He leaned against me, nearly rocking me off balance, and his tree of flesh smeared against my lips. I forced myself to unclench my teeth and part my lips, and it was all the encouragement he needed. He thrust his tree against my mouth so hard that my teeth were parted against my will.

I closed my lips around his flesh in a bid to try and stop the stench of him making me gag. His tree seemed enormous; not as obscenely huge as Big or Bigger's erections—

the two men who had been the enforcers in the Hidden House—but much, much nastier. We had all seen the boys' erect trees in the bath many times and had wondered amongst ourselves how they came not to faint when the blood rushed to their private parts. But Big and Bigger's trees had been clean and smooth. This thing that was invading my mouth tasted vile, as though it hadn't been washed in months. And it was as full of veins as a gnarled tree trunk. I froze, but in spite of my stillness Mac gave a satisfied grunt and pushed further into my mouth, nearly choking me.

Out of habit and training I began to let my mind float away from my body, closing my eyes and pretending the hard floor beneath my knees was tatami matting. After all, what could Mac do to me that many other patrons had already done? I had almost managed the trick of being present in body but not mind when I felt another presence beside me, pressing against me very gently. I heard the rustle of silk and felt warmth and the sweet smell of a freshly washed body.

You do not have to do this, a voice said very softly in my ear, seeming to be beside me and at the same time far, far away. *All this is in the past for you. You need never allow yourself to be used again. Trust me.*

My mind flew back into my body. There was nobody in the kitchen but Mac and me, yet I knew that a moment before we had not been alone. I recalled every word the unseen presence had whispered to me. I did not have to do this. No matter what the training of a lifetime was telling me, I did not have to do this.

"Come on, honey. Let's have a little action here. If you please me enough, I might even let you do it again."

Faint and far away came the echo of that voice. *You do*

not have to do this. Was it really my mother's voice? I hoped it was, but whether it was or not, it gave me courage. If Mac's tree hadn't been brushing the back of my throat, I would have spat it out like a bad shrimp. I could bite it, I thought. Hard. The idea gave me great satisfaction, but at the same time I doubted it would do any good. If I bit him hard enough to hurt, he would simply bash my head against the sink until I was forced to let go. I might be able to make a noise—loud enough for the men to hear—but could I bear for them to find me like this?

I found that my hand was moving without any conscious command from me. I reached up and caressed Mac's kintama gently, and would have smiled if I had been able to as he moaned with pleasure. I slid my fingers around his kintama as slowly as I could and then squeezed. Viciously. I swear I felt his eggs slide apart under my grip, and then his tree was out of my mouth and he was trying to back away. But I did not let go.

Instead, I stood up, all the time gripping his kintama tightly. I smiled gently as he sank to his knees in front of me, his mouth open in a soundless scream of agony. I gave myself a moment of pleasure as I considered how our roles had suddenly been reversed, and then leaned forward and spoke quietly.

"Mac-san, can you understand me?" His bulging eyes looked as if they might pop right out of his head. His teeth —and very nasty teeth they were—were bared in agony. "Please, Mac-san, nod if you understand what I am saying." I released my grip the tiniest amount and he sucked in air, nodding jerkily at the same time. "Good. Now I must explain to you that there is much you do not know about us Japanese. If I tell my husband what you have tried to do to me, he will kill you. It will take a long time, and it will be very painful for you. But he—and I—will enjoy it greatly. Please don't think that he will be found and punished, because I tell you now, he would not care. It is a matter of honor, you understand?"

Mac's face had turned the color of a ripe plum. Saliva flew from his open mouth, and I leaned back to make sure that none of it landed on me.

"I hope you believe me. Perhaps if you remember that a few moments ago you thought I spoke no English it might make you wonder what other secrets us Japanese hold?"

I pursed my lips and watched him. It was only when I realized that he was barely breathing he was in such pain that I relaxed my grip and stood back from him. He fell forward with a groan that was so deep I almost felt sorry for him. And then I remembered all the patrons who had used and abused me in the past, and I had to stop myself from kicking him instead.

"Get out. All of you. This minute," he wheezed.

I shook my head at him in pretended astonishment. "Were you not listening to me, Mac-san? We will stay here for as long as it pleases us to honor your hovel of a home. And you will keep out of our way. You may think that you can go to your police and tell them we owe you rent and get us put in prison." His mouth gawped foolishly and I smiled. What did it matter where a man came from? They all thought in the same way! "But I do not think that that is a good idea. We already have many friends in your country, and a powerful patron who in his turn has many friends in high places. If you leave me—us—in peace, then we will go as soon as our plans are in place. You do not know why we are really here, and it is better for you not to know." I hoped I sounded suitably mysterious and prayed he would not dare to ask what those plans were. "Remember, there is much you do not know about us. Even more that you do not want to know. You do not know us. But we and our friends know you."

I stared down at him, watching his thoughts run across his face. Doubt, worry, and finally fear were clear. He stumbled to his feet and backed away from me, his trousers clutched in his fists.

"I guess if you can keep a secret, then so can I," he mumbled. I nodded and stared at him coldly. The kettle started to hiss at that second, and I turned to look at it in surprise. Had this strangest of dramas really only taken a few minutes to play out? When I looked back, the kitchen door was closing behind him.

I leaned against the stove and laughed until the tears ran down my face, and then realized I was weeping properly, and shaking like a willow tree in a high wind. I smeared my face with my hands and then rubbed it on my kimono until I was sure it was dry and made the tea with shaking hands.

As I walked through back to my husband and friends, the teacups balanced carefully on a tray, I realized that Mac-san had done me a very great favor. He had believed my ridiculous mix of lies and fantasy. And after all, what was the kabuki except a careful manipulation of fairy tale and imagination?

I was no longer worried about whether I would be able to act in Clay-san's strange theater. I knew I could.

8

The gale claws at my
Face, but I cannot see it.
Still, I can feel it!

I lay face-down on the stage. I was panting so hard my ribs hurt, and I barely noticed the rough boards scratching my face. I had ears for nothing but the crowd, and as I listened to the polite applause, I felt my heart break. If we had been in the Floating World, our happy audience would have roared their approval of the play. They would have stamped and cheered. Got to their feet and clapped until their hands were sore. The mannered response I was hearing now was so muted in contrast to the reaction I had hoped to hear, I knew how very bad our performance must have been.

I had failed them all. Danjuro and Ryu and the other actors. I had given it everything that I could. I had followed my hissed cues carefully. I had danced as if I was truly possessed by the evil spirit that was supposed to inhabit my character. In fact, after the first few moments of the dance, I felt that I was a stranger to myself, as if some passing spirit really had been so attracted to me that they had taken my place.

The feeling was so liberating I embraced it joyfully. I whirled and swooped, barely feeling the floor beneath my feet. My costume flowed out from my body and I threw my head back and laughed as I felt my kimono slide down my back. I saw the horror in Danjuro's eyes, and knew my dragon had been clearly revealed to view – not just to the actors beside me, but to the audience as well. At that moment, I didn't care. In fact, I was so drunk with the ecstasy of performing that I actually turned my back on the audience, holding my arms out wide, displaying my hated dragon as if it really was the beautiful work of art Akira had always insisted he had gifted to my body. I heard the ripple of shock from the audience, and I was delighted. I also heard Danjuro's hiss of fury, but I was so drunk with exhilaration at that moment it didn't worry me at all.

At last, my dragon had been vanquished. He was no longer a shameful secret. I was free. I only came to my senses slowly, as the dance wound down. My elation fled, leaving regret in its place. What had I been thinking of? This performance was not about me, it was the only chance the whole kabuki had. My pleasure fled along with my new confidence. From that point on, I followed my instructions to the letter, even though I knew in my heart it was too late.

Of course our performance had been a failure. And it was all my fault. How could I have been so selfish? What had ever made me think that I, who had never even been on stage before, could suddenly be the star performer? I was bitterly ashamed. Of course the failure had been entirely my fault. Danjuro, in his role as the entranced young monk, had been perfect, as always. The other actors had changed costumes as if their lives depended upon it and had been word perfect. Even with all the cuts we had been forced to make to the dialogue, the play still made sense. Clay-san had asked for action, and we had given him plenty of that.

We had all known it would be difficult, of course, but we had been buoyed up by hope. Hope and the knowledge that if this failed, we would truly be riverbed beggars. We would have no money to eat or to pay for our lodgings. Now, as I lay on what was supposed to be the temple floor, the strange curtain in front of the stage came down, cutting me off from the sight of the audience. Tears stung my eyes and I set my mouth in a hard line to stop myself howling. Not only was it my fault that we were going to starve, but my dearest dream was dead. I had acted in the kabuki, and I had not been good enough.

We changed quietly and walked out of the theater without saying a word to Clay-san. We hoped he would understand our loss of face. Tomorrow, Danjuro—and I would insist on going with him—would go back to the theater and apologize. We could not bear to see him tonight, it would be too humiliating. In Mac's horrible lodgings, Danjuro and I lay side by side, cramped together in our narrow, cold bed.

"It was not your fault, Midori No Me-chan," he said quietly. "We all worked as hard as we could. It was my fault. I hoped that the gaijin would understand, at least the plot if not the words, but they were stone."

He hesitated, and I thought he was going to mention my dragon but he did not and I took comfort from his words, even though I knew he was simply being kind.

We had realized it was going wrong from the opening moments of the play. At the kabuki, the audience would have hissed and booed, they would have laughed with us, cried with us. Shouted noisily at the villain and wept at the tender parts. Shaken their fists when the maiden was about to be ravished. They would have enjoyed themselves. Here, the audience was as quiet and still as a rabbit that cowers beneath the shadow of the eagle soaring above. Not a rustle, not a murmur. Even at the end, they had simply clapped. Quite loudly, but that was obviously out of politeness.

We were finished before we had begun.

We ate the last of our rice for breakfast. None of us could face the dreadful gaijin tea, so we did without. Ryu smiled at me and offered to come with us to see Clay-san. It was kind of him, but now we no longer had to hide the fact that I spoke excellent English, I said there was no need for him to go back to the theater. Oddly, I thought he looked disappointed.

We were just about to rise and set off when the door burst open as if it had been thrown off its hinges.

"Here you are! Where on earth did you vanish off to last night? Papa was beside himself. He had lots of people who were just dying to meet you. Have you seen the newspaper review?"

We stared at Evelyn, our jaws dropping like koi carp hoping to be fed. She was hopping from foot to foot with excitement, her cheeks glowing pink. Ryu recovered himself first and rose to his feet, bowing far deeper than politeness dictated.

"Please, Evelyn-san. Sit," he murmured.

Evelyn looked around the crowded room for another chair. There wasn't one, of course, so she accepted Ryu's offer of his chair with an uncertain smile. I watched as her eyes glanced around the squalid room and I was ashamed. I wanted to cry out, to tell her this was not what we were used to! That in Japan we had lived differently, but I didn't get the chance. She was speaking quickly, doing her best to hide her shock.

"Of course you haven't seen the review. I don't suppose even Ryu reads English, does he?"

Ryu was gazing at her raptly, his thoughts obviously not on what she was saying. I spoke for him and smiled as Evelyn's face showed her surprise. Were all these gaijin so very transparent that their every thought showed on their faces? Was that, perhaps, one of the things that had made my mother fall in love with my unknown father, this quality of honesty, almost innocence?

"No, Evelyn-san. We haven't seen anything."

I glanced at the men and got the hint of a nod from Danjuro. It was up to me then to do the honorable thing and apologize for our failure. Of course it was; after all, it was mainly my fault.

"We are so very sorry, Evelyn-san. We did our best, but perhaps the kabuki is so different from American theater that the audience didn't understand. It was very kind of your father to give us a chance, and we are grateful. We will pay him back whatever he lost on our performance as soon as we can."

Evelyn laughed. She laughed until tears came to her eyes and she had to fumble in her purse for a handkerchief to wipe them. We sat like stones, aghast at her rudeness.

"You think they didn't like you?" she spluttered. Hope rose in the smallest of flames in my belly. "They loved you! Didn't you hear the applause when you finished the performance? I thought they would never stop clapping!"

"But..." I paused, searching for words. "But they didn't shout or hiss or anything. Not a single word, all the way through. Not even at the end."

"Well, no. People don't do that in America. If they really

hate a performance at the theater, they will fidget and maybe chat amongst themselves, but it would have to be really awful before they shouted or hissed."

I stared at Evelyn's smiling face, desperate to be sure she was telling the truth. Before I could speak, Evelyn was rattling the paper and reading from it.

"Here you are. On page two! Half a page, all to yourselves! Papa's beside himself. He can't believe he's stolen a march on the rest of the theaters in San Francisco. The reviewer says he's never seen drama like it. He thought you were wonderful, Midori No Me. 'Impassioned,' he says. He's calling you an amazing example of Japanese theater. He's christened you the 'Dragon Geisha,' and says you're as fiery as your namesake."

Instinctively, my hand went to the back of my neck. Ryu was staring at me, his eyes wide. I translated quickly, before he could say anything, and watched Danjuro's face for a clue. There was nothing.

Evelyn stared from one to the other of us, her face suddenly bewildered. She spoke awkwardly.

"Anyway, Papa asked me to give you your share of the takings." She put an envelope on the table. "There's $78 there. Papa says he has a matinee spot free early next week, and he really would love it if you could do the *Dojoji* play again then. Maybe you could come and talk to him later about some more performances? He'll be at the theater all day."

She stood up, and I got to my feet hurriedly.

"Thank you, Evelyn-san. We will come to the theater this afternoon, if that is permitted. Please, allow me to show you out."

It turned out that Evelyn was far shrewder than I had thought. She paused at the door and spoke softly.

"I am so sorry, Midori No Me. I was so excited by the review, I forgot that it should have been Mr. Danjuro that gets all the attention. That's the way it works in Japan, right? It's the man who matters."

"He is not angry, Evelyn-san," I explained. "Danjuro thought that our performance must have been very bad. The kabuki means everything to him, so he was deeply upset. Now it seems we were wrong and he is shocked. And pleased, of course."

Her face brightened. "Great. I'll see you this afternoon, then? You will come, won't you?" I was puzzled; hadn't I just told her that we would be there? Then I realized she was asking if I personally would be coming to the theater. I was touched.

"Yes, of course I will."

"Wonderful! Now that I know you speak such good English, we can be friends."

She leaned forward and kissed me briefly on the cheek. I stared after her in amazement. In the Hidden House, we geisha had kissed each other frequently. Kissed for friendship, for reassurance, for the pleasure of touching without sexuality. But the geisha in the Hidden House were as close as sisters, and Evelyn was virtually a stranger to me! I stayed still as the door closed behind her. Her astonishing kindness had conjured an unexpected and unwanted longing for Japan, for my friends in the Hidden House, for my old life. Even the thought of Akira was suddenly less terrible. I leaned against the door and blinked back tears.

9

Green shoots herald the
Start of spring, but my heart knows
Nothing and still sleeps

*A*nd so our new life began.

Clay-san was delighted to see us when we walked back into his office. Evelyn must have told him that I spoke English, as he launched into business as soon as he had seated us. A matinee of *Dojoji* next week? I did not know the word, so he had to explain. A puzzled Danjuro agreed to an afternoon performance at once; after all, hadn't performances in Edo lasted from morning to the last light? And even later than that? Perhaps an evening performance once a week.

"But I thought you said the theater was fully booked, Clay-san?" I said slyly.

He grinned, his face open. "It is. But if I let you guys go, every theater owner in San Francisco will be ready to scoop you up. Perform whatever you want, the audience will love it. I'll let my regular guys know they can have a break once a week." He stared hopefully at my stone face and then shrugged. "Alright, we can do a deal. I need to cover my expenses, but after that we can make the split of takings seventy percent for you and thirty percent for me. How does that sound?"

I agreed without consulting with Danjuro. He had his kabuki again. It would never have entered his head to haggle about our earnings. Somebody had to ensure that we were fed and clothed, and it seemed as if that somebody was me. Very well; if that was to be my responsibility, I would accept it gladly. Clay-san was holding out his hand, so I shook it on behalf of us all. Clay-san smiled and added delicately that he understood that our lodgings were not all that they might be. He knew of a Japanese widow lady who ran a lodging house locally. Might that suit us better?

I gave thanks to Evelyn, who had obviously seen more than I might have guessed, and agreed at once. We would move tomorrow.

Perhaps it was because I knew we were going to move, but our rooms seemed more squalid than ever. I packed our belongings carefully and pulled a face when a cockroach ran out of our trunk and under the bed. I needed a bath. Badly.

Standing in the stained tub that was the best Mac provided, I poured water over myself clumsily, using one of the clean food dishes. I swiveled fearfully when the bathroom door opened, using my hands to try to cover my black moss and my breasts in case it was Mac, trying again. I relaxed with a sigh when I saw it was Danjuro.

He took the dish off me silently. Ran water over my body, making me shiver. It was icy cold and my nipples stood to attention painfully. But his hands were warm as he soaped me and then rinsed off the suds. He turned me around and ran his finger over the outline of my tattoo.

"Dragon Geisha," he said softly.

I kept my back turned, staring straight at the wall. I was deeply relieved the moment to talk had arrived. I had been anticipating it ever since I realized I had thrown caution to the four winds and displayed my dragon as if I was proud of Akira's symbol of possession.

Normally, a geisha would wear her kimono low at the back to show off the full nape of her neck; to a Japanese man, the most erotic part of her body. Akira had chosen well when he had seared his dragon onto my neck. Not only was I marked as his creature until the day of my death, but he had also ensured that I could never enchant another man by displaying my flawless neck. Danjuro understood, but I hated even him seeing my disfigurement. I had sworn no other man would ever see my hated tattoo. And now a whole theater full of strangers had been shown my shame. Worse still, I had reveled in revealing it, in showing Akira's mark to the world.

"My kimono must have slipped down at the back of my neck during the dance. I had no idea." I lied quickly, although even as spoke I knew Danjuro would see through my words.

"Dragon geisha," he said again. I waited, searching his voice for anger. He leaned his head gently against my back, and I felt his tongue running softly down my spine. "You are truly unique, Midori No Me-chan. The only woman to act in the kabuki. The only geisha to bear the mark of her courage on her back. The only woman who has ever won my heart and my mind. Dragon Geisha the gaijin have called you, and truly you have the spirit and courage of a dragon." Danjuro turned me to face him, and put his arms around me, lifting me from the bath to stand before him. "Akira put his mark on you," he said quietly. "Just as he put his mark on me. We cannot do anything about it. But it doesn't matter. Not now. He cannot hurt us again."

I leaned against him and slumped with relief as I realized that he understood how I had been so carried away by the magic of the kabuki that I had felt the need to flaunt my dragon to the audience. Also did I know that he was not angry with me because of it. I could feel the scar Akira had inflicted on him through the fabric of his robe, and I pushed my finger against it, tracing its terrible length.

"Does it still hurt?"

Danjuro shrugged. "I will not allow it to hurt me. I would not give Akira the satisfaction."

My finger slid lower, past his stomach, down to his black moss. I heard him take a deep breath, and I smiled. We had come so very far from the Floating World, but some things did not change. My nail caught on his moss and I tugged it gently. I smiled and slid to my knees before him. A lifetime ago I had kneeled for patrons in this way because I had to. Because they had demanded it as their right. Now, I did it for nothing more than my own pleasure.

I took the hood of his tree in my lips and ran my tongue gently around it. Bit, less gently. Tugged at the flesh with my teeth. Ran my tongue over the bald head. Tasted him. Listened to his ragged breathing with delight. When I was in the Hidden House, even after Danjuro had honored me by taking me as his lover, Aunty had still expected me to earn my keep by delighting any patron who could pay my high price. Not one of them had given me a fraction of the pleasure I felt just being close to my husband. And that pleasure was multiplied tenfold as Danjuro thrust toward me, his movements mirroring every touch I made to his body.

Much as I was on fire for him, I wanted to prolong the delight as long as I could. When the moment for true pleasure arrived, it would be all the better for being made to wait. I took my head away and just touched the head of his tree with the tip of my tongue. Danjuro gasped, but he knew how the game should be played and stayed perfectly still, waiting for me.

I ran a fingernail down the length of his tree, scratching subtly. Dived into his black moss and cupped his kintama. Leaned forward and licked them, like a cat. Smiled as I felt his flesh tighten beneath my caress. Sat back on my knees and stared up at him, licking my lips. His face was shadowed; I could not read his expression. Nor did he speak. It was up to me, then, to decide what game we would play. I leaned back, my breasts thrusting upward. Very deliberately, I slipped my first finger into my sex, running it down tenderly. The sensation was so exquisite, I sucked in my breath involuntarily.

Danjuro watched me intently. I stroked my sex slowly, enjoying both the feel of it and the effect I knew it was having on him. I took my finger away from myself and held it up to his mouth; his lips parted as he sucked my juices, his tongue flickering hungrily. I laughed with delight, and Danjuro grinned with me. He slid down to the floor in front of me, and lowered his head to my neck. His tongue was quite dry as he licked down my body, pausing to flick at my navel before his lips found my black moss.

I arched backward, all thought of subtlety gone at his touch. Suddenly, I had no time to wait. I was consumed by need and rose to meet his lips with a moan of desire. But Danjuro had other ideas. Just as I had teased him moments before, now he paid me back. His tongue flirted with my black moss. He rubbed his face against me, but so lightly it tickled. I could not wait, I rose and squirmed against him, trying to force his lips into my sex, panting for the pleasure of him seeking the seed with me.

But he would not be hurried. His tongue flicked inside my sex, but briefly. His teeth caught my black moss, and tugged. He took his head away and stared at me. He was laughing silently, and I could take no more. I wriggled from beneath him and pushed his body to the floor. He was very strong; I knew if he had wanted to resist me it would have been like trying to move a mountain. But he slid down almost lazily, lying on his back in front of me. This was the moment, then.

Since we had arrived in our new country, we had barely made love. Everything had been so strange, so fearful, we had fallen into our bed at night and slept badly, hoping only that no dreams would come to trouble us. We had awoken day after day as tired as we had gone to bed. When the need had become so great it could not be denied, we had coupled quickly, like animals rather than lovers. Now, it was time to find each other again. I filled with joy at the knowledge.

I shivered theatrically, watching Danjuro slyly.

"I am cold to my bones, husband," I said. "Do you think you could warm me?"

He pretended to consider my question, pursing his lips seriously. "I might be persuaded to try."

I leaned forward and nipped playfully at his chin, but when I tried to jerk away Danjuro was too quick for me. He snapped a hank of my hair in his mouth, and held me captive. He wagged his head, pulling at my hair until I squealed in surrender. Only then did he let go, laughing at me. He crooked his finger at me and I closed my eyes in pleasure.

But he did not move, and I realized that in this game we were playing I was expected to make the next move. I had no need to think; I knew exactly what I wanted. I slid my leg over his waist and suspended myself over his tree. Supported myself there, waiting. But not for long. Danjuro slid his hands over my flanks and grasped me strongly. Very slowly, he lowered me on to his tree, his gaze on my face all the time. I wriggled in his grip, but he held me effortlessly.

I gave in with pleasure and relaxed in his grasp, knowing I was safe in those strong hands. I had seen Danjuro—when he was taking the role of the villain in a play—lift Tadayo bodily off the ground and flick him to one side as if he were nothing. He would not hurt me. Not unless I wanted him to, of course, but that was a game for another day. He was beginning to pant, but not with the effort of keeping me suspended.

I slid down the last fraction of his tree and felt his black moss tickle my sex. His hands fell away, and I understood that the play was to commence. I raised myself slightly, at the same time gripping him as hard as I knew how with my internal muscles. Danjuro was not the only one who was stronger than he looked! I teased, moving at first slowly, then quickly.

But not for long. I was too excited to keep either of us waiting. I leaned forward, tormenting him by keeping my breast just away from his mouth. But Danjuro had a trick to beat that; he raised his head and poked his tongue out until it could reach my nipple. I shuddered with pleasure as it immediately grew erect and the cold prickled it.

"Enough," he said softly.

I lowered my head in agreement and allowed him to

begin to move with me. Back and forth, the rhythm that I had feared might be forgotten instantly with us again. I felt the heat build within me, and burst the fruit with a small scream of delight. A long time afterward, I reflected irrelevantly that it was no wonder that the Japanese word for orgasm, "yonaki," translates into English as "cries in the night."

Danjuro followed me, and I slid off him reluctantly to lie at his side. He threw his robe over both of us, and we were almost asleep when we heard the rest of the actors enter the lodgings. Guilty and giggling like naughty children, we scampered for our room and slid beneath the prickly blankets.

I had thought that no dream could disturb me that night, but I did dream. In my sleep, Akira's face looked down at me, as if from a great height. There was much light and noise and I knew that I was back in the Floating World. Then Akira was gone, and I shivered as I realized that I was filled with an immense pity for him.

When I woke, there were tears streaming down my cheeks and I rubbed them away against the blankets. Danjuro stirred without waking, and I held my breath in case he did wake up and demanded to know why I was crying.

What would I have said? I had no idea. I didn't understand my sorrow myself.

10

Butterflies spread their
Wings to the light. Do they yet
Enjoy the darkness?

*E*velyn sat down and glanced round approvingly. "Now isn't this so much better than that dump you stayed in at first?"

There was no arguing with that. The lodgings Clay-san had suggested were clean and airy. As he had said, the house was owned by a Japanese widow. She explained shyly that she had left Japan to follow her man, who was a gaijin sailor. He had died not long before, and she was renting out rooms in her house to "make the ends meet" as the quaint gaijin saying was. Even better, she had loved the kabuki when she lived in Edo and was deeply in awe of the great Danjuro. She was honored to have us in her home. We were equally happy to be there.

And it appeared that the good people of San Francisco were equally delighted with us and our kabuki. After our successful first evening performance, Clay-san had quickly rearranged his schedule so that we were performing twice a week, every week. Once in the evening, once in the afternoon.

"They love you," Evelyn said happily. "You are so fashionable. Even the best shops are selling kimonos and hair ornaments like the ones you wear."

I smiled with her, but shook my head. "I have seen those clothes. They are not kimonos."

She shrugged and pointed out shrewdly that the ladies of San Francisco thought they were, and that was all that mattered.

It was true, we were succeeding beyond any hope we might have had. But the gods have a strange sense of humor, and there was the threat of rain in my sky. The kabuki was indeed popular. And I was adored even more. I was bewildered at first. In Edo, Danjuro was the star, the one who could take any role and make the audience laugh or cry as he desired. When he strolled the streets of the Floating World, the crowd parted before him almost as if he were a god, come to walk amongst them. Here, it was me who attracted all the attention. I who had the patrons at her feet.

And I quickly found that I hated it.

I had always thought that the actors in the kabuki must love the attention they got. Perhaps they did; I certainly did not. I knew that Danjuro enjoyed being recognized by his public. But in Japan it was different. Even the great Danjuro could walk the streets of Edo in peace, with no more than bows and murmurs of admiration behind his back to mark his passage. Here, we—and especially me—were never left alone. Whenever we appeared in the streets, we were stopped by gaijin who wanted to talk to us. Often, they asked for our signature. I had no idea why, but at least that was better than having them touch our arms and tug at our clothes. Occasionally, they even patted my face and hair. Eventually, in sheer desperation, I took to wearing Western clothes when we went out. Without my makeup, and wearing a hat with a veil, I found I could pass for a gaijin easily enough. Perhaps people thought I was Danjuro's mistress. I neither knew nor cared; I was left alone. Danjuro seemed to relish the attention; if that was what he wanted, then I was happy for him.

"Ryu's not here?" Evelyn's question was casual, but I was not fooled. Our handsome onnagata was every bit as popular with the ladies in America as he had been in Edo. Clearly, they were not at all fooled by his portrayal of female roles in the kabuki. In fact, I was beginning to worry that perhaps his excesses were finally catching up with him. His cough had not gotten any better, despite me forcing him to swallow some medicine that the pharmacist assured me would work wonders. There were dark circles under his eyes, and—even though our landlady was an excellent cook, and fed us as if we were hungry children—I was sure he was even thinner.

But although Ryu could take his pick of female companions, and I was sure that he certainly did, I was equally sure that he was very attracted to Evelyn. And it worried me. What would Clay-san think if interest turned to action? Evelyn's next words deepened my dread.

"I really like Ryu. You know, he's so different from all the boys I've ever met. I mean, he's traveled. Seen the world." She scratched at the table with her finger nail, not looking at me. "Papa wants me to marry the son of a friend of his."

"Yes? And you do not like this boy?" I spoke carefully, keeping my tone just lightly interested.

"Tom? Oh, sure I like him. We've been best friends

forever. I've known him for years. But you know, I couldn't ever see myself married to him. Not for a minute. What would you do, if you were me?"

I hadn't expected the question. Had Evelyn been Japanese, and the both of us in Japan, the answer would have been simple. Obey your papa and marry the man he had chosen for you. And be grateful that it was somebody that you knew and liked, who was your own age and not an old man. What was there to worry about? He must be suitable, or her doting papa would never have entertained the idea of Evelyn marrying him. Once you were married, you could take a lover. Or several lovers, if you wanted. In Japan, as long as you were discreet it would not have mattered, for surely your husband would also have a number of mistresses, if he was wealthy enough. And although Ryu was low-caste, being nothing but a kabuki actor, he was famous, and as a result highly respected. Most husbands would look benignly on the liaison, as it would reflect favorably on the family name.

I doubted Evelyn would understand all that, so I chose my words with care.

"It is difficult for me to say, Evelyn. In Japan, it is expected that your father will choose your husband for you."

"But your father didn't choose Danjuro for you, did he?" she asked shrewdly. "You chose him for yourself, I know you did. Ryu told me you ran away from Japan with him."

Thank you, Ryu!

"And what else did Ryu tell you?"

Evelyn twisted her fingers together anxiously. "Nothing! Well, not a lot. It was my fault, I was just so interested in you. I kept on asking him. I mean, I know everybody calls you the 'Dragon Geisha' and they all think it must be normal for a geisha to have a tattoo, but I know it's not."

"And did Ryu tell you how I got my tattoo?" Evelyn shook her head, looking at me with wide, adoring eyes.

"The tattoo was put on my back by the man who owned me. The man who Danjuro stole me from," I said bluntly. "He insisted he had put it there as a mark of respect for me, that I was the first woman he had ever allowed to bear the symbol of his clan, but it wasn't that at all. He wanted to humiliate me, and at the same time to let the world know that I was his and his alone."

Evelyn leaned forward, her lips parted. I sighed. Very well. If she wanted to know about my life, then I would tell her.

"Do you really know what it means to be a geisha, Evelyn? Have you found that in your books?"

She shook her head slightly, her whole face eager.

"Very well. I will tell you. In Japan, most geisha are truly slaves. ." I could tell she did not believe me. Evelyn had the most expressive face I had ever seen in a gaijin, and now it clouded with doubt. "It is true. Most geisha are sold to a tea house when they are children. Perhaps their parents have fallen on hard times, or they simply have too many children to feed. In Japan, the boy always comes first. Girl children are not valued."

"That's what happened to you? You were sold?"

I paused. How much of the truth was I going to tell her? Not the whole of it, that much I was sure.

"No. I was born in a tea house. My mother was a very special geisha, the most talented and beautiful geisha in Edo. She could have had her pick of any man as her protec-tor, even taken a high-caste husband, but she didn't want any of them. She fell in love with my father, and she became pregnant by him. They were going to run away together before I was born, but I decided to arrive early. At least my timing was good. It was the night of a great festival and all the rest of the geisha were out of the tea house. I was born without fuss, but my mother and father had to leave me behind. They had very far to go, and I would not have survived. She intended to come back for me later, but fate got in the way and it never happened. So I grew up in the tea house, and when I was old enough, I became a geisha. Like my mother."

"Your father was a foreigner, wasn't he? A gaijin? That was why they had to leave you behind, because you would have slowed them down and your mother would have been bought back and then she would probably have been made to expose you." She spoke breathlessly, in a rush.

"Ryu told you that?"

"Well, he didn't exactly tell me. It's easy to see that you aren't pure Japanese, and so I kept on at him until he told me your story. But is it really true, that you were no more than a slave?"

I was appalled. How could this sweet child be so insensitive as to call me a half-breed to my face? I answered stonily, concentrating on keeping my temper.

"All Japanese women are slaves to some extent. If you marry, then you do exactly as your husband tells you. If you are fortunate enough to have boy children, then you do what they tell you as well." Her brow puckered uncertainly, and I was bitterly pleased. "The only time a married woman has any sort of say in matters is when her sons marry and bring their own wives to live in the family home. Then you can bully your daughter-in-law."

"But you weren't married. You were a geisha!" Evelyn said stubbornly. "I read that geisha can do what they like.

Even take lovers if they want to and nobody minds. You took Danjuro for your lover, didn't you?"

"It doesn't matter how many lovers a geisha chooses to take, she is still not free. She is the property of the tea house, where she lives. Her Aunty—the woman who is in charge of the Tea House—will have paid a great deal of money for her when she bought her as a child. Every meal she eats, every kimono she wears, all are given to her by her Aunty. And each garment, each mouthful of rice, piles up a debt she can never hope to pay, unless she is fortunate enough to find a patron who is so important and rich that he can buy her out, either to live as his mistress, or very occasionally as his wife. And then she is the slave of one man, instead of being at the beck and call of many."

Evelyn looked at me as if she was seeing me for the first time.

"But you escaped." She said in a very small voice. "You ran away with Danjuro. So all Japanese men can't be the same, can they?"

Ryu again. She was pleading with me to tell her he was different, too. To assure her that they might have a future together. I shook my head in exasperation.

"Danjuro is unlike any other Japanese man. He loves me, yes. But even I come second to the kabuki as far as he is concerned." And as I said it, I admitted to myself—for the first time—that it was true. I did come second to the kabuki for Danjuro, and I always would. The knowledge made me speak more harshly than I had intended. "Listen to me, Evelyn. This isn't some romantic novel we're talking about, where everything works out right in the end. Yes, my father was a gaijin. That was why he and my mother had to run away. My mother had brought unforgiveable dishonor on her house by choosing to take a gaijin as her lover. If they had been caught, if my mother was very lucky, she would have been sold on by Aunty and ended up as the lowest common prostitute, available to any man who wandered in from the street with her price in his pocket. And she would have stayed there until she was too old and too ugly even to make a living from that, and then she would have been thrown into the street to beg. Or starve. If Aunty had been angry enough at the loss of face they had caused her, my mother would have simply disappeared, and in all likelihood my father would have died with her. There were very few gaijin in Japan in those days, and the few that were there were very careful to behave themselves. If any of the other gaijin missed him, they wouldn't have dared to ask what had happened to him."

Even as I spoke, I realized that no matter what I said, to Evelyn, this was just a story. One more bit of strangeness to add to the allure of these exotic foreigners. But it had been my life! How could I explain to her how each day that I had looked in the mirror I had seen a mongrel. A nothing. And now, when I had finally thought I had left all that behind me and was simply accepted as myself, this silly girl had come along and spoiled everything. For surely, if she saw through me so easily, then so did the rest of the gaijin. Oh, how they must have laughed behind my back at this silly half-breed who thought she was as good as they were!

And now my dream was shattered, as surely as broken glass. Once more, I was only Midori No Me. The Geisha with the Green Eyes.

I turned my head and waved my hand at her to go away. To leave me alone. She either didn't understand or chose not to care. I heard her moving, and then next minute her arm was around my waist and her sharp little chin was resting on my shoulder.

"Midori No Me, I'm sorry. I've upset you. I didn't mean to. Please, tell me what I've said that was so bad? Are you annoyed with Ryu for telling me about you? It wasn't his fault, honestly. I kept on at him until he told me. I really am sorry."

Her breath was sweet and warm on my cheek. I listened to her anxious voice and heard the truth in it. She really didn't understand.

"I didn't know anybody here realized I was half gaijin," I said reluctantly. "In Japan, it was a very great dishonor. I was treated with as much contempt as one of your slaves is treated by the people who own them. I was thought of as less than human. I believed that I had left all that behind. Now I know I was a fool to think I could ever lose my past. Please go, Evelyn. Leave me alone."

It was unforgivably rude of me to speak to her like that, but I was very upset. But Evelyn did not go. Instead, she tightened her grip on me and rubbed her cheek against mine. She reminded me of Neko when he felt like seeking affection, and I managed a half-smile.

"Nobody would care if they knew, Midori No Me," she said. "But they don't know. I'm the only one that's realized. When you're wearing a kimono and all your makeup and a wig, you look completely Japanese. I don't think you know you're doing it, but whenever you talk to anybody apart from the kabuki troupe, you keep your eyes downcast so they don't notice the color. When you're dressed in Western clothes, and without your white makeup, you look almost as American as I do. But honestly, even if people did notice, it would never occur to them that a Japanese woman should never have green eyes."

She took my hand and held it clasped tightly in her fingers. "I had no idea it mattered so much to you. I would never have said anything if I had known. Please, will you forgive me? Can we still be friends?"

I listened to my heart and nodded. Her face brightened, and I thought not for the first time what a pretty girl she was.

"I don't suppose you know where your father came from, do you?" she asked shyly.

I shrugged tiredly. What did it matter?

"I always thought he must have been Dutch, or perhaps English. Most of the gaijin in Edo at that time were. I suppose it's just possible he might even have been American. His name was Simon."

Evelyn turned the name around in her mouth, tasting it. Finally, she said, "Simon? S-i-m-o-n, that how it was spelled? In that case, he was probably English. Or even American!"

"It's not likely that he was an American." I smiled, interested in spite of myself. "I don't think there were many Americans at all in Edo all those years ago. Until the Americans arrived in their black ships, and changed our lives forever, nobody knew anything about them at all."

"You're wrong," Evelyn said firmly. "I've read all about it. Commander Perry had lots of information about Japan before he sailed. The books don't actually say so, but I reckon there must have been Americans in Japan years and years ago, passing information back to the government here."

Her enthusiasm was infectious. I smiled, remembering Danjuro saying much the same thing.

"You're right. They were all just a bunch of foreigners to us Japanese!" We giggled together, and the ice was broken. "It is odd, now you mention it. I was told that my father spoke such excellent Japanese that if you didn't see he was a gaijin, you would never have guessed. And he even learned to read and write Japanese, which is very, very difficult for a foreigner. A few of the traders spoke a little Japanese, but most of them relied on translators. My father was the only gaijin I ever heard of who was fluent enough to speak Japanese like a native of Edo."

"See? If he had been just a trader, he would never have bothered to learn to speak Japanese as well as read and write it, would he?"

"Perhaps not. But why does that mean he must have been American?"

"Because he was working for the government, of course! He had to be. You know, they don't just unwrap a fresh parcel of warships and send them across the sea just hoping for the best. That kind of thing costs a lot of money and takes a lot of planning. They had to know it was worth it in the first place."

I shook my head. It might make sense to Evelyn, and Danjuro might want it to be true, but she was forgetting one fact.

"Evelyn, I hear what you say. But my father must have been in Japan for a long time before I was born for him to have learned to speak and write Japanese. That would mean he was in Japan for years and years before the American fleet arrived. Do you really think your government would have taken that long to decide to act?"

She tapped her teeth with her finger and then grinned.

"I suppose that would have been too long ago to help plan Commander Perry's visit," she agreed. "But don't forget, Perry wasn't the first American to try and get a deal with Japan. There was another naval commander who was there eight years before Commander Perry arrived."

I nodded cautiously. Suddenly, it seemed more likely

that my father just might have been an American. And now perhaps here I was, in his country. Had I been drawn here by fate? Was it all destiny? Might he and my mother still be here, somewhere? How I longed that it might be the truth, even as I smiled indulgently at Evelyn and shook my head.

"Perhaps," I said.

"I'm sure it's so!" Her cheeks were bright with pleasure. "Look, there aren't any Japanese ladies in society here even now. All that time ago, if your mother was a society lady, she would surely have been noticed. Would you like me to ask around? Tom's mother would remember if she had seen her, I know she would." Seeing the doubt on my face, she added quickly. "Everybody knows I'm mad about anything Japanese. She would just think I was interested. I wouldn't so much as mention you, I promise!"

I smiled. If it would give her pleasure, why not? Suddenly, I wondered. Evelyn was going to ask Tom's mother, not her own mama. She had never spoken about her mother, and now I was curious about her. In Japan, it would have been grossly impolite to pry, but perhaps some of Evelyn's honesty had rubbed off on me.

"What happened to your own mother, Evelyn?"

"She died. When I was quite young. I remember her, though. She was very beautiful. Always smiling, in spite of everything."

"In spite of everything....?" I enquired. Evelyn smiled, but not at me. It was if she was looking through me, into her own past.

"I remember when I was a little girl, we didn't have much money at all. Papa's family was well-off. I knew that because sometimes we went to visit my grandmother, and she always gave me delicious things to eat and quite often she had a new dress for me or some shoes. She lived in a big house as well. Up on Nob Hill. She had servants and every-thing. I never knew my grandfather, he died years before I was born."

"If your grandmother was wealthy, why didn't your papa have money as well?"

"Because she didn't like my mother," Evelyn said simply. "She never actually said anything to me about Mama, but I could tell. Whenever we visited Grandma, Mama always stayed at home. And sometimes Grandma would tell me to go play in the garden, and I heard her and Papa arguing. She called my mother 'poor white trash' once, and we didn't visit with her for nearly a year after that."

I raised my eyebrows in surprise. It seemed I had been wrong about Evelyn; she had seen more of the world than I had thought.

"I asked Papa what Grandma had meant when she called Mama that, and he told me all about it then. My mother had been Grandma's servant before she married Papa. She was just a housemaid, nothing fancy. They met when Papa came home from University. Papa said he fell in love with Mama the instant he saw her, although it took him a long while to convince her he meant it. When Grandma found out, she sacked mother on the spot and forbade Papa ever to see her again. But Papa was having none of it. He said he was going to marry my mother no matter what. Grandma said Grandfather would turn in his grave if he knew how his son had turned out, and Papa said he didn't care. So she threw him out. And that was that. She wouldn't see him again until I was born."

"How did you all live, if you had no money?"

"Mama found a job at another big house, as a kitchen maid. Papa did what he had always wanted to do. He became an actor. I don't know if he was a very good actor," she said thoughtfully. "But I think he was very handsome in those days, so he had lots of parts playing nice, young men. Mama had to stop working when I was born, of course, so then Papa found a job working in a shop during the day, and kept on working in the theater whenever he could get a part. We just lived in a couple of rooms down by the docks."

"You didn't mind being poor?" I asked curiously.

Evelyn shrugged. "We were all poor," she said simply. "All my friends were poor, so nobody thought anything about it. After a while, going to see Grandma and being given nice presents felt like a dream, so I forgot about it. Anyway, Grandma didn't talk to Papa again until after Mama died. She was having another baby, but it wouldn't come and they both died. Papa said it was for the best because they had both gone to heaven together, but I cried and cried and cried. I prayed to God to bring them both back, but He didn't listen to me. I guess that was the last time I prayed."

She sighed and rubbed at her face with her hands. I looked away discreetly and waited for her to begin again.

"Papa told Grandma about Mama being dead. I didn't think it would make any difference, and it might not have, but then Grandma died herself, not long after. I remember going to her funeral, and thinking it wasn't fair that she should have a fancy carriage and all to take her coffin to the cemetery when Mama had had nothing but a cart painted black. Papa said it didn't matter when you were dead, and I suppose he was right. Anyway, it turned out that Grandma had left Papa a lot of money. He said he wouldn't have taken it if she hadn't insisted in her will it was for my benefit, and he was duty bound to do his best for me. That's how he came to have the theater. It was very shabby and run down before he bought it, and it took him years to get it right, but he did it." She grinned. "He says he's much better as a theater manager than he ever was as an actor!"

Restored to her normal good nature, Evelyn pushed her chair back.

"I'll talk to Tom's Mama as soon as I can. Don't worry! I'll be discreet. And I've decided I'm not going to fret about Papa nagging me to marry Tom. I'm not eighteen for nearly a year, and he can't expect me to marry anybody before then."

I saw her go wordlessly. Evelyn was seventeen? This sweet, innocent child was nearly the same age as me? I shook my head in amazement. Truly, her world and mine were so far apart nothing could ever reconcile the two. I jumped as she came back in, a whirlwind of excitement and smiles.

"You know, one of these days I am truly going to forget my own name! This was delivered to the theater by a Japanese man, and he said it was to be given to Midori No Me, and nobody else. If you want to get a message back, he can do that for you. Bye!"

I turned the silk-wrapped package she had taken out of her purse over and over in my hands. It was bound with silken threads, and those in turn were stuck firmly to the silk cloth with large blobs of wax. It was addressed in Japanese quite simply to "Midori Ne Me-San, Geisha, Kabuki, America."

11

Paper was once a
Living thing. Do words written
On it also live?

For a long time, I did not dare to open my package. Akira. It had to be from Akira. He had found us somehow. Neko made my mind up for me. He avoided Evelyn whenever he could. She invariably wanted to pick him up and make a fuss of him, and Neko only wanted petting on his own terms, in his own time. Now that she had gone, he jumped on to the table and sniffed the package, butting his head against it and, I swear, looking at me enquiringly.

"I think it's from Akira," I explained. But Neko was unimpressed. He swiped the package casually with his paw, catching his claws in the silk bindings and tugging at them. I looked from Neko to the package.

"Leave it alone." I patted his paw away. "Alright, I can take a hint."

I tore it open before I could change my mind.

One glance at the clumsy script inside reassured me; if the letter had come from Akira, he would have made sure to employ the best calligrapher, if only to remind me that his wealth and power were endless. After the first few words, I had to put the letter down. I couldn't read anything for the tears that were misting my eyes.

Not from Akira. But Kiku. Somehow, dear Kiku had found me.

I wiped my eyes and tried to concentrate. Kiku's calligraphy was terrible. I wondered why she hadn't asked Mineko to write for her; Mineko had been taught to write by her father, one of the best calligraphers in Edo. In fact, Mineko's handwriting was so good that her father bemoaned the fact that she was not a boy, so she could have followed him in the family business. Then I remembered—how had I ever come to forget?—Kiku was no longer in the Hidden House, no longer in contact with Mineko and the other girls. She had been bought out of slavery by my own old patron, Mori-san, who had found a new favorite in Kiku when Akira had taken me away. Now, she was his wife.

Kiku wrote exactly as she spoke, and for a delicious moment I was transported back to the bathhouse in the Hidden House. I felt almost as if we were sitting side by side, ready to enjoy a good gossip. The wave of nostalgia made my stomach clench with longing for past times. Did Kiku also miss her old life, I wondered? Reading her letter, I thought that perhaps she did.

She herself was well, Kiku wrote. As was her husband, Mori-san. My lips twitched at that; Kiku was Mori-san's second wife. His first wife had died of a fever, and it was generally thought that Mori-san must have gone down on his knees in front of the house shrine and given thanks for her death. She had been a strange woman, very aggressive and domineering, almost mannish in her ways. It was said that she had worn the sword in the family, as the saying goes, and I knew from my own experiences with Mori-san that he was an amiable cushion of a man, unique amongst our patrons in that he had enjoyed being told what to do. Kiku would, I was sure, be far kinder to him than his first wife had ever been. In any event, Mori-san was prospering, Kiku said. He did much trade with the gaijin, and when one of his best customers had mentioned that he had heard the first genuine kabuki theater in America had opened in his hometown of San Francisco, she had immediately decided that it must be Danjuro and me. Rumors had circulated in the Floating World that Akira had had us both executed; never the place to leave gossip unaired, other rumors had said that we had fled to America. Kiku had decided to believe the hopeful version, and never one to have second thoughts, she had picked up her brush at once. Was I—and Danjuro—well? Were we prospering and happy in our strange new country?

The courtesies over with, Kiku got down to business. The Hidden House was still thriving—and how did she know that, I wondered?—and nobody else had left since Mori-san had bought her out. She was sorry to tell me that Akira was still alive, and apparently well, although he was seen less in public, and people were beginning to wonder what he was up to these days. He had bought a substantial share in the new kabuki theater that had been built in Edo, but never attended a performance. Slyly, she added that she had heard that he had set up the strangest of shrines in his beautiful house; a shrine to a goddess who was no longer there.

I picked up Neko and buried my face in his neck. The mention of Akira's name was enough to make me shudder.

Superstitiously, I hoped that Kiku's letter was not an omen, destined to overturn our good fortune. When Danjuro came back from the theater, I pushed it toward him silently. He scanned it quickly.

"Kiku-chan." He smirked and I guessed instinctively that he was delighted with the news that the fame of his new kabuki had reached back to Japan. "Well, when you write back to her, please give her my best wishes for her happiness and prosperity."

And that was it, his interest was gone. I was relieved I had not told him how the mere mention of Akira's name had worried me. No doubt he would have laughed at my silliness. In the next moment, he was telling me how well the plans for the future kabuki production were coming along. I schooled my face to appear as fascinated as he was.

"I think the audience will like it." As always, when he was engrossed in the kabuki, Danjuro could not sit still. He was on his feet, prowling like a guard dog who senses intruders. "It will take a lot of work, but I'm sure it will be worth it. We have decided to amalgamate two plays, *Kanadahon Shushingura* and *Yoshitsune Senbon Zakura*. You know they're both historical plays, with plenty of action. We shall call it *Kizokuno Fukushuu*." He glanced at me and smirked. *Revenge of the Nobles.* "Good title, I think."

"You can't do that to *Kanadahon Shushingura*!" I blurted in surprise. "Even some of the gaijin have heard of *The Legend of The Forty-Seven Ronin*, and *Yoshitsune Senbon Zakura* is nothing like it."

I understood how terribly I had spoken out of turn when Danjuro stopped mid-stride and turned to look at me. A nerve was working beneath one eye, but otherwise his face was blank.

"I did not hear you, Midori No Me," he said quietly. "Go

away and play with Neko. I am sure he would appreciate your company more than I do at the moment."

My immediate instinct was to do as I was told. Danjuro stared at me, and all I wanted to do was to scoop Neko in my arms and leave the room at a run. But I did not move. I raised my head and met his gaze levelly.

"I am sure the new production will be wonderful, Danjuro." Over the thunder of my own heartbeat, I was amazed to hear my voice was still and calm. "Both plays are excellent. But am I right in thinking there will not be a part for me in the new play?" There were no female roles in either *Kanadahon Shushingura* or *Yoshitsune Senbon Zakura.*

"Possibly. I can't say I've really thought about it. I've been working far too hard to get the new production ready to consider your wishes."

He was lying. I could hear it through the bluster in his voice. My husband had not only thought about it, he had deliberately made sure that I was cut out of the new play. *His* new play. I had begun to wonder lately if it was possible that the great Danjuro could be jealous of my success in the kabuki, but I had dismissed the idea as nonsense.

Perhaps he saw the dawning understanding in my expression. In any event, he jerked to his feet and marched across the room. He paused by my side, and for one incredulous moment I thought he was so angry he was going to strike me.

"You forget yourself, geisha," he hissed. "The kabuki is mine. You perform in it by my favor. If it was not for my kindness in trying to give you pleasure, you would never have set foot on the stage. Remember that. *Revenge of the Nobles* is my masterpiece. If I thought you were good enough to be in it, then I would have written a part for you. I have not. Let that be enough for you."

He swept out in the grandest of exits. I heard the outside door slam soon after. I took a deep breath and let it out in a hiss that turned into uncontrollable laughter. I thought it was I who was supposed to leave, not Danjuro!

The laughter left me abruptly. I had spoken out of turn and angered him. That didn't worry me too greatly; when he came back, I would apologize and all would soon be well again. But I knew now that I had not been deceiving myself. Danjuro truly was jealous of my success in the kabuki.

That was a problem that was going to take much more resolution.

No matter. In the meantime, I decided I would answer Kiku's letter at once. I could give it to Evelyn in the morning and ask her to pass it on to the messenger. I wrote carefully, paying attention to every word I brushed on the paper. We were well, I told her. And very happy. My hand trembled as I wrote the last words, but I told myself it had been true, until today. I was acting in the kabuki, I told her, and we had been fortunate enough to be very successful. Almost as an afterthought, I asked Kiku—should she manage to see Mineko—to tell her that the gold I had been forced to leave behind was now hers, to do with as she thought fit. Even as I wrote the words, I knew I was not being as generous as I seemed. We had no aching need for my gold now. Danjuro was simply not interested in money, so I made sure I secured all the takings from our performances. I paid for our lodgings out of it, and gave the other actors their share. What was left, I hid carefully; literally beneath the floorboards in our bedroom. We had accumulated what seemed to me to be a fortune.

I was pleased to think my abandoned gold might help Mineko. I missed her bitterly. Perhaps it might be possible for her to use the gold to buy herself out of the Hidden

House. And if she did that, was it so impossible that she might be able to follow me to America? The thought was a balm to my troubled heart. I finished the letter with a heart-felt plea for Kiku to write back to me with all the gossip of the Floating World.

I lay awake for a long time that night, waiting for Danjuro to come to our bed, but he did not. I heard the clock strike the hours many times; I could never get used to the idea that a mechanical device could tell you the time. What was wrong with the sun, or the moon? Normally the sound of our clock ticking past the minutes had a soothing effect on me, but tonight it taunted me with its determined measure of the passing hours. I had almost given up hope that Danjuro was going to come home when I heard the door bang and the rabble of men's voices speaking far too loudly for the time of night.

He had been out with the rest of the kabuki actors then. Had we been in the Floating World, I knew they would all have gone off to some tea house or other. Been entertained by beautiful, talented geisha. Probably have moved on to see some favored courtesans. And none of it would have cost them a single coin; their visit would have bestowed a great deal of face on any house that could boast it had entertained the entire kabuki troupe.

But here? Here, there were no geisha bowing and greeting the actors with worshipful eyes. Nor even any cour-tesans to welcome them to the arts of love. I was suddenly furiously jealous; had he—all of them—spent the evening with gaijin whores? My lips peeled back into a thin line of anger. I lay perfectly still listening to every movement. Our door opened and closed. I heard Danjuro kick off his sandals and then there was the rustle of his robes falling to the floor. I waited for him to pull on his sleeping robe, but there was nothing. Not a sound. I knew he was standing, watching me pretend to sleep.

He slid beside me, naked. That shocked me. Robes were often discarded during lovemaking, but it would be a strange Japanese man who lay down to sleep—or not!— without at least a thin robe clothing him. In the Hidden House, our patrons had often stripped us naked while they themselves preserved all their clothing. We had all known it was yet one more demonstration of their power over us. Was this strangeness from Danjuro a way of demonstrating his lingering anger with me? Or was it simply that he had spent the evening with a gaijin whore and he had enjoyed the experience so much that he was showing off his new knowledge of Western lovemaking?

I lay still, hardly able to breathe I was so angry. Danjuro was shuffling about, stealing more than his share of the bedding. I sniffed cautiously. If he had truly been with a gaijin whore, then he would stink of her. Even Evelyn poured perfume on herself. It seemed to me that all the gaijin women did, no matter what their class. Very few women in Japan wore perfume; very high caste women might wear a light, floral scent. Sometimes the most expensive courtesans would smooth a little perfumed oil on their skin. For the rest of us, the scent of sweet, clean skin was more than good enough. The first time I had come close enough to a gaijin woman to smell her, I had sneezed until my nose ran. Even Danjuro had noticed the reek and had jerked back impolitely.

But he did not stink of scent. He did smell, a mixture of second-hand tobacco smoke and something it took me a moment to place. Whiskey. That was it. The strong spirit that the gaijin men tossed back as if it was nothing. We had not tasted sake since we came here, but occasionally the men shared a bottle of white wine between them. It was nowhere near as good as sake, they said. At first, they had tried it warm, in the same way that sake is always drunk, and said it tasted terrible. I had tried some, and even cold I didn't think much of it. But a sip of whiskey had burned my throat and made me cough. Danjuro said he didn't like it either, but tonight he smelled as if he had bathed in the stuff.

"Have you been waiting for me, wife?"

His words surprised me. I had expected him to turn his back on me. To try to punish me by simply by ignoring me. My anger began to slip away. I knew where he had been. What he had been up to all evening. He had been out with the boys, drinking as much as he could—and far more than was good for him. It was the typical Japanese man's response to any situation that made him uneasy.

"I have been waiting for you. I could not sleep until I knew you were safe home."

I was careful to sound as if I meant it; I wanted to talk to Danjuro, not antagonize him even more.

"Have you? Then this is a poor welcome for your husband, I think."

I tucked the bedding around his shoulders, to give myself time to think. For all the reek of whiskey, he did not sound drunk. I was thrown off balance; his words said he had forgiven me; his voice was as cold as meltwater. Nor did he help. He simply lay next to me, apparently perfectly relaxed.

"It is very late," I said cautiously. "Are you tired?"

"No, I am far from tired. But if you wish to sleep...?"

"Even if I am tired, for my husband, everything is a pleasure."

I could have bitten my tongue as soon as I spoke. I

sounded sincere, but it was a whore's sincerity, born of long training in the Hidden House. I slid my hand over his belly immediately, and stopped dead. He was already erect. He had not touched me. Not even had a sight of me in the darkness. I was surprised, and at the same time relieved. I was sure now that he had certainly not been with a yujo. A woman of pleasure. Without warning I was aroused myself, just as I had always been whenever he had been with me in the Floating World.

He was no longer my angry, sulky husband. He was my lover again. And I was delighted. Our differences could wait until morning, surely!

I sighed deeply and ran my fingers lightly down to his tree of flesh. Rubbed the silken skin between my fingertips and smiled as I felt him jerk in reaction. I knew that he would not—could not—resist me for long.

"Have you missed me, husband?" I whispered. His reply stopped me dead.

"I have missed Midori No Me. I have not missed the Dragon Geisha."

I felt the hair at the back of my neck prickle erect in a warning to tread very, very carefully. The kabuki was his life, the one thing that he cared about above all else. He had spent years training as an actor. Until I had come into his life, he had cared about nothing else. Now I—a mere woman—had come along and had stolen everything from him. He was no longer the star. I was.

"It is not my fault! I didn't want to steal the attention," I said without thinking. His hand cupped my breast and squeezed hard.

"No? You always longed to act in the kabuki, Midori No Me. You told me that many times. Is that the true reason you came with me to America? Because you knew you would be able to usurp my place?"

His face was very close to mine, and the stink of whiskey was very strong. I would have liked to have turned my face away, but I did not in case it angered him even more. If that was possible!

"I came with you because I loved you. Not for any other reason," I insisted.

"Because you loved me, or because you wanted the kabuki? Or was it because you were tired of Akira, and wanted to escape from him?"

He was relentless, like Neko when he had caught a mouse and would not let it escape. What could I say? Whatever words I tried, he would corrupt them and turn them against me.

"I hated Akira. You know I did," I said desperately. "And I had no idea that the gaijin would be interested in seeing a woman perform in the kabuki. How could I have known?"

"Ah, but you didn't turn the opportunity down, did you? Now, I ask myself would a dutiful wife really want to cause such loss of face to her husband? The husband she says she loves? Well, Kazhua-chan?

I knew then that it was the demon of drink that was speaking, not Danjuro. Kazhua—Green Leaf in Japanese—had been Akira's love name for me. Danjuro had never, ever used it before. I was deeply anxious; in the Floating World, my husband had rarely drunk alcohol and I had never seen him like this. I had no idea what to expect from him. Yet at the same time, I found I was relieved. It was the drink that was in charge of him. In the morning, he would be sober. He would be Danjuro again.

As relief made me relax, I realized suddenly that I was still tense, but with desire, not worry. My hand was still just touching his tree, and I tightened my grip, ready to bring him the stage where he would be unable to resist what I was doing to him. But Danjuro—drunk or sober—was ready for me. Before I could so much as move a fingertip, his hands were on my waist and I was hoisted abruptly on to my back. I gasped with surprise and not a little pain as I hit the futon. But still, I thought I was in command of the situation. I was about to ask what game he wanted to play, when he turned and threw himself on top of me, knocking the wind out of my lungs even as his tree searched for my black moss as though his flesh was some sort of animal, desperate for shelter. It took him no more than a couple of seconds to find his target, but for me in that short space of time the years rolled back. I was no longer a married woman. No longer the Dragon Geisha, the star of the kabuki in a foreign land. In a flash, I was Midori No Me again. A prisoner in the Hidden House, at the mercy of my patron.

I whimpered with shock and not a little fear.

"Please, master, do not hurt me." The words were automatic; back in the Hidden House, more often than not it was what the patron wanted to hear. They had paid handsomely to be the strutting, rutting tiger they had only ever seen in paintings, if only for the space of one evening. And it had been my place to make them feel they were that tiger.

Danjuro grunted deep in his throat. The sound recalled me abruptly to the present. The only time I had ever heard my husband make such a guttural, feral noise was when he was playing a part in the kabuki. That was the noise that the swaggering, arrogant villain used to announce his arrival, more often than not when he had first sighted the innocent village maiden whom he had decided to despoil. In the kabuki, the grunt was greeted with a torrent of boos and hisses.

I laughed silently as I understood that this pretense at anger was all nonsense. He was play-acting. I hid a smile in the darkness and didn't bother with words. Instead, I bit his ear. Hard.

Danjuro reared back as if he had been stung, but I was having none of it. I was the Dragon Geisha, the actress that the patrons paid to see sing and dance, live and die! If Danjuro could act, then certainly so could I. I flung my arms around his neck and forced his mouth down to meet my lips. Kissed him deeply, as if I wanted to suck the life out of him. Danjuro rarely kissed me, and when he did, it was lightly, in a gesture of affection. He obviously found this kiss deeply erotic; as he thrust against me I knew that his body had taken control of his mind and was in charge of him. The knowledge that I had caused this to happen was deeply arousing. I worked with him, meeting him thrust for thrust. All my own self-control began to leave me; if he was an animal, then I was all the elements combined. Wind and rain and storm.

I beat my fists hard on his chest. Stopped only long enough to throw my arms around his shoulders and drag him down to me so that his body slid against my flesh like oiled silk. Bit at his neck and his face. Hissed like a snake when he dragged himself away from me. Wrapped my legs around his waist and held on to him.

I could feel his shock. His skin was hot, everywhere I touched I felt a curious tingling in my fingertips. I arched my back, desperate to force just a little more of him deep into my body.

"Dragon Geisha," he snarled in my ear.

I laughed. "Dragon Geisha, yes. But tonight, for you and you alone."

He liked that, I knew. I could tell. I began to find my

rhythm, moving against him in time to every jerk and piston of his body. But all too soon I read the tell-tale signs that my husband was about to burst his fruit. His movements were becoming increasingly frantic; he alternated between holding his breath and panting. No. Not yet! I nearly screamed aloud in frustration.

Then something I had had no need of since I left the Hidden House came to my rescue. There was no thought behind the movement; before I realized myself what I was going to do, my hand was sliding between our bodies and I pushed my fingers at the very root of his tree of flesh, where it joined his kintama. I joined my fingers around the flesh, and squeezed. Hard. Not hard enough to cause pain, but just hard enough to stop Danjuro's body having its own way before I was ready.

His rhythm faltered and slowed, and I let go quickly, before his whiskey-fuddled mind could focus on what I had done. By the time he had found his pace again, I was ready, and I felt my yonaki build deep in my belly. Danjuro followed me seconds later, bursting his fruit with a shout of pleasure.

He fell asleep almost at once, his head buried against my shoulder. I shifted, unable to get myself comfortable but unwilling to wake him. I drifted toward sleep eventually, but seconds later I was wide awake again.

Danjuro was talking in his sleep. I felt my dragon stir on my back; I was sure it was writhing with pleasure. Danjuro was speaking lines from the play we had first performed in San Francisco—*The Temple at Doji*. His voice was flat, without intonation. But it was not that that worried me.

The words he was speaking were *my* part.

12

Rice in the paddy
Field must always keep its roots
Hidden in water

I told myself constantly that I was the most fortunate of women. I had everything I had ever dreamed of. A loving husband. Wealth. A life that was my own in a country where I was free. I was even acting in the kabuki!

And yet I barely convinced myself. The truth was that I had begun to feel more and more uncomfortable in my new world, and almost a stranger to myself. I had the oddest feeling that I was no longer me, that some unknown woman had taken over my life and I was no more than a spirit, watching myself but unable to intervene. It seemed to me that—adored and famous as I appeared to be in this wonderful new world—I was actually friendless and alone. Even Evelyn appeared to have lost interest in the kabuki. It had been weeks since she had popped in for a chat, her elbows propped on the table and her sweet face alight with interest.

I found it difficult to sleep at night, and when I did, I dreamed of the Floating World. Always, I was back in the Hidden House. Gossiping with the other geisha. Singing and dancing for the patrons. Giggling with Mineko. One day, I awoke abruptly just as Kiku was complimenting my talent with the samisen; she had pointed out the truth of the old saying that if one had three strings, then one would never go hungry—a reference to the three strings of the samisen. I realized I had tears streaming down my face. I had left my samisen in the Floating World when I escaped; would I still be able to play it, even if I had an instrument?

And I was worried about Danjuro. He was drinking, I thought far too much. He had begun to go out more and more frequently, generally with the rest of the actors, but sometimes on his own. Either way, he always came back with his breath stinking of whiskey. In Edo, he had rarely taken more than a single flask of sake. What had happened to change that? The more I thought about it, the more I began to be certain I already knew the answer.

Most Japanese men drank sake as if it was water. The men who came to us in the Hidden House drank flask after flask of it, all the more because it was the best sake in Edo, and very expensive. Often, they reeled home drunk. But never Danjuro.

When he came to visit me at the Hidden House, he would sometimes drink a couple of cups of sake to be polite. But he never had more and often he took only tea. I couldn't remember ever seeing him drink sake at the kabuki, not even to unwind after a performance. Now I wondered if it was because he knew, even then, that drink had too much allure for him. And sake was like water, compared to the whiskey in America. I made my mind up. I would ask Ryu. I was sure I could trust our onnagata to be truthful.

"Of course Danjuro drinks when we are out together. All of us do."

He grinned boyishly at me, but I refused to be placated.

"How much is he drinking, Ryu? Tell me, please. He drank very little in Edo. I'm worried about him."

"No need to worry about Danjuro. He can hold his liquor." But Ryu wasn't looking me straight in the eyes. He was using the old actor's trick of looking at the bridge of my nose. He was lying to me.

"Thank you, Ryu," I said courteously. "I am not just worried for myself, you understand. But also for the kabuki. I can't imagine what would become of us all if Danjuro were not in control."

There was a long, uncomfortable silence, and I took the chance to have a good look at Ryu. He was thinner, I was sure of it. As I waited, he grimaced in pain and put his hand to his stomach. Somebody else who was drinking too much?

"I assure you, there really isn't a problem," he said sincerely. I wanted to believe him, but I could not. Ryu was a very fine actor.

"Oh, Ryu. Tell me, please," I blurted. "Is he really drinking a lot? Why? What's wrong?"

"He isn't drinking any more than the rest of us," Ryu said reluctantly. "It's just that he can't seem to handle it very well. And he knows it, so he drinks even more to prove that it's really having no effect on him at all."

Of course, the typical Japanese man's reaction to something he felt was causing him lack of face. Stare it down. Pretend it wasn't there.

"Please, Ryu. Please. If you can, take care of him. Of course you can't take the drink off him, but perhaps if the rest of you drank less, he would do the same?"

Ryu smiled, but his expression passed into a grimace as he sucked in air.

"What is it? Are you in pain?"

"A little. It's this food we have to eat. After all this time, I still can't get used to it. There are days when I would give a fortune for some good plain rice, properly cooked. And I tried some beef last night. All the gaijin were saying how wonderful it was, so I thought I would give it a go. I think it's disagreed with me."

He pouted and looked at me so dolefully I had to laugh.

"Take care of yourself, Ryu-chan. As well as Danjuro!"

I thought that perhaps Ryu had done as I had asked him. It seemed to me that the boys were at home more frequently on the nights they did not have a performance at the theater, and Danjuro was no longer going out on his own. I was very grateful for that. Perhaps it was because they were all so busy working on the new play, *The Revenge of the Nobles*. I didn't care what the reason was, it was enough that it was so.

And even better, Danjuro was no longer talking in his sleep.

Because things were so much improved, I was reluctant to share Kiku's latest letter with Danjuro. I normally read all of her eagerly-awaited letters to him as soon as I received them. He would listen to me indulgently, smiling when I finished.

"A different world to ours now. We should be very grateful for the fate that led us to this wonderful country, Midori No Me-chan."

He was right, of course. Such a life as we led in America

could never have been dreamed of in the Floating World. The good people of this new country did not regard us as riverbed beggars, but people who mattered. We were respected as talented actors. And above all else, I was free. Free of the Hidden House. And Akira.

But this letter from Kiku made me pause. This one I would have kept to myself as I was reluctant to disturb Danjuro with bad news from Japan. But he came home earlier than I had expected and found it in my hands.

"Ah, Kiku-chan has written! And what does she have to tell you this time?"

I shrugged my shoulders, trying to pretend it wasn't really interesting.

"Oh, the usual gossip. Would you like some tea?"

He stared at me. "Yes, I would like tea. But in a moment. I have heard from Sato-san that strange things are happening in Edo, and in particular in the Floating World. Does Kiku have any news about it?"

I was astonished and hurt. Danjuro already knew that our old world was being turned upside down and he hadn't thought it worthwhile to tell me? Very well, I would read Kiku's letter to him and see what he had to say.

When I had finished, he simply nodded.

"Yes, that is much what I have heard. Well, if Akira is having problems controlling his empire, I cannot say I am sorry. Perhaps the other yakuza will triumph over him in the end. I hope so."

"But it's not just Akira, is it? Look"—I stabbed my finger at the letter. "Kiku says gaijin are being attacked in the streets of Edo, the yakuza have grown so bold. The whole of Edo is in an uproar, nobody feels safe anymore, or even knows what's going to happen next. She says that Akira is letting anybody into the Hidden House who has the price of the geisha in his pocket, no matter who they are. And she is certain that Akira is going to take poor Mineko to be his mistress. Shut her up in his house, just as he did with me."

"Why worry about Mineko?" Danjuro put his finger on the nub of the thing instinctively. "You know she can't feel pain, so it doesn't matter what Akira does to her, does it?"

"But I was her elder sister!" I wailed. "I should be there to look after her."

I stared at him, aghast at his insensitivity. True, the gods had blessed Mineko by giving her the gift of being unable to feel physical pain. But Danjuro knew how I had suffered at Akira's hands. Surely he could understand what mental torment he would be putting Mineko through? He was capable of any cruelty. And it wasn't just physical pain that Akira could inflict, he could be far more subtle than that. I didn't doubt that he was taunting my poor Mineko endlessly, so that each day that passed she would wonder if this was the day he was going to take her, if this was going to be her last hour of existence without being his slave. And when he finally did take her as his mistress, it would be even worse. Akira would delight in playing tricks with her mind, turning her round and round like a blind animal tormented by sadistic thugs. She would see no one except him. Do nothing until he told her she could. Until he tired of her, when he would throw her off like a torn robe. I could imagine only too well the horrors he would inflict on her. I panted for breath as I sought for the words to explain to Danjuro. He stared at me and I was appalled as I saw anger in his face.

"Is it Mineko's welfare that really worries you? He can't hurt her, as he did you. You know that. Or is it just that you're eaten up with jealousy that your lover has finally found somebody to take your place?"

"That's nonsense," I almost shouted, I was so distressed. "How could you ever think that? Mineko is beautiful and talented. It's no surprise that Akira wants her for himself. And you should know that if he had decided on anybody else but her, I wouldn't care at all."

"Really? Do I believe you, I wonder?" He thrust his face so close that I felt his breath on my cheek. "You understand why he's chosen Mineko, don't you? Akira could have his pick of the courtesans in Edo. Each of them would fall at his feet if he so much as looked at them. The real reason he's picked on Mineko is because he knows how fond you are of her. He wants you to be jealous. He's using her as bait, Midori No Me. Bait to lure you back to him."

"That's nonsense," I scoffed. "And even if it were true, how is Akira supposed to know that I'm aware of what's going on Edo? I could be dead for all he knows."

"Akira is more than just a man, you know that. I sometimes think he's a devil in human form. And he loved you. He would surely feel it in his bones if you were dead. In any event, he has ways of finding out things." He paused and stared at me as if he wanted to read my mind. "I've often wondered how much you miss him. And I suppose he was a great lover, wasn't he? You never talk about that. Is it because I can't compare to him?"

"Danjuro, I think the gods have turned you mad." I was almost shouting with the effort of convincing him. "I hated him. You know I did. I don't talk about the time I had to spend with him because it makes me feel ill to think about it."

I tried my best to put the truth of the words in my voice. My dragon shivered, and it felt like Akira running his finger down my spine.

"Really? I find that surprising. After all, you had only to

please him, and in return he showered you with the richest gifts. Anything you wanted, all you had to do was ask. It was the talk of the Floating World, you know. The geisha who had managed to tame the great yakuza. There were even rumors that he was going to take you for his wife. You have no idea how you were envied by the other courtesans."

The other courtesans? I was a geisha, not a courtesan! I stared at Danjuro, wondering if he had really insulted me deliberately. Was that how he thought of me, as a *yujo*? A woman of pleasure? I was speechless. I stood and walked out of the room before I could find words to say something that could never be forgotten.

We didn't speak of it again. For days, we were formally polite with each other, and then Danjuro became so wrapped up in the final preparations for his new play that I thought he had forgotten he was angry with me. Although Danjuro might have forgotten his bitter words, I had not. I was still deeply hurt.

It was not until I saw the first rehearsal of *Revenge of the Nobles* that I finally understood. Danjuro was not angry with me at all. Nor did he really think I was yearning for Akira. He was bitterly jealous of my success in the kabuki. *His* kabuki.

As I watched the rehearsal my first thought was that he had gone mad. Even I, who knew both of the original plays well, still found it difficult to follow the plot. The action seemed to jump from one play to the other without a link. The dialogue was stilted and without life; not that the words would matter to the gaijin, but any Japanese in the audience would pick up on it at once. And there was so little action, I began to fidget from boredom. I knew the other actors were looking at me carefully, so I said nothing at all. When the rehearsal finally finished, Ryu sidled up to me, watching all the time to make sure Danjuro was well away from us.

"I did try and tell him."

"I don't know what you're talking about, Ryu. I'm delighted you have a bigger part at long last, even though it's very different from your normal role as onnagata. You were excellent."

"Not half as good as you would have been. We all know it's you the patrons want to see, Midori No Me-chan. But Danjuro insisted it was time we went back to the traditional kabuki, and there was no arguing with him."

I shrugged, pretending indifference. "He may well have gotten it right. We'll see."

But Danjuro was far from right.

I took my seat at the very back of the theatre. Where I could see both the performance and the audience. The patrons were clearly looking forward to the performance, their anticipation was clear in the muted buzz of conversation and the way they sat forward eagerly as Danjuro strode on stage. I watched the audience watching him, and for a moment thought I had been wrong, that his magic would win them over. But I was not wrong. After only a few minutes, I sensed the puzzlement from the audience. People turned to each other and frowned, raised their eyebrows in question and shrugged. By the end of the first scene, when they had been given nothing but dialogue, the patrons began to fidget and chat to each other. Worse still, a few people actually got up and left, hurrying down the aisles as if they had suddenly recalled an important appointment. I guessed Danjuro knew he had lost his audience as his voice grew louder and his gestures more flamboyant.

At the end of the performance, perhaps a quarter of the

patrons had left early. There was applause from those who remained, but it was more a polite patter of hands than the storm of appreciation the kabuki usually attracted. And instead of remaining seated, calling again and again for the actors to take another bow, the patrons stood and filed out quietly and quickly.

Now, Danjuro's face was empty of expression as we sat with Clay-san in his office behind the theater. Clay-san was clearly agitated. He paced back and forth, lit a cigar—for once, without asking me if I minded—and finally sat opposite us, his elbows on his desk.

"That why you wouldn't let me into rehearsals, Danjuro?" Gooseflesh rose on my arms. Danjuro had told me that Clay-san had told him to just go ahead, that anything he wanted to put on at the theater was fine by him. How many more lies had he told me? "Last night was little short of a disaster. What were you thinking of?" He paused, waiting for Danjuro to speak, but my husband was silent. He stared straight ahead, not even blinking. "Hell, most of the patrons have been to every performance you've put on. They know what to expect, and they love it. What possessed you to overturn everything? Why was there no role for Midori No Me? And all that dialogue, with barely any action! No love interest. Not even a decent suicide to get the tears going at the end. I tell you, half the audience was asleep after the first ten minutes."

"We considered it was time to produce a genuine kabuki play. This play is new, but it is traditional in the way it is performed." Danjuro spoke slowly and carefully. Although his English was excellent by now, he still had to think before he spoke. "In Edo, the kabuki displays new works all the time, mingled with the old. It is not unusual to do this. It is accepted. It pleases the patrons."

"Well this offering sure didn't please your patrons here. To make it worse, Mr. Sato was here with some important Japanese people. He had promised them a real treat, a proper kabuki play by the best actors ever to come out of Edo. And you gave them this rubbish. He said to me afterward that he knew from the first few minutes that you had cobbled it together from two famous plays, and that it wasn't an original work at all. He said the dialogue was so bad, he had begun to wonder if it was supposed to be a comedy, not a tragedy. He even told me he'd had to apologize to his guests about the performance."

Even Danjuro's stone face flinched. Since we had become popular, Sato-san had made it clear to everybody that it was he who had bought us to America from Japan. Even though he had given us little real help since the very early days, he was still our patron, and we owed him much. And now, we had unwittingly caused him to lose face.

Clay-san sucked on his cigar as if he hated it and blew out a blue plume of smoke.

"Now, I know you know your own business, Danjuro. No question of that. You might have gotten away with the new play, if only you had left a decent role for Midori No Me. But you had to go and cut her right out, didn't you? That was all I heard last night, after the performance. 'Oh, Mr. Clay! Where has our lovely Dragon Geisha gone! It wasn't right without her!' No dances. Not so much as a song. I tell you Danjuro, you better come up with something that features Midori No Me big time or you are going to go down like a stone."

"You cannot have things all ways, Clay-san," Danjuro said quietly. "If you want traditional kabuki, then you should not have a woman on stage at all."

The two men glared at each other. Finally, Clay-san shrugged.

"Very well. I'll let the new play run for the rest of the month. I'll spread the word that this is the real kabuki, and not something new at all. The true fans will accept that. But after that, you go back to what they like. Plenty of action. A good few fight scenes. Some singing and dancing. And above all, a *starring* role for Midori No Me."

Danjuro inclined his head and we rose, leaving Clay-san tapping his fingers on his desk like a drum roll. Danjuro did not speak until we arrived at our lodgings. Then, his words were spoken to the air in front of him. He did not look at me at all. His voice was iron.

"I think that Clay-san is very skilled in the ways of the Western theater. But he has no grasp of the intricacies of the kabuki, none at all. It seems as if you have enchanted him as well as the patrons, wife."

"I speak the words you give me, Danjuro," I said firmly. "Dance when you instruct me to. Sing when the play tells me to."

We faced each other. I saw pain in my husband's face. I was about to reach out to touch him, to offer comfort, but allowed my hand to drop to my side as he flinched.

"The gods have been generous to you, Midori No Me. They have given you many natural talents."

His voice was so bitter I was turned to stone. For a moment, I thought he was talking about the talents I had used to such good effect when I was a geisha in the Hidden House and I was cut to my heart. Then I saw he was blinking back tears and I understood he meant the words he had spoken.

"I wanted the kabuki as soon as I first set foot in the theater." I was about to speak, to tell him I understood that, but he lifted his hand, palm toward me, and I swallowed the words. "It has been my life for more years than I can count. But even I had to learn my craft. I had to watch, and listen, and practice. Even now, I doubt myself sometimes. But you. You stroll on to the stage with no training, no background, and the audience loves you. You make it all seem effortless. These days, I walk in your shadow."

"You are wrong. I am nothing compared to you. The patrons who come to our kabuki are knowledgeable. They like me because they understand I'm novel, that's all."

I shrugged helplessly. Danjuro looked at me with weary defeat in his eyes. I was deeply irritated as well as saddened. I loved acting in the kabuki, but that's all it was to me—an act. It had nothing to do with real life, with things that mattered. Nothing to do with Mineko, living each day in dread. Nothing to do with me pining away with homesickness for the flower and willow world I had fled from. Irritation suddenly became true anger. I spoke without considering my words. Later, I told myself I had done it to shock Danjuro out of his self-pity, but I knew I was lying to myself. I spoke from my heart's deepest desire.

"I've been thinking that I would like to go back to Edo." I paused for a beat, watching his face carefully. It was not too late, even then. If Danjuro had said a single word to tell me he didn't want me to go, I would have added hurriedly that of course I would not go. Could not think of leaving him. But he did not. "You know I am very worried about Mineko, and to be honest, I am terribly homesick. I think it would make me appreciate our life here much more if I was to go back. Just for a visit, of course. If Akira has taken Mineko as his mistress, at least I will know the worst. And if there's nothing I can do to help her, then I will understand and it will put my mind at rest."

I trailed to a halt, waiting for his anger. Instead, he simply nodded.

"I'm not surprised. I've known for months that your heart was back in the flower and willow world. Very well, if you're certain that's what you want I will speak to Sato-san, and ask him if he will make the arrangements for you."

Back in the Hidden House, our Chinese geisha, Naruko, had often made us laugh by quoting a Chinese proverb that said, "Be careful what you wish for, you may get it." Now, I did not laugh.

13

The sword inflicts pain
When it strikes. But I do not
Believe it feels pain

 s the days passed before I was due to sail I waited
for Danjuro to swallow his pride and ask me to
stay. Now and then, I thought he was close to speaking, but
each time he did not. I understood that part of it was loss of
face; did I really expect the great Danjuro to demean
himself by begging his own wife not to leave him? But that
was only part of it. If I went down on my knees before him
now and told him that I had changed my mind, that I
wanted to stay, would he be pleased? Then I caught him
looking at me with something I could not interpret in his
eyes, and I knew—if it had ever been there in the first place
—the moment for him to speak had passed.

In spite of the fact that the decision had been mine, I
was dismayed to find that it seemed my new friends had
already begun to forget me. The troupe was beginning
rehearsals for another play, a traditional kabuki with Ryu

taking the female lead. Clay-san seemed pleased with it; when I told him I had to return to Japan for urgent family reasons, fully expecting him to be dismayed about it, I did not get the reaction I expected.

"Oh, that's a shame. Still, if you must go, that's the way of it. The patrons will be sorry about it, but they'll understand, I'm sure."

Even Evelyn accepted my news without much comment.

"You'll be pleased to catch up with all your old friends, I guess," she said dully. "Well, I dare say we'll all still be here when you get back."

I debated trying to get a letter to Kiku to tell her to expect me, but decided against it, both because I thought I might get back to Japan before my letter did, but also from fear. I couldn't shift a stubborn superstitious feeling that if I warned Kiku, somehow Akira would find out. Nonsense, of course, but still I did not write.

As it turned out, I was wrong about one thing, at least. I was wrong about Evelyn; she had not entirely forgotten me. She came to see me a couple of days before I was due to sail. I glanced at her and thought that she looked rather haggard, not her usual pretty self at all. But I pushed the moment of pity away. If it was Ryu she had come looking for, he was not here. Perhaps she would get over her infatuation with him while I was gone; realize that to Ryu she was no more than one more conquest to boast about to his friends. If it was Tom that was worrying her, well, this was a free country. All she had to do was tell her papa that she would not marry him.

Compared to events in the Floating World, Evelyn's worries were no more than shadows to me.

"Ryu's not here," I spoke my thoughts out loud.

"I came to see you, not Ryu. I'm sorry, I guess I've not

been much of a friend lately, but I really did want to give you this before you went."

She pushed a small, square envelope toward me. I looked at it and raised my eyebrows in question.

"I spoke to Tom's mama. You know, about your mother and father?"

I nodded, my mouth suddenly too dry to form words.

"She remembered them really well. Or at least, she remembered a Japanese lady and her American husband landing here at about the right time, so I guess it must have been your mama and papa." She shrugged and fingered the envelope, turning it round and round.

"Please." My voice was hoarse. I cleared my throat and tried again. "Please, Evelyn. Tell me what she said."

"You know, it was really interesting." Her face brightened and for a moment she was her old, eager self. "She said they landed here in San Francisco and stayed for maybe six months, as the Japanese lady was ill and needed to recuperate before they could travel any further. San Francisco was very small then, just an outpost really, and they caused a real stir. Nobody had ever seen a real Japanese lady before, and her husband was a Southern gentleman so everybody was fascinated and wanted to meet them. As soon as she was feeling a bit better they were invited to all the society events. She remembered that the husband said he had been in Japan for some years on a trade mission, and that was where he had met his wife. She didn't speak a word of English, but it didn't matter because he spoke wonderful Japanese and translated for her. She said the lady was like a tiny doll, so perfect she made all the society women feel like elephants."

"Was the man called Simon? Did he have red hair?"

"Maria—that's Tom's mama—couldn't remember his

first name." I slumped with disappointment. "But she did remember that he had the most beautiful auburn hair. Not bright red, but she said it was such a lovely color, all the ladies envied it. He was a very handsome man, she said. And of course, they were intrigued by his wife. All the ladies were very sorry when they went."

Big had said that my father had hair as red as a fox's fur, and that he was ugly. But to Japanese eyes, used to seeing only black hair, surely auburn would have appeared red? And to Big, all the gaijin were ugly. Evelyn obviously followed my thoughts as she spoke eagerly.

"Your hair is almost auburn in some lights, you know! Anyway, she said that once the Japanese lady had recovered enough to travel, they moved on. Went down south somewhere, where the gentleman had plantations. Maybe Virginia, Maria thought, but she couldn't rightly remember."

"Thank you." My voice trembled so much I could say no more.

"I better go. Papa will wonder where I've gotten to. You are coming back, aren't you, Midori No Me?"

Her voice was so small and so hopeful that I smiled and pushed down my own excitement.

"Of course I'm coming back. Just as soon as I can get things sorted out in Edo. A few months, no more."

Or at least I hoped so. Already I was beginning to wonder if, when the time came, I would want to return to my new world. Or if the pull of the flower and willow world would be too strong for me to resist. I had no way of knowing, so I hugged Evelyn and smiled at her. I remembered the envelope she had left just in time. She shook her head when I made to hand it to her.

"No. That's for you. Maria said the couple had their

photograph taken before they left for the South, and they were so popular in society circles that the photographer sold lots of visiting card-sized copies of it. She found this one and gave it to me, and I thought you might like it. Take care, Midori No Me-chan."

I barely heard her go. I turned the envelope over and over in my hands, staring at it. Put it down. Picked it up. Finally told myself it didn't matter; I had no idea what my mother and father looked like, so this photograph would mean nothing to me. Still, my heart was thumping like a galloping horse as I pulled the flap of the envelope back.

The photograph was face down, and I read the inscription on the back before I turned it over. The printed script was so fancy it took me a while to make sense of it, although I suppose that my trembling hand didn't help greatly.

"Mr. and Mrs. Beaumont of High Grove Plantation, Virginia. Mrs. Beaumont was the former Lady Terue, the most beautiful and celebrated geisha in the whole of Japan."

I held my breath for so long, my head was buzzing. Terue. My mother had been called Terue. And even this scrap of pasteboard referred to her as a geisha! I finally turned the card over and was deeply disappointed that the small photograph was so blurred I could barely make out anything except two figures, standing side by side. Then I realized that I was crying, and it was my tears that were at fault. I wiped my eyes with my sleeve and looked again.

I saw a tall man, towering over a woman who barely reached his chest. Both were smiling at the camera, although her smile was more uncertain, as if she did not quite like the idea of some strange machine capturing her likeness. I stared at her hungrily, but the photograph that a moment before had been my hope and salvation could tell me little. She was wearing traditional makeup; her face could have been any pretty Japanese woman's. I took a breath so deep it hurt my chest, and turned my attention to the man.

And I knew, instantly.

I was looking at myself. Although the photograph was old and a little faded, I could see his face reasonably well. His cheekbones were mine. Even his hair, combed straight back from his face had a curious V at the front; Evelyn had told me this was called a widow's peak when she had first seen my own hair loose. It was pretty, she said. And unusual. His eyebrows, too, were naturally arched, just as mine were. Did he have green eyes and red hair? I couldn't tell, but it didn't matter.

This was my father then, this "Mr. Beaumont" from Virginia. And if he was my father, then it was my own, dear, lost mother who was standing at his side.

My heart cried out. This was wrong, so very wrong! After all these years of wondering and longing, I had finally managed to find the first clue to my parents. And all along, they had been here, in this country! Many miles away, I understood that. But we were standing on the same soil, breathing the same air! And now, it was I who was leaving them behind me.

The irony of it made me want to weep all over again.

I put the photograph back in the envelope with shaking fingers. I packed it carefully in my luggage and waited for Danjuro to come home. When he arrived, we were polite to each other, but already it was the politeness of strangers. Did I have everything I needed for the journey? Enough money? Yes, and yes. I did not mention my precious photograph. There was no point.

All the kabuki actors came to the docks to see me off.

They gathered around me and patted my arms in a gesture of familiarity that would have been scandalous in Japan. Only Danjuro stood to one side, seeing but not speaking. Finally, the other actors turned aside politely and chatted amongst themselves to allow us to make our farewells. Danjuro inclined his head, his body a foot away from me.

"Be safe, Midori No Me-chan," he said softly. "You have what you desired in your heart. But take care. What we think we want is not always the right thing for us. When you come back, I will be here. If you want to come back to me."

And again, I wondered. Would I come back?

I turned away wordlessly and walked up the gangplank to board the ship that was taking me home.

14

Life must always move
Forward. Although sometimes it
Is good to look back

Mori-san bowed low.

"Welcome to my humble store." His English was high-pitched and rapid, and I wondered if he had simply learned the greeting by heart or if he had really learned to speak English while I had been gone. So much had changed in Edo, nothing would surprise me.

"Good morning, Mori-san," I said politely, instinctively speaking in Japanese. "It is very good to see you again. May I speak with Kiku-san, please?"

Mori-san had always made me want to giggle. And he did so now. The man who had tried to buy me out of the Hidden House time after time before Akira had stolen me away stood up so slowly I was sure I could hear his bones creak. He stared at me, his mouth sagging as if a ghost had walked into his shop and was demanding to be served. The spell lasted for only a moment before he grabbed my arm and tugged me through into the house.

"Midori No Me? It is you? Really?"

"It is me, Mori-san. I have come back to Edo."

He ran his gaze up and down me, blinking rapidly.

"I thought you were a gaijin!" he bleated. "It is true, then. You did go to America! Kiku insisted that you had, but I didn't believe her. The gossip was that you and Danjuro both were dead. That...somebody had killed you both, for a matter of honor."

How careful he was not to mention Akira's name, even here, where it should be safe. And how grateful I was that Kiku had been equally careful in not telling her husband that she had managed to find me. If the Floating World thought I might be dead, then at least I had the element of surprise on my side. The gods knew, I had little enough else.

"No, Mori-san. We are both alive and well. Both prospering, as you see."

"But what are you doing here?"

I had thought long and hard about this on the voyage from San Francisco and had decided to tell a half-truth.

"I was homesick," I said simply. "We hear some news from Japan, and we understand that there has been much trouble in Edo. I feared for my friends in the Floating World. Feared for them until I could neither eat nor sleep for worry. Danjuro in his turn worried about me. He thought that I might become ill if I did not see for myself that my old friends were well and safe, so he allowed me to return home."

"Ah. So Danjuro is not with you?"

"I am alone."

Relief blossomed on Mori-san's face. I almost giggled as I realized that he was worried that Danjuro might have been jealous of his efforts to buy me out of the Hidden House.

"Please, Midori No Me-chan. Please, come through. Kiku will be delighted to see you."

Kiku did an excellent job of looking astonished to see me. She rose from her chair, her hands clutched to her heart and her eyes rolling dramatically.

"Midori No Me! It really is you, and not some spirit?" She gasped. "I can hardly believe my eyes! We were sure that you were dead. Oh, but I am so pleased to see you! I am overwhelmed with joy!"

Mori-san bowed himself out, bobbing like a boat on choppy water. As soon as the screen door slid closed behind him, Kiku held her arms out to me and I fell against her huge bosom. Finally, I was sure that I was home.

"I knew you would come. I prayed to our household god and I knew he wouldn't let me down." Probably wouldn't dare, I thought! "But why didn't you write and tell me you were coming? We are safe here. You may speak freely. Mori-san will not listen to us; he has more sense. If he knows nothing, then he cannot be made to repeat it." She held me at arms' length and wrinkled her nose. "Come to the bath-house. We shall bathe and gossip and pretend the years have not passed and that nothing is changed in our lives."

I started to laugh and could not stop. Dear, dear Kiku. She meant I stank from the journey and from the strange food I had been eating. Anybody else would have offered me tea and food first, but not Kiku!

"Yes, please," I said simply. "There is much that is wonderful in my new country, Kiku. But the bath is not one of them."

I held my arms out and luxuriated in the silky feel of the water as Kiku's maid soaped me and then poured rinsing water over me repeatedly. I wriggled with sheer pleasure, wondering absently if this was how a snake felt when it had shed its old skin. The comparison was too apt for comfort.

We slid into the steaming bath water, and I relaxed happily.

"You know, I barely recognized you myself when you came in. With your hair dyed that bright red, and the light-colored makeup, you don't look Japanese at all," Kiku said.

"Mori-san didn't recognize me until I spoke to him in Japanese," I said smugly. "I thought it would be safer to return as a gaijin. And as the patrons in the Hidden House always thought I looked like a fox spirit, I decided I might as well truly resemble one. "

"You may look like a gaijin, but you are still Japanese at heart," Kiku said sternly. I smiled; as if there was any doubt about that!

"Tell me what's been happening, Kiku." I glanced around; the maid had gone, but I was still wary. "If you're sure we're safe?"

"We're safe here," she said smugly. "My servants are loyal. More than some are. That's how I know exactly what's happening in the Hidden House. Oh, I persuaded Mori to let me visit once, and Mineko was allowed out to see me when my dear Ichiro was born, but I get most of my gossip from one of the kitchen maids. The maids get to know everything that happens, and it costs me very little to loosen this one's tongue."

"You've seen Mineko?" I asked anxiously. "Is she well? Has Akira taken her yet?"

Kiku smiled. "She's very well. And still at the Hidden House, for the moment at least." She paused, looking complacent. I waited patiently; I knew of old that there was no point in trying to hurry Kiku. "I'll get to Mineko in a minute. You know there is much unrest in Japan?"

"You told me in your letters. But I don't understand. What's happened to stir up such problems with the gaijin all at once?"

"It's the nobles. Oh, not all of them. But a sizeable portion of them think they can turn back time. They believe if they got rid of the gaijin, everything would be as it used to be before the foreign barbarians arrived. They think they would regain their lost power. It's not going to happen, but they don't want to know that. They're plotting amongst themselves to get rid of the gaijin, and they're trying to persuade the government to side with them. They don't bother making a secret of their plans either, and many of the ordinary people agree with them. The yakuza, of course, will bend any way they think will lead to money. They've attacked some of the gaijin in the street, but it turned out not to be such a good idea. One of the yakuza was killed when a gaijin pulled a gun on him."

I nibbled my lip, remembering the group of nobles I had seen on the ship, when Danjuro and I had fled Japan. I had felt something was out of place then, and I felt it now. If the nobles wanted to get rid of the gaijin, why were those important men traveling to America? It just didn't make sense. I decided not to worry about it for the moment. They mattered not at all compared to Mineko. And Akira.

"I see. Well, that's politics, and nothing either of us can do about it. But Mineko is different. Does she know about Akira's plans for her?"

"Yes. She's been worried for a long time, but what can she do? She can't run away from the Hidden House. She knows he would find her and bring her back if she did. Besides, she has something to keep her there. Now."

Kiku's raised eyebrows invited me to ask.

"Something? Or...somebody?" I barely needed to ask; it was clear from her expression what the answer was. She nodded.

"Akira finally felt the need to bring in another man, to take Big's place after he died in the kabuki fire. The new man is called Ken, a martial arts expert from outside Edo. He's odd, not the normal type of yakuza at all. Gossip says that he's actually a noble, and that Akira has some sort of hold over him. Whatever he is or he isn't, Mineko has taken him as her lover."

I digested the information in silence. I watched the steam from the bath rise around us and closed my eyes as I felt each piece of the whole suddenly fit into place. My thoughts were as slippery as the water. I spoke out loud, waiting for Kiku to tell me if I was wrong.

"That's why Akira has moved now, isn't it? He'll have guessed about Mineko and the new man. It's impossible to keep anything secret from him. I used to think he could read my thoughts. Perhaps he could." I shuddered. "But that's why he's decided to take Mineko as his mistress after all this time. Because he knows she has somebody she cares about at last. He wouldn't be able to stand that."

"I think you're right," Kiku said quietly. "But there's something you're forgetting. He's taking Mineko not just because he hates the idea that she's happy, but he's using her to get to you as well. She's bait, Midori No Me. Bait to bring you back to him."

"That's what Danjuro said. Do you think Akira hoped we would both come back? So he could finish Danjuro finally and take me back again?"

"Maybe. But if Danjuro had come with you, I think he would have simply thought it was good luck. It's you he's really interested in. Why should he worry too much about Danjuro? If he gets you back, then he gets revenge on him at the same time. He's been biding his time, brooding about you. I think it's finally tipped him into madness. You know he left your room exactly as it was when you escaped? Nobody is allowed to go in there except him. And he sits there for hours, talking to your spirit." Kiku saw the disbelief on my face and frowned. "He does, you know. He told Mori-san he found comfort in knowing he was somewhere where you had once been. That you were the only woman in his entire life he had cared for."

I could hardly believe her. Akira—the most feared yakuza in the whole of Edo, the man who would murder and torture on a whim—confessing to such nonsense?

"He had taken a lot of sake and opium at the time." Kiku pursed her lips. "My dear husband simply believed what he was saying, but I rather wonder why Akira told him. He doesn't do anything without a good reason, not even when he's drunk. I don't doubt he has made a shrine of your room; he really did love you, you know. Or at least as much as Akira is able to love anybody. But I think telling Mori may have been part of whatever intricate plot he's weaving. He would know that Mori would tell me, and I wouldn't be at all surprised if somehow he knows that I have been in contact with you, and so you would find out. Perhaps he thinks he can win you back, even now."

"He's a monster. Not human at all. I hate him."

"He's a monster with one weakness, Midori No Me. You." I frowned and shook my head, but Kiku was having none of it. "It's true. But it's more complicated than you think. I believe it's true that you're the only woman he's ever cared about. But apart from that, you betrayed him; you escaped from him and ran away with the one man he hated more than any other. He had to try and persuade the whole of Edo that he finally killed you both, because he couldn't take the lack of face if the truth was known. But apart from all that, to make things even worse, you were lucky for him. When you were with him, his businesses prospered like never before."

"That was only because I translated for him, when he was dealing with the gaijin. It amused them that I was half gaijin myself," I pointed out.

"Perhaps, but he doesn't see it that way. As far as Akira is concerned, you not only betrayed him in the worst possible way, but you stole his luck as well."

"If that's true, why is he so desperate to get me back? He must hate me. And anyway, how would he explain how the woman he killed had suddenly come back to life? It doesn't make sense, Kiku."

"It does if you remember he's mad," she pointed out. "If he got you back, he wouldn't care what people thought. He's still so feared, he could say he brought you back from the dead and no one would dare laugh at him. And if he believed in his own luck again, it might be that his fortunes would improve as well."

"Has he lost a lot of money?"

"Not just money. Power as well. He was too greedy. He saw how much many of the other yakuza were making out of the opium trade and he decided that he would like some of that. He has had his own way for so long, I think he just assumed they would let him take what he wanted. But they didn't. Several of his rivals joined forces and began to steal some of Akira's business in their turn. He suddenly found that merchants who had paid him off for years now had other yakuza to protect them. Some of the brothels and tea houses he owned were burned down. And the opium trade wasn't as easy to penetrate as he had thought, so he had to employ more men to guard what he had left, and that in its turn meant spending more money."

"But he still has the Hidden House?" I asked anxiously.

"At the moment, yes. And the Green Tea House. But things are different even there. You know that when Aunty owned the place, the patrons were important men. Powerful men. Only the best were good enough for Aunty. Now, Akira lets anybody in. He doesn't care who they are as long as they have money in their pockets. He would let a leper in if he had the money. I wonder if the shame of it was what caused Aunty to fall ill."

This was news to me. Aunty, ill? Aunty was never ill. She ruled us geisha with slaps of her cane, true, but more than anything with the sheer force of her iron personality.

"Aunty can't be ill," I protested. "She was never less than healthy, in all the years I spent in the Hidden House. You never mentioned it in your letters."

"She's very ill now. It happened not long ago. Mineko found her collapsed in her bed. The doctor says it is a seizure of her brain. She can't speak properly or walk and recognizes nobody. The doctor thinks she may die."

I put my hand to my mouth in shock. Aunty had been the one constant in my life. She had always been there. Never seeming to get a day older, always in charge. And equally, always ready to ensure that a patron did not go too far, no matter how wealthy and powerful he might be. In the strangest of ways, she had been the only mother I had ever known. And now, Kiku was telling me that she might die?

"I know." Kiku sighed, causing the water to ripple around her breasts. "It's unthinkable that Aunty could die, isn't it? It's strange, but knowing she's so ill has made me miss the Hidden House."

I stared at her in surprise, and she shrugged apologetically.

"Silly, I know. After all, I have everything that any of us geisha longed for. A good husband, plenty of money. I probably even have more freedom than any other married woman in the whole of Edo. And here I am, thinking how nice it used to be when we were all together."

"I know. I feel the same. That's part of the reason I had to come back."

We stared at each other and sighed. Was this how men who had fought together felt? Was it the bonds of shared hardships that could not be dissolved? I rather thought it was. And truly, we geisha had been warriors; all of us together, ready to face whatever the Floating World could throw at us.

"So, now that you're here, what do we do?" Kiku asked briskly, nostalgia put firmly aside.

I stared into the steam, wondering where to start.

"Well, if you could give me some tea, it would be a good place to begin!"

We laughed and got to our feet to climb out of the bath. As I turned my back on Kiku, I heard her gasp.

"Your dragon," she whispered fearfully. "I swear I just saw it move."

"I think it did. I felt it." I was whispering as well, as if I didn't want my tattoo to hear me. Nonsense? Perhaps. "I think it knows it's finally near its master, and it's happy about it."

We were both pleased when I was firmly wrapped in a warm robe and the dragon was well hidden.

15

Does the lobster in
Her shell on the seafloor know
How tasty she is?

Kiku wanted me to stay with her and Mori-san, but I refused.

I held her young son Ichiro on my knee, pulling faces to make him laugh.

"I'm staying at a ryokan just inside the Floating World. I remember it was always very popular with the gaijin. It's safer for all of us that way." I looked at Ichiro, and Kiku nodded her understanding. "I would not bring fear to your house, Kiku."

When she learned I wanted to do some shopping when I left her, she insisted I take one of her maids with me, to carry my parcels and so I would look respectable.

"Many of the gaijin women have started having a Japanese maid to wait on them. It seems to have caught their fancy."

My thoughts were whirling as I walked the Floating

World again. I looked around at streets that had once been as familiar as my own face and felt like a stranger. I wished I had worn a kimono and geta, and then remembered that I was now a gaijin, with fiery red hair and pale skin, and I would have attracted unwelcome attention if I had dressed properly. Even in the shops, I had to remember not to speak Japanese and just point at what I wanted. I pretended not understand as the shop keepers smiled and nodded and bowed and insulted me in my own language. I smiled back, and cursed them in my heart.

I held my money out innocently in my palm and bit back a sarcastic retort when the shop keeper helped himself to far more than the few bits and pieces I had purchased were worth.

"If I had known you had such a fat purse, I would have charged you triple." The merchant beamed at me, showing a gold front tooth. "I never knew the gaijin had fox spirits. Go away and play with your thieving friends the foxes, you bitch. Take the rest of the gaijin with you and leave us alone!"

I was aghast. This was not right! In America, it was we who were the gaijin, just as exotic to American eyes as it appeared I was now to my fellow countrymen. But in America we had always been treated with courtesy, apart from my encounter with the horrible Mac, of course. But then, I could barely bring myself to think of him as being human. No, I was sure that hatred and deceit had never lurked behind the smiles in America. Suddenly, as well as being angry with the merchant, I was deeply ashamed of him and all the rest of my countrymen who mocked me behind my back as they robbed me. I smiled at the cheating merchant even as I cordially hoped he would suffer great misfortune.

As I left the shop, I was startled to find that Kiku's sweet little spaniel had somehow gotten loose and followed me. I bent down to pat the dog, and realized immediately that although it had exactly the same markings as Akane, this dog was no more than a puppy. Kiku had mentioned that she had given one of Akane's pups to Mineko and I straightened slowly, searching the jostling street as casually as I could manage. Could the gods possibly have been so kind to me?

My heart pounded as I found myself staring straight across the roadway at my sister. I froze. For the longest moment, I thought that Mineko had seen through my careful disguise. She was frowning, staring at me as if she knew me, but wasn't quite sure if she should cross the road and speak. But then everything changed. Mineko looked down at the spaniel fawning at my feet and clapped her hands briskly to claim its attention; it ran to her eagerly and she simply turned away from me as if I was a stranger. I let my breath go in a long sigh and closed my eyes as I gave a brief prayer of thankfulness. She was still free.

I could ask for no more for the moment.

I watched her retreating back until she turned into a crowded pharmacy a little way down the street. If I had changed, then so had Mineko. Not physically. The change was more in her bearing, in the way she held herself. She appeared worried; I noticed she cast anxious glances around her as she walked. It seemed to me that she was tired; although she walked quickly, her shoulders were slumped, and from time to time she eased her neck as if it was stiff. And I noticed she was alone, without even a maid to chaperone her, and was dressed in an old kimono. What was so urgent that she had been allowed out of the Hidden House on her own, and without her wig and makeup? Was she on an errand for Aunty, perhaps? My own maid was fidgeting, and I decided quickly that it was dangerous to linger until Mineko came out of the pharmacy; I realized that I appeared to be the only gaijin in the crowded street, and already I was attracting inquisitive glances.

I finished my shopping and went back to my inn. I would go and see Kiku again, and soon. Akira was not in Edo, I knew that. If he had been close, I would have sensed his presence. But I guessed that he would come back, and soon. And when he did, he would take Mineko. He would do that out of bravado, as a matter of face. To show his enemies he thought his own amusement more important than fighting them. My dragon shivered with excitement, and suddenly I understood what I had to do. Akira's home —my prison—was calling to me, whispering to me to entice me back. I would go now, while he was away. What I would achieve by going back to that hated place, I had no idea. When I was within his walls again, then I would know.

Kiku cleared the street by the force of her presence, passers-by scattering in front of us. If I hadn't been so worried, it would have made me smile.

"Are you sure you want to do this?" she asked quietly.

I nodded. I could feel my dragon's claws, restless on my back. Was it my imagination, or was it scratching at my skin eagerly? Delighted that I was going back to its master's home, at last.

"I think I need to," I answered. "I have to know it's not my prison any longer, that he has no power over me anymore." As near to his house as this, I was reluctant even to speak Akira's name. "And I want to see this shrine of his."

Kiku shrugged. "Very well."

I put my hand on her arm; she had nearly walked past

the mouth of the short cul-de-sac that led to Akira's front door.

"You haven't forgotten the way, then?" she said wryly.

"I could never forget what he did to me in this place," I said. "Even in America, across a whole sea from him, sometimes I dreamed about being here. I used to wake up and think I was still here." I laughed shortly, a sound without humor. "I hate him. And Danjuro's still jealous of him. No matter how many times I tell him how badly I was treated here, how much I longed to get away from him, he thinks I still feel something for that man."

"Still? Did you ever care for him?" Kiku asked softly.

"No. Of course not. He's a monster. He kept me caged, treated me worse than an animal. Put his mark on my back. Hurt me in ways you couldn't imagine. How could anybody love a man who did that to them?"

"Because he loved you. He was passionate about you," Kiku said simply. "He hurt you because he had to punish you for being cold to him. I think you nearly drove him mad then, by refusing to be cowed by him, no matter what he did to you. He was terrified of losing you. Or did you never work that out?"

I shrugged and shook my head. What nonsense this was.

"I hate him," I said. "I hated him when he had me here. I hate him now. I don't care how he felt about me."

Kiku stared at me for a long moment and then looked away to jangle the bell outside the house. When that got no reaction, she rapped smartly on the door twice. She was about to knock again when the door opened the tiniest crack and a terrified female voice spoke quickly.

"Akira-san is not here. Please go away."

The door began to close in our faces. I frowned,

surprised by this lack of hospitality. I had become so used to the easy informality of San Francisco, where callers were always made welcome regardless of whether they were expected or not, that I had forgotten for a second that I was back in the Floating World. Here, as in the rest of Japan, it was unheard of to visit friends and acquaintances without an invitation. And as far as the maid was concerned, we were total strangers. Apart from anything else, this was Akira's house, and I could not imagine anybody daring to knock on his door unexpectedly. No wonder she was frightened.

Kiku was simply magnificent. Her arm snaked into the doorway before the heavy, Western-style door that had marked the boundary of my prison could close entirely. I guessed the maid had been given instructions to admit nobody in Akira's absence, and she was probably shaking with fear. Kiku shoved the door with her shoulder, and it bounced back. We simply walked in and took our shoes off in the hallway, as good manners demanded.

"Akira-san is not here," the maid wailed. "I cannot let you in. I am on my own here. Please go at once."

Kiku and I glanced at each other. Truly, the gods had decided to favor us today. I saw a discrete glint of gold pass from Kiku's fingers to the maid's hand. When it disappeared into the folds of her obi, I knew greed had won out over fear.

"We know your master is not here," Kiku said superbly. "But my husband is a very good friend of his. My gaijin visitor here," I bowed my head politely as she gestured toward me, "has heard much about how Akira's house is the most beautiful in all of Edo. She would like very much to look around it."

The maid's face drained of color. She shook her head

rapidly. "No, mistress. No. I cannot allow that. If Akira found out, it would be very bad for me."

I almost felt sorry for her, and then remembered the coin she had been so willing to accept. Kiku was obviously not at all sympathetic.

"I will not mention it to Akira-san. I doubt that you will either. And I'm sure you would not wish to offend my friend, would you?" She added the last words meaningfully. The poor maid's eyes were huge as she looked at my bright, red hair. Just to make sure she got the point, I raised my veil so she got a good look at the green of my eyes. Her mouth was opening and closing soundlessly. I was sure she thought I was some sort of fox spirit who would not hesitate to drag her off to torment in the next world if she annoyed me.

"We will come and go in no time." I spoke softly, in Japanese. I thought she was going to faint, she was so terrified. "Your master will never know we have been here."

The poor girl had no option. She closed her eyes tightly and stood back. Kiku grabbed her arm, hustling her in front of us.

"You see, my dear friend? Isn't this the most beautiful house you have ever seen?"

I was surprised to hear real envy in Kiku's voice. Looking at it through her eyes, Akira's house was lovely, I supposed. The furnishings were discreet, but very expensive. The rooms were high and airy, even the carpentry on the joists was perfect. When I had been here last, it had been my prison and I had taken no joy at all from it. Now I saw it through a stranger's eyes and admitted that it was indeed beautiful. We wandered through the rooms, making approving noises.

"My goodness me." Kiku sounded impressed. "What a

lovely bathhouse. I've never seen anything like it." She rolled her eyes at me and I took the hint, slipping away silently as she prattled on to the maid.

I could have found my way to my old room blindfolded. I was inside in a heartbeat, my silk-clad feet silent. And instantly I realized that the rumors were true. I might never have left. Everything was just the same. One screen door was slid back where I had forgotten to close it properly. A shutter was half down to shield the room from the late afternoon sun. It even smelled the same. Like me.

Suddenly, I was frozen with panic. I could not move, could hardly breathe. What had possessed me to want to come here! I managed to turn my head fractionally, hearing the bones in my neck creak with the effort. Kiku's voice echoed down the corridor, but I couldn't make out what she was saying. Was she warning me to hurry? I moved stiffly, like a bunraku puppet wielded by unskilled hands. One step at a time.

But not toward the door.

I was drawn to the closet, where the door was slightly ajar. My hands were trembling as I opened the drawer that contained my kingfisher beak combs. They gleamed with sullen fire, bright red against the wood. Akira had given me a set for each day of the week, and had insisted I wear them whenever we were together. They were expensive beyond belief, but I hated them. Each time he forced me to wear them, I thought of the bright, joyous birds who had been slaughtered for no more than their beaks, and the feel of them against my scalp made me feel sick.

Instantly, I saw that one set was missing. I thought that Akira must have taken them to give to Mineko. My hands moved without me instructing them. I scooped another set of the combs out of the drawer and fastened them into my purse. Even as I fought to fasten the clip against their bulk, I wondered why I wanted them. For sure, I would never wear them. I might have tried to put them back, but the drawer was stuck at an angle and I could neither fully close it nor open it again. I left it ajar; I was in too much of a hurry to worry.

I was deeply relieved when we were out of Akira's house. Suddenly, the stale air of the Floating World smelled very sweet.

Kiku raised her eyebrows at me. "Well? Are you happy now?"

"I'm happy to be out of there," I said. "I had forgotten what it was like. It is a beautiful house, but to me it was a prison." I hesitated, hoping Kiku would understand. "I had to see it again. Apart from anything else, I needed to be sure I could walk away from there any time I wanted. And I needed to know that Akira wasn't there. I felt that he hadn't been there for a long time."

"That's what the maid told me," Kiku said. She looked at me, but I could not read her expression. "What do we do now?"

"Nothing. There's nothing else we can do until Akira comes back. Until we see what he's going to do."

I did not mention the combs to her. I was tempted to throw them away, but they were so very beautiful I could not. Instead I sat with them in my hands, looking at them.

Impulse had made me take them. I had no real idea why at the time. But thinking about it in the safety of the ryokan, I wondered if it was more instinct than impulse. When Akira took Mineko for his concubine, she would surely want to visit my room. Perhaps sit there and wonder how I had passed the endless hours, just as she was doing now. And when she looked through my closets, not just out of curiosity, but to feel my presence, she would find the combs. She knew Akira had given me seven sets; if she had one set herself, she would see at once that another set was missing. And my clever Mineko would surely wonder who had dared to not just disturb Akira's shrine, but to steal from it.

The knowledge gave me great satisfaction.

16

They say that a red
Moon means that it is possessed
By a great evil

"We must leave Edo."

Kiku cradled Ichiro in her arms. She watched her baby rather than me as she spoke.

"Kiku, no! Why now? You've heard the talk, just the same as I have. Things are coming to a head, at last. It can't be long before Akira comes back. We can't leave now!"

Truth to tell, I had probably heard even more gossip than Kiku had. Looking like a gaijin, everybody thought I could not understand them so they chattered freely in front of me. In fact, I had come to see Kiku today to pass on the information that it was whispered that Akira's rival yakuza were almost ready to act, that his days as the greatest yakuza in Edo were numbered. Edo loved excitement, no matter whether it was good or bad. Literally everybody was talking about the war that threatened to disrupt the peace of the flower and willow world. And to add a little spice to the mix,

I had also heard that it was rumored that Akira had taken himself a new concubine, the first woman he had shown any interest in since I had disappeared. The men were almost drooling as they speculated about the amazing talents this new geisha must possess to entice him.

"That's why we must go," Kiku said. "Look at you—you call yourself an actress, and a blind beggar could see how on edge you are. You're starting to forget you're supposed to be a gaijin. You spoke Japanese in front of my maid yesterday, and if I hadn't nudged you, you would have told that merchant the other day that he was over-charging you. Somebody is going to notice you soon, and when they do they're going to recollect the geisha with the green eyes and the red hair."

"But we can't just go. What about Mineko?" I protested. "Akira's taken her as his concubine like we knew he would. We have to at least get a message to her, let her know she's not alone."

"No." Kiku stared at me. Her face was set, and suddenly I was no longer the Dragon Geisha, the star of the kabuki in America and a free woman. I was a humble new geisha in the Hidden House and Kiku was taking no nonsense from me. "If Mineko knew you were here, then Akira would know. She would not be able to hide it; he would sense her excitement. She must know nothing at all, not yet." I thought guiltily of the stolen combs and was grateful when Ichiro claimed his mother's attention at that moment. "We're not going far, just far enough away to be safe. As soon as we're sure that the time is right, we'll come back. Although what we're going to do when we get back, I don't know."

I didn't know either. I just felt that when the time was right, we would triumph. We had to, otherwise all this would have been for nothing. I sighed and thought about what she had said. She was right, of course. I felt Japanese again. Even my Western clothes were beginning to feel strange to me, and I found myself longing for the comfort of a kimono. A sudden thought made me smile; on the journey back to America, I would please myself and nobody else. I would wear a kimono and obi, and if it amused me to do it, full traditional makeup as well. *When* I went back to America. Or did I mean *if*?

"Where are we going?" I raised my hands in surrender. Kiku was right, of course. She was always right.

"To the onsen at Atami. It's not much more than a day or two's journey from Edo, but far enough away to be safe. Mori took me there last year for a short visit. It is very beautiful. You will love it." I smiled at Kiku's certainty and she pretended to frown at me. "You might have been all the way to America and back, but have you ever been anywhere in Japan out of Edo?"

I shrugged; she was perfectly correct. Apart from a couple of boat trips on the river into Edo itself, in all my years in the Hidden House I had never ventured outside the Floating World. Not that I was unusual in that. Apart from the high-caste nobles, few Japanese would ever stray far from their birthplace. Many peasants would never go further than the fields around their own village.

In any event, the onsen was delightful. We bathed in the mineral-rich waters. Walked. Laughed and played with Ichiro in the clean air, blissfully beginning to let go of the worries and woes that had driven us from Edo. For the first time since I had set foot in Japan again, I had no plans, no driving need to do anything. Perhaps it was simply the lack of any stimulation, but gradually I found myself itching for Danjuro. For his touch, his physical presence beside me.

It was so very quiet at night, I could barely sleep. Every few minutes, I propped myself up on my elbow, certain I heard steps in the corridor. But there was nothing. Once the ryokan closed its doors for the night, not even a late returning reveler was allowed in. I knew that nothing could remotely resemble the pleasure my husband's touch could give me. But when I began to wake with my stomach cramping with lust from dreams where he was there, but I could only see and hear him, never feel him, that I decided enough was enough.

I unpacked my love globes.

When I had bought them on impulse in Edo, the merchant had cackled at me.

"Going to wear them as earrings, are you?" He sniggered. "Want me to show you what they're really for, gaijin?"

Not for the first time, I had longed to respond in crisp Japanese, just for the pleasure of wiping the smirk off his fat face. These globes were nowhere near as lovely as the pair a rich patron had given to me when I was in the Hidden House, and the merchant had had the insolence to overcharge me grossly for this inferior pair.

But they would do. I dangled them over my finger and smiled as I remembered when I had learned what my first pair were really used for.

The other geisha had laughed at me when I said that I didn't know what they were. In spite of the fact that my patron had leered at me when he handed them over, I was under the impression that they were some sort of jewelry, although how I was supposed to wear them, I had no idea.

The girls had pried them from my fingers, and little Masaki dangled them in front of me, grinning widely.

"Lie down," she had instructed. I looked suspiciously from face to face, but did as I was told, curiosity overcoming suspicion. "Hitch up your robe, and open your legs. Nice and wide. Pretend I'm a patron who wants to put his tree in you."

I scowled at her, and she grinned.

"Trust me. You'll be happy when I'm finished. I promise you."

She weighed the balls in her hand. They were made of silver, each about the size of a large cherry and very heavy for their size. There was some sort of liquid inside one, and I could hear it sloshing about lazily. Each cherry was tied to the other with a length of what looked like plaited gold thread.

"Goodness me," Masaki said seriously. "You must have pleased your patron greatly. These are very expensive ones."

She leaned forward and I felt her cold little fingers probing at my black moss. I was about to ask what on earth she was doing when she forced me wide open. The other girls shouted with laughter. Obviously anticipating that I would wriggle about, or even try and get away, Kiku and Naruko grabbed my shoulders and shoved me back down on the matting.

Kiku laughed right in my indignant face. "Pretend we're patrons, out for a good time!" she giggled.

I was too breathless with surprise to say anything. Masaki was still trying to keep my sex open, and at the same time was pushing something into me. Something very cold and heavy. Although I still wriggled, it was hardly unpleasant. We in the Hidden House—and I strongly suspected elsewhere, both in the flower and willow world and outside it—were used to each other in the way that only women who live together constantly can be, and we were very aware of each other's bodies. After all, it was by no means unknown for a patron to want to watch a couple of girls enjoying each other rather than taking them himself. Quite often, a patron would demand to see two girls seeking the seed for each other or we would be told to perform a little mutual dew mingling for him. We were always happy to oblige. After all, who but a woman knows how to really please another woman? It also had the advantage that more often than not, the patron would get so excited watching us that he would either burst his fruit on his own, without us so much as laying a finger on him, or at the most only a little twirling of the stem would be required to see him happy and satisfied. Anyway, there I was, flat on my back, legs spread wide, while Masaki fiddled about inside me.

"Keep still," she scolded. I tried, but whatever she was doing tickled, and whatever she was putting inside me was very cold. "There. Done it. Go on, stand up."

I looked at all of them suspiciously. They were all trying to hide huge grins. I stood up carefully, wondering what on earth Masaki had been up to. I got as far as a crouch, and then stopped as suddenly as if I had been turned to stone.

"Oh!" I gasped.

The girls erupted into laughter, literally hanging on to each other for support.

"Told you!" Kiku crowed. "Isn't that nice?"

I moved slowly, feeling the love globes moving sluggishly inside me. The weights in the globes were slightly uneven, and with each movement they moved up and down, up and down. I was sure I could hear a faint click each time they moved. My mouth dropped open in disbelief.

"How long do I leave them in for?" I croaked.

"Long as you like." Kiku laughed. "As long as you can stand it!"

It was no good; I started to laugh with them. And the

more I laughed, the more the love orbs continued their subtle motion until I felt I was on the very verge of a constant yonaki, as though at any minute my fruit might burst and it would go on and on and on. It was a delicious sensation. I scrambled into my clothes, carefully. And still the love globes rocked to and fro.

"After a while, you'll be able to tense and flex and move them about even when you're sitting perfectly still." Masaki smiled knowingly.

It was a long time since I had had any urge to use the globes, and I hesitated as I fumbled to insert my new ones now. Once they were in place, I rocked myself to pleasure, and then to sleep. It wasn't Danjuro, and I could feel that my dragon did not approve, but at least I slept without waking that night.

"We must go back to Edo."

Kiku hefted Ichiro on her hip.

"Why? I mean, why now?" I was startled. Kiku had seemed very content here, and had not even mentioned a date for our return.

"I've had a message. Akira is back, and trouble is about to begin."

"A message from Mori-san?"

"No," she said simply, and I decided not to pry. Even though Kiku looked as untroubled as ever, I sensed she was on edge. It was contagious. All the way back to Edo, I fidgeted, urging the countryside to fly past quicker.

I was surprised to find Mori-san was not waiting for us. More surprised still when I noticed Kiku seemed not at all taken aback by her husband's absence. It was obvious that there was much that I did not know.

"We shall go to the kabuki," she said firmly. I was puzzled.

"Why? Surely, if the message to bring us back was so urgent, then we should stay here, wait to see if more information is going to arrive?"

But Kiku was adamant. We would go to the kabuki. It would be very busy. We would be safe there, she added ominously.

Once we were inside the kabuki theater, I was suddenly, deliciously at ease. Even my gaijin clothes ceased to bother me; I was finally home. The theater itself had been rebuilt after Danjuro's theater had been burned down, on Akira's orders. The yakuza had wanted to buy his way into the theater, but Danjuro had refused him. Probably he was the only man in Edo to dare to stand up to Akira, and the yakuza's revenge had been very terrible. My mother's friend from the Hidden House, Big, had died in the fire. The memories made me deeply sad until the magic of the kabuki conquered me, as it always did, and the sorrow fled. I had no regrets that I was not up on the stage with the other actors. That puzzled me for a while, until I realized that the kabuki I had left behind in America was so unlike this place that it aroused no nostalgia at all. Just as well.

The play was a new one, and I watched it with a growing sense of amazement.

Nothing in the play was as I had expected. I had thought I would sneer at the lead actor as being inferior to Danjuro. But Ebizo, although very different in acting style to Danjuro, was magnificent. And as I watched the complex plot evolve, my stomach knotted. This was so much better than Danjuro's clumsy attempt to knit two existing plays together. It made his efforts look like dross. No wonder Sato-san had been annoyed. I accepted a bowl of steaming udon noodles from a vendor and enjoyed them immensely.

I was so engrossed with the play that it took me a while

to realize that something was wrong. The audience was becoming restless. Patrons were stirring in their seats; some were leaving, others coming back in. And then my back began to prickle as my dragon bared its fangs. I turned to look at Kiku.

"I think it's beginning." She called to the noodle seller, who came at a run.

"What's going on?" She demanded. He smiled, his face the picture of innocence. I threw him a coin and his tongue was loosened instantly.

"Big trouble. At least two yakuza gangs are roaming the streets. The word is that they are on their way to Akira-san's house."

"Is he back?" I forgot myself and spoke in Japanese, but the noodle seller was too excited to notice.

"I don't know. The other yakuza are bragging that if he's not there, they're going to go get his woman and get the truth of where he is out of her."

I rose at once and fumbled my way out of the box, with Kiku behind me. We held hands to keep ourselves together in the packed streets. The Floating World loved theater, and if it was free, so much the better! We had no need to wonder where the trouble was taking place, we were simply carried along by the mob thronging past us. A strange moon had risen since we had entered the kabuki—blood red and full. Edo called such a moon a "hunter's moon," and I felt a superstitious thrill of fear. Was even the great Tsukiyomi, god of the moon, coming to watch the antics of us humans?

"What is it?" Kiku grabbed the sleeve of a passing peasant and hung on. "What is happening?"

"They say Akira's house is burning! The other yakuza have set fire to it."

He yanked his sleeve away and bustled down the street.

"Mineko!" I whispered. Kiku nodded.

By the time the crowd swept us to Akira's house, I was breathless with fear. I could feel my tattoo exulting at the thought that soon it would see its master again, and I wanted to rake my nails across it and tear it off my back. Tears stung my eyes as I remembered the hours I had spent scrubbing at my flesh with a stiff brush, trying to erase it. The only result had been to irritate my skin and make the dragon's colors seem even brighter. Akira had loved to torment me with the knowledge that he had marked me forever. He had taken delight in fastening his teeth in the skin at the nape of my neck and grinding his teeth together until I wanted to weep with the pain and indignity. But even that had never shifted my dragon.

Akira's dragon.

We were blocked by a crowd of people, milling around the entrance to Akira's cul-de-sac. I was much taller than Kiku, and stood on tip-toe to see better.

"Tell me!" she said urgently. "I can't see a thing. What's happening?"

"There are a lot of men, outside the main door. Yakuza, by the look of them, but not Akira's men. I would still recognize most of them."

The crowd around us—mostly men, but with a fair sprinkling of courtesans and geisha, all after their night's entertainment—suddenly gasped. Kiku grabbed my sleeve and tugged it hard.

"What? What's going on?"

"Fire," I whispered. "The house is burning. Flames are shooting up in the garden. Let me go, Kiku. I have to get Mineko out!"

She slid her arms around my waist, and I was stopped dead.

"Stay here," she said. "You're not going to do any good getting yourself killed as well."

I tried to tug myself from her grip, but it was useless. I was ready to lash out at my dear friend, anything to free myself, when the crowd moaned in unison.

"She's come out. Look! They've got her!"

Mineko hesitated in the doorway, but before she could try to run—or even duck back into the burning house—the yakuza were upon her. I heard Kiku moan as we saw Mineko's spaniel run out from behind her kimono, darting through the crowd as if her life depended on it. But Mineko was not as lucky. The yakuza lifted her shoulder high, carrying her triumphantly like some human trophy. I saw her face, contorted with terror, for just a moment, and then they had thrown her down to the hard-packed earth of the street and men closed around her in a ring. I heard one of the yakuza shouting at her, demanding to know where Akira was, and then the terrible sound of a foot kicking hard at flesh and bone. Mineko could feel no pain, but I felt her pain for her.

"Let me go!" I howled at Kiku. Her face was running with tears. "They're going to kill her. Even if she knows where Akira is, she'll never tell them."

"I'm coming with you."

We moved together, shouldering our way through the mob. I had no idea what I thought we could do. Pure instinct drove me onward, toward my sister.

We were never even close.

There was a moment's silence, as terrible as the silence before a tsunami strikes, and then the ring of men around Mineko became a broken chain and the air was filled with howls and screams. Swords flashed red in the twin lights of fire and moon, and I wailed aloud as I watched one of the yakuza fall to the floor, his mouth pumping blood from a terrible wound in his chest. I was frozen for a moment, and then Kiku was pulling me back, bawling in my ear above the row.

"Mineko's all right. Look! She's leaning against the wall, over there. It's Akira, he's come at last."

"Where? I can't see him!"

I peered into the melee of screaming, fighting men. Every now and then, I saw a face I remembered. But never Akira. My heart pounded so hard I could barely breathe. I sent up a frantic silent prayer to the goddess Benzaiten, bringer of good fortune for all us geisha. If ever she was needed, then it was now.

And she smiled upon us.

There was a sudden uproar in the battle. Men fell down and did not rise. Akira. He had come back. His swords flashed redly in the weird light, darting and slashing and stabbing. He was laughing, his head thrown back and— even from this distance—I could see his grey eyes were alight with the joy of battle.

I had told Danjuro I never wanted to see Akira again. I knew then that I had lied. At that moment, there was nobody on earth I wanted to see more.

The fighting men parted before him like a field of grain, bowing down to a strong wind. His teeth were bared, and they were blood red in the firelight. And then there was a man standing beside him. A rival yakuza, his sword raised, ready to strike down. I shrieked out loud, a warning that I knew Akira could not hear above the row of battle.

Kiku and I clung together. I had never felt so helpless in my life, not even in the worst days in the Hidden House. Not even on my mizuage, when I had been bought by a man old enough to be my grandfather, so that he could enjoy the experience of deflowering me.

Perhaps Benzaiten decided to be kind to us once again. I thought so at the time, anyway. Akira turned, but even I could see it was too late. The rival yakuza's sword was flashing down in a deadly arc; Akira had no time to move. And then he did move; another yakuza shoulder-charged him, sending him flying out of harm's way. But the swordsman was too far into his blow to stop; the sword continued downward, cleaving a terrible wound across the unknown man's shoulder and chest. Kiku and I watched him fall, and I thought he must be dead.

But Akira was alive. He climbed to his feet quickly. He took no prisoners; in a moment, the man who had killed his savior was also dead, a crumpled body on the floor. Akira flung his head back and howled at the moon. I thought he looked like a demon in human form. And not just me; the rival yakuza looked at him and began to back away in fear. He had won, then. But not without terrible cost.

I could see Mineko, still half-propped, half-lying against the garden wall. I drew breath to shout at her to crawl out, to get away, but before the words could leave my lips the wall she was leaning against gave a crack so loud it could be heard over the sound of war. I knew that wall. Many, many times had I sat in Akira's garden with my back pressed against the warm stone, thinking sourly that it was high enough and thick enough to withstand a siege.

I was wrong.

The fire had done its terrible work, and now the wall was cracking in a dozen places. It seemed to me that stones were being spat out of it; a rival yakuza howled and hopped as a piece of flint caught him on the ankle. I wasted no pity on him, I screamed and screamed and screamed as I saw the wall falling. Falling on top of Mineko.

She could feel no pain. But she could die.

The hot stones covered her completely. I closed my eyes, my senses swimming. She was dead, then. My sister had died in front of my eyes, and I had done nothing to help her. I was beyond tears. All around me, men were fighting and dying. I didn't care.

I had no idea what I had done to deserve it, but the gods were merciful to me. Perhaps Benzaiten felt my distress and touched me with her divine hand. In a fraction of a heart-beat, I was no longer in the street. I was back in Akira's house. Back in the room where he had kept me prisoner. I felt my dragon stir and then settle with content. We had come home.

I was standing in front of the drawers that contained my hated combs. I picked them up in my hands, but they were no longer solid. The kingfisher beaks were melting, running like hot wax. And then there was heat and flames all around me, and this prison was no longer safe. It was my tomb.

I was going to die here. I would be with Mineko.

I threw my head back and shouted Akira's name, knowing that he was the only one who could save me. I shouted again and again, and then Kiku's hand was squeezing my arm hard, and I was back in my body and out in the street.

Akira was turning slowly, facing the flames of his home. Was I the only one who heard his voice? No other head turned, no other face looked puzzled.

"Kazhua. My love. You have come back to me. I called to you, and I knew you would return. Have no fear. We will face the next life together, as it was always going to be."

He turned and walked into the blazing hell of his house as if he was going to embrace a loved one.

I leaned against the wall. I would have slid down it and sat on the road if it hadn't been for Kiku's sturdy grip.

"Stay there! That peasant woman has grabbed little Kiku. I'll go get her."

I put my hand in front of my face, stifling hysterical laughter. Akira must be dead, or dying. Mineko was undoubtedly dead. But Mineko's pet was alive and yes! Of course we should think of her. Mineko would like that.

By the time Kiku came back, the spaniel whining in her arms, the battle was all but over. Akira's yakuza were swaggering, kicking the fallen enemies and already stripping them of anything of value. The little dog squirmed and leaped out of Kiku's grip, running toward the pile of stones that was Mineko's marker. She scrabbled frantically at the rubble and hope rose like feathers in my throat.

I strode forward, elbowing yakuza aside as if they were nothing. When a couple of them tried to stop me, I tore my hat and veil off and tugged the pins out of my hair, letting it fall in a red flood to my waist. I bared my teeth and hissed at them, and they scattered in terror before the wrath of this green-eyed gaijin fox spirit. I tore at the hot stones with my bare hands. Kiku—sensible as ever—bullied a couple of Akira's yakuza into helping.

It was too late, of course. Mineko was so still; the stillness of death. I choked back a sob but her spaniel had other ideas. The puppy leaped onto her mistress' chest and began to lick her face. Before I could reach down and scoop the dog up, Mineko turned her head. Only the tiniest movement, but it was enough.

I screamed at the nearest of Akira's yakuza to move the rest of the stones, and to pick Mineko up, gently. I think it was the sound of fluent Japanese issuing from gaijin lips that finished them off. They obeyed, digging Mineko out and carrying her in front of us at brisk trot.

"Where shall we take her, lady?"

"To the Hidden House."

Where else? We were going home at last. All of us.

17

In sleep, body and
Mind become one. May I sleep
So we remember

felt as helpless as a stray dog who howls at the moon in frustration. Long ago, when I had been a geisha in the Hidden House, one of my patrons had hunted wolves. It was his passion; although he killed them, he admired the ferocious beasts. And he loved to talk about them.

"To be cast out of the pack is the worst thing that can happen to a wolf," he had instructed me. "To them, even death is not as terrible. To be a lone wolf is to be nothing. It has no home, no friends. It must try to hunt without support, to sleep with no warm bodies beside it. It is a lost soul, wandering until death comes to claim it."

Then he lost interest in his favorite hobby and wagged his tree at me, indicating that a little twirling of the stem was in order. I had forgotten all his words, long ago, but now

I recalled them. And I understood how that outcast wolf felt.

I had thought that Akira's death would mean the end of everything bad. That all threats would be lifted, and I—and the other geisha in the Hidden House—could begin my life anew. And he was dead, I was sure of that. His yakuza had retrieved his body as soon as the ashes had cooled, and I had stared at it until I was sure beyond any doubt that it was him. There was little enough left to recognize, but Akira had twisted as he had fallen and his black moss and belly were relatively unscathed. It was ironic—although I had no desire to laugh at all—that I knew it was him by the tattoo of two hands cupping his tree, and the concentric lines on his kintama. The tattoo, and the fact that he had two of my kingfisher beak combs clutched in his hand so tightly that the tips of the beaks had broken the flesh on his palm before they had melted. Had they, too, taken a final chance to get their revenge on him?

But dead though Akira might be, still his power lingered. And still I was not free of him.

It felt strange beyond belief walking back into the Hidden House. Naruko and Masaki were, thank the gods, just as I remembered them. They had heard what had happened, of course. It was the only topic in the Floating World. But I was astonished to find that the twins, who we had all hated, thinking them Akira's creatures, had suddenly become part of the enchanted circle of the Hidden House. It hurt me greatly to think that they belonged when I no longer felt that I did. Naruko saw my surprise and explained.

"We were wrong about them," she said simply. "This is Hoshimi, and that is Sayo." Both twins rose and bowed deeply as she spoke their names. I wondered how she could tell the difference between them. "They were Akira's spies to begin with. But don't hold it against them. You need to hear their story to understand everything. They're noble by birth. Their brother died in a tragic accident, and their father blamed them for it. He sold them into a lattice brothel when he couldn't stand to see them any longer."

Naruko paused, and I sighed in sympathy. That had been the threat that Aunty had hurled at all us geisha when we displeased her. She would sell us to a lattice brothel, the cheapest one she could find. One of the establishments where the girls were forced to cluster against lattices, open to the streets, so any passing man who had the few coins needed to buy their favors could leer at them, and having made his choice, own them for an hour. Compared to that, life in the Hidden House was truly a haven.

"How did they get here?" It was unbelievably rude of me to speak to Naruko and not directly to the twins, but I was so used to them talking only to each other, I was shocked when one of them answered me.

"I am Hoshimi. This is my sister Sayo," she said politely. "We are honored to meet you again."

I bowed my head humbly in apology. Hoshimi smiled and with superb courtesy continued where Naruko had left off, as if she had not even noticed my bad manners.

"We escaped from that house, during the night. We were lost and very frightened. We had no idea where we were. We decided that we would just walk, and if somebody found us and took us back, then we would kill ourselves rather than face dishonor. It was a very cold and wet night. We were soon soaked through as well as lost. We found a doorway to shelter in, and we were so exhausted we huddled together and fell asleep. We only woke when the door was opened and we fell into the house."

Hoshimi paused, and Sayo took up the tale seamlessly. I smiled inwardly; in some ways the twins were still one.

"Some men were standing around us. We would have run away, but we were too stiff and cramped and frightened to even stand. They laughed at us and called us drowned rats, and then one of the men went and closed the door behind us. It was a very odd door, we had never seen one like it. It was made of wood, and swung open instead of sliding."

"You were at Akira's house, weren't you?" I wasn't surprised. It seemed to me that the gods had decreed that Akira should have a say in all our lives.

"We were. One of the men around us shouted, and Akira came and looked at us. We knew at once that he was in charge, and that he was an important man. He was dressed very richly, but it was more his bearing than anything. One could tell he was a man who was used to being obeyed. Anyway, he ordered that we should be bathed, and he then gave us tea and delicious food. We told him what had happened to us, and he seemed sympathetic. We would have done almost anything not to be sent back to that terrible place, but when he spoke we became his willing slaves.

"'You cannot go back to your father, dear girls. He will just send you back to the brothel. But I can perhaps help you, if you will work with me? Would you like to become geisha?'

"We thought about it. It would, certainly, be much better than being in that other place. Our father had brought geisha to the house frequently, when he had entertained, and we had often thought that the lovely, elegant women were like delicate, beautiful flowers.

"'Yes.' We said, simply.

"'Good,' he said. 'But you will not just be geisha, you will be very special geisha.' And he explained to us about the Hidden House. He was quite blunt; he told us that we would be expected to have relations with our patrons, but that they would all be rich, important men. And that we would never be on public view, but that we would be hidden treasures. We thought about that, but what option—other than taking our own lives—did we have? Surely it would have been much worse had we stayed in the other place?"

I shuddered. We had all been threatened with the lattice brothels from time to time, but how much worse must it have been for the twins, these girls who must have been treated like precious jewels for the whole of their lives? I noticed that even now neither girl would actually refer to the brothel by name.

"That's why you spied for him, then," I said. "Passed on everything you heard."

"No," Sayo said vehemently. "We were grateful to Akira-san for rescuing us, but it was more than just that. He promised that if we did what we were told, he would give us our old life back."

"Even Akira couldn't do that," I protested. "You would never make enough money in the Hidden House to buy yourself out, nobody can. And even if you had managed it somehow, your father would never have taken you back. It would have meant too much loss of face for him."

"We believed him," Sayo said. "Apart from anything else, we had heard of women of our class who had done something dreadful and displeased their husband or their father and who had been sold as courtesans. When their men thought they had been sufficiently punished, they were allowed back into the family as if nothing had ever happened. Akira-san said if we entertained the patrons at the Hidden House and told him everything we saw and heard—not just from the patrons, but you geisha as well —then when he was sufficiently pleased with us, he would talk to our father and persuade him to take us back."

I thought of the aura of power around Akira and decided that in their place I would probably have believed him as well.

"And Sute? What about her?"

At the mention of her name, Sute sat up and looked hopeful, like a dog who expects to be petted. In the short time I had known her, she had alternated between driving me to distraction with her endless chatter and making me want to laugh. That was, once I had recovered from the shock of apparently finding a gaijin playing a geisha in the Hidden House.

"Akira. Again," Masaki said grimly. "He heard about the maiko who looked just like a gaijin and had her bought to the Hidden House for her mizuage. She's been very popular with many of the patrons."

"I don't understand it at all," Sute interrupted. Had it been anybody else, Masaki would have put her firmly in her place. But Sute was irrepressible. "All my patrons say how much they hate the gaijin, but they're delighted to pay for me."

"I expect it's because they can pretend to themselves that you are a gaijin," I explained. "They have to kowtow to all the gaijin who trade with them or buy things from their shops, but they can do what they like with you. It's their way of getting revenge on the real gaijin."

"That's what Masaki and Naruko say, but I can't see it. It was only my great grandfather that was gaijin. I don't even speak their language." Sute frowned, looking like a puzzled child.

"Ignore her," Masaki said. "We've explained it to her time after time, but she still doesn't understand."

Sute looked so woeful, we all burst out laughing. I stared at her in fascination. So strange, hearing perfect Japanese coming from those full, red lips! Then I saw that Sute was staring at me with equal interest, and I saw myself through her eyes and was ashamed of my curiosity.

"Mineko was her elder sister for her mizuage," Masaki said. "It was Akira's idea; he thought it was amusing. But as it turned out, she was a good choice. Mineko was the only one amongst us who had the patience to turn her into a half-way decent geisha."

Mineko. Her name dropped between us like a stone falling into a deep well. Nobody dared say what they were thinking. Except Sute, of course.

"Mineko was very good to me. Do you think she's going to die?"

Pain squeezed my guts. We had called the doctor as soon as we had Mineko safely home. Broken ankle, he had diagnosed. And several broken ribs. But they were the least of Mineko's injuries. He examined her head carefully, probing at her scalp for a long time.

"Her skull seems to be sound. Must have a hard head, like the rest of you in this place." He chuckled at his own wit, but the smile died away as he saw our faces. "When the stones fell on her, they must have injured her brain in some way. Watch." He lifted Mineko's eyelid and rubbed his fingertip on her eyeball. I winced for her, remembering all too clearly how my danna had done the same thing to me at my mizuage to make sure that my eyes really were green, and not artificially tinted. It had hurt me, but of course,

Mineko could not feel pain. I pointed this out to the doctor, and he shrugged.

"I am aware of that. But there should still have been some reaction, even though she is deeply unconscious."

I took a deep breath, and asked the question we were all desperate to have answered.

"Is she going to live?"

"She's young and healthy. It's quite likely that she will." He held his hand up to stop the murmur of relief that came from each of us. "But when I say that, I do not mean that she is going to make a full recovery. She may never wake up. She may stay like this for as long as you coax some food and water down her. If she does wake up, it may well be that she is blind and deaf, and cannot speak. Or perhaps worse, she may no longer be herself. The longer she sleeps, the more likely it is that some mischievous spirit will find its way into her body and steal her soul. If that happens, if she does wake up she will be like a baby again. Alive, but understanding nothing at all no matter how long she lives."

"You can't help her?" I whispered.

He shook his head. "You can do more than I can. You're her friends. Be here for her. Talk to her. Never mind that she doesn't answer you, she may still hear you. If she still has a link to this world, it will help keep the spirits at bay."

Of course we would do that. But the days crept past, and we all began to wonder the same thing. As Mineko lay in the sleep that was so like death, slowly but surely, Aunty began to recover. Was she sucking the life out of Mineko to feed on it herself? Had we been in America, I would have laughed at such superstitious rubbish. But we were in Japan, and all the supernatural beings from my own childhood that haunted my room in the night began to cluster around me again.

Very well. If Aunty was to blame, then I would talk to her.

She knew I was there. I sensed she did. But she refused to open her eyes. I repeated the same thing, over and over again.

"Aunty, speak to me please. It's Midori No Me. Speak to me, Aunty."

Just at the point when I was becoming almost hypnotized by my own voice, her eyes opened a crack. She peered at me and then thrust her head under the bedclothes.

"You're not Midori No Me at all. You're a fox spirit come to get revenge on me. Go away! Leave me alone!"

Exasperated, I pulled her bedclothes down firmly and put my hands on each side of her head, so she could not turn away.

"It is me, Aunty. I've come back." She kept her eyes tight shut. I racked my brains for some way to make her look at me. To make her believe I was me and not some fox spirit come to drag her off to the afterworld. "Aunty, do you remember when I was a little girl? I sat in the sun for too long, and my face freckled badly. You had never seen freckles before, and you thought I had brought smallpox into the Hidden House. You scrubbed my face with lemon juice and vinegar twice a day until they faded and threatened to beat me if I ever sat in the sun again. A fox spirit wouldn't know that, would it?" She opened her eyes and stared at me defiantly. I took a deep breath and seized my chance. "Aunty, Akira is dead. I have seen his body myself. We are safe, now. All of us."

I watched in shock as tears oozed down her cheeks, trembling on the edge of each deep wrinkle before they fell.

"I was always safe with Akira," she whispered. I frowned, wondering if she was rambling. "So it is you after all. You came back whether we wanted you or not. You killed him, didn't you? Had your revenge at last? He couldn't help loving you, you know."

"I didn't kill him," I protested. "The other yakuza did."

"You killed him by coming back here. He didn't want to die without seeing you again. If you hadn't come back, he would still be alive." She stared straight through me, as if I really was some spirit whose place was not on this earth. "My poor Akira. I suppose he died as he would have wanted, fighting to the last. Is Mineko going to die as well?"

The abrupt change of direction surprised me. But I seized my chance.

"She won't die if you stop ill-wishing her," I said firmly. I added slyly, "Akira cared for her as well as he did me, you know that. He would never have taken her as his concubine if he hadn't. Do you think his spirit is going to be happy if you steal her life now?"

Aunty looked at me with sly eyes. "I don't know what you mean. Leave me alone. I need to sleep."

I did as she asked. Perhaps it was just wistful thinking, but when I went in to see Mineko a little later, I was sure she stirred in her sleep. She opened her eyes, and I could swear that—just for a moment at least—she recognized me. I sat at her side and cried with pleasure and hope.

In spite of everything that Danjuro and Kiku—and now Aunty—had told me, I was breathless with disbelief when I found that Akira had left the whole of his wealth to me. Even Kiku was astonished when Mori-san said Akira had dictated his wishes to him some months ago. Mori-san shrugged his shoulders apologetically.

"He made me promise not to tell anybody. He had only distant relatives he did not care for, and he wanted to make sure his money wasn't lost in legal battles. There's not that much left. Only the Green Tea House and the Hidden House. He lost almost everything else in the yakuza war. But what there is all belongs to Midori No Me."

I was literally lost for words. Only the Green Tea House and the Hidden House were left? They were worth a fortune on their own.

Mori-san smiled smugly at my amazement. "Of course, there is much for you to think about, Midori No Me. But in the meantime, perhaps you would you like to visit Ken-san?" He asked. "We have made him as comfortable as possible in my poor house. The doctor says he is well enough now to receive visitors."

Ken—Mineko's lover. The man I had learned had taken the blow that had been meant for Akira. I thought wryly that Kiku's husband had always had an eye to the main chance. If Ken was now free to return to his former life, he would no doubt be very grateful to Mori-san for looking after him.

I felt a flash of irritation. Yet another invalid! This was hardly what I had expected when I had left America behind me. But at the same time, I was intensely curious. The other geisha had smiled slyly when they spoke about Ken. Above all else, Mineko loved him. I decided I would like to see him.

I sank to the floor at the side of Ken's futon. The day was warm and the bedclothes were thrown back. I closed my eyes in horror as I saw the serpentine wound that ran from his breast-bone down past his navel. It was so very like the dreadful gash that Akira had inflicted on Danjuro that I felt the pain in my own body.

"Midori No Me-san. Mineko has spoken of you often. I am deeply grateful to you for coming back to rescue her.

And I am sorry that our first meeting should be so inauspicious."

His voice was deep and warm. I opened my eyes quickly and forced a pleasant smile, doing my best not to stare at him. In spite of his wicked injuries, he was one of the most handsome men I had ever seen. My heart sank; I had hoped all along that I might be able to persuade Mineko to come back to America with me. I had convinced myself that I could coax Danjuro into letting her act in the kabuki; Mineko had longed for that as much as I had. Looking at Ken, listening to his beautiful voice, I felt my dream crumble to dust. If he wanted Mineko, she would go to him. Of course she would.

If she survived.

"You will give her the gift of life," he said.

I blinked; had I worn my thought on my face? Weariness washed over me. How much more did I have to give? Why should it be down to me to bring Mineko back to herself?

"I have no supernatural powers. No magic. It's up to Mineko whether she recovers or not."

"You have come back, that is enough. She said that you were her elder sister, and you would always be there for her. Now that you are here, she will recover."

Wasn't he listening to a word I said? He smiled briefly, and then his expression changed to a grimace.

"Are you in pain?" I asked. I was shocked when he laughed.

"Pain? Yes, I have pain. But it's probably no worse than I've suffered before. Time after time. You're worried I'm not going to take care of Mineko, aren't you?"

I shrugged, but didn't bother to deny it.

"Listen to me, elder sister. Until I saw Mineko, I had no idea what it meant to care about somebody. To love somebody. And then in the blink of an eye, my whole life changed." I had felt that way the moment I first saw Danjuro. If it hadn't been for that, I would probably have laughed at Ken. As it was, I was suddenly disposed to listen to him.

"Mori-san says you are a samurai. Is that true?" He nodded. "What misfortune bound you to Akira, then?"

His eyes closed and I thought he was going to sink back into sleep. I was wrong; he spoke without opening his eyes.

"My father," he said. "My father led me to Akira. It took a long time, but it was all his doing." I wondered for a moment if he was rambling, but his voice was firm and strong. "Give me a moment, and I will explain everything to you. From the day I began to walk, Father instructed me in the samurai code. He was a proud man, and I was his only son. He was determined that I would bear the family name with honor. I undertook training in swordplay and the martial arts every day. If I did not perform to his satisfaction, Father beat me. As I grew, the beatings and the criticisms became more severe. Eventually, rather than becoming the brave warrior Father demanded, I became a coward. I dreaded pain. Still, I suppose he got what he wanted. I made sure I was better than anybody else, so they could never hurt me. I killed him, in the end."

I drew a deep breath. Surely, this was the stuff of a kabuki play, not real life!

"Was it an accident?"

"I killed him with a sword. He had shouted and sneered at me all day. Told me I would never make a samurai, that I bought dishonor on the family name. He snatched up his own sword and said he would show me how it should be done. Somehow, I ducked under his arm and my sword cut into his heart. The wound was nowhere as bad as mine is now, but it killed him all the same. He lived long enough to tell the doctor it had been an accident. But it wasn't. I had wanted to kill him."

"There's a world of difference between wanting to do something and doing it," I said.

He paused for a long time, and when he spoke again his voice wavered.

"Thank you. But whether it was an accident or not, I couldn't live with myself. I couldn't stay in the house where every room reminded me of what I had done. Finally, I decided I would put myself in the gods' hands. I decided I would leave our home and search out every martial arts school I could find. I would present myself to the master, and ask to fight the best man they had. I reasoned that there must be somebody better than me out there, so I would either learn to be the fighter that father had hoped for or be killed in the process."

"And that led you to Akira?"

"Not directly. I soon found that there were many men who could fight better than I did. Fighters who cared nothing for my samurai code and everything for winning. I became more and more skilled, simply to avoid worse beatings than even my father could have inflicted on me. Eventually, I caught the ferry to Honshu Island. I had never left my home island of Kyushu before, but something called me to Honshu. To Edo. My feet had barely touched the soil of the main island when Akira visited me. He had heard about me, he said. And wanted to fight me. I would have laughed at this presumptuous commoner's challenge, but there was something about him that made me hold my tongue."

"Akira was a powerful man," I said quietly. "He was probably as used to getting his own way, as your father was. He beat you, I suppose?"

"Easily. That was one humiliation. The other was even worse. Akira had proposed the wager for the fight, and innocent that I was, I accepted eagerly. If I won, he would give me the freedom of the flower and willow world for as long as it amused me. I could have everything I wanted—for free. Women, sake, gambling, opium. Anything. If I lost, then I was his to command until he decided to free me. And he won. So there I was, his dog."

"You could have walked away. Caught the ferry back to Kyushu. He could hardly have dragged a samurai back from his own castle."

"Ah, but that was just it," Ken said bitterly. "I was—am—a samurai. And I had given him my word. It doesn't matter. When I saw Mineko, I thanked the gods for Akira. She changed everything."

He sighed deeply and his face relaxed. I realized that our conversation had been a huge effort for him, and unconsciousness had claimed him back from me.

I traced the line of his wound with my fingernail, very softly. Very carefully. Had it been just a little to the left, then it would have touched his heart and he would have been dead. As dead as Akira. But clearly the gods had favored him. It had not been his day to die. Even though I knew he could no longer hear me, I talked to him.

"I'll try to bring Mineko back to you, I promise. I'll tell her that I've seen you and that you're going to recover. And then, I suppose, you'll steal her from me. That's not fair, not at all."

Tears clustered in my eyes and I blinked them back. Was I being selfish, wishing my dear friend and sister would recover, and when she did, would choose me over life with this handsome, caring man? I supposed I was. But perhaps —just for once—I was entitled to put myself first?

But just like Ken-san, I had given my word. I went back to the Hidden House and sat beside Mineko. Held her hand and talked to her endlessly. Told her closed face that Ken was alive, and waiting for her to get well in her turn. That Akira was truly dead and would bother us no more. That the Hidden House was finished and all the geisha were free. And finally, so stiff I could hardly move and hoarse from talking, I stood and went to tell Aunty about Akira's final wishes.

The other geisha came with me. Less, I thought, to support me, but rather more out of curiosity as to how Aunty would react to knowing that I was now the owner of the Hidden House. The irony of it was not lost on me, but I was so tired I had no spirit left to crow over Aunty's downfall.

I thought at first that she hadn't heard what I said. Or— more likely—simply didn't want to hear. She had all the stubbornness of the very old, together with the confidence that comes from knowing there was little that life could throw at her that she had not already dealt with. She just sat there, with her head on one side, as if she was listening to a voice that none of the rest of us could hear. I was about to repeat myself when she nodded briskly. Suddenly, she was ordering us about, just like she used to. "Over there," she said, pointing with her stick. When we didn't move, she sighed and rose to her feet. She hobbled to the screen and fiddled with the struts until part of it slid back. She took a silk purse out of the enclosure, and gave it to me. She grinned at my astonished face and patted her nose as if to say, "Wait."

After that, we listened and went where she directed us. There were little hidden closets everywhere. Some had nothing in them, but others contained gold and jewels. By the time Aunty had remembered them all, we had a fortune spilled on the tatami.

"Akira left it all here, with me, when things started to go wrong for him, the dear boy. He knew I would keep it safe for him. I suppose it's all yours now, Midori No Me. I don't want any of it." I raised my eyebrows, wondering when I had offered her anything. "I've made my mind up. I'm an old woman. Now Akira's dead, I've nothing left to live for. I'm going to go into a monastery. Spend my remaining days in prayer and contemplation."

She glared at us, daring us to laugh. She had no need to worry. My eyes were blurred with tears, and I knew the rest of the geisha felt the same pity. Except for Sute, of course. She goggled at Aunty for a moment, and then said, "Won't you get bored?"

Aunty raised her eyes to the heavens and suddenly all of us—even Aunty—were laughing. Only dear Sute looked puzzled.

18

Rich and famous men
Are born and die, but the sun
Continues to rise

*M*ineko was crying in her sleep. Fat tears ran down her cheeks. I wiped them away tenderly and gave thanks to Benzaiten for listening to my pleas. It would, I knew, only be a matter of time now before she came back to us fully.

Every day after that, Mineko's sleep became lighter. Now it was the sleep of recovery, rather than impending death. She stirred from time to time. Snuffled like a contented baby. When we held a cup to her lips, she drank more than she spilled. Now and then, she smiled slightly, as if she was remembering something precious.

One morning I went in to her and nearly screamed with delight as I saw that she had turned over and was lying comfortably on her side. The day after, either sensing that Mineko was on the verge of waking or simply deciding it was time her mistress paid her some attention, little Kiku sneaked in to her and yipped for attention. And Mineko heard her. She cried out and sat up, and when we all dashed in in response to her voice, she stared at us as if it were we who had been on a long and strange journey, not her.

We jostled each other in our eagerness to touch her, to ask if she could hear us, see us? She cleared her throat, but no words came. I realized she must be thirsty and poured a cup of the soothing herbal liquid the pharmacist had prescribed for her. She drank eagerly and then put out her hand, tracing my face.

"Midori No Me-chan? It is you? You are here? I'm not dead? What happened?"

"So many questions!" I spoke as if she were a child. For a moment, I hesitated, and then—looking at her anxious face —decided she had the right to know. "Do you remember what happened? The rival yakuza setting fire Akira's house?" She nodded reluctantly, her face very white. "Akira used you as bait to lure his enemies. He knew if he waited long enough, they would get desperate and try to force you to tell them where he was. He waited until the very last minute, when they were distracted with you, before he moved in on them."

"I saw him. Yes." She shuddered "I remember being thrown down on the ground, and then when the fighting started, I crawled away and I think something heavy fell on me, but after that I remember hardly anything else at all." She hesitated and a cloud passed over her face. "Later, I thought I remembered seeing you looking down at me, Midori No Me. I thought I was dead then, and you were a fox spirit, come to torment me."

"You nearly did die. The yakuza broke your ankle when they threw you down, and you have a couple of broken ribs where those big, brave men gave you a good kicking. But apart from that, you were sheltering against the garden wall when the fire blew it out. One of the stones hit you on the head. You've been unconscious for nearly a month. The doctor said that if you woke up eventually, you could be left deaf and blind. We were beginning to believe him when you wouldn't respond to anything."

We watched her expression change from confusion to amazement and then her eyes began to flicker with exhaustion. I spoke firmly.

"You are alive, and you're going to be well, very soon. That's all that matters for the moment. But enough for now. Go back to sleep, and we'll talk again later."

I watched her struggle to stay awake, but the sleeping draught in the drink I had given her was not to be fought against, and she slid quickly back into restful sleep.

When Mineko woke again, all she wanted was to bathe.

"I smell!" she said indignantly. We helped her down the corridor to the bathhouse and into the steaming water. As I sat next to Kiku, I felt all the troubles that had weighed so heavy on my shoulders lifting. I was home, at last. Back where I belonged. Or so I told myself.

As was only right, we all chattered sociably about nothing in the bath. It was only when we had been dried and were wrapped in clean robes that we got down to business. Over tea, of course. Mineko listened wide-eyed as we told her all that had happened. I thought she was going to weep when I told her that Akira was dead. That the Hidden House was finished.

Finally, she asked the question I had been waiting for.

"Midori No Me-chan, I have prayed that you would come back, but I never really expected that my prayers would ever be answered. What made you come back to us? Kiku told me you were acting in the kabuki in America," her face wrinkled in concentration as she mouthed the difficult gaijin syllables. "That everything was good for you."

"We have been very fortunate in our new world. But the more Kiku told me about how things were going in the Floating World, the more I worried about you all. I wanted to help, if I could. And," I added honestly, "I was terribly homesick."

It was far from the whole truth, but it would do.

Mineko looked at my face and nodded. I knew she understood that there was far more to my return than my words were saying.

"Don't misunderstand me," I said hurriedly. "There is so very much that is wonderful in America. I perform in the kabuki. We have no need to worry whether death is waiting around the corner for us. We are regarded with respect instead of being called riverbed beggars. There is much kindness there and breathtaking marvels in abundance. Things you could not begin to imagine, if you hadn't seen them yourself. Life for us is very good. But still, I missed this." I waved my arms at the light, airy room. "I missed all of you. I used to wake up in the morning and for a moment forgot I wasn't in the Floating World. Then I remembered, and wanted to weep."

"And Danjuro? Does he also miss the Floating World?" Mineko asked.

"No, not really. He has the kabuki, that comes first for him. As far as he is concerned, he carries the Floating World with him, in his heart."

The geisha around me nodded seriously in understanding. Why, I wondered, was this so easy for them to accept when it was so difficult for me to come to terms with?

"Anyway, as I said. The more Kiku wrote and told me what was happening here, the more worried I became, and the more I missed you all. It got to the stage where I couldn't sleep, I was so anxious. Eventually, I persuaded Danjuro that I had to come back, to see for myself. To help, if I could."

All of the geisha drew a sharp breath.

"Danjuro let you come back? On your own?" Mineko marveled.

"Things are different in America," I said. "Women have a voice of their own. Besides, I kept on until he gave in." I lied."

"She means she nagged her way back!" Kiku interrupted. The geisha laughed.

"But if Akira is dead, what's happening to the Hidden House?" Mineko asked. "Is Aunty alive? Is she going to take things over again? Is she well enough?"

"Aunty is alive, and well. Thanks in large part to your care. But she isn't going to be in charge here any longer. She says she wishes to spend her remaining days praying and contemplating in a monastery. It's all arranged." I took her hand and watched her face as I spoke. "Mineko, you always thought that Akira really loved me, didn't you?" She nodded seriously. "Perhaps he did, after all. He has left everything he had to me. I own the Green Tea House now, and the Hidden House. It's all finished. I'm going to knock the Hidden House down. Sow salt on the remains to stop the demons who might want to make their home on the land. You're all free at last."

Why, I wondered, had I said that "they" were free, and not "we?"

Mineko was quiet for a long time, and when she spoke her words were not what I expected.

"Aunty was Akira's wet nurse, did she tell you that?" We stared at her, shocked into silence. "She talked about it when she was so ill she didn't know what she was saying. She was his father's concubine. Had his child, but it died when it was a baby. Akira was born around the same time, so she suckled him in place of her own baby. I think she looked on him as her son."

Perhaps I was not, after all, the only woman Akira had loved. The thought was oddly troubling.

"But if Akira's dead, and you really are going to finish the Hidden House..." I heard the question in Mineko's voice and nodded briskly. "What's going to happen to us geisha? We have no money. No home. No life other than the Hidden House. We know nothing else."

"Tell her about the gold, Midori No Me!" Sute had been fidgeting and could contain herself no longer. Mineko's face clouded at the lack of respect toward me, but I simply shook my head. Annoying as Sute could be, it was impossible to stay cross with her for long, she was so endearing.

"Akira left everything he possessed to me, not just the two houses. I thought at first that there was no more, that he had used everything to fight the other yakuza, but I was wrong. He had left a fortune with Aunty over the years, for her to keep safe, and she has given it all to me."

"Your thirty koban!" Mineko interrupted. "The gold you left with me. I rescued it before the fire could consume it. I must give it back to you, now that you're here."

"No. It's yours. That and your share of Akira's treasure. I don't want it, Mineko. Or at least, not all of it. I've already told the other geisha I'm sharing it between us. We all suffered at Akira's hands. We all deserve a share of what we earned for him. Besides, if I kept all of it, I would never enjoy it. I couldn't. It would be tainted. But shared between us, it's no more than we deserve."

"I'm going to be married!" Sute broke in, her face pink

with pleasure. "Ito-san has asked me to marry him, and I shall take my share as my dowry." Ito-san. The yakuza I had learned Akira had left in charge of the Hidden House. I wondered, not for the first time, if Sute was half as scatter-brained as she appeared to be.

Taking their cue from Sute, the twins spoke up. As always, one of them began a sentence and the other finished it.

"We are going home. We will travel in style. When our father sees that we are rich women, he will accept us back into the family. He will be happy that we have returned. We have heard that father has remarried, a woman who is much younger than he is. He has another son. He will forgive us."

Ah. Another son to replace the lost child. Perhaps it was possible that Akira had kept his incredible promise to them. Even if it was from beyond the grave. I waited for my dragon to stir at the thought of his former master, but there was nothing.

"Naruko? Masaki? What about you?" Mineko smiled at the girls.

They looked at each other. Masaki spoke for both of them.

"Kiku has persuaded Mori-san to rent a house for the two of us. Not in the Floating World, but in Edo. We will be together, which will make us very happy. We think we may travel a little—Naruko would like me to see her home in China." Naruko nodded shyly. "And after that? We will see."

Her face was bursting with happiness, and I had no doubt at all that whatever the girls decided to do, as long as they were together, they would be content.

"And that just leaves you, Mineko-chan." I managed a bright smile. "It was always in my heart that you would come back to America with me. Act in the kabuki at my side. But it seems that the gods don't favor me that much."

Mineko stared at me, her expression flickering from joy to bewilderment.

"If you will take me, I will go with you. I would love that more than anything. You know acting in the kabuki was always as much my dream as yours."

Sute was giggling behind her hand and spoke before I could.

"She doesn't know. I told you all, and you wouldn't believe me. But it's true. She doesn't know."

I wagged my finger at Sute to silence her, but couldn't hide a smile.

"Mineko-chan. If you want to come to America with me and act in the kabuki, then that would be wonderful. But Ken-san says he doesn't think you will. He insists that you are going to marry him and return to his home with him. He says he is going to go back to his family estates, and will take his father's place. And that you will be his bride."

Mineko nodded and smiled absently. It was clear that my words had gone straight over her head. Either that or she simply didn't believe me.

"Mineko." Kiku huffed crossly. Unable to climb to her feet unaided, she shuffled across the tatami toward Mineko, put her hands on her shoulders, and shook her briskly. "Don't you understand? Ken-san is alive. He was terribly injured in the battle, but he's recovering. He wants to marry you. He is going to take you back to his home. You will be a noblewoman. You will have a place in society. You will be safe. Understand?"

Mineko put her head on one side, her lips pursed. She smiled nervously.

"No, you're wrong. Ken is dead, Kiku. I saw him die. He

took the blow that was meant to kill Akira. And then Akira died anyway so Ken gave his life for nothing."

Kiku muttered something under her breath and raised her eyes to the heavens.

"Ken is not dead, Mineko." She spoke slowly and carefully, as if to a child. "He should be dead. The doctor we got for him said if the sword had cut him a finger's breadth further across, it would have cut into his heart and he would have died instantly. He has been very ill, just as you have. But he is alive and is going to be well, and you can see him at any time you like. He's at my home." She added tartly, "Mori recognizes a future customer when he sees one. He's been very happy to welcome a samurai into our humble home."

"We guessed about you and Ken right from the start," Sute chirped happily. "You were both going around with silly smiles on your faces, but when you didn't say anything, we thought you wanted to keep it a secret."

"Quite right, Sute. It was none of your business," I said firmly. "Of course, if you would prefer to come back to the kabuki with me, Mineko, I would be very happy. I mean, I daresay a life of luxury with an adoring husband, far away from Edo and your past life here, might not suit you?"

Even as I said it, I wanted to snatch the words back. I had tried to sound light-hearted, to spare Mineko the pain of choosing, but instead my words were sarcastic. It barely mattered, I knew in my heart what the answer would be. I watched her face as dawning hope vied with indecision. I could take it no longer and smiled at her. Took her hand in mine and squeezed it gently.

"Perhaps, like Naruko and Masaki, we could travel? Visit you in America?" Mineko whispered.

I wiped the tears from her cheeks.

"The gods could never separate us forever, Mineko. We will meet again, I know it. Now, girls. It is time we all got out of this place. Shall we take Mineko to see her husband?"

The scrum to find geta was instant. I watched my sisters indulgently, feeling like a mother hen with her chicks. We were all outside, and I had closed the door when a thought struck me.

"Please, girls. Go on with Kiku-chan. I want to have a last word with Aunty."

"Are you sure?" Sute grinned cheekily. "She said she wanted to be left on her own to wait for her palanquin. She's not in the monastery yet—I just bet she gives you an awful telling off for disturbing her!"

"I'll do my best to bear it."

I watched the girls walking down the street, heads held high, and I was so proud of them I almost cried. My sisters, all of them.

19

All birds must fly the
Nest eventually. Do
They remember it?

"*A*m I never going to get any peace from you, Midori? I thought I heard you all leave, yet here you are still."

Midori. Green. Not even my full name. Not even now, when I owned the very chair Aunty was sitting on. I straightened my back and reminded myself that Aunty was nothing to me now. That I no longer had any need to fear her. Or so I told myself.

"I did not wish to be rude, Aunty. I wanted to say goodbye to you."

"Yes? Well, you have said it. So you can go now. Unless there is something else you want from me?"

I drew a deep breath. She knew then. Of course she did. Aunty had always seen the truth in our faces, no matter how carefully we had lied.

"Aunty, I wanted to ask you about my mother."

"You got the letter she left with Big for you, didn't you? So you know everything there is to know. Go away and leave me alone."

I bit my tongue accidently, and the pain was intense. Aunty grinned at me, and I knew she felt my pain and relished it.

"He would have passed it on to you years ago, but I told him not to. Oh, don't look at me like that. It was for your own good. If you had known what Terue had done, would it have made you any happier?"

I started to speak, to protest that of course it would, but Aunty cut me off.

"No, it would only have upset you. You would have spent all your time mooning about, wondering if she was going to come back and get you. It was better you thought she had just abandoned you without thinking about it. You had the letter in the end, didn't you?"

I nodded. It was all I could do; I was lost for words.

"Well then? What do you want now?"

"I want to know what she was like. You knew her, Aunty. Nobody better. Will you tell me now? Wouldn't you be happier to go into the monastery with a quiet heart? A clear conscience?"

There was a noise like the wind rustling through dry grass and I realized it was Aunty. Laughing.

"My apologies, Aunty." I stood and bowed formally. "Please, forgive me for interrupting your final moments in your home. I will leave now."

Now I knew she was truly incapable of feeling. Now I knew she would rather go to her grave with the certainty of punishment in the next life rather than tell me anything about my mother. I never knew until this moment how much she must have hated her, for the hatred to still burn bright after all these years.

Even as the bitter thoughts tumbled through my mind, I smiled. I would not give Aunty the satisfaction of knowing how much she had hurt me.

She waited until I was at the sliding screen of her room before she spoke.

"I did not say I would not tell you about your mother, Midori. I will, but I need something from you in return."

I turned and walked back to her side. Aunty's expression was open and honest, and I stared at her, not trusting her for a second.

"Sit."

She gestured at the tatami beneath her chair. Aunty had suffered terrible pain in her knees for years. As soon as the gaijin had introduced the fashion for Western-style furniture to Edo, Aunty had bought herself a chair, followed soon after with a bed instead of a futon laid on the floor. They were not exactly comfortable, she said, but it was so much easier for her to sit and lie and stand, it was well worth it.

I sat, positioning myself so I could see her face clearly.

"I will tell you all about your mother, Midori. And your father." She saw the shock in my face and nodded. "Yes, I knew him as well. But this is valuable to you. And I want something in return."

It was in my heart to say, "Anything!" But I kept my lips closed on the word. I did not want Aunty to know how much this meant to me.

"What? What do you want?"

"I want you to leave the Hidden House standing."

I was confused. Aunty was going to spend the rest of her life in a monastery, well away from the Floating World.

What did it matter to her whether the Hidden House was here or not?

"After all the misery it has caused to us geisha over the years?" I said. "Why? It's a terrible place, and better gone. You'll never see it again anyway."

I understood how brutal my words were when I saw Aunty flinch back as if from a blow. I put my hand lightly on her robe in apology, but she shrugged it off angrily.

"I will die in my chosen place. Yes. But for each day of life the gods leave me, I need to know that the Hidden House is still here. That it will be as I remember it. It has been the only home I have known for far more years than you have been on earth, Midori No Me. When I do die, I want to know my spirit can come back and live here just as I did in life, until it is time to move on."

She was leaning forward in her chair, her face thrust toward me. When I saw the tears she was fighting not to shed, I understood how much this meant to her. But even then, I did not entirely trust her. I had never known my parents; Aunty could simply tell me lies about them and I would never know any different.

"Make the bargain with me, child," she said. "I give you my word that I will tell you the truth. Even better, I will show you the truth."

"How?" I said bluntly.

I guessed she had expected me to doubt her. She pulled a sour face and nodded towards a chest that stood against the wall.

"Look in there. At the top, you will find a packet, wrapped in silk. Bring it to me."

I did as she asked and handed her the packet quickly. The oiled silk of the wrapper had become greasy with age, and I did not like the feel of it on my fingers. Aunty took it from me as if it was precious, and folded back the silk with great care.

"Here." She slid out a scrap of paper and gave it to me. A haiku, comparing a woman's beauty to the first dawn of the day. I read it quickly and had almost handed it back with a shrug when I saw the signature. The equivalent of "Seemon" in Japanese characters. My mouth was suddenly very dry.

"Your father wrote that for me, not long after he arrived here in Edo." She pulled out another piece of paper and then another and another. "Here, read them."

I read each one silently. Beautiful, intimate haiku. All signed with my father's name. After the first one, each one headed with the words, "For my Hana. For the loveliest woman in Edo."

"Now, do you understand that I knew your father as well as I knew your mother? In fact better than I knew her."

Aunty stared at me triumphantly. I rose to my feet. Even without geta, I towered over Aunty. I put my hands on her shoulders, keeping her still.

"Aunty, how well *did* you know my father?"

I flinched as Aunty threw her head back and laughed loudly.

"Don't you understand even now? I knew him very well." Her voice was triumphant. "Who would know him better than me? I was his lover when he first came to Edo. Before he even saw your mother."

My hands fell from her shoulders with shock. She could have moved then, walked away from me so easily, but she did not. She raised her head and stared at me hungrily. She reminded me uneasily of a starving dog I had seen once, running from a chicken seller's stall, spitting feathers as he hung on to his prize. I had laughed at the time, but I had no urge to do so now. I stuttered something that made no sense at all, and Aunty smiled.

"I didn't always look like this, you know. I was beautiful once. Beautiful enough for Akira's father to steal me away from my family, to make me his concubine. He wanted to marry me, but I wouldn't have him for a husband. I was far higher caste than he was; it wouldn't have done. I wanted to be able to walk away from him if it became necessary. That was why his son, my darling child Akira, loved you. Because in just the same way as I would never allow his father to own me, you were the only one he could never have. And he knew it. But at least I behaved honorably toward his father. You had to hurt my poor Akira, didn't you?"

I stared at her, my mind whirling. Mineko had said that Aunty had been my Akira's wet nurse, yes. I remembered that. But that wasn't important. Not now.

"My father?" I urged.

"Ah, your father." Aunty was smiling, her expression gloating. "I first saw him not that long after Akira's father had gifted me the Green Tea House and the Hidden House. He was ill and very near death. He wanted to be sure that I was well looked after and safe. He died soon after." She paused and then drew a deep breath, as if she was drawing a line beneath the death of her lover. "A distinguished patron brought your father to the Green Tea House, so of course he was made welcome. He was the first foreign barbarian I had ever seen, and I thought he was so exotic! But it wasn't just that that made him attractive. When he spoke to you, he leaned forward, his eyes fixed on your face as if he found every word you said fascinating. It was as if you had his whole attention. As if you were important to him. So different from our Japanese men. He spoke excellent Japanese, and after that first visit, he came back frequently. We talked for hours. He was so polite, so interested in Japan and in my own life. He told me just a little about what things were like in his own country, but never really spoke about it much. Just enough to intrigue me."

"Take me back with you, when you go home!" I demanded. But he just smiled and shook his head indulgently as if I was making a jest. And the more he denied me, the more I was determined that I would make him fall in love with me. That he would never want to leave my side. That if and when he did go back to his own country, he could not bear to leave me behind. I was older than him, of course, but it didn't matter."

"But my mother? What about her?" I interrupted.

"Your mother!" Aunty mocked. "Always her. Just you sit quiet, Kazhua, and I'll get to her. In my own good time."

I flinched as she called me Kazhua, and she cackled with pleasure at my distress.

"Akira knew that was what Terue named you. He made me tell him all about you. He loved the name as soon as I told him. It was a fluke that he saw you walking back from the kabuki that day, but when he came sniffing round after you, I was delighted. He had been so busy building up his empire it was a long time since I had seen much of him, but when I understood he was interested in you, I encouraged him. If it brought my son back to me, then I reasoned it had to be for the good. If I had known how you were going to hurt him, I would have told Big to finish you off then."

"I hurt Akira?" I said disbelievingly. "He imprisoned me. Beat me. Set his men on me when he was angry with me. Put his mark on me."

"Just as his father put his mark on me," Aunty snapped. Her hand went instinctively to the nape of her neck as she spoke. I flinched; I did the same thing so often it was like watching myself in a mirror. "You see? You're not as special as you think you are. I also bear the mark of Akira's clan, but I wear it with pride, not hatred. It's an honor to enslave men such as them. Don't you understand? Everything they did to us was done through jealousy. They were so afraid that they would lose us, they had to pretend they didn't care."

I wet my lips and tried to find the words to tell Aunty she was wrong. That these things were done in just the same spirit as more minor hurts were inflicted on us geisha by the patrons of the Hidden House. They did it to amuse themselves. Or simply because they could. There was no love involved. The words would not form themselves, and I listened in growing revulsion as she continued.

"As I have grown older, I have wondered if the reason why I wanted your father—Simon—so much was simply because I couldn't have him. I had enslaved my Akira; I had had one of the most powerful men in Japan at my feet. Any man I had wanted to take for a lover, I could have had. But Simon defied me. I smiled at him. Was cold to him. I tried everything. I went to the pharmacist and demanded a love potion. I fed it to Simon in his tea, day after day, but it had no effect. I prayed to Benzaiten, but she did not listen to me. I was nearly distracted. And then the answer came to me; I woke up one morning and I just knew."

Aunty's expression was gloating. She smiled at me, waiting for me to ask. I felt sick; this was my father we were talking about. I stared back at her with a stone face, but it did nothing but increase her amusement.

"I realized he must be lonely in a foreign land with nothing to remind him of home. So I started to ask him about his home. What it was like. About his family. And he mellowed, day by day. When I could see he was deep in sickness for all he had left, I went and sat beside him. Stroked his hand and tried not to show my pleasure when he laid his head on my shoulder. I made sure that I broke away after a moment, as if his actions had not pleased me. He apologized, of course.

"'Forgive me, Hana,' he said. 'I forgot myself for a moment.'

"But I saw the yearning through his words and smiled, opening my arms to him. He hesitated for a moment, and then laid himself against me, wrapping his arms around me and kissing me as if he was a starving man placed in front of a table full of food. I had never been kissed before. You know Japanese men do not kiss. I wasn't sure I liked it at all at first, but after a moment or two, I began to be aroused and I decided I did like it, very much. But for all that, I slid away from his embrace. I smiled at him, and offered him tea.

"I could see he was confused, and I was pleased. From that second, I knew I had him. I thought at first that the knowledge would be enough, that I would no longer want him so badly now that I knew I had caught him. But I was wrong. I went to sleep thinking of his lips on my mouth, and when I woke in the morning, my belly was on fire for him. But I still made him wait, of course. As the days went by, he visited the Green Tea House more frequently. I pressed my best geisha on him, and watched in secret delight as I saw that their singing and dancing no longer fascinated him. But still I was cold to him.

"'Have I displeased you, Hana-chan?' he pleaded. 'You do not seem to welcome my company anymore.'

"'Not at all.' I smiled at him. Waited for a heartbeat. 'I would welcome your...company whenever you wish, Simon.'

She paused, her thoughts far away and long ago. I tried to force myself to think of this as just the memories of an old woman, nothing to do with me personally at all. It was all so confusing; I longed to know the full story of my parents, yet at the same time I felt sick at the thought of my own father lying with Aunty. And in spite of my determination to view this as something that didn't matter to me, I had to ask.

"Big said my father was the ugliest man he had ever seen. Why did you find him attractive?"

She stared at me as if she had forgotten I was there. Then she cackled, her old woman's laugh that sounded like bones breaking.

"Simon? Ugly? Ah, well. I suppose to Big he must have appeared to be truly a foreign devil. He would have hated him no matter what. But he was not ugly. Strange to our eyes, but still a beautiful man. His skin was white, but white with a sheen like white silk. Unblemished. Quite, quite lovely. His hair was much redder than yours, but it was just as lustrous and thick. His eyes were exactly the same color as yours," she added grudgingly. "Like emeralds to look at. All the geisha and courtesans in Edo were at his feet. He was polite to all of them, but took none. Except me," she added gloatingly.

My stomach churned with disgust. I tensed and took a deep breath, held it until I thought I could speak steadily. I was so very close to turning the key on the locked casket of my past, I would not fail now.

"How did you capture him?" I prompted.

"He came to me that same evening. I knew he had read my signals; for a gaijin he was amazingly perceptive. When the last patrons had gone, I took him by the hand to the bathhouse. I soaped and rinsed him myself, and climbed into the bath beside him. He must have used the bath many times, but he was still shy in my presence. He backed himself into a corner and crouched, so his tree was hidden from me. But I was having none of that! I stood beside him and ran my hands over his body. But I was careful only to look at his face, you understand. I did not want him to run away at this last moment. I could see he was aroused from his expression, but still I caressed only his shoulders, lifted his hands and kissed his fingertips."

"'Hana,' He whispered, and bent to kiss me. 'Hana, forgive me if I am clumsy. It is a long time since I have known a woman. If you will permit me, now?'

"Such exquisite courtesy! I was bowled over. I didn't reply in words, but allowed my hand to slide down his belly to cup his tree. And I was pleased. We had all heard tales of how well-endowed the gaijin were, but having been used to seeing Big and Bigger playing together, here in the bath, I had not expected to be impressed. But I was. Simon's tree reared in my hand, seeming to reach for me. But I was not impressed for long. Before I could even begin to play the delicious games I had in mind, Simon had his arms around my waist and was kissing me. Not just on my lips, but on my neck and shoulders. He kissed and bit at my nipples, and I enjoyed that, but next thing he was turning me around and his tree was probing at my black moss. It was very enjoyable, matching the bird to the nest in the hot bath water, but I barely had time to become aroused myself before Simon was bursting his fruit.

"Afterward, I would have known he was not Japanese with my eyes and ears shut. He cuddled me and told me I was beautiful and that I had made him a happy man. Not, I noticed, the most beautiful woman he had ever seen, but I decided that would come in due course.

"There was no keeping him away from me after that. But he tried my patience sorely at first. If he hadn't been the prize I had snatched from so many other women in the Floating World, I think I may have despaired of him entirely. He shocked me." I blinked, my stomach contracting as I wondered what my father could have done that was so bad it shocked Aunty. "For the first few times we matched the bird to the nest, it was over in a flash. First the kissing, which I was beginning to find quite pleasurable. Then a little fumbling of my breasts and a brief exploration of my black moss. No so much as a touch to the nape of my neck. And then he was laying me tenderly on my back and inserting his tree into me. And that was it, he burst his fruit before I had the slightest chance of matching his heat.

"After a while, it became tedious. So I took matters into my own hands. When he tried to lay me down, I turned over and pushed him onto the futon instead. He looked so shocked, I laughed at him.

"'Enough, Simon,' I said. 'The women in your country may like your way of matching the bird to the nest, but you have much to learn about us Japanese.'

"His tried to hide his interest by looking astonished, but I knew better. From that time, I began to educate him in the arts of loving a woman. I made him slow down, using tricks even a maiko would find easy. He was amazed! I taught him the joys to be found in seeking the seed. Responded with delight when eventually he dared to split the melon with me.

"'You liked that? Really?' He was astounded, and I laughed at him.

"'Don't women in your country like it? When you consider how close a woman's black moss is to her rear opening, surely it is obvious that matching the bird to the nest with either is pleasurable?' He shook his head, lost for words.

"Over the months, I taught him to be the sort of lover that any woman would be delighted to have. And once he learned how to satisfy me, I began to realize that I cared for him outside the futon as well as on it. He was always so courteous, so caring. He was a delight to me."

"What happened?" I asked, even though I guessed the answer.

"Your mother. Terue. She happened." Although so many years had passed, a flicker of pure hatred lit Aunty's eyes. "She was going to be the gem of the Green Tea House. She had it all. Beauty and wit and talent. She could sing and play the samisen with exquisite skill. And she had something else, a sweet innocence that made the patrons mad for her. The most important men in Edo drew lots to be the one who was privileged to buy her for her mizuage. The winner was one of the most important daimyo in the whole of Edo. She was a fool, your mother," Aunty growled. "The Lord Dai was mad for her. After her mizuage, he promised he would remain her danna. Look after her. Make sure she wanted for nothing. If she had played the game properly, he would have taken her for his concubine. She would have had it all. Wealth, position, everything. But Terue? Ungrateful bitch that she was, she told me he made her feel sick every time he touched her. Said he was old and ugly and made her cringe. At first, I didn't believe her. In fact, I thought she was being incredibly clever. The more she toyed with him, the more eager her daimyo became. She was playing such a skillful game that eventually I saw he was so mad for her that he would take her as his wife, if that was the only way for him. And for a man of his class, a wife is not disposed of easily. But I was wrong.

"'He will not wait forever,' I warned her. 'He's a very great lord. He may find it tantalizing to be held like this for a while, but he will not tolerate it for long. Eventually, he will simply take you, and neither I nor anyone else has the power to stop him.'

"Still, she shook her beautiful head.

"'If he does take me, he will not find me willing. He is an old, ugly man. I hate it every time he comes near me. How long will he put up with that?'

"I could have slapped her." Aunty stared at me. "She was very like you, in many ways. I remember your mizuage, where you decided to be so upset afterward that you could neither move nor speak. We had to half-drown you, throwing you into the bath, to make you come to your senses."

I shuddered. I remembered the horror of my own mizuage. Being given to a man old enough to be my grandfather. But Aunty was relentless.

"Just like her. You both had to be the center of attention all the time. Me, me, me." I shook my head. It wasn't like that! My mizuage had been horrible. Even now, sometimes I dreamed of Teruki-san, my danna. Felt his wrinkled hands on my body. Smelled his pipe breath on my face.

"No," I said. It was all I could manage.

"Yes! Just the same as Terue. Still, I let her get away with it. I reasoned her daimyo would keep on trailing after her as long as he thought he would get there in the end. And in the meantime, the whole of Edo knew about the affair, and she became the most popular—and the most expensive—geisha in the whole of Japan. And if her daimyo did finally weary of waiting for her, I decided it didn't matter that much. Her reputation would still linger. She was going to make us both rich. I had her, I had Simon for my lover. Oh, I was happy!

"What happened?" I asked again.

Aunty did not answer me directly. She stared into space for so long I thought she had lost the thread of our conversation, as old people are wont to do. But I had underestimated her.

"They say the gods do not like us mere humans to be too happy. We get above ourselves and forget to say our prayers. Perhaps that's what happened to me. Or perhaps I was so happy, I didn't notice what was going on under my nose. Big tried to warn me, but I thought he was just making trouble. He had fallen head over heels for your mother virtually as soon as I bought her off her parents and brought her to the Green Tea House as a maiko. I told him, time and time again, that she was not for the likes of him, but still he hung around her.

"I suppose I should have known Big was right when Simon started making excuses not to come to my futon. First, he was too tired to do me justice. Then he had important business outside Edo. And so on. I decided to put my doubts aside. Fool that I was, I was too deeply in love with my gaijin to see that he was lying to me."

"But how did he come to meet my mother?"

"I introduced him to her, of course. She was my pearl, the best that I had. I even told Simon that she had the most important daimyo in Edo dangling after her, just to impress him." She laughed, the sound totally without humor. "They must both have been better actors than I gave them credit for. Whenever they met in the tea house, they were merely polite." She shrugged. "Or perhaps I didn't want to see the truth. Of course, Terue could go out into the Floating World, and Edo for that matter, whenever she had the free time. They must have been together then. I suppose Simon rented a room in one of the accommodation houses for them. Oh, how the pair of them must have laughed at the way they were deceiving me. Perhaps it added spice to the thing for them."

"And you never suspected?" I could hardly believe it. Surely, Aunty must have sensed my father was no longer interested in her.

"I began to worry when he avoided me for weeks. But what could I do? He was just my lover, not even my danna. Finally, I asked him if I had done something wrong, if he was no longer happy with me. He smiled at me, and reassured me, said it was just business that was keeping him away. I believed him. Why shouldn't I?"

For the first time in my entire life, I felt a spasm of pity for Aunty. I understood what, even after all these years, she did not. Had my father been Japanese, he would simply have told her that he was tired of her. That the affair was over. But that was not the gaijin way. My father had not wanted to hurt her, so he had lied, not understanding that the hurt and loss of face would be all the greater once she found out the truth.

"I believed him right up to the night when both he and Terue vanished out of my life. And left you in their place."

We were both silent for a long time. Finally, I asked the question that had been in my mind since she had begun her story.

"Is that why you didn't expose me? Because you loved my father?"

"You're as sentimental as your stupid mother," she said brutally. "When I came home from the cherry blossom festival, I was happy. It had been a good evening. My geisha had attracted a lot of attention. The blossoms had been beautiful, and even the weather had been kind. And best of all, I had convinced myself that my suspicions about Simon were nonsense. After all, hadn't he told me himself that it was business that was keeping him away from me? I could understand that. Business had to come first. But as soon as I walked into to my apartment, I knew something was very wrong. The screen leading to the secret room was half open."

I frowned at her. Secret room? I had lived for most of my life in the Hidden House and I had never heard of any secret room. Aunty sneered at my expression.

"Think you know it all, don't you? Nobody in the Hidden House knew about that room except me and the boys. And one or two extremely important patrons who had need of it from time to time. It has an entrance off my bedroom and another leading into the garden. It sometimes happened that important men who needed to be unseen for a while or wanted to get out of Edo without being noticed would use it. But it had been empty when I left for the festival, and the door firmly closed. I dithered for a moment, wondering if somebody had had need of it while I was out, and then I heard you crying. I was bewildered. A baby? Not just in the Hidden House, but in my secret room? I decided that somebody very important indeed had found it necessary to hide a child. None of my business, if that was the case. I would have shut the screen and pretended I had seen nothing—it wouldn't have been the first time it had happened—but you were having none of it. You cried and cried until my head ached with the row. So I went in to see if I could shut you up. You had been wrapped in a silk shawl, but you had kicked yourself free of it. The lamp was almost out, but I could still see you. See your red hair. And your eyes. And I knew. I felt it in my belly straight away. I left you there and went to find Big.

"He was awake, of course. Just sitting in his sleeping robe on the tatami.

"'Is she alive still?' he asked. I nodded and he hung his head.

"'I am sorry,' he whispered. 'I promised Terue I would look after her. If it hadn't been for that, I would have killed her myself.'

"'Where is she? Terue? Where is she?'

"'Gone, with her gaijin. The child was born late yesterday afternoon. They wanted to take her with them, but the journey would have killed her, so they left her. By now, they will be on board ship and away from Edo.'

"I nodded. It was too late, already, to bring them back. I was stone. I felt neither sorrow nor anger at that moment. I could even, in a detached sort of way, understand why Big had helped Terue. She had enchanted him just as much as she had her daimyo. And Simon, for that matter. Then you started to cry again.

"'You are a fool, Big,' I said. 'Just as I have been a fool. I should have believed you. But we shall have our revenge on the pair of them. Go and find a wet nurse for Terue's bastard. Many of the brothels will still be open; there's bound to be a whore in one of them who's feeding a baby. I don't care what she's like. As long as she has milk in her breasts she'll do. Promise her what you like, I'll make sure she gets paid.'

"He ran off as though all the vengeful spirits in the after-life were at his heels."

"But why did you save me?" I interrupted. "I used to think it was because you loved my mother. But if it wasn't that, and you no longer cared about my father, why did you keep me? Raise me?"

Aunty stared at me as if was stupid. And beneath her withering gaze, I felt very silly. But still I need to know.

"Why?" I persisted.

"Don't you know? Even now?" I shook my head, mute. "Because I wanted to punish your mother and father, both of them. And you. You should have been my child, not hers! Every time I slept with your father, I hoped I was pregnant. But it never happened. But Terue. Dear, sweet Terue. She managed it with no problem at all. And even escaped from me as well."

My throat was so dry, I couldn't speak. When I parted my lips, nothing came from my mouth but a croak.

"You still don't understand, do you?" Aunty frowned at me as if she suspected I was pretending to be stupid just to annoy her. "I could have killed you. Just left you for a few hours more and you would have died. You had been born early, you were sickly. I was tempted, at first. It would have given me great pleasure to watch you die. Then I told myself not to be greedy. The more I thought about it, the more I realized how much better it would be to keep you alive. To keep you prisoner, here in the Hidden House. To watch you grow, knowing that every day your mother and father would be wondering about you, hoping you were alive and well-cared for. That one day, they might even come back to find you. And if they did that, how exquisite would be my pleasure when they found you were a geisha in the Hidden House. Spending each and every day servicing the patrons in any way they wished. And even if they never came back, I knew from looking at you that you would be very sought after by my patrons. That you would earn me a fortune. And at the same time as I punished them, I would punish you. What revenge could be sweeter? I had you for your lifetime."

She smiled serenely, this terrible old woman. I was tempted to strike her. I raised my arm, and saw anticipation flit across her expression. For a long moment, we stared at each other, and then I lowered my arm. I climbed to my feet —stiffly, for I had been sitting tense as a snake waiting to spring for a long time—and I bowed to her formally.

"Thank you for telling me the truth, at last. I made my promise to you, and I will keep it. The Hidden House will remain standing, at least until you breathe your last. May the gods grant you a long life, Hana, and may you spend every day that remains to you in contemplation of your own soul."

I walked out without looking back, not even when Aunty called my name.

20

The coiled snake hisses
Before it strikes. People show
No such courtesy

I watched San Francisco harbor growing bigger as the ship approached. I knew that appearances were deceptive, and it would be several hours before we docked. As I had promised myself, I had worn a kimono and traditional makeup every day of the voyage. And it had made me as happy as I had anticipated. Only now, as we approached the dockside, did it feel at all odd.

I decided that my touch of unease was only to be expected. I was back in America; I would honor my new country by dressing in an appropriate way. I took a last glance at the approaching land and went back to my cabin to change from my kimono into Western dress: a long skirt and a blouse, topped by a jacket. I pulled the combs out of my hair and tidied my curls so that they could be topped by a hat and a veil. I scrubbed my traditional makeup off and replaced it with no more than a dab of face powder. I checked in the mirror and frowned at my reflection, wondering—not for the first time, and no doubt not for the last—which woman was the real me?

Back on deck, I smiled at my friendly dinner companion from the journey. He had described himself vaguely as a businessman; his own father had been an immigrant to America, he reassured me. His papa had arrived from Ireland with not a cent in his pocket and had founded what was now a substantial business through hard work and a willingness to take risks. He, in his turn, was now looking to extend the family business by trading with Japan. I understood perfectly; in Edo, he would simply have been another merchant, eager to take the chance of a good deal wherever it arose. He seemed delighted with the success of his venture, and I sincerely hoped that my fellow countrymen had not used him too harshly, although given my own experiences, I doubted it.

Henry-san was leaning on the rail, watching intently as San Francisco speeded toward us. He raised his hat uncertainly, and I saw at once that he didn't recognize me. He had been an avuncular companion on the long sea journey across the Pacific, regaling me with stories of his travels the length and breadth of America, telling me constantly how glad he was to be back, and how I would soon come to love his country as much as he did. Politeness forbade me to explain that I had lived in America for the last two years, and it had no fears for me. Instead, I nodded and smiled and allowed him to pick out the choicest dishes at dinner for me, although even politeness couldn't make me accept his choice of rare beefsteak.

"Henry-san?" I smiled politely, watching as his mouth opened and closed but no words came out.

"My God. Midori No Me? I barely recognized you in those clothes, and without your makeup."

I smiled sweetly but didn't speak. I simply lowered my head and watched him from beneath my eyelashes. Obviously flustered by his mistake, Henry-san took my hand and guided it through his arm, giving it a little pat of reassurance as our ship finally bumped and nuzzled into the harbor. It was unforgivably rude of him to touch me uninvited, and I stiffened, fighting the urge to pull away and reclaim a respectable distance from him. He stank as well. He reeked of meat and butter and milk, as if the smell was seeping out through his pores from inside him. As if he was badly in need of a cleansing bath. I had noticed it before, but it was so much more obvious now that he was so very close to me.

I flushed as I realized the mistake was mine. We were no longer in Japan, where even now it was a constant joke that one could smell the gaijin before they could be seen. I had only spent a couple of months in Japan, and already I was thinking like a geisha again!

Leaning comfortably on the rail next to Henry-san I searched the quayside for Danjuro. Useless; there were too many people ranked there to make out a single figure. I thought I saw him and half raised my hand to wave, and then decided I was wrong. It wasn't him. This man was dressed in Western clothes; he even wore one of the fashionable brimmed hats with a round top that Danjuro contemptuously referred to as a "rice bowl hat." Never mind, in a few minutes I would see my husband, and then I really would be home. If he was here.

A wave of anxiety at the thought made it difficult to breathe. I only realized I was squeezing Henry-san's arm against my breast when he coughed politely and withdrew his hand, at the same time waving enthusiastically at the dockside crowds.

"Hi, Maria! Hi!" He bellowed loudly, waving his own hat enthusiastically. "Hi, honey! Henry's home!"

Henry-san moved a step away from me. There had been numerous occasions on the long journey when he had made it all too obvious that he would have welcomed my company in his cabin. No doubt he thought he was being subtle when he told me that he had heard many tales of how Japanese women were trained to please their husbands, and he regretted deeply that he had not had time to visit a couple of what he referred to as "geisha girl houses." I had pretended that I did not understand him, even as I wondered what his reaction would have been had I told him the tiniest bit about my own life as a very special geisha. Truth to tell, there had been one or two nights when I had been so very lonely that even Henry-san's company was tempting. But I had resisted with very little effort, resorting to my love-globes for consolation instead.

Now I watched his face light up at the sight of what I assumed was either his wife or sweetheart, and I was very glad I had not gone to him after all. But still, I couldn't resist wondering if his greeting to Maria would have been quite so enthusiastic if I had accepted his implied invitations. I rather thought not.

"Well, it's been really great spending the journey with you." Henry-san tipped his own rice bowl hat to me. "I really must go and make sure everything is cleared from my cabin ready for landing. You sure you're going to be alright?"

I couldn't resist it. I stood on tiptoe and kissed his cheek, my breath fanning his skin softly. My fingers found his earlobe and nipped it.

"I'll be fine, Henry-san." I breathed, leaning against him. "I just hope Maria is really very pleased to see you back."

As I stood back I had the satisfaction of seeing that his eyes were as round as peaches and his cheeks were mottled deep red. Poor Henry-san; how long would it be before he stopped wondering what he had let slip through his grasp? I waggled my fingers in farewell as the gangway clicked into place and I walked down it, my back straight and my head up, my posture hiding a growing worry.

Danjuro was not here. But he should have been! I had written as soon as my plans were made to leave the Floating World. Kiku had assured me that the letter would reach Danjuro long before I did. True, I had written to him a number of times during my stay in Japan and had not received an answer. But then, I had not really expected one. But I *had* expected him to be here to greet me. Surely, he could not still be angry with me? On the journey across, I had rehearsed our first meeting over and over in my head, planning each scenario I could think of; finding an answer to each and every problem I could imagine.

The only thing that had never occurred to me was that Danjuro might simply not be there.

But he was not. The sense of anti-climax was such a disappointment, I was lost. But not for long. Very well, if he were not here, then I would find my own way. I set my lips and turned, ready to push my way through the throng on the dockside and find a cab. The grip on my arm took me by surprise. I shrugged it off angrily, thinking it was Henry-san who had decided that, after all, I was a better option than his Maria.

"Leave me alone," I snapped.

"Midori No Me-chan, has your memory grown so short since you left America?"

I gasped with surprise. And pleasure. Of course Danjuro was here. How could I ever have thought he would not be? I had just failed to see him in the crowds. I turned, and the smile froze on my lips.

The man with the rice bowl hat. The man I had mistaken for my husband. I had not been mistaken: he *was* Danjuro. And it wasn't just the hat; Danjuro—he who had always disdained gaijin clothes and had insisted on wearing his traditional robes both in the theater and out—was dressed from head to foot in Western garb. Trousers, shirt, and a short jacket. And of course, that hat. He saw my confusion, of course he did, and rather than the anger I had expected he stood back and placed his hands on his hips, grinning and inviting me to inspect him.

I did. Slowly, carefully. Danjuro, the great actor from the Edo kabuki should have looked ridiculous in those clothes. But he did not. In a bizarre way, they suited him. Made him —to my surprised eyes at least—look very attractive. I started to smile, then my eyes fastened on his face and I was confused all over again. The Danjuro in my memory and my mind was the man who had rescued me from Akira and brought me to this new world. His face lean and ascetic, the planes clean and almost angular in their beauty. This man was...different. I raised my hand and traced his cheek with a gentle finger.

"You have changed, husband," I said softly. He shrugged, petulance showing through even the professional mask of the kabuki actor.

"I may have put on a little weight," he said. "After all, with my wife absent for so many months, what did I have to do but eat?"

He laughed, and I smiled weakly. He had put on some

weight, and it did not suit him at all. In fact, his face had become relaxed, almost flabby, with bags beneath his eyes like pouches and the start of a double chin. But apart from that, it was the way he stood, his whole way of showing himself to the world. That was the real change. This Danjuro was no longer the man who had held the whole of Edo in his hand. Would this new husband of mine dare to challenge Akira and snatch me from under his nose with the hounds of death sniffing at his heels? I didn't just doubt it, I knew he would not. I caught myself sniffing for the scent of whiskey on his breath and quickly changed it into a sigh, as if of pleasure. The old Danjuro would not have been fooled for a second. This man? He seemed not to even notice.

"After all, wife. I am only following your lead. Surely, if gaijin dress suits you, then it should also be good for me."

He tucked my hand into his arm and began to steer me through the throng. He had acquired a walking stick to complete his costume and used it to prod at anybody who was in our way. I walked at his side, bewildered. Was Danjuro playing a part in his own head? Or had he simply chosen to forget all that had gone between us before I left? I had no way of knowing.

"Here we are." Danjuro had a cab waiting. "I will send for your luggage later. The main thing is that you are home. Now, tell me. Is everything well in Edo?"

Wrong. Wrong. Wrong. Danjuro was leaning toward me solicitously, as if he was politely interested in what I was going to tell him. Much as if I was a casual acquaintance he had not seen for a while rather than the wife he had parted from with anger and harsh words.

"Have you missed me?" I blurted.

"But of course I have. Do you need to ask?" He sounded hurt. I had my doubts.

"We did not part as friends, husband," I hesitated. "I wrote to you from Japan, but you did not answer. I was worried that time had made the rift between us worse."

"Oh, that." Danjuro shrugged, and I stared at him in disbelief. We had parted in something very like hatred; how could he dismiss it so casually now? "Well, I have thought a lot about that while you were back in the Floating World. I've decided it's best put it behind us. I'm willing to forgive and forget now that you're back home again."

He was nodding seriously, his expression benign. I licked my lips, wondering if he could know how patronizing he sounded. With an effort, I managed a smile. I had been back only moments. Now was not the time to re-open old quarrels.

Later, we would talk.

"I am very glad that it is so, Danjuro." With an effort, I spoke affectionately. "When I left, I felt that we were no longer right together."

"It was good for you to go back to the Floating World," he said promptly. "I think it gave you the chance to reflect on what you were leaving behind, and to value it more."

Ah. In spite of what he had said earlier, it was all my fault. I almost laughed. Danjuro might have changed his coat, but inside he was still Japanese.

"Yes, husband," I said meekly, tongue in cheek. I glanced out of the carriage window to hide my smile. "Where are we? This is not the way to our lodgings. Is the driver taking us the long way around to make money? Does he think we are strangers to San Francisco? I shall tell him he is mistaken."

I was so indignant that I was about to bang on the cab's

roof to tell the driver what I thought of his antics, but Danjuro put his hand on my arm.

"No. Not at all. We are here." As he spoke, the carriage cut across the road and came to a halt in front of a large hotel. I stared at it, speechless. "I felt the lodging house was no longer appropriate for us. We are, after all, stars of the kabuki. All of the actors are here as well, but of course, we have a superior suite to them. Come, Midori No Me-chan."

A uniformed doorman hurried to open the door to allow us to enter. Inside, more uniformed lackeys bowed to us. Danjuro swaggered up to the reception desk but did not speak; he simply held out his hand in the manner of one who is well known and used to being obeyed, and the desk clerk passed him a large key with a deferential smile.

I waited until we were alone in our rooms before I said what I was thinking.

"Danjuro, this place must be costing a fortune! Can we afford it?" I would have many words to say to Ryu, I thought. I had entrusted him with taking care of our finances while I was away, to the extent of telling him where our savings were hidden, and he had let Danjuro do this!

Danjuro shrugged. He had taken his jacket off and thrown it onto a chair. He loosened his tie and rolled his shoulders as though a burden had been lifted from them.

"Oh, don't worry about that. We have plenty of money. Ah, look who has come to greet you!"

Neko strolled across the room and paused, staring at me through slitted eyes. He had put weight on, just like his master, but he had lost none of his old arrogance. He lifted his whiskers in a sneer and turned his back on me, jumping onto an opulent couch and making himself comfortable on a cushion.

I smiled, but the distraction was momentary. I looked

back at Danjuro, and I was convinced I caught an odd expression on his face. Since when, I wondered, had the great actor concerned himself with money?

"Do we? Is Clay-san suddenly paying us more?" Danjuro's expression flickered; just for a second I saw bluster beneath his confidence.

"Please, do not worry." He waved an airy hand, dismissing my anxiety. "A great deal has happened since you left us, but I will explain later. For now, you have returned to me, and that is all that matters."

He held out his arms to me. I hesitated and then made my mind up. I would not question him, not at this moment. He was right. Whatever had been between us before I went back to Japan was resolved. We were together again, and none of the nightmare scenarios I had contemplated had happened. Surely, I should be happy!

His hands slid around my waist and his lips nuzzled my neck. He began to rub himself against me, more like an affectionate pet than a man. His hand moved from my waist and insinuated itself deftly between the buttons on my blouse. Even my stays posed no problem for that searching hand. I found my nipple was being rolled between his fingers in no time at all.

The sensation was deeply pleasurable, but I was puzzled. I have an excellent memory, and I could not remember Danjuro ever making love to me when I was wearing Western clothes. The more I thought about it, the more certain I was. He insisted the various buttons and ties had been invented to thwart love, and that his Japanese hands could not cope with them. Oh, he had been—always! —delighted to watch while I patiently took off each garment. In fact, he had been so delighted that I had quickly learned to strip off each item as slowly as I could, pretending to fumble with buttons to prolong the thrill of waiting. But now it seemed that all thoughts of waiting had gone. Danjuro had already unbuttoned my blouse and taken it off for me. Odder still, I had expected that in his excitement he would simply throw it aside. He did not. He actually folded it neatly over the back of the nearest chair. He must have seen my surprised face as he grinned sheepishly.

"Seems a shame to crease it when it's managed to get all this way in good order."

I giggled at him, refusing to acknowledge the warning thoughts that insisted that this was Danjuro the actor at his finest.

My stays took barely a moment to unlace, and were quickly followed by my skirt. I stood perfectly still, and let him take his time. That seemed to be what he wanted, so why not? Pleasure was surely going to follow, as certain as day follows night. Despite my anticipation, I could not help glancing at the front of Danjuro's ridiculous trousers. I was deeply relieved to see that his tree was rearing happily, barely contained by the thick fabric.

Good to see some things did not change.

As soon as I was naked, Danjuro took me in his arms. He patted kisses on my neck and shoulders. Rubbed his face against my breasts and took my nipple in his mouth and sucked like a hungry infant. Need rose in my belly and I automatically reached for his tree, running my fingers over it and holding it as best I could through his trousers. Now it was my turn to fumble. I could feel buttons—lots of them— under my fingers. I did my best to undo them one-handed, but soon reached the stage where I was tearing at them clumsily, desperate to get this ridiculous garment away from my husband. I wanted to feel his flesh against me, to savor his warmth.

But it was not going to be like that. Danjuro captured my hand and took it away. I raised my head to stare at him in disbelief, but he immediately began to kiss my face, forcing me to close my eyes. I felt him undoing those damned buttons himself, and next second he was pushing me urgently onto the carpet.

His fingers slid immediately into my black moss. He gave a grunt of satisfaction when he found that I was slithery wet, and then to my utter astonishment he immediately heaved himself on top of me and probed at me with his tree. I wriggled beneath him, trying to help, but that obviously was not what he wanted.

"Keep still," he said urgently. "It has been a long time since we were together, wife. I want it to be perfect."

If I hadn't been so shocked, I would have laughed aloud. This uncouth rutting was my husband's idea of perfect? Even the whores in the lattice brothels in Edo would have been insulted had their clients simply walked in and shoved their tree in their black moss. And yet, even as I thought it, I felt desire beginning to rise and take hold.

It had, of course, been months since anybody had made love to me. And I had missed it. But there was something else, as well. The rough feel of his clothes against my naked flesh was intensely arousing. Almost as arousing as the naked need he was showing in wanting me now, this minute. He bit my neck, and I gasped with pleasure. Arched against him, the better to feel his body through his clothes. I tugged and yanked at his shirt until the buttons burst off, and then I thrust my hands inside, running them over his ribs, scratching at his belly. I hissed my pleasure in his ear, and then took that ear in my mouth and bit it, hard. He yowled with desire, and I laughed out loud at his reaction. At the same time, I realized that he was already close to the point of bursting the fruit. He was panting, and his movements were becoming increasingly frantic.

Not yet! I waited until I sensed Danjuro was off balance, and took my chance. I rolled over quickly, gripping his tree as fiercely as I could with the muscles of my sex. I caught a glimpse of his surprised face and then I was riding him entirely to my own rhythm. Fast and then slow. Leaning back so far his tree threatened to pop out of me, and then pushing down so his black moss mingled with mine. When I could stand it no longer, I allowed him to linger deep inside me, all the time grinding my black moss so hard against his flesh that my love button was massaged against him. As my own yonaki erupted, I felt Danjuro tense beneath me and knew I had only just been in time.

The bathroom contained not only a bath, but to my joy a shower over it. I climbed into the tub and let the hot water run over me for many minutes before giving myself a thorough soaping and another rinse. I felt like singing as I wrapped myself in a thick robe. For the first time since I had left Japan, I was truly clean.

Danjuro was calling something to me through the closed door. I thought I must have misheard him, and it was only when he repeated his words that I realized I had not. I walked through to him slowly, still hardly able to believe what he was saying.

"Ryu?" I asked. "Ryu is dead? How? What happened? Did he have an accident?"

Even as I said it, I wondered if he had been captured in another woman's bed—at long last!—and a furious husband had taken his revenge. We had all teased him that it was how he would meet his end.

"No. Not an accident." Danjuro's face was serious. "The doctor said he died of lead poisoning."

"No! How?"

"His kabuki makeup. The doctor said that worn in large quantities for a long time, it was enough for the lead in it to pass through his skin into his body and poison his blood. His art killed him. He would not have wanted to die in any other way."

I wanted to snap that Ryu would not have wanted to die at all, but I was too shocked to speak.

"When did he die?" I whispered.

"A while after you went." Was I imagining it, or did he sound accusing, as if Ryu's death was somehow my fault? "It came as a terrible shock to all of us."

I felt sick as I recalled Ryu's cough, and the way I had shrugged aside the fact that he was getting thin. Should I have done more? If I had insisted he go see a doctor then, would it have saved him? My head said no; my heart said...perhaps.

"He took over your parts, of course," Danjuro said mournfully. "He worked so hard, it was unbelievable. He was determined that the kabuki would not fail just because you had left us."

The remark rubbed salt into my conscience. It stung bitterly. Because of my guilt, I spoke harshly.

"It was all my fault, was it? At least I tried to help Ryu when I was here. I got him some medicine for his cough and tried to persuade him he needed to see a doctor. What did you do? Praised his performances, I suppose? Told him he was working himself to death for the sake of the kabuki and it was all worth it?"

The sarcasm passed straight over Danjuro's head. He glared at me, clearly working himself into a rage. A few years ago, I would have trembled and bowed my head, but now I stared back at him, meeting his gaze without flinching.

"If you hadn't deserted me and gone running back to find Akira when you thought he was in trouble none of this would have happened!" he shouted.

"That's not true. You know it's not."

"Do I?" He stalked forward, pushed his face so close to mine that our noses were almost touching. "Hate is a strong emotion, just as love is. All I know is that you ran away from me as if I was nothing to you. You went back to him. To your lover. I always knew you would. I knew from the start that I would never be able to satisfy you. Nothing I could give you was any more than flower money compared to what you could get from Akira just by opening your legs for him. Once a yujo, always a yujo."

I was frozen with shock. Words fought to get out from beneath my clenched lips, but even in my own mind none of them made sense. My silence clearly infuriated Danjuro still more. He put his hands on my shoulders and shook me so hard that my teeth clicked together.

"You see! You don't even bother to deny it! You're just like your mother. I heard the tales about her. How she rejected the greatest lord in Edo to follow her whims. Would a decent woman have run off with a gaijin? She was a whore, and so are you. If Akira hadn't died, would you have come back to me? Would you?"

He was yelling at me so loudly his words echoed around the bedroom, bouncing off the walls and seeming to strike me with their fury. I stared at him and my shock and hurt died within me, leaving me cold.

"Danjuro," I said coolly. I spoke slowly, carefully, as if I was talking to a dangerous animal that had to be calmed at all costs. "Akira was never my lover. He was my jailer. He kept me in prison until you rescued me. He tortured me in ways you couldn't begin to imagine. I felt I had to go back to the Floating World, but not because of Akira. I was home-sick, so homesick I was making myself ill. Apart from that, I was afraid for Mineko and my sisters in the Hidden House. Listen to me." I paused and took a deep breath, reluctant even now to show weakness to him. "If you had told me just once that you wanted me to stay, I would never have gone back. Never left you for as much as a day. If I didn't love you, would I have crossed an ocean to be back at your side?"

He stared at me, a muscle below his eye working.

"Truly," he said. "You are really a very great actress, Midori No Me. I'd forgotten how gifted you are in the arts of deception. But you will find that a great deal has happened since you ran away from me, and your acting talents no longer matter greatly. Clay-san made it clear some time ago that we were no longer welcome in his theater. But the gods were kind to us. They've shown me the way forward. I no longer have any need to kowtow to the likes of Clay-san, or even a petty merchant like Sato-san. We have a new, powerful patron. A nobleman who is a true patron of the kabuki theater. We're leaving for his home in Boston shortly. Of course you can come with us if you want, you are my wife and your place is with me. But I would not try and force you. If you really wish it, you can stay here in San Francisco, although you may find you have fewer friends here than you thought you had. As you seem to have decided that you can do exactly as you like, I will leave the decision up to you."

He bowed and I thought he was about to say something

else, but he did not. It was only after he had walked out of the room, closing the door with exaggerated courtesy behind him, that I understood that he had been waiting for me to speak. For a while, I was angry with myself for not trying to mend our quarrel, then I realized I had had no words to offer him.

21

A stain on the earth
Is far more obvious than
A stain on the soul

I sat opposite Clay-san and watched his stony expression with hurt concern. We had always been good friends, Clay-san and I. How could I have offended him so when I had not even been in America for many months? Was it suddenly my karma, to upset everybody I cared for?

"Clay-san?"

He stared over my shoulder, his eyes flinty. "What can I do for you, Midori No Me? I hardly expected to see you before the kabuki left for Boston. I believe you're all going very soon?"

"Next week, Danjuro tells me. I've decided I'm going with them." I smiled and shrugged my shoulders. "My homecoming was quite overshadowed by poor Ryu's death, I'm afraid. Danjuro was clearly very upset."

Not at all the truth, but it was as good a way as any of explaining the dark shadows under my eyes to Clay-san.

Danjuro had not returned to our room until very late that night. I waited restlessly for him in the never-quite-darkness from the streetlamps outside; in the hours he had been gone, I had convinced myself that our quarrel had been nothing but a lover's tiff. That we had both been on edge and that it was only natural for our mutual worries to explode into anger. After all, we were both from the flower and willow world, where everybody's emotions always ran high. And of course, I understood that beneath all the bluster, Danjuro blamed himself for Ryu's death. Just as I blamed myself.

We still loved each other. That was all that mattered.

I would welcome him back properly when he came in. He would apologize for his rash words, and all would be well between us again. I was still bewildered by the need for a move to Boston, but did it really matter to me? I understood now that—much as I loved my new country—in my deepest heart, the Floating World would always be my home. In that case, what did it matter if I lived in San Francisco or Boston? Besides, on the voyage back to America, I had had time to think about my mother and father. I had no reason to believe they were not still in Virginia. I knew now that America was a huge county, and that Virginia was further away than I could comprehend from San Francisco—or Boston, I supposed—but for all that, we were still in the same country. I had made my mind up; somehow, I would find them.

The knowledge delighted me.

I was thinking about my parents when Danjuro finally came back. I heard the click of his key in the bedroom door, and I quickly pulled the bedclothes up to my neck. A slow reveal would excite him, I decided. Remind him again—but properly this time!—of all he had missed while I had been away. I lay still, waiting for my moment.

There was no need to see what Danjuro was doing; my ears told me. He heeled his shoes off quickly. His trousers followed, so quickly I guessed he had not bothered with undoing buttons. I smiled to myself in anticipation. His jacket and shirt followed with equal speed. I was about to sit up, to allow the bed linen to slide down my body, when he literally threw himself into the bed beside me. At the same time, he tugged at sheets and blankets, forcing them into a ridge between us to make an impenetrable barrier. Only a few seconds later, he was snoring gently.

I lay back in the uncomfortable Western bed. So much for my careful plans. Danjuro was obviously even angrier with me than I had thought. I wriggled, trying to get myself comfortable, but it was no good. Danjuro's breathing rhythm was ragged and uneven, and I found myself holding my own breath as I willed him to breathe properly. Apart from that, lust gnawed at my belly. I had been looking forward to our reconciliation. So much so that if Neko had not chosen that moment to forgive me, and snuggle up against my back, I would have retreated to the bathroom with my love globes for consolation.

I could not move without making a major disturbance, so instead I lay sleepless and frustrated until the morning light began to show, when I finally fell asleep from sheer exhaustion. I woke barely an hour later and found Danjuro had gone from my side.

Very well. If my husband was determined to sulk, then I would go where I was sure of a welcome. Or so I thought.

"I came to say good-bye to you." I smiled uncertainly at Clay-san. "And Evelyn, of course. I hope she is well?"

His eyes swiveled to look at me full in the face, and I saw such deep anger and—yes, pain—in his expression that I almost jerked back from him.

"I don't know why you came to see me. But I really don't have time to talk."

He stood and walked to the door, holding it open in a brutal signal that I should leave. I sat for a moment, too stunned to even get up. And then all at once, this last—relatively minor—rejection piled on top of everything else and tears welled in my eyes. They stung, and I gasped as they rolled down my cheeks.

What had I done wrong? Why had my whole world suddenly turned to poison in my mouth? As if poor Ryu's death and Danjuro's coldness were not enough, now even the man I had thought of as our first real friend in America was acting as if he hated me.

"I'm sorry," I mumbled. "I just wanted to say goodbye to you."

I got to my feet, but blinded by my own tears I caught my foot in the mat and stumbled. I would have fallen if Clay-san hadn't caught me.

"You're either a far better actress than even I thought you were or you really don't know," he said gruffly and helped me sit down again.

"I don't know anything," I wailed, hiccuping like a distressed child through my tears. "I only arrived back yesterday and everything has changed. Ryu is dead and Danjuro says we're moving to Boston. And now you're angry with me as well."

I blinked the tears away and wiped my cheeks with my hand. Clay-san handed me a large, clean handkerchief and ordered me to blow my nose. I obeyed meekly.

"I know you don't normally drink, Midori No Me," he

said. "But I'm going to have a brandy and I think it would be a good idea if you joined me."

He poured the spirit into two glasses and handed me one. I sniffed it suspiciously and then shrugged my shoulders wearily. He was right. Today I would drink. It seemed to amuse Danjuro to drink this vile stuff, so perhaps it would be good for me as well. I took a healthy gulp and coughed.

"Sip it." I couldn't see Clay-san through my watering eyes, but I could tell from his voice that he was smiling, so I took another very careful sip. Whatever it was, it tasted better than whiskey smelled. I cradled the glass in my hands and focused on Clay-san.

"Please. If I have offended you somehow, at least tell me why."

Clay-san rolled his glass in his fingers and took another mouthful of the brandy before he answered me.

"You don't know about Evelyn?"

Dread grasped my heart with hard, cold fingers. I had thought Evelyn had been distracted when I had seen her last. Had I been so wrapped up in my own plans that I hadn't noticed that my friend needed my help? I had no words and simply shook my head.

"She lost a baby."

I stared at the brandy left in my glass for a long moment and then drained the lot. Held it out for more. "Baby," I repeated dully. "She didn't tell me. I had no idea."

Yet another hurt. Evelyn had been—was—my friend. Yet she hadn't trusted me enough to tell me this. Something clicked in my wandering thoughts and I stared at Clay-san, praying I was wrong.

"Was it Tom's baby?" I asked, more in hope than belief.

"Not Tom's. Ryu's," He said brutally. "She didn't tell

anybody about it. Not even me. When Ryu died, she took it real hard. I wasn't surprised about that. It was easy to see she had a big crush on him. I mean, we were all real sorry; he was a likable kind of guy. But Evelyn couldn't seem to shake it off. I did my best with her. Tried to distract her by pushing her toward Tom." I winced, and he nodded sadly. "Now, of course, I realize it was the worst thing I could have done, but I didn't know at the time. Maybe if I had just let her alone, she would have gotten over it. If she had told me what the trouble was, I would have helped her. Sure, I would have played roasting hell with her at first, but she's my little girl. I would have looked after her. She should have known that. My poor Evelyn."

I heard the pain in his voice and felt my heart ache for him. We both sat silently, the two of us buried in our own grief and guilt. A sudden thought brought me out in gooseflesh.

"Evelyn. She is all right, isn't she?"

"The doctors say she is. Young and strong, they reckon. Once she pulls herself round, she'll be none the worse."

"What happened?" I asked quietly. How polite I sounded! We might have been chatting about a mutual acquaintance, who had suffered a minor accident. "What happened to the baby?"

"She...she got rid of it." Clay-san closed his eyes. He looked ten years older than I remembered him and weary to the heart. "She didn't tell anybody what she was going to do. God knows how she found somebody to do it, but she did. Told me she was going out for lunch with some of her girlfriends and that they might do a little shopping as well so not to expect her back until evening. I was pleased, Midori No Me. I thought she was pulling round at last. I gave her some cash to spend and laughed when she asked for a little more, just in case she found something nice in the shops."

I put my empty glass down. Kneeled at his side, putting my arms around him. He leaned into me as if he was glad of the support, and my guilt increased tenfold. What were my own problems compared to this? He was shaking; I felt him take a deep breath as he tried to get control, but it was useless. His sobs came and I cried with him. He spoke through his tears, his voice hoarse.

"I should have known something was wrong. When Ryu died, she was inconsolable. She wouldn't talk to me, not to anybody. But I thought she was coming around a bit, I really did. I didn't see her when she came back from her shopping trip. She just called out she was worn out and was going straight to bed. When she didn't come down for breakfast, I sent a maid up to ask if she wanted her breakfast in bed. She was down again in a second, her face as white as paper." I closed my eyes; I didn't want to hear this. But Clay-san needed to talk to somebody; I had to listen. It was literally the least I could do. "The girl said Evelyn was still in bed and she was moaning and looked awful. I was up there like a shot, you can bet. Evelyn tried to sit up and when I put my arms around her, she screamed. I still didn't understand until the doctor arrived. He pulled the sheets back from my little girl and she was covered in blood. He wouldn't tell me what was wrong until I shouted at him, and then he took me out of Evelyn's bedroom and spoke to me as if I was a child myself. Told me she was suffering a miscarriage. I laughed at him. Told him he was talking rubbish and that if that was the best he could do, he should get out of my house and I would get a real doctor in. He was a saint, that doctor. He calmed me down and said he was sure. Told me we had to get Evelyn to the hospital straight away. She had lost a lot of blood and was still bleeding."

"I'm sorry, Clay-san," I whispered. Sorry, not just for poor Evelyn, not just for him, but for my own lack of understanding. I had seen Ryu and Evelyn lusting for one another. Seen and dismissed it as not being important. If I had intervened, told Ryu to keep away, would it have done any good? I didn't know. I would never know. Guilt filled me and left me feeling sick. "I am so sorry."

"Not your fault, Midori No Me," Clay-san said gently, and I wondered if he knew how I felt. When he went on, I was sure that he did. "I daresay you saw how Evelyn and Ryu were, same as I did. But if anybody should have done something about it, it should have been me. But I did nothing. Hell, the last man I wanted for a son-law-was a Jap— begging your pardon, Midori No Me. But if Evelyn had trusted me enough to tell me, I would have given in. It wouldn't have saved Ryu, but at least I would still have had my grandchild."

"Yes," I said wearily. So much death; Akira and Ryu and now Evelyn's baby. I was tired all at once; I longed to lay my head on Clay-san's knee and just sleep. But I could not. If I mourned for poor Evelyn and Ryu, what pain was she enduring? I was filled with guilt.

"May I see Evelyn, please?"

"She isn't here."

I lifted my head and stared at Clay-san. He had said she was well. Surely, she was not still in hospital? He patted my shoulder gently.

"She's married, Midori No Me. She married Tom, a month after she lost the baby."

We stared at each other, the knowledge of things that could not be spoken out loud heavy in the air between us.

"He's a good man," he said defensively. "Evelyn told him all about the baby. How she had felt about Ryu. And he said he didn't care. If she was willing to accept him as her husband, then he still wanted to marry her. She agreed, and I believe they are very happy together."

I swallowed. My eyes were burning with the tears I had shed; Clay-san's face was out of focus. It didn't matter. I didn't have to see him to know that he sensed exactly what my own instinct told me. Not now, perhaps not for years, but one day Tom would look at his wife and wonder if she still thought of Ryu. If she still cared more for her lover than she did for him. If she would ever have married him if Ryu had lived. And when that day came, Tom would no longer love his wife. Nor she him, even if she thought she loved him now. The seeds of the cancer were there, and they would grow and grow until there was no happiness for either of them.

Poor Evelyn!

"I am pleased for them both," I said politely. Clay-san avoided my gaze. I changed the subject quickly. "I understand now why the kabuki had to leave your theater. It would have been impossible for you."

"Danjuro didn't tell you?" He sounded startled, and I shook my head, watching him cautiously. "The kabuki left me before Evelyn's miscarriage. It had nothing to do with that."

I frowned, trying to absorb this new information. The brandy I had drunk earlier was making its presence felt, and I found it difficult to concentrate. Clay-san helped me to my feet and sat me back on my chair. We smiled at each other, and I knew that this good man was suddenly deeply embarrassed by the confidences that had passed between us.

"I'm sorry." I groped for the right words with great care. "I don't understand. Danjuro led me to believe that the decision for them to leave had come from you, not him."

"Danjuro hasn't told you about Lilly, then? Lilly Goto?" His words left me bewildered. I shook my head slightly, wondering for a second why the name sounded familiar. Then I remembered. Of course, the half-Japanese gaijin that Tadayo had introduced to us proudly, not long after we had landed in San Francisco. The girl who had annoyed me by being so very rude.

"Lilly? Yes, I've met her. But what's she got to do with it?"

"Ah." Clay-san cleared his throat, his eyes suddenly fixed on his desk. "Well, I guess it's something you need to talk to Danjuro about."

I chose my words with care.

"Things have been...difficult between Danjuro and me since I came back. Apart from the news about Ryu, he hasn't told me anything that has been happening. You were always my friend, Clay-chan. Please, will you tell me what my husband apparently cannot?"

I looked at him appealingly.

"I'm sure there's nothing that he won't tell you himself, when he gets round to it," he said hurriedly. "I guess he was in a real fix when Ryu died. I had persuaded him that he needed to go back to the plays with a decent female lead. Ryu was great—not you, of course, but the ladies loved him and that was half the battle." We both smiled, remembering Ryu's cheeky, appealing grin. "But of course, with Ryu gone there was nobody to take his place. For a while, I thought we were going to have to close the kabuki down altogether, but then Tadayo suggested Lilly might do. You probably know she's the daughter of one of his Japanese gambling cronies. She was born here in San Francisco—her mother's

American. Tadayo insisted she looked a little like you, and seeing as she'd worked in a music hall, singing and dancing, she was used to performing in front of an audience."

"That's hardly the kabuki." I said quietly.

Clay-san shrugged. "I know. I can't say I was happy, but I had to give her a chance. I had no option. After just one performance, I was appalled. She was terrible. She can't even speak Japanese, so they had to cut virtually all your—her—dialogue, so all she had to do was dance and wave her arms about and scream occasionally. And she couldn't even do that very well. She was so over the top, the patrons asked me if this was some new form of experimental theater Danjuro was trying out."

In spite of my horror, I giggled. "What did you tell them?"

"I lied," he said simply. "I said it was, and asked if they would give it a week or two to see how it went. Eventually one of the patrons realized he had seen Lilly performing at a music hall, and that was that. The patrons voted with their feet, and within a month Danjuro was playing to an almost empty theater. I tried to reason with him. But when I told him bluntly that the problem was with Lilly, that she belonged on the music hall stage, not the legitimate theater, he just went off at the deep end. He shouted at me—I have no idea what he was saying, as it was all in Japanese—and that made it even worse. When he saw I didn't understand a word of it, he switched to English, but it was obvious he was deeply embarrassed by his own mistake."

"Yes," I said quietly. "He would have been furious with himself. In Japan, such a thing is called 'loss of face,' and it matters much more than it could ever do in the West. He didn't apologize, I suppose?"

"He certainly did not. He told me that if Lilly wasn't

good enough for me, then none of them were. He was with-drawing the kabuki immediately. I tried to reason with him, Midori No Me. Honestly, I did. Told him we could discuss things later, when we were both calmer. But it was no good. He said his mind was made up. He even told me I would be sorry to lose the kabuki. That nobody would come to my theater if it was gone."

I winced. Clay-san had given us our first chance in America. He had befriended us when nobody else would. We owed him a debt of gratitude so strong we could never repay it. Even as I thought that, I understood that that was a big part of the problem. The great Danjuro—the man who had owned most of the kabuki theater in Edo, who had been the star actor in it, worshipped and recognized by everybody—owed a debt of honor to this gaijin he could never repay. It must have crushed him, made him feel help-less. Lilly, I thought, was no more than an excuse for his anger.

"I am sorry, Clay-san," I said sadly. Suddenly, the gap between our two cultures yawned so widely I could see no way of bridging it.

He smiled at me. "Don't worry. It's forgotten. I don't suppose there's any chance that you could persuade Danjuro to change his plans and stay? If you're back as the female lead, I would be only too pleased to see you all back. And so would the patrons."

"I wish I could. But he won't listen to me. It would be a matter of honor, anyway. He says the kabuki has a new patron, a nobleman, and if he has promised him that the kabuki is to move to Boston, he cannot go back on his word. I'm very sorry."

We were both silent for so long, it became embarrass-ing. Finally, I stood awkwardly.

"I am sorry our farewell has not been happier, Clay-san. Please, give Evelyn my best wishes. I will think about her, often."

He escorted me to the door, put his hand on my shoulder, and held me back for a moment.

"It's none of my business, Midori No Me. But if I were you, I would ask Danjuro if he has any plans for Lilly going to Boston with you."

I shook my head, hiding a smile. What was he thinking of? What would Danjuro want with Lilly when I was back? But Clay-san persisted.

"You need to be real careful about Lilly. As soon as she joined the kabuki she started calling herself the Dragon Geisha."

The absurdity of it lifted my spirits and I laughed out loud. "Did she? And how does she claim that title?"

Clay-san spoke very seriously. "Don't underestimate her. She can't act, but she's far from stupid. She had a hell of a reputation at the music hall for hooking men, bleeding them dry, and then dropping them. As soon as Danjuro took her up, she had a dragon tattooed on her back. It's not a work of art like your tattoo; in fact, hers is a nasty, crude thing. But it's there. You got to remember that nobody has ever actually seen you in Boston, although I'm sure your reputation will have reached that far. If a woman who's half Japanese, who looks a bit like you and who sports a dragon tattoo on her back turns up calling herself the Dragon Geisha, who's going to know in Boston that she isn't you? I might be talking out of turn, but I've heard that she's vanished from sight, so who knows where she is. You take good care of yourself, Midori No Me."

To my surprise, he took my hand and kissed it gently. "You take care of yourself," he repeated.

My thoughts were bitter as I walked back to the hotel. I shrugged Clay-san's concerns about Lilly Goto aside. I wasn't surprised Danjuro had not mentioned her; he was no doubt deeply ashamed of his error of judgment in allowing her to act in the kabuki in the first place. If she was determined to try and hold on to her place in the kabuki and dared to follow us to Boston, I was sure he would simply tell her she was no longer wanted or needed. Rather, I dwelt on poor Ryu, and my dear Evelyn. I should have listened to my instincts about those two. Clay-san had been truly kind, taking the blame himself. But he was wrong. It was my fault that Evelyn had been forced to undergo such heart-breaking loss. Perhaps even Ryu's death was down to me. I should have insisted that he visit a doctor before I returned to the Floating World.

And it wasn't just the horror of death and loss suffered by my two dear friends that finally soured my homecoming for me. Every last coin of the money I had brought back from Edo was gone, spent before we left San Francisco. I had nothing left at all of Akira's treasure but a few loose gems, and those I was determined to hold on to.

I had found all too soon that the savings I had left with Ryu had been spent long ago. Now, word had obviously gotten out that we were leaving, and I began to dread each knock on our door, knowing there would be yet another creditor standing outside. The hotel demanded an amount that made me gasp with disbelief. Costumes had been made and worn and not paid for. Many meals had been taken at expensive restaurants and put on account. Ryu's doctor had been apologetic, but his bill had not been paid.

I turned over his sheets of carefully noted visits and medications and raised my eyebrows in amazement.

"I'm sorry, ma'am." The doctor turned his hat in his

hands nervously. "I know it's a large amount, but at first Mr. Ryu wouldn't tell me exactly what his symptoms were. I was treating him for stomach upsets for weeks. When that didn't work, I thought maybe it was just nervous exhaustion, so I tried giving him tonics. When he did finally tell me exactly what was he was going through, it was too late. I did my best, but there was nothing I could do to save him. I sure hate to ask for payment when my patient has died, but what can I do?"

I found a smile from somewhere and reassured the poor man that it wasn't his fault. Even worse than the doctor's bill, I found that poor Ryu's funeral had gone unpaid, and that was one debt that I was glad to pay. The idea that my playful, wicked Ryu was buried alone and forgotten in cold, foreign soil was very terrible. I hoped that perhaps Evelyn might be able to visit him, but I doubted it.

Danjuro simply ignored it all, as if he was above such things. Not once did he thank me for paying off his debts; he didn't even acknowledge that they existed.

As I walked away from the theater and from my friend Clay-san, the sun hid behind a cloud and with it any pleasure I had left from returning to San Francisco fled as well. Suddenly, I wanted no more than to get away from this place, where everything had gone so very wrong.

To go somewhere I could make a fresh start, yet again. My spirits were lifted by the prospect. I began to smile at Danjuro, and was delighted when he responded with cautious pleasure. My optimism rose still further as I realized that we were talking to each other again. Really talking, rather than simply being polite.

I should, I suppose, have been content to leave the situation as it was. But I could not. My thoughts returned again and again to the conversation I had had with Clay-san about

Lilly Goto. I understood how deeply Danjuro must have regretted hiring her in my – and poor Ryu's – place. But the more I dwelt on it, the less I could understand why he hadn't simply told me about it.

So I asked him. Carefully, as I had no wish to upset the happiness that had come to live with us again.

"Husband, how did the kabuki manage to carry on when poor Ryu died?"

I should have known then that I was treading on dangerous ground. Danjuro stared into space for so long that I wondered if he had not heard me. Finally, he frowned in irritation and knowing him as well as I did, I understood that he was going to pretend he had no idea what I was talking about. So I persisted.

"I mean, where did you find a female lead from? Did one of the other actor's take Ryu's part?"

"Why do you ask? You didn't think about it when you went off and left me, did you? You didn't worry about the kabuki then." He snapped angrily.

At first, I thought he was acting his fury. And very well, as always. Then I looked into his eyes and saw hurt as well as anger reflected back at me.

"My thoughts were with you, always." I said simply. "It was always my intention to come back to you as soon as I could, you knew that. To you, and the kabuki. If I had known how ill Ryu really was, I would have put my own plans aside and stayed with you here." Especially if I had known Lilly was waiting to step into my shoes! Despite my good intentions, I was angry and I forgot my tact. "I'm surprised that you seem to have forgotten my part in making the kabuki a success in San Francisco."

"You made the kabuki a success?" He sounded incredulous. "Have you forgotten that my kabuki theater was the most loved in the whole of Edo? That it took me years of working and careful study to perfect my art while you simply wandered on to the stage and sang a few songs, performed the odd dance? You really think it was you the patrons came to see? I'm sorry that you seem to have risen above yourself. You're wrong, anyway. I had no problems at all in filling your role after Ryu died.."

"Lilly Goto." My words obviously hit home. Danjuro stared at me wordlessly in shock. "Yes, I know all about that. I also know that she was so bad that she nearly ruined the kabuki."

"You know nothing at all." A tic was working under his eye. It made him look as if he was winking, and I almost laughed. But my good humor was crushed when he went on. "You abandoned me. Ryu was dead. If it hadn't been for Lilly taking your place, the kabuki could never have carried on. She barely got the chance to prove herself before Clay-san decided he didn't like her."

I felt absurdly guilty. There was, I supposed, at least a shred of truth in Danjuro's words. If I hadn't felt impelled to go back to Japan, then there would have been no need for Lilly to join the kabuki. I took a deep breath and spoke quietly.

"I am sorry, husband, that you feel like that. I understand now why you felt it necessary to cast Lilly in my place. But why didn't you tell me about her?"

I stared at his face, willing him to understand that this was the question I needed answering.

"Because I knew you would make a fuss about it." He said promptly. "That you would consider another woman could never be good enough to take your place."

I was so astounded that it took a long moment before I

realized that somehow Danjuro had skillfully turned the tables on me.

"That's nonsense." I protested. "Of course I would have understood that you needed a female lead. And all the other kabuki actors are far too masculine to even think about taking the onnagata's role."

Even as I spoke, I realized the truth of my words. The other actors would have been so out of place in a woman's role, the audience would have laughed until they cried. And yet ....

"You should have told me about her." I said again. "I would have understood."

"Would you?" He stared at me curiously. "In that case, why are you making such a fuss about it now?"

For once, I had no answer for him.

22

Winter possesses
Me. Is there to be a spring
To awaken me?

Ironically, in spite of my urgent need to leave San Francisco and its bitter legacy behind me, Boston seemed very unwelcoming. It had none of San Francisco's light and gaiety. It was sober and drab and cold, as were the people, bundled into their autumn clothes. The journey across our new land had taken weeks, changing trains so frequently I lost count. It barely mattered. All of the trains were crowded and uncomfortable, hot at first and then increasingly cold. The food had been the worst I had ever been offered in America. I was appalled to find that I hated Boston on sight, and told Danjuro so in no uncertain words.

"This is our new home," he said impatiently. "You must become used to it. We will be here for a long time. Our new patron has been here for some years. He has made a theater ready for us. A real kabuki theater, Midori No Me. He is a generous man. And a very rich man. The gods have smiled on us." His eyes lit up with delight.

"Who is he, then?" I demanded. "Another merchant, like Sato-san, I suppose?"

Danjuro looked so smug I was determined to provoke him. I was even more annoyed when he simply smiled condescendingly at me.

"You do not know him. But he is no merchant. He is a true nobleman, a daimyo. He has not only money, but tradition and high birth."

"Who is he?" Despite myself, I was intrigued, and also very doubtful. If our new patron was really a daimyo, a noble lord, what was he doing here, in America?

"His name will not mean anything to you. He is Lord Takishima, a nobleman who is a true patron of the arts."

I sucked in a breath. Danjuro was wrong; I did know him. Lord Takishima, the oldest of the nobles I had spoken to on the ship that first bought us to America. I closed my eyes and saw his face clearly in my mind. At the time, I had been deeply puzzled as to why a group of nobles were fleeing Japan. Now, I understood. It had been the topic of much gossip in the Floating World. Lord Takishima and his friends were just as much in exile as Danjuro and I had been. But in their case, they had volunteered to leave behind everything that was precious to them. They were *tozamu daimyo*—outside lords; nobles who had been denied power by the ruling shoguns for hundreds of years. When the gaijin forced their way into Japan, they saw their chance to seize power once again. It was said that these men had decided that the traditional ways would never be strong enough to allow them to regain power in Japan. They wanted to fight fire with fire. To understand the military strengths of the gaijin, and eventually use them to not only force the gaijin out of Japan, but also to win back their place in government.

So they had sailed for America, leaving behind everything that was precious to them. No wonder Lord Takishima was so pleased to have a kabuki theater at his disposal. It would be a constant reminder of Japan, of his home. And to a man of his wealth, it would be nothing.

I was about to tell Danjuro this when I saw his face. He was smiling broadly, and I guessed from the glitter in his eyes that he was thinking of nothing but his precious kabuki. It would hurt him deeply if I told him the truth— that it was not *his* kabuki that had attracted Lord Takishima. Any kabuki theater would have done as well. So I closed the words behind my lips and smiled with him.

He was so much like the Danjuro I had first known in the Floating World that I felt a little of the ice melt from my thoughts. My foolish heart leaped; it must be that there was hope for us both yet. The love that had been between us was too rare and precious to be lost, surely.

"That is wonderful, husband. I am sure the kabuki will be as great a success here as it was in San Francisco."

He straightened his shoulders and raised his chin proudly. "It will be better. We are no longer riverbed beggars. Now, we have a rich and powerful patron. A man of standing. He knows the kabuki well, and is interested in what productions I am going to offer."

I? Instinctively, I was concerned. What about me, the original Dragon Geisha that the audiences in San Francisco had loved? I was about to ask when I saw the good humor fade from Danjuro's face. I realized at once that my expression had given me away. He frowned at me as if I were a child who had been denied a treat for her own good and was about to throw a tantrum.

"There will be many changes from San Francisco." He nodded, his eyes half closed as he looked to the future. "Here, the kabuki will be the true art. I am sure Lord Takishima would have it no other way."

"I am very happy for you, husband." I tried to speak calmly, but my voice was shaking. "Am I to understand that I no longer have a part in your kabuki, then?"

I spoke quietly, my eyes never leaving his face as I watched for his reaction. Perhaps it was because I was watching him so carefully that I saw the extent of the changes in the man I had followed without question halfway across the world. He was still undeniably handsome. But the lean lines of his face were blurred slightly. There were lines across the bridge of his nose that not been there before. His eyes—always so bright, so passionate— were slightly bloodshot and dull. My heart cried out, and without thinking, I raised my hand to stroke his face in tenderness. He was still beneath my touch. My hand moved away slowly as I wondered if the flame of the love that had burned so brightly in the flower and willow world had truly gone forever.

"Is that the real reason why you came back? For the kabuki, rather than me?" Danjuro asked flatly.

"Of course not. That's nonsense." I protested. "I came back to be with you."

"Did you? You are the one who changed everything, Midori No Me. Not me." He said. "You made your decision when you left me, and ran back to your friends in the Floating World. You seem to think that you can just stroll back to me, and take things up where you left off. But when you went, I found that I – and my kabuki – can manage without you. I am going out now, wife. I feel the need for some fresh air."

He turned from me abruptly. But not so quickly that I didn't see the tears that were gathered in his eyes. I called out to him that it was raining, and he needed an umbrella, but he was gone already and did not hear me. I sat with my thoughts, and Neko came and brushed against my face, offering such much comfort as he could.

I put my face in his soft fur and wondered how things had come to go so very wrong.

23

I long to pluck the
Topmost fruit, yet I fear to
Break the living bough

*I*t was a small consolation, but at least our lodgings in Boston were comfortable. The other actors each had a room of their own, but Danjuro and I had what he grandly called a "suite," a large bedroom with its own bathroom and a much smaller room for living in, day to day. The separate room opened on to a large garden, and I was delighted that I would be able to sit in the open air and enjoy the flowers and birdsong.

"Lord Takishima feels it is better for us to be here than in a hotel." Danjuro's mouth turned down at the corners, and I knew he would have preferred the grandeur of an elegant hotel. "As he is paying for it, I suppose it will have to do."

I was not alone in liking my new home. Neko loved it. He had hated the journey to Boston; each train guard had insisted that he had to be put in the luggage van, confined in his box. No matter how often I visited him, he mewled and looked at me piteously. He obviously felt our new lodgings were far superior, and he quickly established his rights to the garden over the local tomcats.

Sadly, I soon discovered that my home was the only consolation I was to find waiting for me in Boston. Danjuro —together with the other actors—spent most of each day away from our lodgings. When I asked him where he had been, what he had been doing, he looked at me as if I was mad.

"I am overseeing the final work on our new theater," he said. "The troupe is working through our repertoire. The final choice for the first play will rest with Lord Takishima, of course, but we want to be sure that everything is ready when he comes to a decision."

I shrugged listlessly. I wasn't just unhappy, I was also ill. I told Danjuro so.

"I'm tired all the time. It's an effort to get out of bed in the morning." That cursed Western bed! I hated it, and longed for a futon. When I told Danjuro that, he raised his eyes to the heavens and told me I should be grateful for a decent place to sleep. "My vital spirit is gone. Even when the rain stops, it seems to me that everywhere is still grey. I have no appetite. When I do eat, I don't enjoy it. If we were still in the Floating World, I would be convinced that a spirit had visited me in the night and sucked all the life from me."

I tailed off, willing him to understand what I could not put into words. I was lonely, that was part of it, for sure. Since I came back from Japan, I had had no word at all from my sisters in the Hidden House. Wearily, I thought that they had forgotten me already in the excitement of their own new lives. Mineko was no doubt so taken up with her new husband that she had no time to spare a thought for her elder sister. Even Evelyn, who I thought was my best friend in this new country, hadn't bothered to write. I didn't waste my breath trying to explain any of that to Danjuro; as I had told my sisters in the Floating World, he carried the kabuki—and Japan—deep in his heart, and it was enough for him.

"Do you have any pain?" he asked, quite kindly. I shook my head. Oddly, I felt that pain would almost have been welcome. If I had felt pain, I would have understood what was wrong with me. As it was, I was bewildered, unable to understand myself.

"Well, we are not in Japan. Spirits do not exist here in America." He chuckled at his own wisdom. "Still, if you are not well, wife, then you must see a doctor. Whatever is wrong with you is obviously a Western malady, so you need a Western doctor."

I shuddered, remembering poor Ryu.

The doctor was not at all what I expected. He was a young man, and very brisk. Before his serious face, my list of symptoms seemed very trivial.

"You have no pains anywhere?" Echoes of my husband! I shook my head. "Very well, Mrs. Danjuro, I will examine you. Please take your clothes off."

"All of them?"

"All of them. And then lay down on the couch."

He turned his back as I disrobed, writing something at his desk and uninterested in my body. It was disconcerting. I had taken my clothes off for so many strange men in my time at the Hidden House, but they had always awaited the sight of my naked body with huge anticipation. This total lack of attention was somehow far more demeaning.

"Ready? Good."

He rubbed his hands together briskly before parting my legs and delving into my black moss. I gasped indignantly.

"Please, Mrs. Danjuro. I am a doctor. It's essential that I examine you properly. I assure you, my interest in you is purely professional."

Finally satisfied with probing my private parts, he moved on to my breasts, squeezing and stroking each one. I heard what he said, but it seemed to me that his examination was far more enthusiastic than was strictly necessary.

Finally, he sat back and steepled his fingers beneath his chin.

"Well, now. Physically, I would say that you're in A1 shape. Nothing to worry about there at all. So perhaps we need to look at the mind."

"Are you saying I have something wrong mentally, doctor?"

This was not at all what I had expected! Had I been right all along; could it be possible that an evil spirit had indeed visited me in my dreams and stolen my vital energy? But the doctor was smiling at me indulgently.

"No, no. Not at all. But I think I may know what the problem is. You're a young and very beautiful woman, Mrs. Danjuro. Does your husband understand that? Is he aware of your needs?"

I was deeply puzzled. My confusion must have shown on my face. The doctor wagged his head from side to side, smiling at me.

"Does your husband appreciate you as he should? Are your relations with your husband all they should be?" When I continued to stare at him blankly, he sighed. "If I may be frank with you, are you intimate with him at night? In bed?"

I felt my face flame. Danjuro had not made love to me

in weeks. At first, I thought it was because he was still angry with me. Then he had taken to going to bed early, claiming he was exhausted. I had begun to question myself, wondering if I no longer attracted him. Me, who had once been able to arouse any patron with no more than a smile! And now this doctor was rubbing salt into my wounds by telling me my "illness" was caused by frustration?

"Yes," I snapped. He seemed to be taken aback by my abruptness. I was pleased.

"Ah. Well. Perhaps then it's just women's problems. Your courses are on time? You have no problems with them?" I shook my head again, honestly this time. "Not that, then. Well, it seems to me that you are basically a very healthy young woman. I'll give you a tonic, which you must take twice a day. Other than that, I suggest you take some exercise. A brisk walk every day will get you out of the house and give you something to do. It'll do you the world of good."

I glanced incredulously out of the window. The rain was streaming down, blown against the glass by a stiff, cold wind. The doctor seemed not to notice.

"Perhaps I'll feel better when the sun shines," I joked weakly. To my surprise, he took me seriously.

"Indeed, you may. Our Boston weather is sometimes difficult to adapt to, particularly for ladies who have been used to heat and sunshine. In any event, if you find that your symptoms don't improve, please do come back and see me. I just I wish all of my patients were as young and healthy as you are!"

I turned my back to put on my clothes, and this time I was sure he was watching me intently. The thought cheered me up greatly.

When I told Danjuro what the doctor had said, he shrugged.

"These Western doctors know little compared to our own men. But I suppose as we are in America, we must heed his words. As it happens, we are to go to the theater this evening. Does that please you?"

"The theater?" I echoed. "But the kabuki isn't ready, is it?"

"No. Not the kabuki. A Western-style theater. We are to be Lord Takishima's guests for the evening. He's arranged everything."

Danjuro was clearly delighted with the daimyo's generosity, but I was nervous.

"He is happy for me to attend?"

"Indeed, he is. In fact, he made a point of asking me to bring you."

I hovered between worry and pleasure. Of course I was delighted, but what if Lord Takishima recognized me from the journey? How was I going to explain to Danjuro how I had never come to mention the meeting to him?

I soon found I had no need to worry. Our new patron's eyes wandered happily over the front of my kimono and finally glanced briefly at my face with no sign of recognition. Once he was satisfied that I was presentable, I was seated at the back of the private box, behind Danjuro and him. And his other guest. The youngest noble from our journey to America. I puzzled for a moment and then his name came to me. Lord Shimazu.

I had no doubts at all that this man *did* recognize me. He smiled at me, his eyes lighting up with interest, and I thought that he was going to speak. Then Lord Takishima claimed his attention, and he turned reluctantly away from me. He had not changed at all in the two years or so since I had last seen him, and I remembered him perfectly. His lean, acetic face reminded me disturbingly of Danjuro when I first knew him. Even though I worried that he might mention our meeting on the ship, I was disappointed that we did not get the chance to speak again. He was undoubtedly an attractive man, but it was not just that that roused my interest. When he inclined his head to listen to Danjuro, or to speak to Lord Takishima, his whole attention was focused on them. It was if they were the most important thing in his world at that moment. I was envious; I wanted that gaze to fasten on me and find me equally fascinating. But even though we did not speak, I noticed with a spark of surprise that he made an error. Danjuro had simply introduced me as his wife. During the interval, when Lord Takishima ordered wine, and drank a lot of it himself, Lord Shimazu politely told the waiter to bring a glass for "Midori No Me-san." I pretended I had not noticed. But I was pleased, all the same.

The performance entranced me. It was the first Western play I had ever seen, but once I got used to the rhythm of the production I decided it was not so different to the kabuki. The thing that did astonish me was the two main actors. Both of them were women! And not only that, I quickly understood that they were each taking two parts; twin sisters at first, and then later—with their hair tucked up and wearing men's clothes—twin brothers. I longed to discuss this with Danjuro, but I was not given the chance.

Lord Takishima, that noted patron of the arts, was obviously not following the action on stage at all. He chatted all the way through, munching on the Western sweetmeats that I knew were called "chocolates" happily. He obviously approved of the women actors. He leered at them to the extent that I was glad the theater lights had been dimmed for the performance. Occasionally, he nudged Shimazu and raised his eyebrows at one or other of the women on the stage. Shimazu smiled politely, but I was sure he was irritated by the interruption. The fact that the women were also acting as men passed Lord Takishima by entirely. When we got back home, I mentioned our patron's behavior to Danjuro, but he shrugged it away.

"His money's as good as anybody's," he said simply. "Besides, once the Japanese community learns that our patron is such a distinguished noble, they'll be impressed."

"I noticed Lord Shimazu found the play fascinating."

"Do not speak of him," Danjuro snapped. His anger was so fierce, I almost jerked back in surprise. "He used to be a great patron of the kabuki in Edo. He came every time we had a new production."

And what was so bad about that, I wondered? I was about to ask when Danjuro answered my silent question. His voice was tight with hatred.

"He was a rich and important man in Edo. I was forced to sit and listen to him, to pretend I was interested in what he was saying. Do you know he had the insolence to try and tell me I should change my productions? Several times he said he had seen the same play performed in the kabuki in Kyoto, and that they had presented it in a different way, one that I might like to consider? How dare he!"

I nodded in understanding. I knew there was no point in arguing with Danjuro when the kabuki was under discussion. Lord Shimazu obviously did not!

Danjuro had taken a great deal of wine, and he was asleep in moments. As he snored, I marveled to myself about the strangeness of karma. How odd that I should have met both nobles before we even landed in America! And stranger still that Danjuro should know both of them already as well. Surely, there must be more than simple coincidence behind it. I tried to put it aside; there was nothing that I, a mere mortal, could do to untangle the puzzle.

Yet still, I wondered.

The next day, Danjuro bought me a bird, in fact, two birds. Both were exactly alike, smaller than the palm of my hand and prettily colored in shades of green and pink. I named them after the twins, Hoshimi and Sayo, and just like the twins I could never tell them apart.

"There, wife. Something to amuse you, apart from Neko." He poked his finger through the bars of the cage and both birds fluttered away from him. "Lovebirds make wonderful pets. I believe with a little patience, it is even possible to teach them to speak."

Lovebirds. Had Danjuro chosen my twins on purpose, to hurt me? I looked at his grinning face and realized he had not even thought of it. In spite of his kindness, I would have liked to have released my caged birds, but I knew only too well that the garden birds, jealous of their lovely plumage, would mob them and they would be dead in minutes.

Neko clearly approved of the birds. He spent hours sitting in front of the cage, his tail twitching every time one of them fluttered. When he dared to poke his paw through the bars, I smacked him and then felt absurdly guilty about it.

Unlike my birds, I, of course, was free. Free to sit in our rooms and read. Play on the wonderful new samisen I had purchased in the Floating World; I was very gentle with it, for fear it might split in the persistent wet weather. I could walk out or sit in the garden if the weather was fine. Talk to my birds. Play with Neko, if he was in the mood. We had an excellent cook, and a maid, and even a gaijin woman who came in to clean for us—all provided and paid for by Lord Takishima—so I had no need to do anything about the house at all. Danjuro reminded me constantly that I had great good fortune; I had nobody to please except myself. He was right, of course, but no matter how often I told myself that, my intense sadness seemed to deepen each day.

As the time neared for the kabuki to open, I sensed his excitement. Perhaps it was contagious, but I felt my own spirits begin to rise. Lord Takishima had clearly enjoyed seeing women perform on the stage, so why would he not approve of a woman in the kabuki? In my dreams, I acted in the kabuki again, and it was so very wonderful that my terrible lethargy began to leave me, at long last. I smiled at Danjuro when he returned home, and I was sure that he noticed and was pleased by the change in me.

I decided it was time I made a real effort. My sun was shining again at last. I would take a bath, and when Danjuro came home I would welcome him as a wife should. I would ensure that he could not resist me. And then, we would talk about the kabuki. About my part in it. I was singing softly to myself as I toweled my hair dry. The door to our apartment opened and closed, and I heard Danjuro moving about.

"Danjuro-san."

I listened, puzzled. Was I hearing things? The voice was soft, but unmistakably feminine. And it was certainly not our maid. Besides, I was sure I had not heard a knock at the door. As I opened the connecting door between the bathroom and our bedroom, I heard Danjuro speak. Loudly.

"Ah, Lilly-chan. Come in. Here you are at last. You remember my wife, of course. You met briefly in San Francisco."

"Of course. Tadayo introduced us." She smiled sweetly.

I felt as if I had been punched hard in the stomach. I was bewildered; Lilly Goto had been left behind in San Francisco. How could she be here? *Why* was she here? And then Clay-san's warning ripped through my thoughts. And almost as disturbingly, I realized that this whole conversation was eerily familiar. I was listening to a few lines of dialogue from a kabuki play, the conversation carefully rehearsed and slightly stilted. The only really strange thing about it was that my husband and Lilly were speaking in English.

I was dumbstruck with shock and disbelief. And above all a very deep jealousy of this woman who was trying to be me. This woman who was *here,* where she had no business to be at all.

"Ah, Midori No Me-chan. There you are." Danjuro smiled widely. Odd; if he was so very pleased to see me, why, I wondered, did I feel as if I was the stranger in the room? "We have a visitor. No doubt you remember we spoke about Lilly before we left San Francisco, and I'm sure you remember Tadayo introducing her to you."

Lilly was bowing repeatedly. And very clumsily. I stared at her wordlessly and felt a deep stab of anger; how dare she stroll into our home as if she belonged here, and was sure of her welcome? I felt the bones in my neck grind together as I turned to stare at Danjuro.

"Lilly. Yes." My voice was very level; I was amazed at my own composure. "Of course, she took my place in the kabuki briefly while I was in Japan. After poor Ryu died."

Danjuro was smiling broadly; what an excellent actor my dear husband was! Pain gripped my stomach so fiercely I almost retched. My lethargy vanished in a flash as apprehension surged through my veins. Lilly was here, yes. But *why?* I was about to demand an explanation from Danjuro when Lilly forestalled me.

"I was very honored when Danjuro chose me to act in the kabuki," Lilly chirped up happily. "I guess it was lucky that I was available to help him out."

She smiled at us both, clearly unconcerned by the tension that was almost heating the air between us.

"It has been interesting meeting you again, Lilly-san. But as you can see, I'm not yet dressed from my bath. Perhaps you could go now?"

I spoke through clenched teeth. I wanted this bobbing, smiling intruder out of my bedroom. Now. And even more did I want her out of our life.

"Oh, sure." Lilly's smile never faltered for a second. I was surprised; I had half expected her to smoke and catch fire from the intensity of my anger. "I'll see you later."

I knew the words were aimed at Danjuro, not me.

"What is she doing here?" I demanded angrily. Danjuro shrugged sulkily.

"It's nothing to do with me at all. Our new patron is interested in her."

"Is he? I'm surprised a man who has the taste and refinement to sponsor the kabuki is also interested in the music hall. I don't believe you. I think she's just chased after you here." I said bluntly. I rather thought Danjuro looked pleased at the idea. I wanted to slap him.

"That's nonsense." He scoffed. "You're just jealous of her, because you thought nobody would be able to take your place when you took it into your head to go back to Japan and left me to cope on my own."

I took a deep, steadying breath before I answered.

"I'm so sorry, husband, that my actions put you in such a

difficult situation." I spoke sarcastically, but Danjuro seized my words and turned them against me.

"So you should be. You left me in San Francisco for months, just so you could run back to your friends in the Floating World, and then you marched back into my life as though you expected to find nothing had changed. If it hadn't been for Lilly, we could never have carried on. And while we're on the subject, just how did you get all that money that you bought back with you?"

"What?" I knew I was shrieking, but I couldn't help it. The injustice of his words maddened me. "You know where the money came from. Akira left it to me in his will. There would have been more, but I felt I had to share it with the other geisha from the Hidden House. You should be grateful I had it. I spent every coin I had clearing your debts."

"Ah. Your friends. Of course. The other...geisha. I imagine they were so very pleased to see you back. I can just see all of you huddled together in the bath, reminiscing about old times. Chatting about all your old lovers. Did you bring me into the conversation, I wonder? Or didn't I measure up to them?"

He stared at me, his face working. I didn't need to hear him say the name to know what he was talking about. Akira. Always Akira. I searched for the words to tell him that he was wrong. That it hadn't been like that. Not now, not ever. But I didn't get the chance.

"Don't bother to lie to me," he snarled. "You're right about one thing, Midori No Me. You are a far better actress than Lilly ever will be."

My anger boiled over into action. I darted across to him and grabbed him by the lapels of his coat, shaking him with all my strength. It was like trying to rock an iron girder.

"How dare you?" I shouted into his face. "How dare you compare me to that...that creature? She can't act. She can't sing. She even stole my name! Calls herself the Dragon Geisha when she can't even speak Japanese. And how dare you tell me that it was my fault that she took my place in the kabuki?"

For a moment, I thought he was about to strike me. I flinched, but did not back down. We stared at each other, panting. I looked into Danjuro's eyes and saw the man I loved looking back at me. Did I imagine it, or was it tears that made his eyes so bright?

Very slowly, as if I was calming a wild beast, I raised my hand and stroked his cheek. Danjuro turned his head and licked the length of my little finger. His tongue found my palm and lingered there.

"Ah." Not a word, more of a release of breath. Suddenly, I was hungry. Not for food, but for my husband. I thought I saw him nod slightly, but I could not be sure as I was already raising my head to find his lips. I slid my arms around his neck, sliding against him and rubbing my cheek against his face. He needed to shave; the roughness of his skin was immensely arousing.

I had no warning. His hands slid around my waist, dragging me toward to him. His teeth bit my neck, hard enough to make me moan. In a flash, Lilly—and our quarrel—were forgotten.

Danjuro slid to his knees before me, parting my robe with his face. His lips probed my black moss, his tongue sliding into my sex as easily as if we had never been cold to each other. I exhaled noisily and then screamed out loud as his tongue found my love bud and nipped it gently with his teeth. I grabbed his head and forced him further into me.

I would have been overjoyed if he had sought the seed

with me for hours, but he did not. After a few moments, he pulled his head away and staying on his knees, pulled me down to face him. Danjuro had long legs; kneeling, we were much of a height. He was smiling at me, his lips parted and I saw a thread of saliva, thickened with my own juices, joining his teeth. For a moment, I fancied myself a morsel of food, caught between his teeth, and I shuddered with delight at the notion.

I was about to speak, but he shook his head.

"No." His voice was throaty. Just the one word, and in the midst of my arousal, I had no time to wonder what he meant. It didn't matter, anyway. I leaned against him, pushing aside his robe and rubbing him with my breasts. I slid down, finding his tree and taking it in my mouth. Let him say no now! But he did not. He groaned, and thrust into me until his tree filled my mouth. I gulped his flesh, determined that not a shred of him would go from me.

Danjuro arched his back into me, hanging onto my back with his hands. Perhaps it was the heat from his palms, but I felt my dragon warm everywhere he touched. It had been quiet for so long, I had thought it tamed. Now I knew differently. It distracted me, and I realized suddenly that Danjuro was panting and thrusting at me violently. He was close—far too close—to bursting the fruit.

I pulled my head back, allowing his tree to slip out of my mouth. When only the hood was left, I allowed it to linger, roaming my tongue around it softly. Danjuro hissed with pleasure and I lifted my head, looking at him, my face almost touching his.

He lay back, watching me. Just as he used to when I went to him in the kabuki. Then, I had been his willing slave. Now, it was different. I paused, asking myself what I wanted. The answer wasn't at all difficult to find.

I threw my leg across him, and lowered myself on his tree of flesh as slowly as I could stand. When I was sure that he had no more to give, I began to move up and down; barely raising myself up at first, and then with increasing motion as my need arouse. Danjuro put his hands on my waist, and supported me. When I could take no more and felt my yonaki approaching, I leaned forward and bit his lips, hard.

We burst our fruit together; I felt his seed hot inside me and screamed out loud with pleasure.

When I had cooled a little, I propped myself on my elbow and watched Danjuro's face. He was sinking into sleep rapidly, but I nudged him back to awareness with my elbow in his ribs.

"Tell me, Danjuro. Why is Lilly really here? *Did* you invite her to come?" I demanded.

I wasn't at all sure if Danjuro was feigning sleepiness or if I had truly worn him out. Either way, he spoke drowsily.

"I told you. It was nothing to do with me. Lord Takishima insisted that I send for her. In fact, he made it a condition of sponsoring us. He saw her act in the kabuki in San Francisco and he's taken a great fancy to her, so he thinks the patrons in Boston will love her as well. He doesn't care that she doesn't speak Japanese. He says it doesn't matter. I kept meaning to tell you, but things were so good between us again, I honestly didn't want to upset you."

He turned over and was asleep in seconds. I lay at his side and stared at the ceiling, listening to the rain falling outside. It found an echo in my heart. If Danjuro was speaking the truth I knew that Lilly had stolen my place in the kabuki, and there was nothing I could do about it.

Although that barely mattered, as long as that was all that Lilly had stolen.

24

Memories can be
More pleasant than the present.
The past is perfect

On reflection, I decided that I might as well forgive Danjuro for Lilly's sudden appearance. After all, neither he nor I had any choice in the matter; it had not been his decision to bring her to Boston. And if his kabuki depended upon it, then he would never deny his patron anything. I shrugged her aside as a relatively minor irritation. I was here with him; what power to interfere in our lives could this so-called Dragon Geisha have?

Besides, after our passionate lovemaking, I was smugly sure that things were right between us again. Whenever he was not occupied with the final arrangements for the kabuki, Danjuro came to our bed early these days. And when he did, it was to reach for me eagerly. I said nothing about Lilly, or her place in the kabuki. The time would come—and I hoped very soon—when I would persuade Danjuro to set her aside. I was sure that once Lord

Takishima saw me act in the kabuki, he would recognize that Lilly was nothing more than a false and pitiful imitation of the true Dragon Geisha.

But I had reckoned without fate.

The day before the kabuki was to open, I woke late. Danjuro had been restless, and as a result I had had little sleep. He was gone before I opened my eyes. I stretched and swung my legs out of bed, and suddenly the room was spinning around me. So violent was the motion that I felt nauseous; I clutched the sheets to stop myself falling to the floor. I must have made a noise, as our maid came in and helped me to lie down again. And that was the last thing I really comprehended.

Life took on the dreadful quality of an unending nightmare. Every time I sat up, the room rocked violently around me. I could not eat, but I had a raging thirst. When I drank, I immediately vomited it back again. If the bed covers were pulled around me, I was too hot. When I kicked them off, I shivered with cold. And worst of all, I had no balance at all —I, who had once danced with so much grace that my feet barely kissed the floor. When I needed to pass water, I had to ask the maid to bring me a chamber pot. I wept with the humiliation of it.

Faces came and hung over me. The doctor—he who had so much enjoyed poking at my private parts—came and barked questions at me. I decided he was trying to hurt me and answered him in Japanese. He left bitter powders for me to take that made me want to vomit even more. Danjuro appeared often, his face unreadable. When I put out my hand to touch him, his flesh was as insubstantial as water. I was sure that Lilly came and leered at me. I screamed at her to leave me alone, and she vanished. Even Lord Shimazu haunted my dreams, and oddly he was more real than the rest of them. I thought he sat on my bed and laid cool fingers on my brow, but I knew it was all my imagination.

I had no idea how long I was ill. Day and night melted into one long fever-ridden lifetime. My mind wandered; I was sure I was back in the Hidden House, gossiping with the other geisha. Eventually, even that consolation was denied to me; I became convinced that Akira lay beside me as I slept.

I knew I was beginning to get better when I saw Neko crouching beside my lovebirds, putting a crafty paw through the bars of their cage. I called to him to leave them alone, and he immediately came and jumped onto my breasts and butted his head against my chin.

"How long have I been ill?" Danjuro sat beside me, staring at me. It was nighttime, and he had been drinking. I had to turn my head aside from the whiskey stink of his breath.

"Nearly a month."

I gasped. "No! It can't be so long."

But he insisted it was.

"The kabuki. I missed your opening." That suddenly seemed more important than anything. "Did it go well?"

I hoped he was going to say that Lilly was dreadful, that the patrons had seen through her clumsy performance, but he did not. His eyes gleamed happily.

"It was wonderful." He was on his feet, striding about with excitement. I smiled for him, in spite of my own disappointment. "Lord Takishima was delighted with us. We've been playing to a full theater for every performance since."

He sat down again on the bed and his weight tipped me slightly. I winced as my sore chest hurt.

"Ah, I'm sorry." He shifted again and I tried not to groan as the pain grew worse. "I've been sleeping in one of the other rooms since you've been ill. I think perhaps I should stay there for a while, until you're properly well."

I wanted to protest that I would be all the better for having him at my side, but my ribs and stomach hurt so much, I gave in and agreed.

It was wonderful being able to stand and walk again. The doctor visited and I apologized for shouting at him. He shrugged off my apologies.

"Luckily, I don't speak Japanese, so I have no idea what you said." He smiled.

"What was wrong with me?" I asked curiously.

"You had a severe fever. I thought at first it was cholera, but fortunately it wasn't. You would have been dead if it was," he said bluntly. I shuddered and gave thanks to Baizenten for my recovery. "Now, you need to eat. If you feel you are up to it, you can take a little exercise. Drink plenty of milk, that will do you good."

I pulled a face. I had never tasted milk until we came to America, and I didn't like it all. Tea, I decided, would be much better for me.

When he went, I swung my legs out of bed and walked slowly and carefully to the bathroom. I have never enjoyed a bath more.

I didn't share my plans with Danjuro. I wanted it to be a surprise for him. How delighted he would be when he found I had made my own way to the kabuki!

The carriage dropped me off outside the theater. Once inside, I stared around curiously, disappointed. Danjuro had said that his patron had made him a true kabuki theater, but to my eyes this was simply a Western theater decorated with vaguely Japanese looking hangings and bits of furniture. To honor the kabuki, I was wearing a kimono and full geisha makeup. I felt disconcertingly out of place, as though it was me who was the imposter.

I scurried to a box at the side of the stage, aware that the other theatergoers were staring at me with undisguised interest. It didn't matter. The kabuki captured my heart at once, as it always did. Lilly was better than I had expected, which annoyed me. I understood at once that she had obviously simply learned her lines without understanding what the words meant. Her accent was terrible, but the audience didn't notice. I was amazed that most of them were gaijin, with barely a sprinkling of Japanese. Danjuro was superb, as always. I smiled into the darkness, proud of my husband.

I lingered in my box after the play ended, caught up in the magic of it. Eventually, I followed the rest of the audience into the lobby, surprised that so many people were still left. I smiled to myself as I saw that many of the patrons looked at me curiously; I guessed they were wondering who I was, why I was there. They didn't bother to lower their voices, obviously assuming I spoke no English.

"Is she something to do with the kabuki, do you think?" A richly dressed gaijin woman spoke to her companion, another woman. "I've heard the delicious Danjuro has a wife tucked away somewhere. Do you think that's her?"

"Can't be." The response was prompt. "I heard his wife is old and ugly and that he only tolerates her for her money. She's supposed to be as rich as sin. Probably one of those arranged marriages they go in for in Japan, and now that he's got her he's stuck with her."

"Shame. Who's this one, then? Mistress, maybe?"

The other woman snickered, putting her gloved hand in front of her mouth.

"If she is, you've got to admire Danjuro's nerve. Everybody

knows Lilly, the one who calls herself 'Dragon Geisha,' is his mistress. My God, if he's got two of them on the go and a wife as well, I'd like to know where he gets his energy from!"

Both women giggled and passed from my hearing.

I stood as the audience surged around me. Instead of going out of the main entrance, I turned and pushed my way in the opposite direction, behind the stage. I walked blindly, instinct carrying me forward. The layout was the same as Clay-san's theater; I knew my way. Voices grew louder as I walked down the main corridor; Japanese and English mingled. The door to the main dressing room opened at my touch.

Nobody noticed me for a moment. Then Tadayo glanced toward me, and his mouth sagged open. His hand went up sharply, although I could not tell if the gesture was a warning or to tell me to go away. It didn't matter. I had seen enough.

Danjuro was standing opposite Tadayo. He had a glass in one hand, and his other arm was wrapped around Lilly. She was leaning against him, her head on his chest, looking up at him adoringly. As I watched, she went up on tiptoe and presented her lips to him. Danjuro dipped his head and kissed her lingeringly, his arm tightening around her waist, pulling her against him.

They were the last ones to see me. I felt the ripple of shock pass around the room as the other actors followed Tadayo's gaze. The conversation faltered and died, but Danjuro and Lilly were so wrapped up in each other it was only when total silence fell that Danjuro broke the kiss and glanced up.

I waited until he had taken a good look at me before I turned and walked away. Fool that I was, even then I expected him to run after me, to shower me in apologies, to beg me to forgive him.

But he did not.

I took a cab home and sat and waited for him until the early hours of the morning. Eventually, I understood that he was not going to come home.

25

*Plums shed their fruit to
The fury of the storm. The
Earth below is blood*

The night was retreating into that curious light where darkness reluctantly gives way to true daylight when I heard the door open. I was slow to rise; I had been sitting for a long time and my bones were stiff. When I saw who had come in, I stayed where I was.

Lilly obviously didn't see me. She walked over to the bird cage, and both birds fluttered away from her, thrown into a panic by her silent approach.

> *"She's only a bird in a gilded cage,
> A beautiful sight to see.
> You may think she's happy and free
> From care,
> She's not, though she seems to be."*

She sang the words gently, and her voice was soft and surprisingly sweet now that it was not trying to fill a theater.

"Take them as my parting gift to you." She jumped and put her hand to her heart in a theatrical gesture of surprise at the sound of my voice. "They will soon get used to you. After a while, you will find you can let them out to fly around the room. But you must always make sure there are no windows open. If they get out, the other birds will kill them."

I expected her to stutter out her excuses. To beg me to forgive her—and her lover. To tell me why she—and not Danjuro—was here. But she shocked me.

"Is that how you feel?" She turned her head and stared at me. "That something as lovely as you are will never be tolerated by ordinary people? That they would be jealous of you? That's you, isn't it? A bird in a gilded cage."

I poked my own finger through the cage bars and stroked the nearest bird gently. It cooed and rubbed its head against my nail.

"Is that what I am? A prisoner?" I said softly.

I thought about it, and realized that she was right. I had always been a prisoner. In the Hidden House, of course. And even more so when Akira had taken me. And now I understood that even the freedom I had thought I had found with Danjuro was no more than an illusion. But I had no intention of sharing that insight with Lilly.

"Did Danjuro send you here? Was he afraid to come and face me himself?"

"No. He didn't know I was coming here. He would have forbidden me to come if he had known. I left him sobbing his heart out."

I stared at her stonily. "Perhaps he should have thought

twice about taking you as his lover if he's that sorry about it. So why have you come to see me?"

If I had been surprised to find her here, it was nothing to the shock I felt at her words now.

"Danjuro says you have no feelings. That you don't care about anybody."

I shook my head. "I loved him," I said tightly. "He was my life. It's not me who changed, it's him."

"Is that what you really think? I always thought he was wrong about you, but I guess he wasn't." Her voice was hoarse with emotion. "Well, I care about him. He's mine now, and I'm going to keep him. That's why I came here, to tell you that. He thinks you'll forgive him if he crawls to you. That you'll take him back. But that's not going to happen. I'm not going to let it happen. You've never cared about him, not like I do. You just used him, that's all."

I had a sudden recollection of Clay-san warning me about Lilly. What was it he had said? Be careful of her. She's far from stupid. She had a hell of a reputation at the music hall for hooking men, bleeding them dry, and then dropping them. And she was accusing me of using Danjuro! But I was not going to argue with her. There was no point. All that had been wonderful between Danjuro and me was dead, and the dead can never be made to live again.

"My bags are packed. You can tell Danjuro that I no longer have any part in his life," I said quietly. A thought struck me, and I put my hand on her arm. Lilly stared at it as if I might try to hurt her. "But before I go, will you do one thing for me? May I see your dragon?"

She licked her lips, staring at me warily. Then shrugged. "Why not?"

She unbuttoned her blouse and turned her back to me, shrugging the silk away from her shoulders. I stared at her tattoo curiously, wondering how she had ever come to think that this ugly thing could enhance her body. It was a clumsy creature, far smaller and less colorful than my tattoo, and looked to my eyes more like a seahorse than a dragon. It had no enchantment at all. I ran my finger around it and watched as Lilly's flesh rippled in distaste at my touch.

"Thank you." I stood back quietly. Watched as she fumbled her blouse buttons back up.

"I'm never going to match you, am I?" She spoke sadly, and against all odds, I felt pity for her.

"No," I said simply. "The man who put this dragon on my back loved me after his fashion." Odd that I should acknowledge that now. "He wanted to mark me as his property, but that is no way to keep love. Danjuro loved me as well, once, and I loved him. But there is no way back for him and me now."

I walked away from her and went and sat in the kitchen, waiting until I heard the door close when she left. Then, I picked up my suitcase and samisen. Neko would just have to follow at my heels, as he had done in the Floating World.

I stepped outside and walked away without a backward glance.

26

The threads of life do
Not make a pattern that I
Find easy to know

It had stopped raining, but the puddles still lay everywhere. Neko picked his way on fastidious paws. I walked quietly, my mind still and clear. At the first shop we came to—a stationery store—I walked inside and waited until another customer had been served.

"Help you, ma'am?" The shopkeeper smiled at me, and I regretted that I had no use for his wares.

"Could you tell me where the Japanese quarter is, please?"

He blinked at me, clearly surprised, and scratched his hairy arm while he thought about it.

"You mean the place where all the Jap immigrants flock together?"

I nodded. He obviously didn't mean to be rude, and I needed to know.

"Well, I guess that would be around the Porter Street

area. But I don't think it's somewhere that a lady should be going on her own, if you don't mind me saying so."

"Thank you. Is it far?"

He shook his head at my stubbornness and then shrugged. "You couldn't walk. If you really want to go there, you need to take a cab."

Mentally, I counted the money in my wallet. I had a couple of dollars and some change. It would be enough. I hoped.

I knew the gods were smiling on me when a cab idled past as soon as I walked out of the shop.

A gang of half-naked Japanese children watched me climb out of the cab, their eyes huge with interest as they saw Neko.

"Hello." I squatted down to their level. "I need somewhere to stay. Do you know anybody who wants a lodger?"

Instinct had made me speak in Japanese. The children glanced at one another and then stared at the eldest boy, who must have been all of five, waiting for him to speak. He frowned importantly as he stood up.

"I might do. Li-san's eldest daughter married last week, and so she has a room spare. Would you like to talk to her?"

"Yes please."

As my hands were full, the child grabbed a fold of my skirt and tugged me importantly down the street and into a side alley. The rest of the children followed at a respectable distance behind us, giggling and nudging one another.

If Li-san was surprised to find a Japanese-speaking gaijin in her house, she showed no sign. She did indeed have a room to spare, and would be pleased for me to have it. The room and my food would be five dollars a week.

"I have no money." I said, and watched her face fall. "But I can pay you with this."

I reached into my purse and slid my fingers into the small leather pouch containing the few gems I had managed to hold on to after clearing Danjuro's debts in San Francisco. I had no need to look; I found the gem I wanted by feel. I handed the flawless pearl to Li-san reluctantly. She rubbed it cautiously against her teeth, feeling for the slight grittiness that told her it was a genuine pearl.

"A month?"

I shook my head. The pearl was worth hundreds of dollars.

"As long as I want to stay," I said firmly. Even as I said the words, I found myself rejoicing at the knowledge that suddenly my time, my life, was my own.

Li-san slipped the pearl into her obi and nodded.

My room was tiny. There was a futon on the floor and hooks on the wall. When I put my suitcase and samisen case down, it was crowded. Supper was rice and a few vegetables. It was delicious and I cleaned my bowl.

I slept well until the early hours when Neko yowled to be let in and—clearly pleased with himself—presented me with a fat, dead rat. I threw it out of the window by its tail and was barely surprised when there were a few shreds of meat in everybody's rice bowl later.

Li-san asked me nothing about myself. Her children—and she seemed to have many—were far less polite. They chattered to me constantly, demanding to know if I was really Japanese. Why was I here? Was I going to stay for long? I told them, laughing, that I was a princess who had escaped from a terrible dragon and that I was hiding here. Even as I said it, I thought wryly that it was not so far from the truth.

Without thinking about it, I switched from Japanese to English. The children stared at me in blank puzzlement, and I realized that none of them—not even the two youngest who told me proudly they had been born in America—spoke a word of English. I switched back to Japanese quickly and apologized to Li-san for my mistake.

"You speak good English?" she asked. I smiled.

"Yes. I learned in Edo in the first place."

"You can read it as well?"

"Yes."

If I was surprised by her sudden interest in me, I was even more surprised when she handed my pearl back to me.

"My children need to learn to speak English. If they do not, then they will never leave this place." She gestured with her hands, and I understood she meant this area of Boston. "It's too late for me, I'm too old to learn. But they are clever children. Will you teach them to read and write English in return for your room and food?"

"Of course."

For the first time, I thought kindly of Akira. He had made me learn English so I could translate for him in his dealings with the gaijin. He would, I thought, have been deeply amused if he knew what use I was making of it now.

Our schoolroom was the dusty yard of Li-san's little house. I scratched letters in the dust with a stick, doing my best to make a game of it. And day by day, my class grew until the children were packed in like rice grains in the bowl. Some of the parents were too poor to pay with money. Those who could afford a few cents paid proudly. Those who could not gave Li-san presents of rice and a little dried fish. She was overjoyed and, I swear, grew a couple of inches in height with pride at her gaijin lodger who had somehow turned out to be a sensei.

And I soon found my language skills were in demand

elsewhere. A local merchant approached me shyly, clutching an official-looking letter. Could I translate it for him? It was from City Hall, and he was deeply alarmed by it. It was nothing he needed to worry about, I explained, but it did need a reply. Would he like me to go with him to City Hall? He was almost in tears of gratitude, and when the problem was resolved, he pressed a couple of dollars into my hand. After that, I translated regularly for local merchants, and I soon found I had quite a stash of money in my samisen case.

It came as a surprise to me, but when I thought about it I realized that I was happy. I was free. I had no one but myself to please. And for the first time since I had walked out of his life, I allowed myself to think about Danjuro. Did I still feel the pain of losing him? Yes, but it was no longer so bitter. Did I still love him? I had to think carefully about the answer to that one, and I sighed as I guessed it meant that I did not. I stared at my bare wall and realized I could no longer remember his face as it had been the last time I saw him. The Danjuro I did remember was the man who had risked his life to snatch me from Akira, and I understood sadly that that was the man I had loved. The Danjuro that Lilly had stolen from me was no more than a pale shadow of *my* man. I could not yet forgive them, but perhaps that would come.

Perhaps.

27

Birds should sing from joy
Of living. Not because they
Escape from their cage

*L*i-san listened carefully as I read the newspaper article out loud to her. War. With every day that passed, it seemed it was becoming more certain. The knowledge troubled me greatly. War between different nations was bad enough, but I could not comprehend how terrible it would be when a country was so divided it had to fight against itself.

Li-san seemed unconcerned. She pulled at her earlobe and shrugged when I finished the article.

"Typical men. They always have to find something to squabble about. Still, it might do us some good. If there's going to be a war, then there will be a demand for men who can work with their hands. I daresay my husband will do well out of it."

I stared at her in surprise. Li-san had never mentioned a

husband, and I had assumed she was a widow. She grinned at my expression, obviously reading my thoughts correctly.

"My husband goes where the work is. It's been over a year since I saw him last. But he sends me money regularly, so I know he's alive and well. He's a clever man. He can read and write very well, but he knows I wouldn't be able to read a word, so he doesn't bother sending me a letter. He can turn his hand to almost anything." She beamed, clearly proud of her husband.

Intrigued, I asked, "How did you all come to be here, in America?"

"It was his idea. In Japan, we were never well off. His parents were very poor, and they couldn't afford to buy him a place to learn a trade so he had nothing and nobody to say that he could do this and that. Because of that, he had to take any job that was offered and work for whatever wages he could get. We lived in a shack that nearly fell to pieces every winter. My husband's cousin found his way here, and we heard that he was doing very well for himself, so we saved as best we could, hoping to follow. We would never have managed it if we hadn't had a stroke of very great fortune. One day, I was out cutting reeds to repair our hut and I heard a baby crying. It was a little girl, a newborn I thought. I couldn't bear to leave her to die on her own, so I took her home. My husband just shook his head at me—yet another mouth to feed. But it all turned out well in the end. I had given birth to my second son not long before, and I had milk enough for her as well. And then I heard from a neighbor that a very well-off woman in a nearby village had given birth to twins—a boy and a girl. As you know, it's very unlucky to have twins, so her husband had given orders that the girl child was to be taken away and exposed."

I nodded, and we were both silent for a moment,

saddened by the fate of so many unwanted girl babies. Li-san went on briskly.

"Anyway, the neighbor said that she had heard that the woman didn't really want to part with her daughter. She had spent many years unable to have children, and had come to think she was barren, so to her twins were no misfortune at all. I wrapped the girl child up in a clean cloth and went to see her mother. After all, the worst she could do was to turn me away. But she didn't. I could see she was delighted that I had found her baby, and that she was alive. She called for her husband, and he agreed that the gods had decided the baby should live and be returned to them, so that was it. The woman didn't have enough milk to feed both babies, so she asked me if I would nurse her daughter along with my own son. When she was weaned, I was given more gold than I had ever seen in my whole life. It was wonderful. We decided at once that we would spend the money on our passage here. If the gods were pleased to save the baby's life, then surely they would also be pleased to help us in our new life. And as you can see, they were."

She stared around her modest home with huge pride. "Now, I have all this. My children are fed and clothed. And thanks to you, they can now speak English. They will have a good future here."

I was pleased for her, and said so.

"For us, it is a wonderful home. Compared to what we had in Japan, it's luxury beyond belief. But you will not stay with us much longer, will you?"

"Are you tired of having me as a lodger?"

"Not at all." She peered into my face, her expression serious. "You bring great honor on to our house. But this place is not for you."

I shrugged helplessly. Compared to the Hidden House,

Li-san's house was a hovel. But it was clean and I was happy here, teaching the children. I was about to tell her that when she shook her head.

"When you first came to us, you were hurting. Here." She made a fist of her hand, and placed it between her breasts. "Life had not been good to you. You were tired, and full of sorrow. But as time has passed, you have healed. I have seen it with my own eyes. Now, your heart is well again. You do not belong with us, Midori No Me-chan. You are too clever and too beautiful to spend your life here."

Her words reminded me of Lilly, and I sighed.

"I like being here," I protested. But even as I spoke, I knew Li-san was right. I still enjoyed teaching the children, but I knew in my heart that the life I was leading was no longer enough. I itched to be out in the world again. To see whether my healed wings would carry me. *Where* they might carry me. And lately, I had begun to realize that I knew exactly where I wanted to be. What I wanted to do.

The kabuki. Always, the kabuki. It had called to me from the first performance I had ever seen, and now it was calling to me alluringly, demanding me back again.

Li-san smiled at me and bowed, leaving me alone with my thoughts.

I sat and plucked out a melody on my samisen. My thoughts chased around my head like bees flocking to flowers. And slowly, I understood that I already knew what I had to do. And I would do it, because I was the Dragon Geisha, and I had only myself in the whole world to please. But not for the first time did I regret leaving Mineko a world away in Japan, with her new husband. Everything would have been so much easier, so much better, if she had been at my side. She was my sister and I missed her terribly.

The clerk at City Hall—where by now I was a regular

visitor—was very helpful. It took him no time to find Lord Shimazu's address for me. It had to be Lord Shimazu— there was no other who would understand. I had watched him at the theater, when Lord Takishima had been so bored with the performance. Shimazu had concentrated on every word, every gesture, on the stage. If he loved Western theater so much, then how much more must he care about the kabuki? I remembered Danjuro's fury that Shimazu dared to think himself such an expert that he could inter- fere, and knew I had to be right.

Standing in front of his door, I took three deep, delib- erate breaths. It had no doorbell, or door knocker, and oddly that raised my spirits. Traditional Japanese houses might have a bell hanging outside, but otherwise one knocked on the door to be admitted. So I did knock. Quite loudly.

"Yes?" The Japanese manservant who answered the door looked me up and down coolly, clearly assessing the worth of my kimono to the last cent.

"I wish to see Lord Shimazu."

The servant should have been an actor. His face displayed the full range of his emotions, running through amazement to annoyance and finally settling on disdain.

"You do not have an appointment. Lord Shimazu sees nobody without an appointment."

He was closing the door in my face, but I was too quick for him. I put my hand on it, and shoved back. For a moment, there was a ludicrous push and shove contest until he opened it again and glared at me. I spoke before he could find words.

"Please, tell Lord Shimazu that Midori No Me is here to see him. He will not refuse me."

The servant hesitated, and I realized that he was waiting

for me to bribe him. I did not; my money was too hard earned to throw at this sneering underling. I won the battle of wills. Finally, he shrugged and stepped back to let me into the hall.

"Wait here. Don't bother to take off your shoes."

The sub-text was insultingly obvious. He was sure that Lord Shimazu would give orders to have me thrown out. He was gone for so long that I was relieved when he came back, and I saw instantly from his posture that I had won.

"Lord Shimazu has graciously agreed to see you, Midori No Me-san. Please, come this way."

I glanced pointedly at my geta, which I had already taken off. The servant pretended not to notice.

"Midori No Me-san. It is very good to see you again. Please, sit down. Gaku, we will have tea."

I slid to my knees gracefully and waited, expecting Lord Shimazu to demand to know what I wanted. Why I was here, bothering him without even the politeness of making an appointment? At least he remembered me!

"Lord Shimazu, I thank you for your courtesy."

"Not at all," he said politely, his voice calm and without emphasis.

We sat in—for me at least—an awkward silence until our tea arrived. Gaku poured the boiling water onto the tea powder and whisked it briskly, but without any grace. I frowned at him, and he was so taken aback that he almost spilled my tea.

"You must forgive Gaku." Shimazu sounded as if he was laughing, but his face was expressionless. "He is a mere man. He has never had the advantage of being trained in the art of the tea ceremony."

"I will make the next cup," I said firmly. "It will taste better if it's done properly."

"Of course it will." We sipped our hot tea. "I'm delighted to welcome you to my house, Midori No Me-san. What brings you to me?"

"I want you to make a kabuki theater for me."

I spoke quite casually, as if I was asking for the smallest favor. I supposed I should have dressed the raw request up a little. Begged for this great lord's favor, smoothed his vanity. But I was past all that. He would either laugh at me and throw me out or he would be intrigued enough to want to know more. As the proverb has it, to wait for luck is the same as waiting for death.

And I was tired of waiting.

"I see." He paused, his lips pursed as he considered my request. When he spoke, I was astonished. It was as if my words were no surprise at all to him. I felt as if we had discussed this before but had been interrupted in our conversation and were now simply carrying on from where we had left off. "You would, of course, take the female lead? You would be the onnagata?"

"Yes. I took the role many times in the kabuki in San Francisco, when we first arrived in America. I was very successful. The audience loved me," I said defensively.

"Yes? So why did Lilly take over your role?"

Ah. He knew she had stolen my place, then. Just as she had taken Danjuro from me, now she was stealing my hopes for the future. I felt at once that there was no point in going on. My shoulders slumped as my hopes drained away with the last of my tea. I managed a polite smile.

"Sumimasen deshita, Lord Shimazu." *I am very sorry.* "I have obviously wasted your time by coming here. Thank you for the tea."

I was climbing to my feet when his voice froze me into place.

"Please, do not leave, Kazhua-chan."

Kazhua. Nobody had called me Kazhua—*Green Leaf* —except for Akira. It had been his love name for me. Ironic that the name he used to show his power over me should also have been the name that my dear mother had wanted me to be known by. But it was not the name the world called me. This man had no right to even know it. Still less right to use it. He was mocking me, and I would not stand for it.

"My name is Midori No Me. *Green Eyes*. An ugly name, but mine. I am not Kazhua to you, lord. I am sorry to have bothered you."

I stared at him. My anger and disappointment melted into confusion as I saw his expression, as honest and open and—yes, innocent—as any one of the children I had taught at Li-san's house.

"You have not bothered me," he said urgently. "You don't know it, but I've been searching Boston for you since you disappeared. I even had inquiries made in San Francisco, in case you had gone back there. But there was no trace of you anywhere."

My legs folded underneath me. To give myself time to think, I reached for our empty teacups and automatically went through the graceful motions of the tea ceremony, whisking the tea powder just so, and handing Lord Shimazu's cup to him elegantly. He took it with a polite bow.

"I've been here on Porter Street all along," I said. "Not even the other side of the city. You must have been looking in the wrong places, or didn't try very hard!"

I sounded accusing, almost as if it was Lord Shimazu's fault he had not been able to find me.

"I did my best. I had no idea where to start, so I hired

one of Mr. Pinkerton's famous detectives to find you. Alas, she didn't live up to the reputation of the company."

"She?" I interrupted fascinated.

"Indeed. It seemed to me that it was better for a woman to look for a woman. But even Miss Warne could not find you. She hinted that perhaps Danjuro had had you killed, to leave the way open for him to marry Lilly."

The absurdity of his words made me laugh out loud. Tears came to my eyes and I had to wipe them away with the palms of my hands.

"You spent your money for nothing!" I gasped. "I always considered Danjuro to be my husband, but in truth, it was never made legal. Not so much as the traditional three-three-nine-times sips of sake ceremony passed between us. He was free to put me aside and take Lilly any time he wanted. I don't suppose a Western woman would ever understand that." Abruptly, all desire to laugh fled. "Why were you searching for me?"

"Because I needed to find you." I considered his words. *Needed*, rather than wanted?

"You don't even know me. Why was it so important that you found me?"

"Because I have been stupid enough to let you slip away from me in the past. I was determined it wasn't going to happen yet again."

"Why?" I said suspiciously. "We've only met a couple of times. Why would you be so interested that you would bother going to all that trouble to find me?"

"You don't believe in karma?" I shrugged. "No, neither did I until fate kept throwing us together in the most unlikely ways. I first saw you on the ship that brought us all to America. Remember?" I nodded, I was hardly likely to forget it. "I was intrigued by you, even then. I had always loved the kabuki. I saw the great Danjuro perform many times. Before I left Edo, there were rumors flying about that Akira had murdered him. He had disappeared, and so everybody thought the gossip was probably true. And then you popped up out of nowhere, telling us he was not only alive, but on the very same ship with us. And there were other rumors, as well. Rumors that the terrible Akira had been tamed by a very special woman, a geisha who could enchant any man she chose to glance at. A geisha that nobody ever saw. Some said you were not human at all, but an elemental spirit. When I saw you, I knew that if you were a spirit, then you were a spirit made flesh."

I shook my head. "No. The rumors were all wrong. The truth is that Akira kept me as his prisoner. I was no more than his slave."

"You really think that? I wonder myself who was the slave and who the mistress."

"I was no more than a green girl then," I said softly. "Akira took me against my will. I couldn't do anything about it."

"And now?"

"Now?" I thought about it, and finally said, "I am no longer a child. I'm nobody's slave. I'm my own woman. Carry on, please."

I met his gaze. There was silence for so long I wondered if he had lost track of his thoughts. But I was wrong.

"I thought about you on the journey often, but you never appeared again. When we docked in San Francisco, Takishima-san and I came straight here, to Boston. The others went elsewhere in America. I suppose you know why we are here?"

"You and the other nobles are *tozamu daimyo*—outside lords. You left Japan to study the ways of the gaijin. You hope that by learning their military secrets you'll eventually be able to use their own strengths against them to not only force them out of Japan but also to win back your rightful place ruling Japan."

Shimazu blinked. I was pleased by his surprise.

"Truly, I think you're far more talented than any of Mr. Pinkerton's famous detectives."

I shrugged impatiently. I was on fire with curiosity. I wanted him to get on with his story, not pay me absurd compliments.

"You really didn't forget me, then?"

"That I didn't." He said. "I had business in San Francisco. I was there for a couple of months, and I went to the kabuki at every opportunity I had. I saw you perform time after time. You were magnificent. I have always loved the kabuki, but you made it fresh and new and very special. I became obsessed with you. I could think of nothing and nobody else. In the end, I decided I had to speak to Danjuro, to try and persuade him to bring the kabuki to Boston. I asked him to come to my hotel. I told him that if he would come to Boston, then I would be honored to be his patron. That I would provide him with anything he wanted. He could name his own price."

"I don't understand," I interrupted. "You couldn't have done that. Danjuro would have told me about it. Besides, if that was the case, why did Lord Takishima end up as his patron, not you?"

"Because Danjuro turned my offer down. I told him his kabuki was wonderful, but that it was you who made it so special. If he would come to Boston, then you must take the role of the onnagata. He was polite, but adamant. He thanked me for my generous offer but said his theater was very happy in San Francisco. It was obvious there was no point in trying to persuade him."

That I understood. Danjuro would never accept that he might not be the star attraction of the kabuki. Without knowing that he had done it, Shimazu had offended his pride, yet again. Danjuro would never accept anything that put him into second place. Even more so when that offer came from a man he already hated.

"I see," I said cautiously. "But if you failed, how did Lord Takishima come to persuade him to move? And why was he so interested? I thought that the night we spent at the theater with him, he seemed bored. But of course, that was Western-style theater, and not the kabuki."

Shimazu laughed softly.

"Like me, he had business in San Francisco. And of course, he had to visit the only kabuki theater in America. My old friend Takishima loves to think of himself as a great patron of the arts, but he's not. He has a fine collection of woodcuts, but rarely looks at them. Apart from the shunga, of course. Those examples of erotic art he finds very interesting indeed. When we were in Edo, he patronized the bunraku puppet theater frequently, but often fell asleep in the middle of a performance. It's just the same with the kabuki."

"So why did he want to bring the kabuki to Boston? It must have cost him a fortune," I protested. "And it wouldn't even give him the sort of kudos he would earn in Japan by supporting it. I don't understand."

"Don't you? He wasn't interested greatly in the kabuki itself, but one aspect of it appealed to his tastes greatly. Lilly."

"No!"

"It's true. When he came back from San Francisco, he

could speak about nothing but the Dragon Geisha. He was entranced, so deeply in lust he couldn't rest. At first, I was absolutely horrified. I thought it was you he was after. When he told me that the gods had smiled on him, and Danjuro had readily agreed to come to Boston, I was in despair. I thought you must know all about my offer being rejected, and didn't care. When I saw you at the theater that night I longed to speak to you, but with Danjuro on one side and Takishima on the other, what could I have said? I attended the first kabuki performance with Takishima with a heavy heart. I almost laughed out loud when I realized that the Dragon Geisha on stage was only a sad imitation of the real thing. I couldn't understand what had happened to you. I asked Danjuro, and he shrugged off my questions. You had gone back to Japan, he said, while the kabuki was still in San Francisco. When you came back, you had decided you were bored with the kabuki and you were no longer interested in performing."

"I did go back to Japan, but I left a male onnagata in my place. Not Lilly! Poor Ryu died before I came back," I said sadly.

"I know. Danjuro told me at least that much. He insisted he had been immensely fortunate to find Lilly to take the female lead. He must have realized how interested I was in you. He smiled at me when he told me that now you were back, you had lost interest in the kabuki, so Lilly had taken your place permanently."

"That was a lie!" I said indignantly. "When I got back to America, I found that Danjuro had already made plans to move the kabuki to Boston. He told me that Lord Takishima had made having Lilly as the onnagata a condition of sponsoring the kabuki."

"Another lie. Takishima simply assumed that Lilly was

the real Dragon Geisha. He probably told Danjuro how much he admired her, but I doubt he would have even thought about insisting she came with the kabuki. He would just have taken it for granted that she would."

I shook my head slowly. And I had believed Danjuro. What an absolute fool I had been.

"Even if you weren't performing, I expected to meet you at the kabuki." Shimazu watched my face carefully as he spoke. "I went often, in hopes of seeing you. But you eluded me yet again."

"I was ill. So ill that for many weeks I couldn't leave my bed. When I did recover enough to go, I went to a performance without telling Danjuro. I wanted to surprise him," I said bitterly. "And I certainly managed to do that. I found him with Lilly in his arms. It seemed that everybody except me knew that they were lovers. I was ashamed of my own naivety. How unbelievably stupid of me, not to see what was right under my nose. I came home straight afterward and packed my things. Told Lilly she could have him."

"That was incredibly brave of you. Did you know people in Porter Street? Did you have somewhere to go?"

"No. I asked somebody where all the Japanese people lived and then went there. I lodged with a Japanese family and taught the children English to pay for my keep. I thought I was happy, at last. But I came to realize that there was no future for me there. That I wanted one thing, and one thing only. I wanted the kabuki back. You were my only hope, that's why I came here today. It seemed to me that perhaps you loved the kabuki as much as I do. Perhaps I was just being foolish, again. But perhaps not. Were you really searching for me?"

"Unlike the rest of the men in your life, I do not lie. I told you, I was fascinated by you from our first meeting. I was sure that karma had thrown us together, and that all the problems that kept us apart were no more than minor obstacles along the way. In fact, the more I couldn't have you, the more I wanted you."

"You are obviously a man who is used to getting his own way," I said drily. "But I am sorry. This time, you will not get what you want. I am no longer a geisha in the Hidden House to be sold to the highest bidder. I am no longer slave to a man I hate. I am a free woman, in a free country. I will not prostitute myself again, no matter how much the goal means to me."

My belly was tight with tension. Ah, such a shame! The kabuki that had been within touch of my fingers a moment ago was gone, as surely as if Shimazu had laughed at me and thrown me out straight away. He was a handsome man; I had been greatly attracted to him at the theater. And now, after just a little time in his company, I realized I was comfortable with him. It was as if we were old friends, united after a long absence. Under other circumstances, I had no doubt at all that there could have been something between us. If that something could only have been given and taken freely between the two of us, with no strings attached. But he had made his meaning plain. He wanted me in exchange for my beloved kabuki. My body and my soul in exchange for my dream

"You do me a great injustice. Do you really think I would want you if you were willing to sell yourself? I'm not Takishima, besotted with a pretty face and willing to pay for my pleasures. I neither want to buy you or bribe you"

"Really?" The vision of my kabuki hung in the air for a moment, and then vanished like mist before the sun. I wanted to believe his words, but I could not. "Thank you for your kindness. But I see I was wrong to come here today. I'm afraid I`m going to disappoint you yet again."

I straightened my back, ready to stand, but froze as Shimazu spoke.

"You are no Lilly, thank the gods. But you are very like your mother. She was beautiful and courageous and determined, just as you are."

All desire to leave the room fled.

"You knew her?"

"I met her several times." Shimazu smiled, his expression far away. "My father was one of the nobles who competed to be her danna for her mizuage. She came to our house several times when she was a maiko. Even then, she was enchanting. She had no need to coax a shy, young boy out of his shell, but she did. She spoke to me and it felt as if I was the only person in the whole room that she wanted to be with. To tell the truth, I was relieved that my father didn't win her. I was so infatuated with her, I would have died to think my father was with her when I could not be."

He laughed and shook his head.

"You see? Even after all these years, I think fondly of her. And you have her very special talents. Your reputation does no honor to you. You are more than special."

"I am her shadow." I sighed. "I never knew her. She was forced to run from Edo the day I was born, with my father. He was a gaijin, and nobody even knew she had taken him for her lover. If they had stayed, it was likely that they would both have been killed. My mother for the dishonor she had brought on the tea house, and my father for the dishonor he had brought on her. Gaijin were not much thought of in Edo, in those days."

"Why did they leave you behind?"

"They had no choice. I arrived early, and I would never

have survived the journey. I think it really is karma that led me here, to this country. I found out a while ago that my father was an American, from Virginia. I hope that they are both there still, and that I may see them again."

"The gods sometimes steer us in our journey through life, even though we have no idea of it. Don't you see, Kazhua? Your karma brought you here, to America, to find what you thought was lost forever. My karma also brought me to these shores. The same karma has brought us together, at last."

When he spoke, it all seemed so *right*. But I doubted it. When had my life ever been easy? Besides, there were other things I wanted to know.

"Why do you call me Kazhua? You know my name is Midori No Me."

"Because Midori No Me is not a beautiful name, but Kazhua is. I have always thought of you as Kazhua. Does it offend you?"

"Kazhua was the name Akira gave me. I hated it when he called me that. But then I found out it was the name my mother wanted me to be known by, and I hated it even more that Akira had dared to steal her name for me."

"Do you hate it when I call you Kazhua?"

I thought for so long before I answered, it must have seemed to Shimazu that I was avoiding his question.

"No," I said finally. "You had no way of knowing it was to be my name. I think perhaps it is right in your mouth."

"Thank you. Then I shall always call you Kazhua. I always have, in my heart."

We sat silently for a moment. I spoke first.

"Lord Shimazu. I came to you today in the hopes that I could persuade you to give me what I wanted. A kabuki theater. I am sorry, now, that I came."

The blood left his face, leaving him ashen. I had to fight an absurd urge to stroke his hand, to give him comfort for the very words I had spoken.

"I have offended you?" he asked. I shook my head.

"You have honored me," I said simply. "But you spoke about karma earlier. Until very recently, I spent the whole of my life certain that I had no say in my own fate. That my place was to do as I was told. First in the Hidden House, where I was expected to entertain the patrons however they wished." I paused, glancing at his face to see if he understood. He nodded.

"I have heard of that place. Some of my friends went and came back with tales about geisha that were like no others in the whole of Edo. I was supposed to go, once, but something interfered with the plans and I didn't make it."

"I'm pleased that you never saw me there," I said quietly. He nodded, his eyes fixed on my face.

"And Akira? It was Akira who took you from there?"

"He did. And made me his prisoner. I went from one jail to another. I had even less freedom with Akira than I had enjoyed at the Hidden House. At least there, all we geisha had each other. With Akira, I was alone. And then Danjuro rescued me from him, and I thought that I had found freedom at last. But love binds more tightly than any ropes, and I truly loved him."

"Loved?" Shimazu picked up on the word hungrily. "Do you still love him now?"

"No," I said softly. "The Danjuro I loved is dead and gone. Lilly may think she's taken him from me, but the man she has isn't Danjuro. I can't love a dead man. I can mourn for what I've lost, but I can't love somebody who no longer exists."

"Lilly thinks you broke him," Shimazu said hesitantly. I stared at him in astonishment.

"You've seen Lilly? Why?"

"I went to see her to find out if she had any idea where you had gone. I knew there was no point asking Danjuro. Even if he knew, he wouldn't have told me. Lilly said she had no idea either, and I believed her. If she had known, she would have told me."

"Why? I imagine she would have been happier if she thought I was dead."

"Perhaps. But I offered her a lot of money to tell me where you were, and her eyes were very hungry. Did you know the kabuki was not in a good state?"

"It was when I left," I said tartly. "What happened? Did the patrons actually come to see through Lilly?"

"No. Don't forget, most of the patrons are gaijin. They all thought that was how kabuki should be. The problem was with Danjuro. I went to see a couple of performances, and I was embarrassed for him."

I stared at him incredulously. Danjuro, the great actor, performing badly? He saw my expression and nodded.

"Truly. He forgot his lines. He mumbled. Came in late for his cues. At one performance, he didn't appear at all when he was supposed to. The other actors covered up for him, but even the gaijin could see something was wrong. And the poorer Danjuro became the more confused and upset the others were. The last performance I saw was so bad it was cut short, halfway through the final scene."

"That's not possible," I said flatly. "Not Danjuro. Never. The kabuki is his life."

"Lilly said it was all your fault." I gawped at him, my mouth open but words refusing to come. "She said that Danjuro still loved you to distraction. That he was only half

a man without you. That was why he was trying to drink
your memory away. She said he cared for nothing, not even
the kabuki, without you in his life."

"That's nonsense," I managed to say. "I left him when I
found out he had taken Lilly for his concubine. I suppose in
Japan, it would have been expected. But things are different
here. I had no intention of living a lie."

"You were wrong. When you went back to Japan, he was
mad with jealousy. Lilly admits that she threw herself at
him, and he was flattered. Things only got worse when your
patron in San Francisco told him that the kabuki was hope-
less without you. You understand? He was—literally—crazy
that you had undermined every area that mattered in his
life. Lilly says he was convinced you had run back to Japan
because you loved Akira, and that he was the only man you
had every truly cared about. That would have been bad
enough, but then when he thought you had stolen the
kabuki from him as well, it finished him."

"No. That's not true at all. I told him time and time again
that I hated Akira, that I was only driven to go back to Japan
for fear of what was happening to my sisters in the Hidden
House. Especially Mineko, my younger sister." I thought
Shimazu was going to say something, but he gestured for
me to carry on. "And I could never steal the kabuki from
him. It was always his creation, it was Danjuro who made it
special. Anyway, if he was so jealous and worried about me,
why would he take Lilly as his mistress?"

"Because he was trying to make you jealous in your
turn. Think what he did. He put a woman with no talent at
all into the kabuki in your place. Even worse, a woman who
was trying to be you. When that didn't appear to worry you,
he took Lilly to his bed. He was convinced that would make
you furious, that you would insist that he got rid of her and

welcome him back to your arms. But it didn't work, did it? When you found out about her, instead of behaving as he expected, you turned around and walked out of his life without a word. Lilly said that was when he started drinking, very heavily."

"He never could take his drink," I agreed sadly. "It must have been very bad if he couldn't even remember his lines."

"According to Lilly, he's barely sober at any time. She's at her wits' end. Takishima has been watching events, and he's started making blatant offers for her. She's refused so far, but if things get any worse, she may go to him. They have no money, she says. He spends it all on drink."

"I'm sorry," I said simply. I felt absurdly guilty, as if I really had caused Danjuro's problems. But I had not, I told myself fiercely. I had been there for him, always. Everything I had done in the time we had been together had been to support him, to please him. My own hopes and desires had always bowed before him. "How are they coping, if there's no money? The actors have to be paid, they must eat."

"She says they have nothing. That was why she was willing to sell this to me."

He stood and stretched, lithe as a cat, and walked across to a cedar wood chest. He lifted out a sealed packed and handed it to me. I turned it over in my hands, just as—a lifetime ago—I had turned the first letter from Kiku. But I knew instantly this was not from her. The calligraphy was beautiful. It was addressed to me, at the theater in San Francisco. Somebody had added the Boston address, in English, beneath the Japanese characters.

I knew instantly who it was from. Mineko. I had seen her calligraphy before, and had always envied her sublime art with the brush. While the news about Danjuro had failed to move me, the knowledge that I had not, after all, been forgotten by my friends reduced me to the brink of tears.

"Did Danjuro know about this?" I asked hoarsely, my throat very dry.

"Lilly said it had only just arrived, and he had not seen it." He paused and then added gently, "She said that many letters had come for you since the move to Boston. Some from San Francisco, some from Japan. Apparently Danjuro didn't even open them. He just threw them all on the fire. This one would have followed, if he'd seen it. Are you going to open it?"

"If you don't mind?" It was a thick package, and would take me a while to read it. The knowledge that my friends had not forgotten me filled my heart to overflowing with gratitude. I was tempted to put Mineko's letter to one side and read it when I was on my own, but I was too excited to wait. It would contain only gossip about her new life, but it didn't matter. I would hear her dear voice in the written words.

I read the letter quickly, and then again, far more slowly. Lord Shimazu was polite; he stood and walked about the room, pretending he needed to stretch. Finally, I put the pages down and stared into space.

"Bad news from Edo?" he asked. I blinked at him. "I read it in your face."

"My younger sister, Mineko. When I left Edo she was about to marry a samurai, a man who had been tricked by Akira to be bound to him. With Akira's death he was free. They were very much in love, and her samurai was willing to forget all the traditional needs to have her adopted into a good family before they were married. He just wanted to take her back home with him, as his wife."

"There was gossip about it." I stared at Shimazu in

amazement. He had heard about Mineko and Ken, an ocean away? He shrugged. "It was so unusual, and Ken-san was so high-born, there was bound to be a huge amount of talk. A noble who had heard about it mentioned it in a letter to me. But I understood that they actually married. Has something happened?"

"Ken is dead."

Surprise flared in his expression. "He was a young man, surely? Was it an accident?"

I closed my eyes, feeling Mineko's hurt. Shook my head.

"No. I mean, yes. Oh, it's so difficult! Did you know that Ken's father mistreated him terribly? He was determined that his only son would be a great warrior, one who would live up to the family name, so he beat him every time he made a mistake with the sword or in the arts of body fighting. Ken killed him eventually. It was a terrible accident, but even in the little time I knew him, it was easy to see that Ken blamed himself for it, and that the pain of it would never leave him. Mineko says that he was teaching his cousin—a boy he was very fond of, and intended to adopt as his own son —sword fighting. Somehow, the boy got under Ken's guard and the blow killed him. She said he was smiling when he died, and she was sure he was happy because he thought he had finally paid his debt. She writes that Ken had a melancholy temperament, and nothing she could do made him as happy in life as his death."

"That is very tragic. Mineko must be deeply upset. I'm sorry that when you finally get news from your friend, it has to be so distressing. Sorrier still that it was my hand that delivered it to you."

I shrugged aside his polite words. He hadn't known either of them; he couldn't hope to understand.

"It's worse than you might think." I picked up the letter

and sorted through the sheets until I found the page I wanted. "Mineko writes that Ken's relatives have gathered in his home like a flock of vultures. He hadn't made a new will when they married, and now all his relations are squabbling amongst each other as to who should inherit his estate. Even the boy who killed him wants his share. She thinks she'll be left with very little. She doesn't care. With Ken gone, she has nothing left for her in Japan. She asks me if it's possible for her to come to America, to be with me and —perhaps—to take a small part in the kabuki. Like me, it was always her dearest dream."

"Then at least that will be good news for her. If she can act, then there is no reason why your kabuki can't welcome her."

I stared at him. In spite of everything I had said, could he still think he could buy me with the price of my dreams?

"Lord." I paused, gathering my words.

How many times had I called the patrons in the Hidden House "Lord" when they were no more than rich merchants at best? But how they loved to hear the title fall sweetly from our even sweeter lips! And how simple would it be now to smile and promise Shimazu future reward in return for my kabuki. There was no doubt at all that he was a very attractive man. Besides, I liked him; it would be no hardship at all to forget my principles. I hesitated and heard the faint echo of my mother's words as I kneeled before the unspeakable Mac. *You do not have to do this.* If I took the easy path now, would she forgive me? I was sure she would. But could I ever forgive myself? I doubted it.

"Lord Shimazu, I have told you. I am not willing to give myself in exchange for a kabuki theater. Not even poor Mineko can make me change my mind. She wouldn't expect it, I know that."

"I see. If that's how you feel then it's better for you to go now."

I froze. I had expected him to plead with me. To beg me to change my mind. But I had been wrong all along. He was not the man I had thought he was. I stood and bowed, as politely as I could. Sorrow—for the dream I knew was lost forever, for my poor Mineko, and even for what might have been with Shimazu—rose in my throat and drowned any words I might have found. I turned my back on him and took a single step.

"You're a proud, stubborn woman, Dragon Geisha. Your pride matters more to you than anything, I think. And you let it rule your heart and your head both."

I turned my head and glared at Shimazu, still seated comfortably on the tatami.

"And are you always so offensive when you don't get your own way?" I was shocked by my own discourtesy. If we had still been in Japan, he would have been perfectly justified in striking me. He smiled and patted the tatami at his side.

"Not normally, no. But it was the only way I could think of to bring you to your senses, Kazhua."

It was the final straw. I was across the room in a heartbeat. I leaned down and grabbed his robe, shaking him and shouting in his face.

"You've no right to call me Kazhua. You've got no rights at all over me. I'm not Lilly, to be bought and sold by anybody who takes a fancy to her. No man will ever do that to me again. If I starve in the gutter, it will be worth it to keep my self-respect."

"If you starve in the gutter, it will be only what you deserve."

I was so surprised, the anger died in my mouth. He took

my hands from his shoulders and got to his feet, his movements fluid and graceful. We stared at each other silently.

"I do not intend to starve," I said finally. "I have many talents. I can sing and dance, and play the samisen. I can act. I can read and write, both in English and Japanese. I will find my own way forward, whether the gods are with me or not."

And, I thought bitterly, if all else fails I can always rely on my greatest talent. I could become a high-class yujo again. And even that would give me a certain freedom; at least I would be able to choose my own patrons with no Aunty to fear.

He smiled at my words. Or had he somehow gotten inside my mind and it was my thoughts that made him smile?

"And talented as you undoubtedly are, at this moment you look exactly like a little girl who has had her favorite toy taken from her."

I would have walked away finally then, but Shimazu caught my shoulders and held on. He spoke to my back.

"Dragon Geisha, you have no idea how long I've dreamed of the day that you would walk into my house. And now that it has happened, everything has gone badly. I've said all the wrong things. Done everything wrong. Forgive me. Please. Or if you can't forgive me, at least listen to me."

"I have listened to many men in my life, Lord Shimazu." My voice was shaking. I cleared my throat and tried again. "I believed Danjuro, and he betrayed me. Why should you be any different?"

"Because I would not try and make you my possession. I would never try and take your freedom from you. What would be the point? I have always hated caged birds. Birds need to be free, to fly where they will. Put them in a cage, and they're miserable. Just like you've been miserable. I would never make a cage for you. I would only want you to stay with me because you were happy, because you wanted to, not because you had to."

I searched his face for the truth behind his words. Did I believe him? I wanted to, but I couldn't be certain. I chose each word with care.

"I came here to ask you for my heart's desire. For the kabuki. Will you give me that, freely and without any ropes to bind me?" I saw he was about to speak, but I held my hand up, stopping his words. "Listen to what I am saying. It will be purely a business arrangement. If you agree, I will write to Mineko and tell her to come here, at once. You remember the play we watched together, where the two girls played the part of both women and men?" He nodded, obviously puzzled. "That is what Mineko and I can do in the kabuki. The world has moved on, but the kabuki has not. It is time it changed. I want to turn it on its head. I will take the part of the female lead. I will truly be the Dragon Geisha again. And Mineko will take the lead male actor's part. Together, we can make something wonderful."

He nodded slowly. "Yes, I believe that you could. But not on your own, not even with Mineko. You'll need supporting actors as well. Lilly said that Danjuro has offended many of his actors. She was worried that they were going to leave him anyway. They would come to your kabuki, I'm sure."

My heart soared. He had said *my* kabuki. Then I thought of Danjuro, suffering because of me. I had never intended it, but I had loved him once, and I was sad for him.

"I can't take Danjuro's actors. It would kill him."

"His kabuki is going to die, no matter what. And it's not your fault." I was surprised by his intuition, and watched his face carefully as he spoke. "You've never tried to hurt him. He's bought it on himself, but he'll never understand that. He'll always blame you for his misfortunes. From what Lilly said, I believe he would like to go back to Japan. Not to Edo, she thinks it would be too much loss of face for him. But there are kabuki elsewhere in Japan that would welcome him with great honor. And it may be that a long sea voyage, with no chance of any drink, would help to bring him to his senses. Lilly thinks so, anyway."

"And is she willing to go with him?"

"She loves him," Shimazu said simply. I sighed. I understood that well enough; hadn't I come with Danjuro to this new world myself for love? "I think it would be the best thing for him. It would surely kill him to see you succeed in a new kabuki, breaking all the rules he would never change himself."

"You're willing to persuade Lilly?" I asked.

"I'll talk to her. Tell her I'll fund the voyage back to Edo for both of them. I'll also give her some more money, so she can keep them fed and housed until they find their feet again. If I do all that, will you take up my offer?"

My heart shouted at me to say yes, immediately, but my head urged caution, and I made myself listen.

"I will, but only if you agree to my terms. It will be a legal agreement, a properly drawn up contract. I will pay you back for every cent that you invest. You must understand, you will have no hold on me. No right to anything outside our business agreement. No right to me."

He steepled his fingers beneath his eyes, so most of his face was hidden.

"So, what you are proposing is that I pay out large amounts of money to set you up in a totally new venture, with no guarantee of success. I am also to pay Lilly and

Danjuro to get them safely back to Japan, and I suppose pay for Mineko to come to America as well?" I nodded. "And in return, I have your word that eventually I will make my money back."

I thought about it for a moment.

"Yes. That's about it."

"Now why should I do that, when I could probably get at least ten percent return on that money every year, perfectly safely?"

Answers rolled around my head. *Because you are a rich man, and the money means nothing to you. Because you love the kabuki. Because I am sure you would find the gamble enticing. So you could triumph over Lord Takishima.*

"Because I am the Dragon Geisha. Because you want to do it to please me," I said finally.

"And in return? You offer me nothing more at all?"

"I offer you my friendship."

I expected him to be angry. Instead, he moved his fingers so I could see his face. His expression was unreadable.

"It is always good to have a friend," he said quietly. "I would greatly value your friendship, Kazhua. And may I live in hope—nothing more, you understand—that someday we might be more than friends?"

I had the curious feeling that I was suspended in space, looking down on myself. The whole of my life that had already passed, I could not change. But every day of the future was mine to do with as I pleased.

And Shimazu pleased me.

"No ropes," I repeated. "Nothing to bind me, nothing to make me a prisoner. No promises that can be broken. But for the future, who knows?"

"I understand," he said, and I believed that he did.

"There is just one more thing." I smiled as I saw the worry in his eyes. "Before my new life begins, there is a journey I have promised myself I would make one day. It's a long journey, but I hope it will be worth the effort. I would be pleased if you would come with me."

"I would be honored."

Gaku broke the moment by coming in to clear away the remains of our tea. We sat in silence until he had gone.

"If our journey is in America, we had better go soon, Kazhua. War is coming. It's going to be dangerous for anybody to venture far."

"Yes," I said simply. "I'm ready to go, if you are."

He laughed. After a moment, the laughter became a smile. He leaned toward me and ran the tip of his finger gently across my cheek.

"You have freckles. Did you know that means that you have been kissed by the sun god?"

I was sure I heard Aunty draw in her breath with a hiss of fury. I smiled with him.

T he carriage slowed. I cleaned the filthy window with my hand, and peered out anxiously.

"This is the right place? You're sure?"

"I'm sure, ma'am. I've lived in these parts all my life, and this is the Beaumont place, alright. High Grove Plantation, just like you asked for."

I bit my lip, hesitating.

"You want to go in, ma'am? I guess there must be somebody about the place still."

"I think we must," Shimazu said quietly. "You have come too far to turn around at the last minute, Kazhua."

I drew a deep breath and nearly choked on the cloud of dust that was rising around our carriage. He was right. I had to know.

"We stay."

The coachman came around and opened my door, handing me down courteously.

"Want me to wait?" I nodded, and he strolled off to tend to his horses. Shimazu jumped down to stand beside me, and together we stared at what had once obviously been a great and gracious house.

Now, the paint had peeled off in great scrapes. The rail that ran around a long, shady veranda had slats missing. Even the steps leading to the front door looked rickety. And there was a stink of rotting fruit. Shimazu took my hand and squeezed it gently.

I was bewildered. We had traveled for many hundreds of miles; with each passing mile, my excitement had grown. At last, I was going to meet my mother and father. I had practiced my first words over and over, debating endlessly whether it would be better to speak in English or Japanese. I wondered how much they would have changed from my photograph; still more did I worry what their reaction would be to the daughter they had left behind on the day of her birth. Shimazu reassured me.

"You have to know," he said quietly. "Even if you find you're not welcome, you must know. If you don't find out, it will haunt you for the rest of your life."

He was right, of course.

Now, I stood in front of their house, and nothing was as

it should have been. I took a hesitant step forward and stopped as a man, his skin the color of weathered mahogany, stepped down from the shadows of the veranda. He gawped at us, his mouth hanging open.

Shimazu put his hand warningly on my arm. I turned to look at him and shrugged and shook my head at his unspoken question. I jumped with surprise as a large dog jumped down the steps and flung himself at my feet to roll in the dust, almost trapping his lolling tongue beneath his own ribs. He was irresistible in his enthusiasm; I bent to pat him, blinking as the bright sun bounced off the white dust, dazzling me. The strange man gazed down at me, and sucked in his breath sharply.

I froze in shock as he spoke.

"Welcome home, ma'am. I suppose you come looking for your mama and papa. I'm real sorry, they been gone one way and another for a long time." He hesitated and then added shyly, "I'm William. I guess I'm your uncle."

The next book about the women of the Hidden House is coming soon! Subscribe to our mailing list to be the first to be notified about new releases.
http://redempresspublishing.com/subscribe/

ABOUT THE PUBLISHER

VISIT OUR WEBSITE
TO SEE ALL OF OUR HIGH QUALITY BOOKS:

http://www.redempresspublishing.com

Red Empress Publishing

Quality trade paperbacks, downloads, audio books, and books in foreign languages in genres such as historical, romance, mystery, and fantasy.

ABOUT THE AUTHOR

India Millar started her career in heavy industry at British Gas and ended it in the rarefied atmosphere of the British Library. She now lives on Spain's glorious Costa Blanca North in an entirely male dominated household comprised of her husband, a dog, and a cat. In addition to historical romances, India also writes popular guides to living in Spain under a different name.

Website: www.indiamillar.co.uk

Made in the USA
San Bernardino, CA
06 June 2018